OTHER BOOKS BY
JENNIFER L. ARMENTROUT

The Titan Series
(New Adult Paranormal)
The Return
The Power
The Struggle

Wicked Trilogy
Wicked
Torn

Covenant Series
(Full series completed—Young Adult Paranormal)
Daimon
Half-Blood
Pure
Deity
Elixir
Apollyon
Sentinel

Lux Series
(Full series completed—Young Adult Paranormal)
Shadows
Obsidian
Onyx
Opal
Origin
Opposition
Oblivion (Daemon's POV of Obsidian)

The Dark Elements
(Full series completed—Young Adult Paranormal)
Bitter Sweet Love
White Hot Kiss
Stone Cold Touch
Every Last Breath

Standalone Titles:
The Problem with Forever
(Young Adult contemporary)
Don't Look Back
(Young Adult romantic suspense)
Cursed
(Young Adult paranormal)
Obsession
(Adult spin-off the Lux Series)
Frigid
Scorched
(New Adult Contemporary Romance)
Unchained
(Adult Paranormal Romance)

Wait for You Series
(Read in any order, as standalones.
Contemporary New Adult)
Wait for You
Trust In Me (Cam's POV of Wait for You)
Be With Me
Believe in Me (short story in the anthology Fifty Firsts)
Stay With Me
Fall With Me
Forever With You
Fire In You

The Gamble Brothers Series
(Full series complete—Adult Contemporary Romance)
Tempting the Best Man
Tempting the Player
Tempting the Bodyguard

For details about current and upcoming titles from
Jennifer L. Armentrout,
please visit www.jenniferlarmentrout.com

The Dead List
Published by Jennifer L. Armentrout
Copyright © 2017 by Jennifer L. Armentrout
All rights reserved

Library of Congress Cataloging-in-Publication Data
The Dead List/Jennifer L. Armentrout—First edition
ISBN: 978-0-9979691-4-6

Interior Design & Formatting by:
Christine Borgford, Type A Formatting

THE
DEAD
LIST

1 NEW YORK TIMES AND INTERNATIONAL BESTSELLING AUTHOR
JENNIFER L. ARMENTROUT

For the readers who still picked up The Dead List even though there was sort of, kind of a clown in it.

THEN

PENN DEATON LOOKED three years younger than thirteen. With his thin arms and legs, he was the tiniest out of the four of us, and always picked last during gym class, if picked at all. He was more into bird watching with the telescope his grandfather had given him for Christmas two years ago than he was chasing a ball around.

I didn't really get the whole bird thing and couldn't pick out a northern mockingbird to save my life, but I sat with him in the tree house nestled deep in the woods behind his house, my backpack forgotten in the corner, my legs dangling over the edge. One of my flip-flops had fallen to the ground below. The other hung precariously from my toes. The drop was steep, scary high. Falling would probably end with more than a visit to urgent care. I was always surprised that Penn would come up here since he was afraid of heights, but I guessed he was into birds more than he was scared.

There were other things I could be doing instead of sitting here waiting for Penn to see whatever he wanted to see before we made our way over to Gavin's. Running, for starters. I loved doing that. The feeling of my muscles tensing and releasing, my lungs burning as my sneakers thumped off the pavement, provided such a rush. When I got to high school, I was going to join the cross county team and the track team.

I could've already gone to Gavin's house. He wasn't allowed out after school right now because he'd set off the bottle rockets he found in his parents' garage last weekend. He was still grounded for another billion years. But he'd gotten a new game system that hadn't been taken away from him and we were still allowed to visit. Jensen was probably already over there, waiting on Penn and me. He didn't have the patience required to sit quietly in a tree house and watch for birds. Jensen was always picked first in gym class, and if a game controller wasn't in his hands, he'd rather be chasing a ball around.

None of our parents ever tried to keep the four of us apart, even if we were in major trouble. Since elementary school, we had always found a way to be together. We were peas to each other's pods, as my Grammy would say, and I though that was kind of a weird saying, but we were our own little group and we were best friends.

Things . . . things were starting to change though, and I really didn't understand why.

Gavin didn't like spending time in the tree house anymore and sometimes he blushed and acted weird. Everyone wanted to be around Jensen at school, especially the girls.

I bit down on my lip as my stomach tumbled like my flip-flop had.

My mom said Jensen was growing like a weed, and he was, towering over the three of us. I wasn't growing at all. Glancing down at my T-shirt, I sighed. I was the same as I was last year and the year before and the year before that. Still incredibly flat chested. Still mistaken for a boy if I had my hair up and under a hat. I was convinced I'd never grow boobs like the other girls in my class, which meant Jensen would probably never think of me as anything other than the girl who was often mistaken for 'one of the boys' he hung out with.

Ugh.

I don't even know why I cared if he woke up tomorrow and realized I was a girl. It was stupid, I decided as I picked at my nail instead of chewing on it, a habit my mom was trying to break me of. It didn't matter if I never changed, because neither had Penn, and even though with each passing month school was getting harder and harder for him, he was still the same old Penn. I sort of loved him more for that.

"There!" Penn whispered excitedly. "Right there, Ella."

I looked up, frowning and squinting toward the tree he was pointing at. It took me a few seconds to find the bird with black and white wings with a splash of red across its breast.

I shuddered as the bird hopped to the branch below it, shaking the leaves. "I don't like that kind."

Penn glanced down at me, clutching the silvery shaft near the eyepiece lens. His dark brown eyes glimmered with excitement. "Why? They're beautiful."

"I don't know." I pulled my foot up as the bird took flight, disappearing further into the tree, where it found a leafy hidey-hole. I took off my one lonely flip-flop. "It looks like its throat was slit and it bled all over itself."

His mouth dropped open. "That's . . . that's sick."

I giggled. "It's true."

"Never looked at it that way. Huh." He dipped his head back to the eyepiece and I swallowed a sigh. We weren't heading to Gavin's anytime soon. "They're my favorite species."

I hadn't forgotten that.

Cardinals were Penn's favorite.

NOW

ONE

STARS BLANKETED THE sky like tiny tiki torches, casting pinpricks of light on the dark field that butted up to the edge of an obsessively manicured backyard. I scratched at the label on the bottle I held and tipped my chin up, closing my eyes as the warm, end-of-summer breeze washed over my face. The dry, rough grass scratched at my bare legs and I was probably sitting on or near a fire-ant hill, about to be devoured alive, but I didn't care.

In less than forty-eight hours, I'd be starting my senior year, and by this time next year, instead of staring up at stars, I'd be gazing at the twinkling city lights outside the University of Maryland.

I would be so done with this place.

"Ella, what in the hell are you doing?"

I jerked at the sound of Lindsey Roach's voice and twisted at the waist. She stood behind me, holding two bottles of beer in her hands.

"Double fisting tonight?" I asked, raising my eyebrows. "Hardcore, Linds."

She laughed as she dropped down beside me, curling long dark legs underneath her. Handing one of the bottles to me, she wrinkled her nose. "Yeah, no. I'm not going to be one of those girls who gets drunk at Brock's party, takes off their clothes, and jumps into his pool, among other things."

I opened my mouth.

Linds held up a hand, silencing me. "Not trying to judge, but you know what's going to go down. It happens every year. One of the giggling chicks back there is going to strip down and show the world, God, and baby Jesus her goodies."

My lips twitched. Linds and I had been best friends since freshman year, when we'd been paired together to work on a social sciences project. She'd always been a hell of a lot more opinionated than me. Linds really couldn't be called *pretty*. Not with her curly black hair that looked perfect whether it was pulled back tight at the crown or cascading down her back. Pretty wasn't a word I'd use for her near flawless deep brown skin, or cat-shaped eyes and lips ready-made for a makeup ad.

Nope.

Linds was the kind of beautiful that made you want to kick her in the lady bits when she donned a two-piece bikini. She was *gorgeous*.

"Remember last year?" She took a drink and rested the bottle on the hem of her denim shorts. "Vee Bartol took off her clothes and danced on the diving board? Like dropped low on the diving board?"

I winced, easily recalling that incident. Not because Vee got up and did that, but because of the fallout that occurred afterward. But it happened every year since we were sophomores. The parties Brock Cochran threw the weekend before school started had become a religion to the student body. They were *notorious*. His parents were always on the absentee list Saturday night, and his older brother supplied the alcohol in various forms. And someone always did something they'd spend the upcoming school year regretting on an epic level.

My smile faded away like the last days of summer as I stretched out my legs. I glanced over at Linds, and in the silvery moonlight, I could see that she was no longer smiling.

She bit down on her plump lower lip. "I heard that the police still think she ran away."

Wiggling my toes, I cast my gaze to the sky again. Everyone wants to believe that Vee ran away. I do. The only other options are horrifying and ugly, but when she went missing two weeks ago, her family had appeared on the local TV stations, tearfully begging for her return. It was well known, as all things are in small towns, that none of her personal belongings had disappeared.

Who ran away without money, an ID, or extra clothes?

Or even their cellphone?

It didn't make sense.

Linds tipped back her beer and I forced my thoughts away from Vee. I'd never been close to her, but her situation, whatever it was, was still difficult to really comprehend.

The silence between us was full of soft chirps from an army of crickets probably about to descend on us. I hated bugs. All kinds of bugs except ladybugs. They were kosher in my book. There was also probably a stinkbug in my hair. I'd heard one a few moments before and nothing made me freak out quicker than one of those archaic looking monsters, and they were *everywhere*. Having invaded West Virginia like we were its own personal version of D-Day, they had made our town their bug bitch. Bugs were useless. I didn't care about cross-pollination. They could go cross-pollinate my ass and—

"Can you believe it?" Linds said, pulling me away from my bug obsession before I jumped from the grass and ran screaming into the nearest shelter. "We're going to start our senior year. Freaking finally."

My smile returned and a ridiculous flutter began in the pit of my stomach. Senior year was a big deal. Besides the fact I could just coast through classes, I was so ready to be out of this town. The University of Maryland wasn't as far as I could go, but it would work for now. My stomach twisted around the beer. Part of me was happy and the other part felt like a balloon that had been let go and was unexpectedly floating up into the sky.

I made a face at that thought as I looked at the two beers I was holding. God, I needed to drink more. Or less. Probably less.

Linds rested her cheek on my shoulder and I leaned into her. Her cool bottle ended up resting against my leg. "But you suck. You're not going to WVU. What am I going to do without you?"

"Run your mouth more than you do already?" I laughed as she jerked away from me and gaped, feigning shock. "You'll be fine. And we're going to visit each other every other weekend, remember? And we have breaks where both of us will be home."

"I know. And you know what else I know? You will find a new guy and you won't even remember Gavin's name. You're going to be like Gavin who? Who is that lame, piece of poo-poo on a poo-poo platter?"

"Poo-poo platter?" A laugh bubbled up and broke free. "Are you drunk?"

"Nope." She knocked her shoulder against mine. "You know, I'm kind of surprised he isn't here."

"He's still at the beach with his parents. He's not getting back until tomorrow."

Her lips turned down at the corners. "Are you still talking to him?"

Contrary to what Linds believed, when Gavin and I broke up at the end of May, it was mutual . . . for the most part. He wanted to take our relationship further than I wanted to go with him. He hadn't been a dick about it. Frankly, he seemed kind of relieved that I wasn't as into him as I'd been telling myself I was. We'd known each other since elementary school and had been best friends since forever. We'd been dating for almost two years, and it had been fun . . . and *easy*. Things used to feel good—feel exciting whenever we were alone, but it had gotten to the point that doing anything naughty began to feel like I was making out with my brother.

And that was just really disgusting.

And I didn't even have a brother.

"Gavin and I are still friends, Linds. You know that." I took a sip out of my old bottle and nearly threw up as warm beer sloshed down my throat. Gross. "And I really don't want to date anyone. What's the point? I'll be leaving for UM."

Linds glanced up at the stars, scrunching up her face. "Do you know who else I heard was going to UM?"

I raised a brow and waited. Everyone and their sister and brother and Mary, Mother of God, was going to WVU or Shepherd. When she didn't respond, I nudged her with my elbow. "Who?"

"Jensen Carver. Apparently, he's going to UM. You could totally get with him."

I stared at her and blinked a couple of times. "Jensen? I don't think I've spoken more than an entire sentence to Jensen in, like, almost four years. So I don't see how him going to the same college is really relevant to anything."

"No time like now to take that one sentence to two sentences and turn it into some bow-chick-a-yum-yum." She giggled as I gaped at her. "What?"

"*What?* He's a stuck-up asshole!"

"Shh," she said, laughing as she glanced over her shoulder. Talking bad about hot boys—and Jensen was hot with an extra T and a side of Linds' yum-yum sauce—was apparently the only thing she wasn't vocal about. We were far enough away from the pool anyway. "I still don't understand your problem with him."

I cocked my head, shooting her a death glare. "Uh, yes you do."

"That was, like, a long time ago, Ella." She rolled her eyes. "Anyway, I don't think he's stuck up."

"He doesn't really talk to people outside of his inner group of guys or whoever he's dating this month. I don't even know how he's as popular as he is."

That was a lie. I did know.

Even though Jensen didn't hail from a super-rich family like Brock and he'd spent freshman through most of his junior year in a different state, he was attractive and athletic—first-string quarter-back. Throw in asshole and you had the "A" trifecta of popularity.

Attractive. Athletic. Asshole.

Politics of high school at its finest.

I took a long gulp of my newest beer.

"Maybe he's just quiet?" she protested.

The truth was that Jensen had always been a bit on the quiet side. Had, being the key word. I had no idea how Jensen was now. I shook my head and then tucked a strand of hair behind my ear. "Why are we talking about this?"

"Whatever. We'll both be single our senior year. Probably better that way." Grinning in a way that would've lit up her dark eyes if I could see them, she held her bottle high between us. "To our senior year! Cheers, baby!"

Unsure of which beer to toast now that I was the one double fisting, I raised the half-empty one. "This is going to be a great year."

"Yes, it is. It's going to be even greater if we stop sitting out here by ourselves like total freaks."

I laughed. "All right. Let me, uh . . ." Not wanting to leave a bottle out in the field, I shrugged. "Never mind."

Rising to my feet, I shimmied my hips until my dress situated itself. "Do I have any dirt on my butt? Or bugs? Are there any bugs on me? You'd let—"

Linds snorted. "There are no bugs on you. Here . . ." She smacked at my butt with enough force to move me a couple of inches. "If you did, not anymore."

"Thanks." I turned around, eyeing her. "I feel like I've just been violated, by the way."

"Shut up." Looping her arm through mine, she grinned. "You liked it. Everyone likes a Lindsey level of butt fondling."

"That's what I hear."

She sucked in a sharp gasp. "Bitch."

"Ho."

A laugh curled through the night air as her arm tightened around mine. "Love you."

"Love you long time," I replied, grinning as we hoofed it up the slight hill and the party came into view once more. Apparently I'd been hiding out for longer than I'd realized. "Wow."

Bright light streamed over the large patio and packed pool. Little dots fluttered in the stream of light, almost like glitter . . . if glitter wasn't in the form of bugs that most likely bit the every loving crap out of you.

I really needed to stop thinking about bugs.

The thump of music was broken up by shouts and laughter. Water sprayed into the air as a guy on the football team power bombed the pool, dousing a cluster of girls in heels that stood too close and causing a splash big enough to drench half of our senior class.

My eyes scanned for friendly faces and ended up on a whole lot of male flesh. The group of shirtless guys standing near the gas grill was the who's who of hot guys at MHS. All of them played one sport or another—football, soccer, baseball, or basketball. And all of them took keeping their bodies sports-ready very, very seriously.

Thank God and Lind's baby Jesus for that.

Their dedication to various favorite American pastimes packed on the biceps and cut those stomachs in a way that made a girl think about doing stupid things. Lots of stupid things.

Whoever said that only boys were visual creatures wasn't looking in the right place, because there was all kinds of eye candy going on in front of us.

Brock was the one closest to the grill, wearing black swimming trunks. His close-cropped dark hair gave him away, as did the way he tipped his head back and let out a loud laugh. He was always friendly and fun to be around . . . when he wanted to be.

During my freshman year I might have harbored a split-second crush on him, but he'd been dating Monica Graham—one of the high-heeled and now wet girls by the pool—on and off. He'd never been available to really hardcore crush on, but according to his Facebook relationship status updated two weeks ago, he was now single. And when Brock was single, he liked to play. Everyone at school knew that.

Beside him was Mason Broome—a soccer player slash stoner. His blond hair was loose and reached his shoulders. Currently, he was thrusting his hips . . . at the air. Interesting. Linds had hooked up with Mason over the summer. It didn't go anywhere, but I think she still had the hots for him based on the way she was eyeing that hip motion.

Across from them, staring into the pool like he wanted to be anywhere than where he was at that moment, was the one and only Jensen Carver.

I was totally woman enough to admit that he was at a level of hotness that was code panty-dropping. Bad attitude and our past history together aside, he was the best-looking guy I'd ever seen in real life.

Jensen had light brown hair that would almost look dirty blond if he was out in the sun. It was wavy and had a habit of falling onto his forehead. When he was younger, it had been long enough to constantly be in his eyes. He had broad, high cheekbones, and a strong, cut jaw, and lips that were . . . well, the kind of full lips on a guy that sort of made the knees weak when the idea of kissing him popped into your head. The slight hook in his nose, an injury from a football game years before, when he had played in a different state, somehow added to his looks. His eyes were a light blue, sometimes gray. Not that I paid *that* much attention to his eyes. And his body?

Boy worked out. Hard, too.

Out of all the guys standing there, he was probably the leanest and the tallest. While Brock and the rest were broad with linebacker shoulders, he was a good foot taller than the rest of them and had the kind of abs I wanted to poke to see if they were real.

"I wonder if that chick knows I can see her pink bra through her shirt?" Linds said. "Nice."

I had no idea who she was talking about, but I was grateful for the distraction. I didn't need to be staring at Jensen. Linds shouted something and the boys turned. One of them raised a cellphone.

"Hey!" I lifted the bottles and popped out my hip, cheesing it up for the camera right along with Linds. The flash went off like a mini sun explosion. "How stupid did I look?"

Brock cocked his head to the side, assessing me. That look . . . well, the center of my cheeks heated. "You look hot. As always."

So was not expecting that response.

My cheeks continued to burn as I lowered the bottles so I wasn't standing there like a drunk Muppet Baby. I glanced at Linds, and her eyes were darting back and forth between Brock and me. "Um, thanks," I said.

He grinned. "No problem. You drinking for two tonight?"

Instead of saying no and explaining that I wasn't quite sure how I ended up holding two beers, I shrugged. "Sure. Why not?

"Cool." Brock glanced over his shoulder at something Charlie Lopez said. Charlie was a big guy with a big smile. I had no idea what he'd just said, but Brock nodded.

"You girls having fun?" Mason asked, returning Linds' earlier look, except he made it seem like she wasn't wearing any clothes.

She nodded. "Yeah, we're ready for this party to get interesting."

I gave her a look that said *we are*? But the boys opened up into a half circle, and somehow I managed to get rid of the warm beer bottle and had enough sense to pass on the Jello shooters. I was a lightweight, and since I'd driven myself to the party, I didn't want to end up being some tragic statistic they constantly talked about in health class. The conversation flowed back and forth, with the exception of Jensen. He was now staring into the field I'd just come from, his angular jaw tense.

"You're not going to WVU, are you?" Brock asked, angling his large body toward mine, surprising me. How in the world had he known? He grinned, and I realized I'd asked the question out loud. *Niiice.* "Linds must've told Mason. He was telling me a few weeks back."

Made sense, I guessed. "Yeah, I want to get out of the state and see some different faces, you know?"

"True. I get that. If it wasn't for football, I'd be doing the same thing." He flashed a smile which was full of perfect white teeth. He moved closer, his arm brushing mine every time he raised the bottle to his lips. "We're going to miss you. I know I will."

My lips curved up at the corners at the unexpected statement, though I doubted the sincerity behind it. "Thanks." I frowned, wondering what the hell I was thanking him for. His smile spread. "I mean, I'm going to miss everyone—you, too—when school ends."

"But we have this whole year ahead of us. We've got to make it memorable." He caught a strand of my black hair and tucked it behind my ear, and I swore the conversation around us grinded to a halt for a moment or two. "Right?"

I found myself nodding as my gaze slid away from Brock's and collided with Jensen's. He was staring at me. It was too dark for me to pick out his current eye color, and now I was staring at him. For the life of me, I couldn't look away. A muscle thrummed steadily along his jaw as he raised a bottle to his lips, eyeing me over the rim as he took a drink.

And yep, I was still staring at him.

I looked away quickly, blinking rapidly. Monica was now standing at the fringe of our little group. She was gorgeous, just like Shawna and Wendy, her closest friends since the days of the sandbox.

Jensen and Wendy had dated for a whole two weeks last year, after he moved back to town. The perky, tiny blonde had been all over him during that short period of time, turning the cafeteria and hallways into a soft porn film set. And now she was beside him, leaning in so close that her boobs were practically mating with his chest.

It was a lovely chest to mate with.

Monica smiled at me as she tossed her super-shiny mane of black hair over her shoulder, and I wiggled my fingers around the bottle in return, thinking she should be in a Pantene commercial.

Linds' sudden wild giggle whipped my head around. Mason's face was buried in her neck, and he was either whispering something or licking her. Everyone was breaking off into couples, and somehow I was standing with Brock.

What in the world was happening here?

He drifted closer, his shoulder pressing into mine. "You wanna talk for a few? Someplace away from these idiots?"

My mouth felt dry. Momma didn't raise no fool. Talk was code for anything other than talking. As handsome as I found Brock, I was so not going to turn into his friend with benefits until he decided he could no longer live without Monica and got back together with her, turning me into public enemy number one.

I started to step away just as Jensen turned, tossing his bottle into a nearby trashcan. My gaze tripped across his face and my heart skipped a beat. His complexion looked darker, as if he'd been blushing, and his lips were tightened into a thin line.

"I'm out," he announced, digging a set of keys out of the pocket of his swim trunks.

"What?" shouted Charlie, moving to follow Jensen, dragging Shawna behind him. "You are so not out!"

Jensen kept walking.

"Leave him be!" yelled Brock as he snaked an arm around my waist. "Something's done crawled up his ass. Let him go spend some alone time with it."

As Jensen strode down the side of the pool, he tossed his arm up, flipping us off. Brock threw his head back, letting out a loud laugh. With Charlie chasing after Jensen and Linds one step closer to making babies with Mason, I was left alone with Brock.

Whose hand had slipped down the curve of my back and then

lower. He squeezed, and I squeaked.

"Jumpy?" he asked, dipping his head toward my neck. I darted to the side before he could complete whatever he was trying to accomplish. He looked up, frowning. "What? Don't you want to talk?"

"Uh . . ."

His almost sleepy stare crawled down the front of me once more. "I like the dress. Is it new?"

Actually, it was. I'd gotten the yellow strapless sundress just for this party. My mom said yellow was best for my fair skin and dark hair, and for once, she was right. Forcing a smile, I took a step back. "It is."

"It's nice. You look hot in it."

"Thank you," I murmured, backing into the flat wall of the pool house.

Brock stepped forward, the bottle of beer dangling from his fingers. "You're so hot."

My eyes widened as he planted his hand next to my head. I darted under his arm. He spun around, frowning again, in a confused way.

"Where are you going?" he asked.

"I've got to get home. Curfew and all," I lied. It had been many moons since I worried about a curfew, but if he said hot one more time I might vomit. "But it's been fun. Got to go. Bye!"

Brock started toward me, then his gaze darted to the right and his brows slammed down. "Hey!" he shouted. "Who the hell let you all in here?"

I looked over, spying three skinny underclassmen that looked like they also had no idea what they were doing here. The three boys huddled together, throwing panicky looks at one another. Something about the sight of them pierced my chest, reminding me of—I shook my head, clearing my thoughts.

Brock tossed his beer bottle to the side, where it bounced off a shrub and then shattered on the walkway. "Charlie!" he yelled, grinning in a way that caused my stomach to dip. He looked like a lion about to pounce on a three-legged gazelle. "Look what we have here."

I had no idea where Charlie was, but I took full use of the distraction and spun around, hurrying back to the cluster of dancing bodies, dropping my almost full beer bottle in the trash. My eyes searched for Linds, but she and Mason were nowhere to be found.

Deciding it was way past time for me to make an exit so I didn't end up hanging around and doing something stupid, I dipped inside and grabbed my keys from where I'd left them near an unused breadbox. I figured when I got home, I could pick up the last Black Dagger Brotherhood book that was patiently waiting for me on my pillow. I don't know what it was about bad-mouthing vampires that made me about seven different kinds of happy, but it did. The only other books to do that were the Kristen Ashley romance books I stole from Mom when she wasn't paying attention.

They made me want to move to Colorado.

Linds liked to give me a hard time about having my nose stuck in a book, but sometimes I needed to get my head out of real life, and reading was the best and quickest way to do it.

Back outside, I headed toward the gate leading to the front of the house. As I crossed the lawn, the sounds of the party faded into the background.

I needed to text Linds to let her know I'd left, but my cell was in my car. Telling myself not to forget, I passed the tall hedges blocking the yard from the dark road in front of Brock's house.

His house was the only one for at least a mile on an isolated stretch of road, but tonight the sides of the street were packed with cars, and I had to park what felt like a million miles away from the house.

Wrapping my arms around my waist, I picked up my pace. My sandals smacked off the cracked asphalt, echoing around me. As dark as it was, with no street lamps and only thin slivers of moonlight stretching across the road, it was an eerie, too long walk.

I kept waiting for Big Foot to barrel out of the thick stand of trees crowding the road. Or maybe Mothman; after all, I did live in West Virginia.

A shiver coursed down my spine as I pictured a giant winged creature flying out of the trees, and then I cursed my imagination. This was not what I needed to be thinking about when there was no one around.

When I spotted my car, a wide smile broke out across my face. Almost there. My fingers tightened on the keys as I stopped at the driver's side door, pushing my finger down on the unlock button.

My car chirped a hello.

My sandals still smacked off the asphalt.

No. Wait. Another shiver tiptoed down my spine. I wasn't walking, so those footsteps . . . they weren't mine.

Tiny hairs rose along the back of my neck and I whirled around, quickly scanning the dark road around me. A breath caught in my throat as I squinted into the thick shadows between the cars.

I saw nothing.

Seconds passed and I didn't dare move or breathe too loudly. My ears strained to hear the footsteps, but there was nothing but the low hum of insects that came out at night. What if there really was a Big Foot? Or a chupacabra?

Or a giant, flesh eating stinkbug?

Now I was just being stupid.

No one was out there. It was just another case of Ella's overactive imagination. Instead of planning on attending college for a law degree, I should major in creative writing. The way I could creep myself out over something so harmless, I could be the low-rent version of Stephen King or something.

Laughing softly, I turned back to my car and reached for the door handle. The tips of my fingers brushed over the metal just as a rush of warm air stirred the hair next to my temple.

That was the only warning.

Every instinct in my body flared alive, screaming out a warning, but it was too late. A hand smacked down on my mouth. Jerking back suddenly, my keys slipped from my fingers, clanging off the road.

My brain ground to a halt, unable to process what was happening. In the next second, my feet were off the ground and space was increasing between my car and me. I was being hauled away—carried backward.

Horror seized my insides in an icy grip, snapping me out of my shock-induced immobility. Instinct roared back online. My heart pounding, I struggled against the hold, throwing my weight forward and then back again, trying to dislodge the arm that felt like a steel band under my chest.

The attacker grunted, but held on. Panic rose inside me like a great wave crashing over a beach. I clawed at the hand over my mouth, but my fingernails only scratched rough gloves. Air puffed out from my nose in short, wheezy wisps.

This isn't happening. Oh my God, this isn't happening.

I swung my arm back, desperately trying to make purchase, but I hit nothing, only air. My car was several feet away from me now, the woods close at our backs. Deep down, in a part of my brain that was still functioning beyond the terror, I knew that if he got me in the woods, it would be bad—really bad on a stranger-danger kind of level.

Not knowing how to fight or defend myself, the panic took over. I kicked out my legs, losing my sandals, but the sudden movement caused the attacker to stumble. I kicked my legs out again, and his footing slipped on the embankment.

We went down in a tangle of legs and arms. I hit the ground hard, knocking the air out of my lungs. My survival instinct had taken hold of me. Ignoring the spark of pain in my ribs, I rolled onto my knees and scrambled up the small slope. I dug my feet into the damp earth, kicking up grass and soil.

A scream burst out of my mouth, breaking the silence. Birds

took flight, their wings beating together as they rattled the thick tree limbs above me. My feet hit the warm asphalt as another scream tore out of me.

"Help!" I shrieked into the empty road. "Someone, help—"

Weight crashed into my back, forcing me down. My knees and palms skidded across the coarse road, tearing open my skin. The pain was overshadowed by my growing terror.

My cries ended in a grunt as something slammed into my lower back, stunning me. My cheek smashed against the pavement. Flipped roughly onto my back, I found myself staring up into a face shadowed by a dark hood. The glint of a zipper reflected briefly, but there was nothing under the hood but darkness.

A gloved hand slid over my cheek, the touch almost tender, almost loving, and that punched a whole new wave of terror through me.

I immediately flailed under his weight, bucking my hips and trying to force him off, but his strong legs pressed down on either side of mine, trapping them together. His hands wrapped around my throat, cutting off my scream. I lost my next breath before I even realized I'd taken my last.

I opened my mouth to drag in oxygen, but nothing flowed through my parted lips. Nothing. Not a wisp of anything. The pressure increased, bruising my neck. I could feel the muscles and bones grinding together, and my lungs cramped.

Reality washed over me like a draft of frigid winter wind. Whatever he wanted was worse than what could happen in the darkness of the woods. He was going to kill me.

Oh God. Oh God, not like this.

I didn't want to die like this, on the side of the road. I didn't want to die at all.

A different kind of panic took root in me, and I swung my arms out, pounding them at his arms and chest, but nothing seemed to faze him. He leaned back, avoiding a direct hit to the face, but my fingers grabbed ahold of the hood. With a burst of energy, I yanked it back.

Horror took away the last little bit of oxygen my lungs had desperately tried to hang on to.

What stared back at me was something out of a horror movie. The attacker's face was covered by a clown's mask—the hard, plastic kind. Ghostly white skin with small, red blush on the cheeks greeted my horrified stare. The eyes were wide, with three lashes painted in black. Above the holes were two half circles painted in black. The tiny, pert tip of the nose was painted red, and the lips were carved into an obscenely wide smile, revealing fake buck teeth.

Full of terror, I reached for the mask, but the thing holding me down jerked out of the way. The hood slipped further down, revealing a blue frizzy, curled wig.

A cramp seized my entire body, causing me to jerk against the road. This . . . this was going to be the last thing I saw, I realized dumbly as I tried to smack at him again, but my arms weren't co-operating with me. My muscles were useless, and my arms fell to my sides, lying at what felt like an unnatural angle.

The clown mask grew closer as it leaned in, stopping a mere inch or so from my face. The pounding in my chest slowed as it tilted its head to the side, watching me from somewhere in the dark holes.

My lips worked around a word that couldn't be uttered. *Please.* I repeated it over and over, mindlessly. *Please.*

A soft tsking sound radiated from behind the mask, and it shook its head side to side slowly. Tears welled in my eyes, spilling down my cheeks, and the image of the *thing* blurred as darkness crept across my vision.

Without warning, its hands were gone. My lungs expanded frantically as I dragged in greedy gulps of air. I didn't understand how, but I could breathe!

I felt it lifting my body by my shoulders, raising me up like dead weight and—

Bright lights flooded the road, and the thing above me froze. It stilled for a second and then slammed me down. The back of my head cracked off the road, blinding me as darkness exploded all around.

Arms were around me again. There were voices—voices I recognized that should've meant safety of some sort. Someone was yelling. Feet pounded in every direction. I couldn't lift my head, but I could see again and all I could see were the stars in the night sky.

They were blurry, but they still looked like tiny tiki torches. The embrace tightened, lifting me up as a voice rasped in my ear, "I got you."

TWO

ATTEMPTED MURDER BROUGHT in all the cops from the land I liked to call *everywhere*.

I tried to sit up in the hospital bed, ignoring the tender pull against my ribs and the dull ache in the back of my head. Mom was right by my side, gently coaxing me to lie back. Her normally coifed dark brown hair was a mess of waves reaching her shoulders, and her hazel eyes, more green than brown, were full of concern.

"Baby, just relax," she murmured, smoothing the thin blue blanket over my hips. "Don't move around too much."

"Listen to your mother," a voice said from the edge of the bed.

My gaze darted over to where my father sat. The fact that the two of them were in the same room together, let alone within touching distance of each other, signified how big of a deal this was.

My brain hurt.

"Mom," I sighed, glancing at the two troopers from the state police standing behind her. More officers waited in the hallway—city, county and state. From the moment I'd woken up in the ambulance, police and people had been asking questions at a rapid clip. "I'm okay. Really, I am."

Mom shook her head as she sat beside my hip. "You were

almost . . ." She drew in a shuddering breath. "You could've been . . ."

My stomach knotted painfully. Even though she couldn't finish the sentence, I knew what she meant. Dad reached over, placing his hand where my foot poked up from under the blanket.

I could've died, but the attacker had stopped—he'd been lifting me up as if he planned on taking me away from the road. He wanted me to be incoherent but not dead.

And that was far scarier than anything else.

Bile rose up in my sore throat and I leaned back against the flat pillows stacked behind my head. A shudder worked its way through my body as I slowly let out a breath.

Trooper Ritter shifted his weight behind Mom. "I'm sorry to keep asking questions when I know you're exhausted. . . ."

"It's okay." I lifted my hands and started to smooth them down my face, but stopped. The skin on my palms was scratched and raw from where the pavement had torn them open. Unable to really look at them, I lowered them to my sides. "This is important. I know."

"You kept referring to the attacker as a he, but how can you be sure it was a male?" he asked, holding his hat under his arm. "You said the attacker was wearing a mask and a wig."

"A clown mask," Dad muttered, rubbing a hand through his neatly trimmed brown hair. "What is this town turning into?"

Town? What was the world coming to? I swallowed hard, wincing against the pain. Clowns had never scared me before, but now I'd never be able to look at one the same way. "I was lifted up like I weighed nothing, and I sure as hell weigh a good—"

"Honey," Dad said softly, eyeing me. "I think he gets the point."

The trooper nodded. "But there are a lot of strong women out there, Ella. I'm only pointing that out because we want to be sure we have everything we need to find this person."

My gaze shifted to my torn hands. In a flash, I saw them reaching for the door handle. I had been so close to getting into my car—to safety. The memory of being jerked back and picked up was too fresh. I sucked in an unsteady breath.

"Ella," whispered Mom, placing a trembling hand on my arm as Dad squeezed my foot. "Are you okay?"

I nodded as I raised my gaze to the trooper. "When he first grabbed me, he pulled me back against him." I bit down on my lip as Dad let go of my foot and shifted away. Tension coursed through his body, pouring into the stuffy room. "I didn't feel any . . . you know . . ."

Boobs. Breasts. Tits. Tatas. Boobies. I couldn't bring myself to say any of those words in front of Dad, especially when he looked like he was about to dive-bomb under the bed.

Thankfully the trooper nodded in understanding, and I wasn't forced to elaborate. He asked a couple more questions and then one that totally caught me off guard. "You've been seeing Dr. Oliver. Is that correct?"

"Yeah." I glanced at my parents, but the question didn't seem like a big concern to them.

"May I ask why you're seeing a therapist?"

Heat flooded my cheeks. It seemed stupid to be embarrassed about something like that considering I almost just died on a back road, but I didn't like the look creeping across the trooper's face. Like he was wondering what was wrong with me that forced me to see a psychologist.

"We insisted that she see one after the divorce," Mom answered, and well, that was kind of not a lie. *Kind of.* "It's just something she's stuck with."

"Okay." Trooper Ritter glanced over at one of his coworkers, his green uniform stretching against his broad shoulders. "I just have one more question for you, all right?" When I nodded gingerly, he gave me what I guessed was supposed to be a reassuring smile, but it made me shift uncomfortably. "Were you close with Vee Bartol?"

Dad stiffened at the foot of the bed. He turned to the trooper, his face paling. "Isn't that the girl who went missing?"

"Two weeks ago," I whispered, reaching up and gently touching my neck with my fingertips. "I didn't know her very well. I mean, we kind of grew up together, but we weren't friends beyond saying hello to one another."

Mom's forehead wrinkled as she leaned back, idly brushing at strands of my hair. "I heard on the news that the authorities believe she may have run away. So what does she have to do with what happened to Ella?"

"We do believe that she ran away," Trooper Ritter answered evenly. "But in these situations, we have to look at every possible option. Her disappearance and this attack, while most likely not related, we still have to check it out."

"Understandable," Dad said, shaking his head. "My daughter is safe. Right?"

My body seemed to freeze up while the trooper answered the question. My thoughts whirled around Vee Bartol. Did the police suspect something else had happened to her, but weren't being entirely truthful when it came to what they were telling the public? I didn't know and I also couldn't see how anything with Vee could be related to what had happened to me. I hadn't lied. Vee and I weren't friends.

"There's still some people we need to talk to—those who were at the party and were leaving while you were," Trooper Ritter continued.

A different kind of stillness settled over me as I remembered the voice—*his* voice. *I've got you.* My chest squeezed. I imagined they had already talked to him. I looked at the door, for some reason expecting to see him standing out in the hallway too, but he wasn't.

"If you can think of anything else, please don't hesitate to call us." Trooper Ritter handed a small white card to my mom. He turned and then stopped at the door, looking back at me. "You are a very lucky young lady."

My breath caught as I squeezed my eyes shut. I didn't need him to tell me that. I already knew it. I was officially part of a small percentage of those who had *luckily* escaped their attacker.

"HAVE YOU SEEN the news?" Linds' voice traveled from my bedroom. "You're all over it. They even got ahold of last year's school picture. The one where you thought it was a good idea to wear pigtails? You looked like you were twelve."

My reflection winced and then I groaned. The skin along my right cheek looked like I'd unloaded a compact of blush on it. Worse yet, upon closer inspection, my cheek resembled a strawberry.

I pulled back, picking up a tube of mascara. Even without the giant red mark, my face couldn't handle a lot of makeup. Anything more than some lip-gloss and mascara, and I looked like a clo—

I couldn't finish the thought, so I concentrated on my reflection.

For the most part, everything about my face was too large. My eyes. My cheekbones. My mouth. By the grace of God or my father's DNA, I had a small nose. Not up to doing anything special with my hair this morning, I let it fall in dark waves around my face.

Placing the lip gloss back, I frowned when my hand shook. I sternly told myself that I was ready to go to school, that I didn't need any time off, and as I stared at my pale face, I told myself I was okay. I was fine.

I was alive.

A shudder rolled through me as the gaping, dark empty black holes where eyes had appeared ghosted through my thoughts. My throat ached as I swallowed hard. I glanced at the open bathroom door where Linds' voice traveled toward me. She was still talking about the news. Last night, I barely slept. My body ached and throbbed in places I didn't know it could. And there was a teeny, tiny part of me that didn't want to go to school.

That didn't want to leave the house.

Cold fear balled in the pit of my stomach. What haunted me the most was the fact I hadn't been able to defend myself. I had fought the attacker like a cornered animal about to be slaughtered. If luck hadn't been on my side Saturday night . . .

I needed to stop thinking about it.

Taking a deep breath, I pushed away from the sink and hurried out of the en-suite bathroom. Our house on Rosemont Avenue was old, like potentially standing during the Civil War old and maybe a little haunted kind of old. Before the divorce and before the housing market collapsed, and before . . . well, before *everything* changed, Mom and Dad had gutted the entire house, which turned the small useless bedroom next to mine into a bathroom.

Linds was sitting on my bed, her legs tucked under her while she held an old blue Care Bear I'd never had the heart to get rid of.

She smiled slightly. "Oh, Ella . . ."

"What? It looks bad, right? My face?" I sighed, tugging the hem of my shirt down. Linds was wearing a cute dress, but I was in jeans and a t-shirt. She made me feel like I needed to put more effort into my first day of school outfit.

"It's not your face." She bit down on her lower lip as her gaze dipped.

To my neck.

I had done everything to not look or think about it, because the first time I'd seen it in the hospital room it made my knees go weak. Bruises covered both sides of my neck, mottling into a deep purplish-red, a painful reminder of the hands clenching tight, cutting off my air.

Shaking my head, I let my hair fall forward. The edges reached past my chest. "How does this look? It's too warm to wear a scarf."

"Better." Placing the Care Bear aside, she unfolded her legs and hopped to her feet. "It really doesn't matter. You look great."

"Plus the fact that everyone in the entire county knows that someone strangled me, right?" I forced a casual shrug. "There's no reason to even worry about hiding it."

Linds' tight curls bounced as she bopped over to me, wrapping her arms around my shoulders, careful to avoid my ribs even though they really didn't hurt anymore. "God, Ella, I'm so happy that you're okay." She squeezed me as her voice thickened. "I wouldn't know what to do with myself. The whole thing is just so damn crazy and scary."

I folded my arms around her. "It really is." And that was the God's honest truth. Trooper Ritter had stopped by Sunday evening, checking in. The young officer believed that whoever had been responsible for the attack had probably skipped town, that I didn't have anything to worry about, but on the news last night, another officer—a deputy—had stressed that people, especially young women, needed to be on the lookout and stay aware of their surroundings.

Statistically, I should be safe. Who ended up being attacked twice by the same maniac? But the cold ball of fear still rested like a stone in my stomach.

"Are you doing okay?" she whispered, hanging on to me like cling wrap.

"Yeah." I was doing okay by not thinking about what could've happened if those headlights hadn't flicked on. Last night had been hard, though. As I laid awake staring at the ceiling, all I could think about was those too long moments where I couldn't breathe, couldn't do anything to defend myself.

A shiver coursed through me and I pulled back before Linds could feel it. I took a deep breath. "There is something I've been thinking about."

"What?" She picked up her bag.

I grabbed mine off the floor. "I'll tell you on the way to school. We'll be late if we don't leave now."

Mom was in the kitchen, pouring her coffee into a mug. Dressed in black slacks and a white blouse, the frazzled woman from the night before was gone as she turned to me. Being the branch manager at a local bank meant Mom kept her own hours and was always home before I left for school. Wednesdays were rough, though. She had to be in Huntington on Thursday mornings for face to face meetings, so she always left after work Wednesday to make the drive and returned home late Thursday night.

Otherwise, the morning meet and greet was a tradition that started after Dad left.

She reached behind her and handed over a toasted Pop Tart wrapped in a napkin. One for me and one for Linds. "You ready for everything?" she asked.

"For anything," I replied, taking the sugary goodness. "Thank you."

Linds leaned over, kissing my mom's cheek. "You're the bomb. Toasted Pop Tarts. My mom hands me a cup of coffee."

Mom laughed. "Ah, hold off on the coffee as long as you can." She propped her hip against the counter as she turned to me. "You sure about today? I know the school would understand if you didn't go, and I can call the bank. They'd understand, too."

She had hovered over me all day yesterday like a momma bear. As much as I appreciated being waited on hand and foot, there was no way I could miss the first day of school. "I'm okay. Seriously. I want to go to school."

Linds passed by me, making a face.

"Look, we've got to go," I told her, backing away. "I love you."

"I love you, too." Her chest rose in a deep breath as she plucked her suit jacket off the back of the kitchen chair. "Text me when you get to school and when you're leaving, okay?"

I nodded, figuring I was going to be doing a lot of checking in over the coming months.

Out in the early morning sunlight, I slipped on my sunglasses and hopped down the porch steps two at a time. When my feet hit the sidewalk, an odd sensation curled around my spine. Tiny hairs on my arms rose. The feeling. . . .

I tightened my hold on my messenger bag. In spite of the strong glare of the sun, I suddenly felt like I'd been encased in ice. The breath I took lodged in my sore throat.

Linds stopped next to me, frowning. "What?"

Turning around, I expected to find Mom at the door, watching us, but it was empty. So was the porch. The old wooden swing swayed at the end of the porch in the light breeze. Facing the front, I scanned the yard and sidewalk in front of the house. I could see the hood of my Jetta from where I stood.

The icy feeling remained, but I forced myself to draw in a breath and take a step forward, chalking it up to paranoia. Which was totally understandable. Less than forty-eight hours ago, I'd faced something I never in my life thought I would. Of course I'd be a wee bit paranoid.

I smiled as Linds started to shift nervously. "Nothing."

Eyeing me closely, she hesitated for a moment and then started forward. Shaking off the weird sensation, I inhaled the scent of freshly cut grass as I crossed the front yard and hit the sidewalk. I drew up short, stopping at where my car was parked along the curb.

Son-of-a-basket weaver.

There was a demonic brown stinkbug on my windshield.

Squealing like a small child, I darted around the front of the Jetta and yanked open the door. I lurched into the car and slammed the door shut just in case the stinkbug was ninja stealth, which most were.

I turned the car on and hit the windshield wipers, grinning like the Mad Hatter as the wipers flung the bug into next week.

Linds raised a brow from where she waited on the sidewalk.

"Sorry!" I hit the unlock button.

She climbed in, casting me a long look. "It was just a small, harmless bug."

"They are not harmless," I told her, easing away from the curb. "They are the scourge of the Earth."

In reality, I could walk to school if I was feeling, I don't know, active, which was something I hadn't really felt in a while. Once upon a time, in a galaxy far—whatever—I used to love running. It was something I looked forward to every morning or after school, and I used to plan on joining the track or cross country team, but I hadn't run in almost four years.

As I drove down the street, I did something I always did. Three blocks down, I looked to my left, to the large brick house so much like my own. The glance was short, but the impact lasted far too long.

I gripped the steering wheel as I sped up. The narrow streets of Martinsburg were crowded with cars. The town was small, with a town square that was literally just a square with flowers, but the population was growing every month it seemed, making travel equivalent to getting your eyelashes plucked out.

"Everyone is going to stare at me," I blurted as we waited at a red light in front of the library. "Aren't they?"

She didn't answer immediately. "Do you want me to lie?"

Little knots formed in my stomach. "No. Okay. Probably. Yes, please."

"No one is going to stare at you," she said solemnly. "And if they do, I'll kick their asses. How about that?"

The corners of my lips rose up. "That would be awesome. Thank you." I paused, twisting my fingers around a lock of hair as I kept my other hand on the steering wheel. "I . . ."

"What?" she asked, and I could feel her eyes on me.

I thought about telling her what I'd been thinking about last night while I lay awake, but the desire to talk about it—to even think about Saturday night—vanished. I shook my head, unsettled more than I cared to admit. "I . . . hope today doesn't suck."

"It won't."

We ended up arriving at school with less than two minutes to book it to our homerooms. I was in such a hurry to get to my class that I didn't even have a chance to worry if people were staring at me.

As I came out of the stairwell on the second floor, I nearly ran into the back of Wendy—the blonde with boobs that should be illegal on a high school girl. I'd finally grown a pair myself, but compared to her, it was like being thirteen all over again.

She and her friends—Monica and Shawna—were literally standing in the middle of the hall like it wasn't a place where people walked, and they were also talking loudly enough that anyone inside the school and the middle school next door could hear.

"I don't care if he was the last guy on Earth and it was up to me to repopulate civilization, I wouldn't get with him," Wendy announced, flipping a sheet of shiny blonde hair over her shoulder. "Like, there's not enough Jello shooters in the world for that."

Monica giggled as she slid a sly look to where the metal lockers lined the wall. "Don't be so mean, Wendy. I think he's, you know, *special*."

Then I realized that the boy they were talking about—Luis Clayton—was standing at his locker. The back of his neck was beet red and his shoulders were unnaturally tense.

Bitches.

The whole conversation reeked of a hundred similar scenarios I'd witnessed, reminding me of things that struck too close to home.

Skating around them, I hurried down the hall so I wouldn't be late to class, but as soon as I walked into homeroom, I was turned right back around with a note to take my happy butt to Ms. Reed's office, guidance counselor extraordinaire *and* art teacher of the year.

Christ on a cracker, this was the last thing I wanted to do.

Slipping back down to the first floor, I groaned as the bell rang, signaling the start of homeroom. If Ms. Reed sucked up my time, I'd be late for first period, which meant everyone *would* stare at me as I entered the classroom.

Ugh.

My flip-flops slid over the recently polished face of a bulldog, then I made a sharp left, slowing down as I hit the rotunda. The offices to the right were packed with staff, but before I could pay any attention to who was in there, I caught sight of my reflection.

Even in the glass, I could see the red stain on my cheek. Shifting my chin down, I let my hair slide forward, covering the mark. I passed through the rotunda and the door to Ms. Reed's office burst open, a dark shape stepping out. There was no stopping the collision as the door swung closed.

I bounced off a chest—a hard, male chest. Stumbling a step, I almost fell back into the rotunda, but an arm shot out and a hand caught my arm, steadying me.

"Whoa, you okay?"

My body locked up at the sound of his voice, and my gaze started at the tan hiking boots and traveled up denim clad thighs, over an old t-shirt that clung to abs and then a broad chest and shoulders. I forced my eyes all the way up, and they met pale blue ones.

Jensen.

Stepping free from his hold, my mouth went dry and my brain conveniently emptied. One brown eyebrow rose as he stared at me, and all I could think was this was the closest we'd been in four years.

Four. Years.

Ms. Reed's door opened, drawing my attention. Her plump cheeks rose in a smile when she spotted me. "Ah, there you are, Ella. Come on in." Stepping aside, she opened the door as she adjusted her square glasses. "It will only take a few minutes."

I glanced back at Jensen, knowing I needed to say something—anything—to him, but no words came to mind. I wondered if I'd suffered brain damage when my head hit the road Saturday night.

Like a complete doofus, I turned toward Ms. Reed.

"Wait." Jensen shifted forward, blocking me. "You have one of those damn stinkbugs in your hair."

"What?" I gasped, my heart wrenching to an abrupt stop.

"Bug," he repeated in that smooth, deep voice. "In your hair."

I raised my hands, swallowing my banshee-like shriek. "Get it out! Get it out! Get it out!"

"Oh dear," Mrs. Reed murmured from the doorway—her bug-free doorway.

Jensen's lips twitched as he stepped closer. "It's just a bug, Ella."

"I don't care. I don't care." I squeezed my eyes shut. "Please get it out. *Please.*"

With my eyes closed, I couldn't see jack, but I knew the very second he got close. The light scent of cologne mixed with the outdoors filled the next breath I took, and then I felt his warm breath along my forehead.

In an instant, I forgot about the bug as a shiver of awareness skated over my skin. Was it necessary for him to get *that* close to just get a bug out of my hair? My breath halted in my throat.

"Got it." He moved back, and I opened my eyes to see him flicking the brown bug into what was hopefully the afterlife. "It's gone now."

I didn't move. He was still so close. The tips of his boots touched my toes. His arm was close to mine, and I knew if I drew in a deep breath, my chest would brush his.

That one side of his lips curled up again, forming a lopsided smile. "You're totally okay and have officially entered a bug-free zone."

I still stood there.

Ms. Reed cleared her throat loudly. "Yes. I'm pretty sure the bug crisis has been averted. All is well in the world once more."

I blinked once, then twice. And then my body was burning again. Jensen cocked his head and his eyes traveled over my face, lingering on my scratched cheek. He started to lift his hand, but with a little shake of his head, he spun around gracefully and walked away.

"Jensen!" I called out.

He stopped, and as my heart pounded against my ribs, he slowly faced me. His expression was empty, but his pale blue eyes were locked on mine with the intensity those eyes always held. I took a step forward. "Thank you. I didn't get a chance before . . ."

A muscle popped along his jaw as he watched me with a look that said he wasn't quite sure he knew what I was thanking him for, but the words *I got you* cycled over and over again in my head.

"Thank you," I repeated, holding his gaze. "For helping me Saturday night."

THREE

JENSEN DIDN'T REPLY. All he did was nod and turn back around. I probably would've stood there forever watching his retreating form if Ms. Reed hadn't motioned me into her office.

I still couldn't believe it had been Jensen of all people that had been the one to show up when he did, startling the attacker. If he hadn't been getting into his truck and turning on the lights at that exact moment, God only knows what would've happened.

One thing I didn't understand, and hadn't been able to figure out, was why Jensen was still out there by the road. He'd left a good five to ten minutes before I had. Or at least I thought he had.

"Why was Jensen here?" I blurted out the question before I could stop myself. I flushed as I sat down. "That's probably none of my business."

"You're right. It wouldn't be any of your business." She sat behind her desk, folding her hands atop a closed file. A lock of dark hair fell across her forehead. "Normally. But I wanted to see him this morning for the same reason I wanted to see you. I wanted to make sure he was okay after everything since he was the one who found you."

Ms. Reed wasn't too much older than us, and everyone liked her as far as I knew. She was relatable in a way that most of the staff in school weren't. I enjoyed my time with her at the end of last year when I'd picked out my classes for senior year and she'd piled on the forms for financial aid and college applications, but that didn't mean I wanted to do the whole care and share thing with her.

"I really don't want to talk about Saturday night," I said, sitting rigidly still.

A sympathetic smile crossed her face. "Too soon?"

"You could say that." I reached up, twisting a lock of hair around my finger, a nervous habit I'd never been able to break. "Before you ask, I'm totally okay."

"Are you?"

My gaze flicked up, meeting hers.

"I know you can't be a hundred percent okay, Ella. What happened Saturday night had to have been terrifying for you."

Really, Captain Obvious?

The chair squeaked when she shifted, leaning back. "That kind of event is going to leave an impact on anyone, especially someone who—"

"I know," I interrupted, feeling my stomach dip. Closing my eyes, I curled my hands into fists until my sore palms ached. The mask—the porcelain looking clown face—flashed before me, forcing my eyes open. "But I don't want to talk about it or anything else."

Ms. Reed held my gaze for a moment longer and then nodded. "Is there anything I can help you with?"

I started to tell her no, but that's not what came out of my mouth. "Can you help me defend myself?"

She blinked slowly. "Come again?"

"I couldn't fight him off," I said. My voice came out unexpectedly hoarse, and I struggled with my next breath. "I didn't know how to. I couldn't *fight* him, and the only reason why I got away was luck—that's it. Luck. I was helpless." My voice cracked and I felt my cheeks heat. "And I don't want to feel that way again. So, unless you can help me become a ninja, there's really no reason for me to be sitting here."

A beat of silence passed. "Well, I don't know if I can help you become a ninja."

"Of course not," I muttered.

But she smiled widely, surprising me. "But I do know something about self-defense classes—more like someone who helped teach the one I was in during the summer. The classes are over, but I'm sure he'll make an exception for you."

I so wasn't expecting that. "Are you serious?"

"Yes." She looked happy to be helpful. "And to be honest, I think this is a brilliant idea. I think all women should take a course in self-defense. I wish we lived in a world where that wasn't necessary and we didn't have to worry about our safety, but until society wakes up and acknowledges we have a huge, misogynist problem on our hands, I'd rather be prepared to defend myself than not."

I nodded so quickly my throat hurt. I was so relieved that Miss Reed hadn't laughed in my face. "Exactly."

"It's also very empowering, and I'm proud that you are taking a step to gain back the power in the situation rather than doing nothing. Come back here at the end of the day and I should have the information for you."

I stared at her.

Ms. Reed laughed softly. "Look, like I said, I think it's a great idea for girls to learn how to defend themselves. Besides the fact that sadly a lot of teenage boys have been raised to believe that girls are put on Earth simply for them—"

My brows climbed up my forehead.

"—You can never be too safe. And I think that it will help you feel . . . better about things," she continued, taking off her glasses. "Everyone talks about women needing to have 'girl power,' as if that's something we're just born with. I mean, really, what is girl power? A pill or a drink we can take? Is it having a ton of female friends? Playing sports? Knowing how to kickbox coming out of the uterus? Being incredibly wise or a general smartass?" She snorted while I openly gaped at her. "What exactly are we teaching our girls? What about self-worth as empowerment? Instead of acting like a girl, or hitting like a girl being an insult, it's something to be proud of. Because let me tell you, I hit like a girl and I can knock someone into next week."

I glanced around the office, my eyes wide. "Um . . ."

"In my opinion, being empowered isn't so much the act or what you do, it's the driving force behind playing sports, having friends, knowing how to fight, and so on. It's knowing when you need help and the conscious decision to seek it out instead of doing nothing. Being proactive and taking back the control I know you feel like you've lost even though you don't want to tell me."

"I . . . I did feel like I lost control," I admitted, and I liked the idea that I was empowering myself by doing this. I wasn't just going to hide in my room or go about my life like nothing had happened. I was doing *something* at least.

"I know, Ella. This will help. It will bring only good things, and in the unlikely situation something happens again, even later in life, you'll be better prepared. That's real empowerment, making that choice to not be a statistic no matter what."

While I liked everything she was preaching—*girl power, roar!*—my brain got hung up on one thing. "Again?" I whispered, thinking about my belief in the statistical improbability of that occurring.

Ms. Reed's smile faded as she slipped her glasses back on. "Better safe than sorry, Ella."

I GLANCED DOWN at the slip of paper Ms. Reed had handed to me as I shuffled out the back door of the school, following the steady stream of students walking to the parking lot. I'd swung by her office after classes had ended, got another sermon on empowerment, and then was on my way. There was an address to a warehouse off of Airport Road and a cellphone number I didn't recognize in case I got lost.

My throat went dry as the paper fluttered between my fingers. Was I really going to do this? Ms. Reed told me my 'instructor' would be waiting for me after school and had been 'extremely willing' to help out.

Self-defense classes.

I almost laughed because the only form of exercise I had done recently was walking from my front door to my car, and I imagined that self-defense lessons were going to be one hell of a workout.

An almost familiar buzz of excitement trilled through my veins. I recognized the feeling before it could slip away from me. It was the same sensation I got when I used to lace up my running sneakers.

A sudden whooping drew my attention to the weight and locker rooms. The football team barreled out the door, heading to the football field on the hill for practice. Some carried their shoulder pads, others wore them over white shirts.

Brock was among them—the one hollering. He was pushing a scrawny boy, laughing as one of the towels he carried floated into the air and fell to the ground.

Shaking my head, I picked up my pace and then stumbled a step when I saw my Jetta. A small smile broke out across my face.

Gavin Grimes was leaning against my car, his hands shoved into the pockets of his khaki shorts. It had been at least two months since I'd seen him. Even though he lived on the same street as me, he hadn't really been around during the summer.

When he saw me, he pulled a hand out of his pocket and smiled, thrusting his hand through his coppery colored hair. A dimple appeared in his left cheek and he pushed away from my car. I opened my mouth, but his arms went around me, sweeping me up in a mammoth bear hug that didn't feel that great on my bruised ribs.

The hug caught me a little off guard. Our breakup had been

totally civil, but we hadn't so much as brushed arms since then. But the hug felt good on an emotional level—great, even. It was warm and familiar and so damn easy.

Gavin was half a head taller than me—he wasn't as tall as Jensen, but he was broader and longer limbed, something that he had trouble dealing with in middle school. The kids used to call him spider boy. Well, namely it had been Brock and Mason calling him that, but Gavin had grown into it. He was a cutie and he was all tan from the beach. As he hugged me tighter, my face was mushed against the top of his chest.

"Good God, Ella, I heard what happened to you," he said, and as I leaned back I could see others watching us as they got into their cars. "Are you okay?" Then his gaze moved to my cheek and below, to my neck. "Shit. You can't be okay."

"I'm totally fine," I told him, which is what I told everyone who had asked today—teachers, classmates, and the school resource officer who I'd ran into after lunch.

"But you—"

"Gavin, I'm okay. Just a little scratched and bruised. Not a big deal." The clown mask formed in the back of my thoughts, and I violently pushed it aside. "You weren't in class today. They called your name in English."

His arms were still around me. "Yeah, we didn't get back from the beach until late and I decided to skip today. I was going to call you later, but I needed to see that you were okay. I figured you went to school when I didn't see your car in front of your house." He paused, scanning my face and stopping on the strawberry mark. "Damn, Ella . . ."

I drew in a breath, but it got stuck in my throat. Heat flashed across my skin, and suddenly I was too hot. Slipping out of his embrace, I took a step back, needing space. Tugging a lock of hair around my finger, I fixed my gaze on an old Mustang a few spaces down. The engine kept turning over but not kicking on. "So . . . we have AP English together, and I'm on A lunch. Are you?"

He scrunched up his face, a habit when he was thinking hard. "I think I have B lunch."

"That sucks." I forced a smile as my gaze shifted back to him. "I want to chat . . . catch up, but I have to get going." I raised the piece of paper. "I'm going to take a self-defense class."

His brows shot up and his light green eyes widened. "You're what?"

I cringed. "I know I'm as coordinated as a two-legged llama, but don't tell me it's stupid because I think it's a smart thing to do. All things considered, you know?"

He coughed out a laugh as he shoved his hands into his pockets. "Yeah, that's kind of true, the whole llama thing, but I don't think it's stupid."

Relief sparked in my chest. "Really?"

"Yeah, why not?" He shifted his weight. "Where are you doing it at?"

I shrugged. "I really have no idea. Some kind of private lessons Ms. Reed took or something."

"That's cool. You're going to have let me know how it turns out for you," he said, idly scratching his jaw. "I've got to go. Dad wants me to help out tonight. I think it's payback for skipping school today."

I smiled at that. Gavin's parents owned a successful cleaning business considering they were pretty much the only ones in town. Every so often, his father had him help out. Something about learning responsibility. Gavin hated it—and the smell of cleaner and disinfectant—but he also got paid when he helped out, so he dealt with it.

"Call me later?" I asked, squinting into the sun.

"Of course." He stepped forward, hugging me again, and this time I relaxed into his embrace. "I wouldn't know what to do if something happened to you. Please be careful."

My face flushed as I squeezed my eyes shut. Before Gavin and

I tried to do the couple thing, we had been best friends. When we were eight years old, he helped me rescue a box turtle with a cracked shell we'd found in Back Creek. For Halloween one year, we dressed up as Jack and Jill. And when my grandmother passed away my freshman year, he'd brought me a plate of red velvet cupcakes and didn't wig out when I started crying.

And when the entire town had been turned upside down while we were in the seventh grade, he'd been there right along with me. I would never, ever forget that.

"I'll be careful," I said, hugging him back just as tightly. "I promise."

We broke apart then, promising to call each other later, and when I got into my car, I glanced out my window to see him still standing there. I wiggled my fingers.

Gavin waved back.

For the hundredth time since we broke up, I wished so hard that things hadn't been so easy with him—that I felt more, because he was a good guy—a *great* guy. And as I pulled out of the parking lot, I wished I were seeing him later tonight, curling up on the couch together and watching stupid movies. It would be nice to have him there right now, and if I asked, he'd be there, but that wasn't fair. The last thing I wanted to do was mislead him if he still had more than friendly feelings for me. Our relationship hadn't been the same since we broke up, and I'd give anything for it to go back to the way it was before we dated. Back to middle school actually, when we had this perfect little group of friends.

But no one could travel back in time.

And I was no longer so incredibly naïve. My childhood friends— the four of us. We hadn't been perfect. None of us. Far from it.

TRAFFIC CAME TO a complete standstill on Route 11. Stuck behind a fleet of orange buses, I wanted to bang my head against the steering wheel. Ms. Reed hadn't given me an exact time to show up, but I also didn't want this person waiting around forever for me.

When I finally reached the turn on Airport Road, I almost missed it. I had to hook a sharp right onto a narrow two lane road crowded by single family ranch homes that all looked identical. I winced as my tires squealed. An older gentleman out watering his grass sent me a sharp look when his head jerked up.

Perhaps I also needed driving lessons.

Glancing at the street number on the address given to me, I frowned and slowed down to a crawl, following the road. Up ahead, the houses all but disappeared, replaced by a restaurant that appeared to be in an old plane hangar. The only other building was the giant gray warehouse situated to the left, surrounded by fields full of yellowy reeds.

My stomach took a tumble as I parked my Jetta near a dark blue truck that looked vaguely familiar. Too nervous to pay it much attention, I took my sunglasses off since the sun had all but disappeared, and picked up the crumbled piece of paper, along with my cellphone, holding both tight in my grasp as I stepped out.

Wind whipped across the parking lot, stirring my loose hair. There were a few cars spotted throughout the lot, but as I stared at the darkened doors leading to the warehouse, my feet felt like they were cemented to the ground.

The place looked foreboding and empty, a perfect place to host a Halloween haunt in October, and pretty much the last place I wanted to enter.

Chills radiated up and down my back and a strange sort of pressure clamped down on my chest, squeezing my lungs until air wheezed in my throat, much like Saturday night when hands had circled my—

"Stop," I gasped out, swallowing hard. "Stop it right now."

Talking out loud was a sure sign of veering into cray-cray land, but I forced my heart to slow down and my feet to move. Clenching the phone to my chest, I crossed the parking lot.

The dark glass doors opened before I reached them and two older guys stepped out, gym bags flung over their shoulders. I had to be in the right place, but there were no signs outside indicating that I was.

As they passed me they smiled and I forced my lips to do the same thing, but the smile felt weak and weird—overly strained. The one closest to me was wearing black wraparound shades even though heavy clouds fat with rain had rolled in. He got halfway past me and then stopped.

"Hey," he called out.

My heart plummeted as a wave of fear crashed over me. The reaction stole my breath. I'd never been jumpy before, but now? I felt like I was going to crawl out of my skin.

"Ella Mansfield?" he said, and I turned around at the sound of my name. His buddy's brows rose in recollection as I stood there, thoroughly confused. The one who called my name stepped forward, taking off his sunglasses. Dark brown eyes met mine. He wasn't that old, maybe approaching his late twenties or early thirties. Something about his face was vaguely familiar.

I took a step back. "Hi?"

"You don't recognize me?" His smile didn't fade. "Totally understandable. I was one of the officers to . . . uh, respond Saturday night. I'm a deputy—Jordan Shaw. This idiot next to me is also a deputy—Neil Bryant."

"I wasn't there," Neil said, running a hand over his shaved head. "But glad to see you're doing good."

"Oh!" Heat crept across my cheeks. For some reason, the more I looked at Deputy Jordan Shaw, the more familiar he looked. Not from this past weekend, but like I should know his name. "Hi."

Shaw glanced over my shoulder, his eyes squinting. "I've never seen you here before. . . ."

He left the statement open, giving me a chance to explain my presence. "This is my first time. I . . . um, came here because I wanted to take a self-defense class." The heat turned to scalding. "I thought it would be a great idea and one of the staff at school knew someone who offered instruction."

"That's a damn smart idea," Neil said, nodding his approval.

"Thank you." I looked over my shoulder. "So I'm in the right place?"

"You are. That must be why the lights were on in room four. I can show you where to go. It's a bit of a maze in there." Shaw turned to his buddy. "I'll be right out."

Neil nodded. "See you later."

I gave him a little wave and then turned to Shaw. "You don't have to do this."

He was already at the door, holding it open. "It's no problem. It'll just take me a few seconds."

Biting the inside of my cheek, I shuffled forward and into a dimly lit corridor that smelled of . . . *apples*. I murmured my thanks and, as I sneaked a peek at the off-duty deputy, I got the sense that he wasn't doing this because he was normally Deputy Helpful, but more likely because he felt sorry for me.

And that made me want to go hide in a corner.

"So how are you holding up?" he asked, closing the door behind us.

"Okay."

He watched me for a second, his expression doubtful as we passed an empty glass case. "A lot of officers train here. If you go straight ahead, there's a gymnasium. Some of us come and play ball." When I nodded, he gestured to a set of closed double doors on his right. His damp white cotton shirt stretched across his arms. "That's where they teach Krav Maga. That will teach you self-defense real quick, but the classes being taught there aren't for beginners."

In other words, not ideal for what I was looking for.

"You want to go down here." Shaw pointed down the hallway

to our left. "Second set of double doors on your left is room four. That's where they usually teach the self-defense classes."

"Thank you." I stopped in front of the blue doors. Black paper had been taped over the windows, blocking the view inside, and I resisted the urge to peel the paper away and peek inside.

Shaw hesitated a moment. "Like my buddy said back there, this is a smart idea. Hell, I think it should be mandatory in schools."

Maybe if it had been, I would've been able to get away from the freak Saturday without needing luck.

I started to reach for the door when it struck me how I knew him. "Wait a second. Are you related to Gavin?"

"Yeah, I'm his cousin. His father and my father are brothers." He tilted his head to the side. "You guys were dating for a while, right? But not anymore?"

Nodding absently, I now remembered that Gavin had mentioned having an older cousin named Jordan who was a cop, but they weren't close due to the gap in their age. Never once in my entire life had I seen Jordan and Gavin together, but there was something else lingering at the fringe of my memory.

"Well . . ." He took a step back. "If you need anything, don't hesitate to call. I know the state has your case, but all you have to do is call the sheriff's office and ask for Jordan Shaw. They'll get you in touch with me."

"Thanks," I said, since it appeared to be the only thing I was capable of saying. Then I gave him a lame, awkward wave.

Shaw turned and then stopped, facing me. His dark eyebrows, the same color as his crew-cut hair, furrowed together. "We've met before—before Saturday night."

I frowned as I searched my memories, coming up empty. "I'm sorry. My brain has been scattered lately. Was it at one of Gavin's family things?"

"I can understand that." He flashed me a quick grin. "It wasn't at a family get together. It was a couple of years ago. I think you were about twelve or thirteen, the same age as Gavin. I responded to a call in the woods."

An icy rush of tingles exploded across the back of my skull and spread down my neck. I still didn't remember him, but I knew what he was talking about, and knots formed in my belly. "I was thirteen."

He nodded as his eyes met mine. "Some calls . . . well, some calls are harder to forget than others, and that was one of them. That kid . . ."

The floor seemed to swell underneath me. Every muscle in my body locked up, and I was seconds from being thrown into the past, into stumbling into something so horrifying it had taken *years* to erase those images.

"Anyway," Shaw said, giving a little shake of his head. "Don't forget what I said. If you need anything, don't hesitate."

I nodded slowly as he walked down the hall, disappearing around the corner. Closing my eyes, I swore under my breath. The good news was that those ghastly images from almost four years ago didn't resurface, but the ball of acidic emotions did curl around those knots.

That was the last thing I needed to think about.

I inhaled deeply and pushed open the door, ready to do anything to get my mind off the past . . . and the present.

I came to a complete stop, the air whooshing out of me as the door swung shut behind me.

Holy mountain roads take me home . . .

There was a half-naked dude in front of me. His back was to the door and the intricate play of muscles that rippled and flexed across his shoulders and back were fascinating to watch as he lowered a punching bag to the floor, next to where a gray shirt rested in a heap. His dark blue nylon pants hung low on his hips, showing of a taut band of lower back muscles. But it wasn't just any half-naked dude, and suddenly the blue truck outside made sense.

Oh dear God, it was *him*.

As he turned sideways, looking over to where I stood, I felt like I needed to go sit down on one of the metal chairs. I got an eyeful of rock hard abs, a little bit of dusky brown male nipple, and then he was bent over, swiping his shirt off the floor.

One side of his mouth curved up. "I was wondering when you were going to get here."

A healthy dose of intelligence escaped me as I stared at him. "I'm in the wrong room."

He chuckled under his breath, straightening and facing me fully. Beautiful eyes, the color of the morning sky, met mine. "You're in the right room, Ella."

My heart kicked against my ribs and my brain raced to come up with a different alternative to what—or who—was staring me right in the face, but there were no other answers.

He's extremely willing to help out, Ms. Reed had claimed, but she must've been toking off the crack pipe or something, because she had sent me to meet with Jensen Carver.

FOUR

I HAD NO idea how I was standing in front of him. "You teach self-defense?"

Jensen strolled over to me, taking long, purposeful strides, and lordy-lord, he so needed to put that shirt on because I was having a hard time keeping my eyes trained on his face. "I've helped the instructor a time or two during his classes, so I know what I'm doing."

My gaze dropped to those indents on either side of his hips. He *so* knew what he was doing. "I don't understand. Shouldn't you be at football practice?"

Jensen stopped a few feet in front of me, casually fixing his shirt so it wasn't inside out. "I'm not playing football this year."

"Why?" I demanded like I had a right to know. "I mean, I heard you were going to start as quarterback. You tried out for the team last spring. You made it." My cheeks heated as he cocked a brow at me, and I realized it might be a little odd that I knew that since I hadn't spoken to him when he'd showed up halfway through my junior year. "I mean, everyone was talking about it."

He looked up at me through thick lower lashes as he tugged the sleeves out. The density of those lashes should be illegal. "I'm trying to get a scholarship to UM. Football isn't going to pay my way there, so I decided that focusing on my classes was a smarter idea."

How had I not heard that he wasn't playing football this year? Then again, since he had returned, we weren't running in the same crowds, not anymore. I just assumed that he'd changed. That he was like Brock and Mason, only caring about chasing balls and girls. Okay, that was judgy. Jensen was not one-dimensional. The guy was super smart. I just didn't know him anymore.

Watching him pull the shirt over his head, I now didn't know if I should be happy or disappointed he was covering up the kind of body fantasies were built upon.

"So," he said, letting the shirt slide down his abs. "You want to learn self-defense?"

I was stunned. "Did you know it was me when Ms. Reed asked you?"

His eyes glinted in the bright fluorescent lights. "Yes."

"And you agreed to do it?"

He laughed under his breath, like something was funny. "Yes."

"I don't get it."

Jensen ran his fingers through his hair as he titled his head to the side, eyeing me with a look of barely restrained exasperation. "Okay. Did you ask Ms. Reed to help you find someone who can teach you self-defense?"

"Yes, but—"

"And that's what she did. She caught me before lunch and asked if I would teach you a few things. I said yes." He lowered his hand. "And here we are. That's not too hard to figure out."

My eyes narrowed. "I'm not stupid. I can follow along with the chain of events."

"I know you're not. You're the opposite of stupid."

"But I don't know why you'd agree to help me. You don't . . ."

Now his eyes tapered into thin slits as he took a step forward, his arms at his sides. "I don't what?"

Every instinct demanded that I take a step back, but I held my ground. "You don't like me."

The lopsided grin spread. "I've never in my entire life ever said I didn't like you, Ella."

The way he said my name brought a flush of heat to my cheeks. He had never said my name like that before. Suddenly, he was right in front of me, standing so close that his sneakers were brushing my toes like they had been this morning. Before today and before Saturday, the last time we'd been this close was when . . .

Jensen had been my first kiss.

My heart jumped as the memory tugged at it. We were kids, and neither of us had any idea what we were doing, but that kiss had been better than all the kisses that had come afterward. A flutter started between my ribs, like a little hummingbird trying to beat its way out. And I hadn't ever felt that with Gavin or anyone else.

"I think it's obvious," I managed to say.

One eyebrow lifted. "How so?"

"You haven't talked to me in four years."

"Ella, I moved away."

Anger flashed through me, bright like the sun. "Um, the last time I checked, there's a nifty invention called the telephone and the Internet."

"Yeah, I think I've heard of that, but . . . you know, there was some shit going on. More than you think, but you know what else? I'm pretty sure the whole communication thing goes both ways. You didn't try to contact me either," he added before I could question the whole 'more than you think' comment. He shifted just the slightest, keeping his eyes trained on mine with an intensity that had always been his. "And if I remember correctly, I did try to talk to you when I came back to Martinsburg. At school my very first day here, and you told me to stay away from you. That was the second time you've told me that."

He had a point with that and I wanted to ignore it. "I think this was—"

Jensen moved so quickly I didn't have the chance to do anything. He grabbed my upper arms and whirled me around. My grip tightened on my keys and phone, but they were of little use as his arms came down around me, clamping my arms to my sides.

Air whooshed out of my lungs as he jerked me back against his chest. Momentarily stunned, I was torn between being wholly aware of the feel of him pressed against me, and the memory of the last time I was snared in such a grip.

"What are you doing?" I shrieked.

His chin grazed my cheek as he lowered his head. "Starting your first lesson. Probably the most important."

My eyes felt like they were going to pop out of my head. This was a bad idea, the height of all my bad ideas combined into one giant stupid idea. "My first lesson?"

"You know, the whole self-defense thing?" Amusement clung to his tone.

"B-But I'm not even wearing workout clothing," I stammered, irritated with him and myself and the world and the Queen of England.

"That's good. You know why?"

I frowned as I tried to pull forward, but there was no breaking his hold. "I bet you're going to tell me."

"Your movements are restricted in normal clothes, and the likelihood of you being attacked walking out of gym class while wearing gym clothes sounds a bit unlikely, right?"

For a second, I pictured myself breaking free like a ninja and karate-chopping him across the head. That was also as unlikely as being attacked moments after leaving gym class. "You don't have to be a smartass about it."

His deep chuckle rumbled through me, eliciting a shiver from my body. His laugh died off and a heartbeat passed between us. The warmth of his body rolled into me, loosening a bit of the knots in my stomach. His grip didn't loosen, but his body tensed behind mine. In that tiny span of time, it felt like something had shifted between us, something potent and consuming.

And then he opened his mouth.

"How did he grab you?" When I didn't answer, he tried again. "How did he grab you, Ella? Like this? From behind?"

I blinked a couple of times, and my heart leaped into my throat. In a nanosecond, ice trickled into my veins. "Yeah."

"And what did you do?"

What did I do? Memories rushed over me like a disturbing photo album. As I stared at the closed doors with covered windows, my mind drifted, no longer in this room. I was back on the long dark stretch of road, right near my car, so close and yet so very far away.

"Let me go," I said.

The muscles in his arms twitched. "Is that how you got free? I don't think that worked."

Of course it hadn't. I squeezed my eyes shut, feeling my feet suddenly in the air and the horror of being weightless as I was dragged away from my car, toward the woods. My chest rose and fell rapidly. "He slipped," I gasped out. "When I threw my weight back, he slipped and fell, but I didn't get very far." I dragged in a deep breath, forcing my eyes wide. He . . ." Horror seized me, and again, I was struck by the stupidity of this. "It's too soon. I don't want to do this."

Jensen held on. "Ella—"

"Let me go." I jerked forward, but he held on. Panic crawled up my throat. "I'm not ready for this. Please. I don't want to—"

"It's okay. You're safe here. I'm not going to hurt you," he said, his voice low. "You know that, Ella. You probably still know me better than most."

No. I didn't know him anymore. I stopped knowing him years ago, but I stilled, realizing only then how much I was struggling against him.

His cheek was pressed against my temple. "You're safe here."

My chest rose sharply once more and I whispered, "I know."

"I'm just here to help you and I'm going to. Okay? You want that, right?"

I nodded as his words sunk in, and I forced my breathing to slow. I came here for a reason. Freaking out was not helping me at all. As my heart slowed, embarrassment reared its ugly head.

"How are you hanging in there?"

"Now or . . . ?" I bit down on my lower lip.

He shifted his head and his breath was warm against my ear. "You're okay now. I can tell."

"How?"

"Your breathing has changed," he explained, and boy, that's how close we were. He could *feel* the patterns in my breathing. "What about the other stuff?"

The other stuff . . .

My fingers twitched around my cell and keys. "Do you know how many times I've been asked that today?"

"Well, you've just been asked once more."

The corners of my lips twitched, and I started to say what I'd been saying to everyone. Maybe even change it up with 'all right,' but that's not what came out of my mouth. "Not that great."

"I can imagine." The muscles in his arms flexed again. "Maybe this will help."

"Maybe," I murmured.

His chest rose against my back. "All right, first things first. You can always trick the assailant. Pretend to be weak. Fake a faint."

"What?" That just made no sense.

"If you're grabbed and your attacker thinks you're weak when you're not, you have the upper hand—the element of surprise, especially when you have a weapon in your hand. You probably did Saturday night. Did you know that? It's your keys."

My keys? "I dropped them."

"You don't want to do that. Look at them. You have . . . holy crap, how many keys do you have on that thing? Jesus. Like twenty?"

I rolled my eyes as I flushed. "Not that many. Geez."

"I think you have a key for every house on Rosemont Avenue," he said, chuckling, and my blush deepened even further. It was something I tried not to think about—that he only lived three blocks from my house; moved right back into the house he'd grown up in—that I'd grown up in. When he moved away, his parents had rented it out, but I still looked for him every time I drove past his house. "Anyway, move the keys so that the jagged parts are sticking up between your fingers." When I did as he asked, I could hear the smile in his voice when he spoke next. "See? You got yourself a hell of a weapon now. Slam those keys into any body part and you may just get the upper hand, but you've got to get free first."

Staring at the jagged key edges, I tried to picture myself shoving them into someone's face. Before Saturday night, I never would've thought I could do something like that. The only thing I could easily hurt was bugs. With an icky sinking feeling, I realized I could easily do that to someone now.

Saturday night had irrevocably changed me.

"There's a couple of ways to break this kind of hold that doesn't involve throwing your weight around. That doesn't always work. The first one is going to be the easiest and something people don't think of," he explained. "All you have to do is stomp a foot."

"Stomp a foot?" My brows rose.

"Yep. Bring your leg up—you're right-handed, right? Use your right leg and slam your foot down on mine as hard as you can."

Jensen walked me through it and then he switched to a different tactic. In a smooth, rolling voice, he taught me the different ways to break a bear hug. One involved shifting to the side and bending down. By extending my arm back, I could get a good crotch shot in.

Swinging back toward that area on him was about seven kinds of awkward.

"Come on," he coaxed. "There have been plenty of times you've wanted to hit me in the balls, so I know you can do better than that."

I grinned despite everything. "Now that you mention it . . ." I swung my arm back, stopping at the last possible moment. When I felt his chest rise sharply, a disturbing amount of satisfaction whipped through me. "How's that?"

"Uh, yeah, that's much better."

I dropped my phone on the mat but kept my keys for the next round. This one involved bringing my knee up and kicking it back into the assailant's knee. He went over that until I got the hang of the motion, and then a few more utilizing the same kind of technique.

"I want you to go through this—the crotch shot. Don't hit me," he said. "I just want to throw that out there. When I let go, you have two options. Run like hell."

"Sounds like a good option."

He ignored that. "Or you fight. Okay? We're going to start from the beginning." He released his hold and when I started to look back at him, he snapped forward, wrapping his arms around me and pulling me back.

I did as he instructed. First, I raised my right leg and stomped my foot down on his. Jensen grunted and his grip loosened enough to give me some room. Holding on to my keys, I shifted to my left as I bent at the waist. Extending my right arm, I swung it back, my hand knocking off his inner thigh. Close enough for him to suck in an unsteady breath. He let go as I wrenched forward.

Two options. Fight. Or flight.

I didn't think it through as I spun around, facing him. Jensen had started forward, but drew up short when I raised my hand with the keys.

His brows, darker than his sandy hair, rose. "You're going to fight?"

Breathing heavily, I watched him. Would I fight? I'd gotten free Saturday night and I ran. I hadn't gotten very far. "A smart thing to do would be to injure the person and then run."

"It would be, but I would rather you run."

I frowned, thinking that by choosing to fight I'd done the right thing. "Why?"

He looked away for only a moment, and then he shot forward, wrapping his large hand clean around my wrist. He hauled me against him, chest to chest. The contact frazzled my senses and I dropped the keys.

Like a total loser.

Jensen lowered his head, coming so close that his mouth was inches from mine. "You probably should have held on to those keys."

"No shit."

"Though there's not much you can do with the keys when I'm holding your wrist."

"Double no shit."

"When did you get such a mouth on you?"

"When you weren't around," I shot back without really thinking about it.

"Good point." His gaze dropped for a moment and then rose, the hue of his eyes deepening to a magnetic blue. "See how easy that was? That's why I'd want you to run. Not to mention, you have no idea where to even shove your keys."

"How about in your face?"

"All I have to do is lean back." He didn't lean back, though. If anything, it felt like he got closer. A low, sweet simmering warmth washed down my neck. "If you're going to fight, you need to really know how to fight, Ella. If not, you need to get away. That's the smart thing to do. That's what we teach in self-defense. How to utilize these moves to get away. Not to turn around and engage."

"But I did get away," I whispered, and my lashes lowered. I could almost feel my toes slipping through the grass and the dirt. "But he caught me again."

"Is that how this happened?" he asked, and when I must've given him a "huh" look, he twisted his hand, barely brushing his thumb under the scratches on my palm. They ached from how tight I'd been holding the keys. "And this?" With his other hand, he trailed his fingers under the mark on my cheek.

The soft whisper of his touch rattled me. My breath was coming in and out a little too fast. "Yes, but . . . you can teach me where to hit. You can teach me how to fight."

His fingers drifted off my cheek. "I can."

"Then teach me."

He shook his head. "You need to know how to get away—"

"I already told you that I got away, but he *caught* me. I don't want to know how to run. I want to know what to do when I get caught. Okay?" I swallowed the sudden burn of tears. "I don't need to know how to run."

"I know you know how to run. If I remember correctly, you could run fast." His eyes searched mine. "Why aren't you on track or cross country like you planned?"

The question caught me off guard. "I don't run anymore."

He blinked. "What? You loved—"

"I just don't do it anymore. I . . . got bored with it." Frustration rose. "I want to learn to fight, Jensen. That's why I'm here."

His brows knitted as he stared down at me. He didn't respond for a long moment and then said, "I get it. I do, Ella."

I let out a shaky breath. "Thank you."

Jensen's lips split into a real smile, one that reached his eyes, and I was a little awed by that. It had been far too long since I'd been on the receiving end of a Jensen Carver smile. "Against my better judgement, I can teach you how to fight, but not tonight. It's getting late."

I hadn't even thought of the time.

Jensen hadn't moved and neither had I. Our chests were still getting to know each other, and if I stretched up on the tips of my toes, my lips would meet his, but that would be wrong. All kinds of wrong.

I just couldn't remember exactly why that would be a bad idea.

"I'm glad you're okay," he said, breaking the silence.

My fingers curled inward. "I'm . . . I'm glad you were there."

His eyes met mine and then flitted away. "Yeah, me too."

Jensen let go and backed off, thrusting his hand through his hair. "That's enough for tonight."

The sudden change was like walking into a freezer. I turned, picking up my phone and collecting my useless brain cells. "So, how much do I owe you for this . . . ?"

He shook his head as he strode past me. "You don't owe me anything."

"But I need to pay you for this. I don't have a lot, but—"

"I'm not taking your money," he interrupted, reaching the door. Holding it open, he motioned me forward. "Come on. I've got to turn the lights off."

I didn't like the idea of not paying him, but I could see I wasn't going to win this argument right now. I let him usher me outside, and as he locked up the room, I realized his intentions. "You don't need to walk me to my car."

He fell in step beside me, which meant he was slowing down his long-legged pace. "But what if a bug jumps out and tries to bug molest you again?"

His teasing tone tugged at my lips. "What? Do you make a habit of rescuing damsels in distress from bugs?"

"Only from stinkbugs," he said. "And only pretty girls."

I tripped as I looked at him sharply. "Don't say that."

His brows snapped together. "Why not?"

There were a multitude of reasons. "Just don't."

He was quiet as we continued down the dimly lit hall. Grunts echoed from the closed doors surrounding us. "Should I not compliment you? Would you prefer that I insult you?"

A laugh escaped me. His tone was light, still teasing. "How about you just stay . . . I don't know, real with me."

"Okay. I can do that." He opened the door for me. "I can keep it real."

There seemed to be a message in there that I wasn't getting.

"We can talk about what times you want to get together. You're on A lunch, right?"

I stopped in front of my car, brushing back the strands of hair the wind had tossed across my face. "Yeah. Are you? I didn't see you today."

"I saw you." He shrugged a shoulder. "Anyway, I'll catch up with you tomorrow." He started to turn and then he stopped. Our eyes met from across the parking space separating us. "I'll wait until you're in the car."

It was ridiculous, but the flutter was back in my chest, banging off my ribs. I raised my hand and waved awkwardly like a crossing guard with a broken arm. "See you tomorrow . . . Jensen."

A little smile appeared on his lips, just a tiny tip at the corners as he nodded. Over his shoulder, the sun had started to disappear behind the horizon, turning the sky along the mountains a deep pink and vibrant blue. He waited until I got into the car and turned it on. Only when I shifted it out of park did he turn and jog over to his truck. I didn't realize I was smiling like a total fool until my cheeks started to ache.

The smile stayed on my face all the way home.

I all but ran inside my house, delayed only by how long it took me to unlock the front door. Darting into the kitchen, I grabbed a bottle of water and then made my way upstairs.

The noise from the TV in Mom's bedroom traveled out into the hall. I thought about going in there and plopping my butt down on her bed and stealing the ice cream—the pint of ice cream I knew she had with her—but I headed to my bedroom first to change.

Flipping on the light with my elbow, I toed my shoes off and started to pull off my shirt, wincing when the skin along my ribs pulled as I lifted my arms. Stepping in the middle of my room, I stilled when a warm rush of air blew across my exposed stomach.

Odd.

I tugged my shirt off as I turned toward my bedroom window. In an instant, everything but my heart slowed down, like someone had pushed the giant remote control on life and hit slow-mo.

The thin white curtains billowed out from my window, rippling in gentle waves as they fell back down.

My toes sunk into the carpet as I walked toward the window. Reaching out, I curled my fingers around the soft curtains, slowly pulling them back. The window was open.

No screen.

Nothing but the night air filling the void.

My heart stopped as I straightened and turned toward my bed. My gaze made a slow crawl across my room, skipping erratically when something—the bathroom door—creaked. I wheeled toward the bathroom, but stopped when my gaze landed on the bed.

I stumbled back a step, the shirt falling from my limp fingers to the carpet. "Oh my God . . ."

On my bed, nestled between the two king-size pillows and placed on top of my blue Care Bear, was a mask—the same mask I saw every time I closed my eyes. And there it was, staring back at me with those empty eyes and the overly wide, disturbing smile.

The clown mask was on my bed with a post-it note attached to it, just above the holes were eyes should've been. The crudely written message screamed at me.

It's your fault.

FIVE

IT WAS HERE—*HE* was here.

I backpedaled, stumbling into the computer chair as a scream burst from my mouth. Ice drenched my veins as I wheeled around and took off. Throwing open my bedroom door, I raced down the hall.

"Mom!" I screamed. "Mom!"

Oh my God, what if something had happened to her? My stomach lurched as I reached for the closed door at the end of the hall, but it sprang open before I could get there.

Mom rushed out, her face pale as she took me in. "Ella, what is going on? Why don't you—"

"He's here!" I grabbed her arm, pulling at her. "The window is open and a mask on my bed! With a note! He's in my bathroom!"

Confusion flickered across her face and then she spun around, darting back into the bedroom.

"Mom!" I shouted, looking over my shoulder as my heart pounded so fast that I was afraid I was going to have a heart attack. Was she grabbing her ice cream? "We need to get out of here. What are you doing?"

She returned, her cellphone in one hand, and she tossed me a shirt. Only then did I realize I was standing in the hall in my jeans and a bra.

Horror sunk my stomach to a new low when I realized I'd been in my room half naked and so had that—that *thing*.

Mom grabbed my arm, pulling me toward the stairs as she spoke into the phone. Breathless, she gave the dispatcher her name and address. "Yes, we're leaving the house right now."

We rushed outside and across the front yard, the grass warm and wet under my feet. I stopped at the thick hedges and turned back, raising my gaze. My bedroom was in the back of the house, over-looking the backyard, and there was nothing I could see from here.

My chest hurt as I shuddered. "He had to have gotten in through the window. The front door was locked. He had to have climbed the tree and opened the window."

Mom said nothing as she wrapped her arms around me. Within seconds, I could hear the blaring of sirens and the steady approach calmed my nerves a little bit, but all I could think about was that thing being in the house with Mom and for God knows how long.

Three city police cruisers arrived, one after another. One of the cops hustled us out to the sidewalk as two of them went inside, guns drawn.

I sat down on the curb, watching the red and blue lights whirl over the road as Mom repeated to the officer what I had said. He immediately asked if it was the same kind of mask the attacker had worn Saturday night.

I nodded. "Yes. It was the same mask. I'm a hundred percent pos-itive on that. And there was a note on it. You'll see. It said it was my fault." I looked at my mom. "I don't understand what that meant."

She folded her arm around my shoulders. "I don't know, honey."

Mom stayed with me until one of the deputies called her over to where he was standing near the porch.

Shoving the hair back from my face, I rested my forehead on my knees. What was the monster doing back? Trooper Ritter had insisted that the attacker most likely fled not only the county, but also the state. So why would he be here?

For some horrible reason I thought of how the trooper had asked about Vee and the worst kind of idea popped into my head. What if she hadn't run away? What if she was grabbed just like I was, but she hadn't gotten away? And now the guy was coming back . . .

It didn't matter. The cops were here and they had to have found him. This would be all over and my life would be normal again.

"Ella?" Mom's soft voice called.

I sat up, spying the other two officers, and I jumped to my feet. I searched behind them, looking for some creep in handcuffs, but there was no one with them. Unease blossomed in my belly. "Did you find him?"

One of the officers, older with hair graying at the temples, glanced at the other cop. He cleared his throat. "We checked the entire house, top to bottom, and there was no one in your home."

"No." I balled my hands into fists, wanting to hit something. "He must've climbed back out the window." I looked over at Mom and the pinch to her expression confused me. "Did you at least get the mask off the bed? The note?"

Because I was so not going back into that bedroom with that thing in there. On second thought, I never wanted to go back in there and touch anything he'd had his hands on.

The cop shifted his weight. "There was no mask on the bed, nothing, and the bedroom window was closed. There's no evidence that anyone was in the house."

It took a few moments for what he said to sink in, and then I understood the look on Mom's face and the reason why the officers looked so uncomfortable. "No." And then I said it again. "*No.*"

"These things are common after traumatic events." The officer who'd remained outside turned to my mom, speaking quietly. "Stress can do some strange things, make people believe they've seen something not there."

I zoned them out as I turned back to the house. There was no way I was so stressed out that I had imagined *all* of that. I wasn't crazy.

Red-hot anger bubbled up inside me, and I was walking toward my house before I even knew what I was doing.

"Ella!" Mom called out.

I ignored her and took the porch steps two at a time. I threw open the storm door and rushed up the stairs. I didn't stop until I reached my bedroom. I stood in the doorway, breathing heavily.

The window was closed.

The bathroom door was open as were the closet doors. My gaze shifted to the bed and another wave of anger burst like a firecracker, a mixture of humiliation and frustration.

My Care Bear sat on the pillows, minus the creepy clown mask and note.

The cops probably thought I was crazy. So did my mom. But there was no way I could've imagined all of that.

I crossed the bedroom, tugging the curtains back. The window was down. There was no lock on it, so it was entirely possibly that he'd bolted once I ran screaming from the room, taking the mask with him and closing the window behind him. Getting up or down wasn't hard. The tree was right up against the roof, and I knew it was possible. It had been done over and over before.

But why?

Did he plan on grabbing me or . . . or just scaring me? And if he wanted to scare me, what was the point? I was already scared.

I was *terrified*.

"Baby."

Turning at the sound of her voice, I drew in a shallow breath. She came into the room and sat on the edge of the bed. "How could I have imagined that? I *saw* the mask on my bed. And I read the note. I *felt* the breeze from the open window. I *heard* my bathroom door move. How can you hallucinate all of that?"

"I don't think you hallucinated anything."

I folded my arms across my chest. "Then you believe me."

She lowered her gaze as she patted the spot next to her. Reluctantly I made my way over to sit beside her. "I believe you think you saw something. I heard the fear in your voice, but . . ."

I scanned the room. Nothing was out of place.

"But I do think it's a good idea to call Dr. Oliver tomorrow," she continued, smiling gently when I turned a sharp look on her. "I think you need to talk to him."

"I don't need to talk to him," I said, freezing up.

She smoothed her hand down my hair. "All I'm saying is that it wouldn't hurt to see Dr. Oliver. You haven't been to him in a while."

My lips pressed into a thin line.

"Ella, baby, you've been through a horrific event." She reached down, pulling my arm away from my body. She threaded her fingers through mine. "And you're going to have some leftover . . . issues from that. Look at it this way. You're taking self-defense, right? Consider talking to Dr. Oliver as another lesson."

More like a lesson in feeling like a maladjusted teenager. Dr. Oliver wasn't bad or anything, but I always left his office feeling like I needed a cartload of meds or something.

"Okay," I whispered, not liking it, but also knowing there was no other way out of it.

Mom nodded as she squeezed my hand. "How was your lesson today? Did you learn anything?"

I welcomed the change in subject as I eyed the bedroom, waiting for some creep to appear out of thin air. "Yeah. You're not going to believe who's teaching it."

"Who?"

"Jensen Carver."

Mom blinked slowly. Of course she knew him. Mom had been like a . . . second mother to Jensen growing up. Just like Jensen's mom had helped raise me.

"Really," she said finally, like that was the only thing she could say in response.

At least that brought a wry grin to my face. "Yeah. I was surprised he agreed to do it, but he said he'd teach me, so . . ."

Mom reached over, pulling my free hand away from my hair. "I think that will be good. You know, for you two to reconnect."

My stomach did a weird little flip at the thought of *reconnecting*.

Creases appeared in her brow. "But doesn't he play football?"

"Not anymore."

"Hmm," she murmured. "How is Jensen doing?"

I shrugged. Mom knew we hadn't talked. Not since seventh grade, around the time Jensen grew into his long limbs and those beautiful lips. Overnight, he'd become popular, and I remained . . . well, painfully average. And that was before he moved away.

A lot had happened before he moved away.

She shook her head. "Every time I think of him, I think of his brother. What was his name?"

An ache pierced my chest at the mention of Jensen's older brother, someone I hadn't thought of in a very long time. "His name was Jonathan."

"Such a tragedy." Mom sighed sadly. "For a young man like that to just die in his sleep. I feel so terrible for him and his parents."

Pressing my lips together, I nodded. Jonathan had been five years older than Jensen. The two had been close when we were . . . friends. A lifetime ago. I'd heard that his brother had been home from college when he'd died in his—

My eyes widened as I realized why Jensen wanted to go to the University of Maryland. Or at least I thought I did. That was where Jonathan had been going to school. Was Jensen following in his brother's footsteps as some way to honor his memory? If so, that was . . . God, I didn't even know and I had no idea what to do with that piece of information.

"This town has seen enough tragedy," she said.

I froze again. Was she going to talk about *it*? No one ever talked about *it* anymore, but before she could continue, the doorbell clanged throughout the house, causing me to jump.

Mom frowned as she stood up. "Probably one of our nosey neighbors." She paused at the door. "Are you okay?"

Not really, but I nodded.

When she left the room, I was alone and still too creeped out to sit in here. Hopping to my feet, I made it to the door just as Mom called for me. I stopped at the top of the stairs. She was at the bottom, an odd little smile on her face.

"What?" I asked.

"It's for you." And that's all she said.

Having no idea who it could be, I came down the stairs. If it was Linds, Mom would've just let her upstairs. Even Gavin. The fluttering was back in my chest as I hurried up, practically hopping down the steps.

I passed Mom, shooting her a look when she all but pranced from the room. Taking a deep breath, I opened the door and my suspicions—or hope, but whatever—were confirmed.

Jensen stood on my porch, dressed as he was earlier, wearing nylon pants and a cotton shirt. Our eyes locked, and I swore some kind of unseen tension eased from his stare.

"You're okay." It was a statement, not a question.

Glancing behind me, I saw the top of Mom's head poking out from the living room. I stepped outside, closing the door behind me. "I'm okay."

Jensen stared at me like he was trying to see something not easily visible. "I just got home and Dad said there was a bunch of police cars here."

"And you came to check it out?"

An eyebrow arched up. "Uh, yeah. I'm here."

I flushed because that was a stupid question. "Everything's fine. They were just . . . um, checking out the house."

A look of doubt crossed his striking face. "But you're okay?"

Earlier, when I mentioned how many times I'd been asked that question, I didn't think I could stand being asked one more time, but for some reason, it didn't irritate me now. "I'm really fine."

His eyes met mine again, and as we stood there, I could clearly remember the last time he'd been on my porch. I'd told him I never wanted to talk to him again. Tears had streamed down my face, and I'd been so angry and so embarrassed.

And so heartbroken.

Jensen opened his mouth as if he was about to say something, and then he tilted his head to the side, causing a wavy strand of hair to topple across his forehead. "You know that number Ms. Reed gave you?"

I nodded.

"That's my phone number," he said. I had sort of figured that out at this point. "Do me a favor and save it on your phone. If you need anything, call me. All right?"

The note was burning a hole in my jean pocket at that very moment. "Sure."

He held my stare a moment longer, then nodded and pivoted around with the kind of grace I'd never have. He got to the pathway before I stopped him.

"Jensen."

He turned, head tilted to the side again. Standing in the dark with only the moonlight slicing over his broad cheekbones and cut jaw, he looked like some kind of fairytale prince come to life.

Oh God, I had no idea why I was comparing him to a Disney prince or stopping him. I needed to stop reading so much. But I wanted to invite him inside, and I wanted to sit next to him. And I wanted to somehow reclaim the missing years between us.

And he'd make a really hot Disney prince, too.

But I couldn't say any of that, so I latched on to the first thing that popped into my head. "The reason you want to go to the

University of Maryland . . . is it because of your brother?"

Surprise flickered over Jensen's face as he rubbed his hand across his chest. "Wow. That was a random question."

"Yeah, it kind of was." I raised my hands and shrugged. "Probably also none of my business, so you don't—"

"Yeah, it is." He lowered his hand, and a tight, one-sided smile appeared. "He couldn't finish college, so I thought I'd do it for him."

"That's . . . that's really nice." I wish I had something better to say. "I mean it, Jensen. That's really a good way of honoring him."

He nodded slowly. "Yeah . . . I've got to get back, but I'll see you tomorrow."

Once again, I found myself waving at him awkwardly. I watched him disappear around the tall hedges, hanging a right toward his house.

"Interesting," Mom said the moment I stepped a foot back in the house. "And might I add that Jensen has turned into one fine looking young man?"

"Ew. Mom."

She shrugged. "I may be old, but I'm not blind."

I ignored that as I climbed the stairs, and it wasn't until much later, when I was lying in my bed clutching the stupid bear to my chest as I stared at the closed window, that the thought from earlier—the one about the tree and roof—popped back into my head.

There was a reason why I knew anyone could climb that tree and make the jump to the roof. After all, it had been done so many times in the past that I'd lost count.

When I was younger and it was way past our bedtime but we wanted to hang out, Jensen would sneak out of his house and scale the tree like a little monkey. He'd land on the roof and shuffle right up to my window.

He'd taught me how to do it.

He'd also taught Gavin.

And he'd taught *Penn*.

THEN

"I DON'T KNOW about this," Penn called out. His thin arms were practically glued to the trunk of the tree that was at least five sizes wider than him. "I don't think that limb is strong enough."

Gavin groaned from where he stood at my bedroom window. "Dude, Jensen and I both just walked on it and we're bigger than you."

"Everyone is bigger than me," Penn shot back. "But that doesn't mean it won't break."

I poked my head out the window. "The tree's been there longer than this house. It's not going to break."

"How do you know it's been here longer than the house?" he challenged. "Did you count the tree's whorls?"

"The what?" replied Gavin, his forehead wrinkling.

Penn shook his head. "The whorls on the tree trunk. Counting them will tell you how old a tree is."

"Who knows that?" he retorted. "No wonder you get picked on, dude. Seriously."

I smacked Gavin's arm even though Penn appeared largely unfazed by the comment. Behind us, my bedsprings creaked. I glanced over my shoulder. Jensen was standing, all long limbs and hair.

"I know what whorls are," Jensen said, crossing my bedroom and joining Gavin on the other side. He waved at Penn. "Do exactly what I showed you. It worked for Gavin."

Penn glanced down.

"Don't do that," Jensen ordered. "Don't look at the ground. Look at us." When Penn lifted his gaze, Jensen nodded. "Just pretend . . . I don't know, that you're walking to your telescope or something."

"I wouldn't put my telescope on a branch or a roof."

I smiled.

Gavin sighed. "Look, I'll come out on the roof." He reached up, gripping the top of the window as he put a knee on the windowsill. The moment his head hit the sun, his hair turned a burnt reddish color. "Does that make you feel better?"

"No! I don't trust you!"

Gavin froze.

"I mean, if I fall, you aren't going to be able to stop me," Penn added. "You're not much bigger than me."

"Geez. Thanks." Gavin glanced back at us. His eyes were wide and the center of his cheeks pink. "Did you guys hear that?"

I smashed my hand over my mouth to stop from giggling.

Jensen grinned at me before he shouldered Gavin out of the way. He placed one hand on the windowsill and hopped up, agile like the neighbor's cat. He dipped through the window and then straightened once he was on the shingled roof.

Biting my lip, I watched Jensen tread carefully toward the edge of the roof, where the thickest branches met the gutters. "I really hope my mom doesn't come home soon. If she looks up and sees Jensen and Penn, she'll die."

Gavin nodded. "You're going to be in so much trouble."

"It's all Jensen's fault," I reasoned. "He started this."

Jensen looked over his shoulder. "I can hear you two."

I crossed my eyes and stuck out my tongue.

He laughed as he turned back to where Penn was still clinging to the tree. Extending an arm, he wiggled his fingers. "Come on, Penn. You can do this. I know you can."

Time seemed to have stopped as Jensen and Penn stared at one another. I really didn't think Penn was going to do it, and I started to panic. Because there was no way he was going to climb back down that tree. We were going to have to call 911 and they'd bring the fire truck. Instead of rescuing kittens, they'd be rescuing Penn.

I was going to be in so much trouble.

"Okay," Penn announced, and then he let go of the tree trunk. I held my breath as he reached up and gripped the branch above where he stood. He took a step forward, his gaze trained on Jensen. "I trust you."

Jensen smiled.

SIX

LINDS MET ME inside the school and immediately wrapped her arm around mine, drawing me out of the stream of students, to the side of the hall. "You look like crap."

"I feel like crap."

"No sleep?" she asked, concern pinching her expression.

I shook my head. I hadn't told her about what I saw last night, or at least thought I saw. Maybe Mom and the police were right and it was stress. Or maybe it had been the creeper.

Trying and failing to suppress a shudder, I let Linds lead me down the hall, toward the stairwell. I told her about my self-defense lessons and when I got to who was teaching them, she almost fell flat on her face in the stairway.

"Jensen?" she whispered, her dark eyes wide as she pulled me to a stop. "Are you serious?"

I smiled apologetically to the guy who almost slammed into Linds' back. "Yeah, he's going to be helping me. I guess." Last night, around two a.m., I'd added his number to my phone. It felt like such a major step. "Yeah, so . . ."

"So? So!" She tugged on my hand and her tight curls bounced. "Wow. I was so not expecting you to break that kind of news to me."

"It's really not a big deal." I pulled my hand free.

Linds darted around me, almost sending a small girl flying down the stairs, and blocked my path. "This is big," she said, her voice barely audible above the conversations surrounding us. "This is huge. You guys are going to make up. Like after all this time, you're going to—"

"Excuse me?"

I turned, spying Shawna and Wendy behind me, obviously waiting for Linds and me to move out of their way. Besides the fact they could easily walk around us, it was pretty damn ironic considering they had blocked the *entire* hall yesterday.

"I'm sure there's enough room for you to walk around." Linds gestured at the empty area next to us. "So walk around."

"Or you could just move?" Wendy snapped back.

Linds came down a step, folding her arms. "Or not."

Knowing that this was going to escalate as quickly as a rocket ship, I stepped aside. "Come on, Linds, we're going to be late."

She didn't move.

Wendy's bright blue gaze snapped toward me. "You really should cover up your face."

My eyebrows flew up. "Excuse me?"

"Your face." She pointed at my face as she moved her finger in a circle. "It's gross. It looks like you shoved a vacuum hose against your cheek."

As I stared at her, I kind of wondered what the hell Jensen was smoking when he dated her. "Wow," I said, because really, what could I say to that? I mean, that wasn't even a really good insult. It was kind of stupid.

Linds had something to add. "That's funny, because at least the ugliness will fade from Ella's face. That shit on yours is forever."

Damn.

"Oh!" someone shouted from below us.

Wendy's cheeks flushed pink, but before she could reply, Linds leaned over, shoved her middle finger right in her face, and then spun around. Gripping my arm, she all but dragged me up the stairs.

"God, I have no idea what crawled up her ass, but I am so not dealing with it," Linds then yelled over her shoulder as the doors swung shut. "Not today, Satan!"

I glanced behind me, but I didn't see Wendy or Shawna. It was weird—her attitude toward us. Without Monica by their side, they were usually like little fluffy bunny rabbits, especially Wendy. I didn't get a chance to put a thought to it.

Gavin was there, waiting at my locker. He practically pounced on Linds and me. "Mom said there were cop cars at your house last night. I called but—"

"I know. I just forgot to call you back. I'm sorry." I opened the locker door and yanked out my English textbook. "They were over . . . um, to just check out the house. Nothing major."

Doubt crossed his face. "She said there were like three cop cars there."

"They roll deep?" I said, shrugging. How many people on our street had noticed? Gavin lived further down than Jensen. "Really, everything was fine. They were just checking out the house."

"God," Linds exhaled deeply, tipping her head against the nearby locker. Two red circles blossomed across her cheeks. "She's such a bitch!"

Gavin looked at her, confused. "Huh?"

"Wendy," I told him, closing my locker door. "She's talking about Wendy Brewer."

"Oh." He didn't look surprised to hear that name as he straightened the hem on his dark blue polo shirt. "What did she do?"

Linds pushed off the locker beside me. "Breathed her bitchiness on me?"

Sliding the strap of my bag up my shoulder, I laughed. "I've got to go to class. See you guys later?"

"Yeah." Linds started down the opposite hallway but whirled

back around. "Oh! Before I forget, you're helping out with the haunted house this year."

"What?" I stared at her while a slight grin appeared on Gavin's face. "It's like, not even September. Why are we even talking about this?"

"Because I had my Leadership of Tomorrow meeting yesterday, and they're already planning for this year's Halloween crap." She didn't even have the decency to look ashamed as she trotted backward. "And they need volunteers. So thank you for volunteering."

I gaped at her.

Holding her notebook close to her chest, she grinned like a cat that had eaten an entire cage full of canaries then moved on to a poor family of mice. "Our first meeting is Saturday afternoon. I'll give you more details later. Bye!"

Tipping my head back, I groaned. "What the hell?"

Gavin chuckled as he draped an arm over my shoulders. "Well, that should be fun."

I slid him a dry look. "Last year I ended up being—"

"The girl dissected on the table," Gavin finished, grinning down at me. "I remember. You were so thrilled about being covered with corn syrup and food coloring."

Squeezing my eyes shut, I groaned again. "I refuse to play the stupid half dead chick this year."

There was a pause and then he said, "Too close for comfort kind of thing?"

I smacked his arm and a sheepish look crossed his face. "Yeah. That."

SPYING THE REDHEAD I was looking for, I hurried to where Heidi Madison was sitting at the end of the table, her bag on the seat beside her. I picked it up, setting it aside, and then dropped my tray down.

Heidi raised her chin as she pulled out her white earbuds. She dropped them into the lap of her flowery, flowing dress that was colored with pinks and purples. A headband pushed her vibrant red hair back. With her baby face full of freckles, she looked like a freshman instead of a senior, something that bugged the hell out of her. I told her all the time that when she turned forty, she'd appreciate the fact she always looked younger.

Linds and Heidi couldn't be any more different. One was super vocal while the other only spoke when she had something to say. Linds loved the outdoors and hated the idea of wild animals. Heidi preferred books to people and wanted to be a veterinarian. Linds was a meat lover and Heidi was a holy granola roller. I was somewhere in-between the two, the glue that forced the two opposites together.

"You're late," she said, closing the paperback she was reading. Her food sat untouched.

Picking at the bottle of water I grabbed, I heard Brock laugh and glanced over to the table full of football players, then there was the sound of a tray hitting the floor. I turned around just in time to see a smaller student bending down and chasing peas across the floor.

Why did they have to be such jerks?

And why did I even think for two seconds that Brock was cute? A sense of betrayal rushed through me, because Brock and his crew of boys had always acted like that, ever since I had known them. This was nothing new, so it was more of a case of me forgetting.

Forcing myself to forget a lot of things, actually.

I flipped back to Heidi. "I couldn't get my dumbass locker open."

"I don't know why you have so many problems with it." She slid her tray closer and picked up a fork. Interest sparked in her light green, almost hazel, eyes. "Every year it's the epic battle of the locker for you."

"I know." I sighed, feeling pitiful. "Hey, did Linds corner you over the stupid haunted barnyard crap?"

"She knows better than that." She laughed softly. "She got you again, didn't she?"

"Yes!" I picked off a slice of pepperoni and then another, resisting the urge to beat my head on the table. "It's not even September and I have to think about this."

She giggled. "And you know you guys will start building the props within weeks."

"Ugh. Don't remind me." Over my shoulder, I scanned the cafeteria. Not that I was looking for anyone in particular, but my insides twisted in a funny way when my eyes stopped on Brock's table.

Wendy was sitting beside Monica, flashing super-white and super-straight teeth at the guy next to her, who just happened to be Jensen. If it wasn't for the fact that he was leaning back with his arms across his chest, looking pisstastic, I'd be a lot less—

That very second he looked over to where I was sitting, and I swear that even though there were several tables separating us and many heads in the way, our eyes met.

One side of his lips quirked up.

My cheeks flushed as I turned back around, meeting Heidi's look. "So," she said, drawing the word out. "Were you just eye screwing Jensen Carver?"

"What? No." I picked up my pizza. "Why would I do that?"

"I can think of a few good reasons," she said dryly.

I coughed out a laugh. Heidi didn't know about my history with Jensen and, as much as I loved the girl, I was so not going there. "Whatever. I mean, he is good looking—okay, he's more than good looking and very few girls or guys would kick him out of their beds, but eye screwing?"

Her gaze flicked over my shoulder. "Uh, Ella—"

"If I'm going to eye screw someone, it would not take place in the cafeteria. That just seems unsanitary."

"Um—"

"I would eye screw in class," I decided, winging my pizza around. "Like in biology. While we're dissecting frogs, I'd eye screw the hell out of him then, but he's not in the class and that also seems unsanitary, so I guess I'm not eye screwing—"

"Me?"

I swallowed the mouthful of pizza as I squeezed my eyes shut. He was not standing there. He was so not standing there. Oh no, no, no, no.

The chuckle that came next was too familiar, and I forced my eyes open. He dropped in the seat next to me, angling his body toward Heidi and me as he propped his chin on his palm. "I have bio after lunch, but if you tell me when your class is, I'll do all kinds of terrible things to get mine changed."

Oh my God, even the tips of my ears were burning.

Heidi took a hefty drink of her all natural root tea or whatever gross concoction was mixed in her plastic bottle. "Well, we now know that Jensen is a fan of eye screwing."

His eyes darkened to a blue on a bright sunny day. "That I am."

I wanted to crawl under the table and die.

Stretching his leg out, he knocked his knee against mine. "So I hear you had a little run-in with Wendy this morning."

Heidi placed her bottle on the table, frowning. "You did?"

I sighed. "I didn't think it was a big enough deal that anyone would hear about it."

"She was regaling the entire table with tales of your viciousness," he added, eyes glimmering.

"Me?" Forgetting about the whole eye screwing thing, I twisted toward him, which caused his knee to slide against the inside of my leg. My breath caught in my throat, and our gazes locked. I waited for him to pull back, but he didn't. Neither did I. The grin on his face went up a notch.

His lashes lowered. "You."

For a moment I had no idea what he was talking about. Something to do with . . . ah, yes. Bitchiness. "Wendy said I needed to cover up my face."

He frowned. "She said what?"

I pointed at the strawberry mark. "Said I was grossing her out."

"Well, that's rude." Heidi stuck out her lower lip. "It's not like you can help it."

"She's a charmer," Jensen murmured.

"And you dated her." I grinned when his lips thinned a bit. "Just saying."

He shifted in his seat, dragging his leg alongside mine, and I thanked God and Buddha that Heidi couldn't see it, because I was convinced that Jensen was leg screwing me. "I wouldn't say I *dated* her."

My skin prickled. Wasn't jealousy. Absolutely not. "That's nice."

He shrugged his shoulder as he glanced over at Heidi, who watched us like she needed a bowl of popcorn in front of her. "So Ella was eye screwing me?"

"Oh my God!" I shot her a death glare when she started to respond. "I was not eye screwing anyone. What are you doing over here anyway? This is not your table."

"We have assigned tables?" he asked.

Heidi pursed her lips. "I don't think we do."

I rolled my eyes. "You have always sat with *them* since you came back."

His eyes had regained that playful, lazy quality. "So?"

"So?" I took a drink of my water. "You're here."

"I am." He knocked his knee off mine again. "I wanted to visit you."

Heidi made a cooing sound. "Aw, that's so sweet."

My fingers curled along the edge of the table and I shot her another look.

"What?" She pouted. "It *is* sweet. He crossed the brutal sea of the cafeteria just to visit you."

"I think it's incredibly sweet, too," Jensen said, biting down on his lower lip.

My mouth twitched as I fought a smile. "You know, both of you—"

A high-pitched shriek cut me off. The sound was so loud and clear that it whipped through the noisy cafeteria, silencing everyone. I jumped to my feet just as Jensen did the same.

The shrieking sound came again. It was coming from Brock's table. Without thinking, I stepped forward, but suddenly Jensen was there. He wrapped his hand around mine as he pulled me back.

At Brock's table, Wendy was standing up, her hands pressed to her pale cheeks. She was still screaming—she hadn't stopped. And everyone at the table had scattered, backing away with identical expressions of horror and disgust. Someone—Monica—had bent over at the waist, her long black hair shielding her face as she started to gag.

"What the . . . ?" I trailed off as I saw what lie on the table, next to Wendy's backpack. "Oh my God."

Pulling my hand free from Jensen's, I smacked both over my mouth. Lying on the table was a red bird—a cardinal. The official state bird, I thought dumbly. Its wings were tucked neatly behind its back, and in the center of its little chest were a handful of mini stakes. Dozens stabbed clean through it.

SEVEN

A HORRIBLE PRANK.

That was what the staff said once one of them had decided to check out why Wendy was screaming. That was what the teachers said in the afternoon classes, where each one lectured us on the virtues of maturity.

I'd never known anyone to stab a bird and place it in someone's backpack as a prank. It was sick and disturbing, and not even remotely funny. Not to mention, when had it happened? Wendy had the bag on her all morning. Wouldn't she have, I don't know, noticed a dead bird in there before lunch?

The sight of the dead bird lingered all day, and I imagined it was the same for everyone. Well, everyone except Linds, who, while in art class, had expressed her disappointment at not seeing Wendy freak out. But it was more than just the grotesque sight. The bird—the type of bird—made me think of the past, a place I didn't need to dwell on.

When I got home that afternoon, the house was quiet and empty. Normally Mom would be driving to Huntington tonight, but after what happened this weekend, she was not making the trip.

But I was still alone until she got off.

Trying to concentrate, to have some sort of normality in my life, I plopped myself down on the couch and cracked open my history text. It wasn't until I read the same two pages four times that I dropped my highlighter in the crease of the book.

I pressed the tips of my fingers against my temples, massaging away the slight ache there. Weariness tugged at me, urging me to curl up and take a nap, but the idea of falling asleep while I was alone in the house wasn't on the top of my to-do list.

Maybe seeing Dr. Oliver really wasn't a bad idea.

Opening my eyes, I shifted my attention to the archway leading out into the hall and to the stairs. Coldness seized my insides. I stared at the empty foyer, unsure if I'd heard something or if it was just my imagination, but the tips of my ears tingled.

There had been a noise, a soft thud upstairs—

The doorbell rang, throwing my heart against my ribs. "Jesus," I gasped, jumping to my feet. I hurried to the door and peered through the tiny peephole.

"Whoa," I murmured, spying the chiseled profile of Jensen.

Two visits in less than twenty-four hours? Er, well, three if I considered the lunch thing a visit. Maybe four if I added in the self-defense class.

Beyond curious, I quickly unlocked the door and opened it. When he turned, the late afternoon sun kissed his cheek. "Hey," I said lamely.

A half smile appeared. "Can I come in?"

Nodding, I stepped aside, a little caught off guard by his presence. It had been years since he'd been inside my house. Shoving his hands into the pockets of his jeans, he walked toward the living room but stopped, turning to me.

Our gazes locked, and the moment stretched into what felt like forever. An awareness cloaked my skin like a warm blanket. Several feet separated us, but as the intensity in his stare rooted me in place, it felt like he was right in front of me. Why was he here? Had he just wanted to see me? Many years ago, he would just randomly show up, and I always looked forward to his impromptu visits, but that was then. We weren't the same people anymore.

I really needed to say something. "Would you, um, like to sit down?"

He tilted his head to the side. "Sure."

Feeling the back of my neck heat, I led Jensen into the living room. He went straight to the couch, picked up my history text and carefully closed it, keeping the highlighter in it so I didn't lose my place.

He dropped to the couch, leaning into the cushions and extending his left arm along the back. "We didn't get a chance to talk about when you wanted to do the lessons."

"Oh!" I wanted to smack myself. Of course he had a valid reason to be here that didn't involve his sudden inability to stay away from me. Forcing myself to act like I had some common sense, I sat beside him. "Yeah, the whole . . . bird thing kind of distracted everyone."

"Yeah, wasn't expecting to see that during lunch." He paused and his jaw tightened as his gaze dipped beyond my face. He cursed under his breath.

I stiffened, not understanding at first, and then I became aware of what he was staring at. With my hair pulled back, my neck was visible. I hadn't expected anyone to stop by. Conscious of the ugly bruises that were mostly hidden when my hair was down, I reached up to take out my hair tie, but like a snake striking, he moved before I saw him.

Jensen caught my wrist and lowered my hand. "You don't have to do that."

Heat rushed across my cheeks and then zinged through my veins as his hand slid up my arm, his long fingers reaching the sensitive skin on the inside of my elbow. My mouth dried as a shiver of responsiveness danced across my skin.

"Does it hurt at all?" he asked.

I shook my head. "Not really." The truth was, my throat, like my cheek and ribs, ached every so often. Nothing major. Could be worse kind of thing.

"It looks like it does." His thumb moved in a slow, small circle along the inside of my elbow. "You came so close to . . ." He trailed off as he let go of my arm, his fingers trailing downward as he leaned back. "You know what I was thinking today?"

Swallowing a breath, I shook my head again. The contact had left me a bit frazzled. "What?"

"When I saw the bird on the table at lunch?" He looked away, a muscle thrumming along his jaw. "I thought about . . . I thought about Penn."

I jerked back as if I'd been slapped. I didn't know what to say. My tongue tied into a knot, like the one forming in my stomach.

His gaze slid back to mine. "Remember how he loved birds?"

My pulse kicked up and it took a few moments to speak. "Yeah, I do."

"Cardinals were his favorite," he said quietly, watching me intently. "So were bluebirds, but the cardinals . . ."

An ache pierced my chest, like it always did whenever I thought about Penn, which was something I tried not to do often. But I missed him something fierce. "He liked their mohawks and the black mask. Thought they looked badass."

"Yeah." His lips curved up slightly. A few moments passed and he cleared his throat. "Anyway, it was a weird thing to think, right?"

"I don't think so. I thought it, too," I admitted, nervously toying with the hem of my shirt. If anything, that had haunted me more.

"He used to—"

"I don't want to talk about him," I interrupted, unable to help myself. "I'm sorry, but I just don't want to."

Jensen studied me. "Okay. So what about lessons? You still down for them?"

"Are you?"

He lowered his hand, tapping his fingers off my arm. "I wouldn't be here if I wasn't."

"Why?" I blurted out before I could stop myself.

He cocked his head to the side. "Why what?"

"Why do you want to help me?" The moment the question came out, an entire buttload of things I shouldn't say spilled forth. "I mean, I don't get it. I know you said yesterday that you didn't hate me, but we haven't talked in *years* and neither of us have taken the opportunity to do so, but you're here now, and I . . . I just don't understand why, after all this time, you're here again."

He rubbed his palm along his smooth jaw. "You want to know the truth?"

"What? Ms. Reed is paying you to help me?"

Jensen gave me a long look. "Uh. No. That's not the truth."

"Well, that's good," I murmured, leaning back against the cushions.

"Okay. I'm going to be real with you." Jensen leaned forward and the distance between us evaporated like water on a hot summer day. He was right there, eye level with me, and my heart did a little cartwheel. "There have been many times I've wanted to talk to you. That I thought about picking up the phone and calling you. Or seeing if your email address was still the same. And when I came back? Every time I drove past your house, I wanted to stop and talk to you. Every. Single. Time."

Now my heart did a backflip—a perfect one.

"But I never did. I don't know why." His eyes deepened to that darker blue, almost cobalt. "Maybe it's because I never knew what to really say. Or maybe it had to do with the fact I knew you were with Gavin, because yeah, I looked at your Facebook."

My eyes widened. I'd totally Facebook stalked him. Or at least tried. His profile was private and his tweets protected.

"And you were still with him when I came back here. Didn't mean we couldn't be friends. I get that. I just . . . don't know. I wish I could tell you why, but I can't. And I'm sorry, and I know that doesn't change anything, but after Saturday . . ." Jensen closed his eyes briefly, and I stilled until the only thing moving was my pounding heart. "After what happened Saturday, it seemed stupid to continue the way we were, because what if my headlights hadn't turned on? What if I wasn't walking to my truck at that very moment?"

I shivered, knowing the answer.

"And when Ms. Reed called me into her office, she practically handed me a way of weaseling back into your life on a silver platter. I took it and that's why I'm here. Because we were . . . God." He laughed sadly. "We were best friends, Ella, and I screwed that up. I know I did, but we were friends and I want to be friends again."

Jensen dipped his chin, staring up at me through impossibly long lashes. "And after being with you for an hour yesterday, I realized just how much I've missed you."

Friends—he wanted to be friends again, and while I wasn't sure how I could really be *just* a friend to him, my breath caught. And since he put it out there, I was going to put it out there, too. It was only fair. "I've . . . I've missed you, too. A lot."

He was still for a moment, and I wasn't even sure he was breathing, but then he smiled—a real smile, and it reached his eyes, transforming his coolly handsome face into something breathtaking. "That's good," he said in a low voice. "That's a start."

A start to what?

But the question floated away as he leaned in, pressing his forehead against mine. It was so not-a-friend move that I was left speechless. My eyes drifted shut as his warm breath danced over my lips, and even though I knew he wouldn't kiss me, because who kissed a girl after asking to be friends, my imagination went there. I could almost feel his lips, and I could almost taste the mint on his breath. Muscles throughout my body and in some very, very interesting places clenched.

"So," he murmured. "Friends?"

I sucked in a breath as he tilted his head just the slightest. "Friends."

"Good." There was a pause. "About those self-defense lessons . . . ?"

"What about them?" I wanted him to touch me—to put his arms around me. Friends did that, right? I mean, really close friends did. Totally.

As if he knew what I was thinking, what I wanted, he shifted his body, drawing his leg up until it pressed against mine. He still hadn't pulled back. "I can do whenever."

"Me too."

The very tips of his fingers brushed the curve of my jaw, and that was decidedly not friendly, but I didn't care. "Then tomorrow?"

"After school?"

"Yeah," he said, our mouths so close that we were sharing the same breath. "Cool for you?"

I nodded, causing our noses to brush, and Jensen sucked in a deep breath. His fingers trailed up my jaw, reaching the tiny pieces of hair that had escaped my ponytail. Something was about to happen. I could feel the shift in him and a spark of nervousness rose within me, but there was more. A yearning—a sweet, fiery anticipation that overshadowed common sense. It washed away our past. I wanted nothing—

The doorbell rang, thrusting us apart. Breathing heavily, my eyes fluttered open, and I saw that Jensen was watching me, the pupils of his eyes dilated.

Had we been seconds away from kissing?

The doorbell rang again, jarring in the silence.

One side of his mouth quirked up. "You gonna get that?"

"Yeah. Yeah," I repeated, pushing to my feet. I moved through the living room in a daze, thinking that it better be Santa Claus on the other side of the damn door.

It wasn't Santa.

Or his elves.

Or reindeer.

It was Gavin.

"Hey," I said, proving I was the queen of greetings.

He smiled. "Can I come in?" Before I could say a word, he strolled through the door. "I thought I'd keep you company until your mom got home. I figured you probably didn't want to be sitting around . . ."

Gavin trailed off as he entered the living room and realized that I wasn't alone. He stopped right in front of me, and I bounced off his back.

From the couch, Jensen tipped his head up in greeting. "What's up?"

The atmosphere shifted the very second Gavin spotted Jensen, whose lazy, arrogant sprawl on the couch suddenly felt very misleading, as if he could pop to his feet at any given second and without warning.

"Hey," Gavin said slowly, and then glanced back at me. Confusion flickered across his face. "I didn't know he was here."

"Yeah." I stepped around him, looking back and forth between the two guys. "He stopped by not too long ago."

"Oh," Gavin said.

And that was all he said.

I shifted my weight, turning my attention to Jensen, expecting him to do or say something, but he just raised his brows.

God, it was so weird, the three of us being in my living room. It was like jumping back in time, except . . . well, Gavin and Jensen wouldn't have been eyeballing each other like they were now.

Which made this all kinds of awkward.

But when we were younger . . . well, we teased each other mercilessly and we laughed all the time. The three of us—Jensen, Gavin, and me—had been inseparable from elementary school until eighth grade. Jensen had been the one to bring the box for the turtle with the cracked shell we'd rescued. He'd dressed up as the hill, using cardboard boxes, grass clippings, and a ton of superglue, when Gavin and I went as Jack and Jill. And Jensen and I had shared the shameful guilt from the weekend the whole landscape of our town changed. So yeah, the three of us.

No.

Not the three of us.

The *four* of us.

The half smile was back on Jensen's face, but there was no humor in the smug quirk of his lips. "So, what've you been up to, Gav?"

Gav. I winced, remembering how much Gavin hated that nickname. Hell, when he ticked me off, I'd call him that.

Gavin's shoulders tensed. "Nothing much. Just going to school and helping out with Mom and Dad."

"Ah, yeah, the cleaning business thing." There wasn't any arrogance in the way he said that, but Gavin's cheeks flushed.

"Do you want anything to drink?" I asked, hoping to defuse the situation.

Gavin's lips were thin as he nodded. "Sure."

"How about you?" I asked Jensen.

Sliding his arm off the back of the couch, he dropped his hands on his knees and turned his pale eyes on me. "Thanks, but I'm going to go ahead and get out of here."

"You don't have to leave," I said quickly.

Gavin crossed his arms. "Yeah, you don't have to leave."

His tone was so not welcoming, and I shot him a look he largely ignored. Jensen chuckled under his breath as he rose. He brushed past Gavin, not paying him any attention.

"I'll be right back," I said, trailing after Jensen. "You really don't have to leave, you know."

"No. I think I kind of do." Jensen stopped at the door, not even looking at Gavin. "Tomorrow after school? Same place."

I nodded. "I'll be there."

"Good." Only then did his gaze flick behind me. "I'm looking forward to it."

Gavin was standing in the center of the living room when I returned, arms still crossed across his chest. "What was he doing here?"

"Um, like he said, he was just stopping by." I walked past him, determined not to be too irritated. Gavin and Jensen hadn't been friends for a long time either, but I had to believe they missed that friendship too. "And I told you he was helping with the whole self-defense thing."

He followed me into the kitchen. "Is he teaching you at home?"

"No." I sighed, reaching into the fridge. I handed him a Coke. "But we were just setting up a time to meet again." He was silent as I hopped up onto the kitchen counter, letting my legs dangle off the edge.

"You know what I don't get?"

"No."

His forehead crinkled. "Where did Jensen learn self-defense?"

I opened my mouth, but I really didn't have an answer for that. Good question.

"I mean, that's not something you just know how to do, so shouldn't you be learning from someone who knows what they're doing?" he asked, popping the tab on his soda. The liquid fizzed. "Instead of someone who just says he knows what he's doing?"

"He knows what he's doing."

"Really?" He took a long drink.

"Yes. Really."

"Uh-huh."

Forget trying to not be irritated. My scalp started to tingle. "What's your deal?"

"Okay." He placed the soda down on the table and walked over to where I sat. Placing his hands on either side of my legs, he leaned in. "You just went through some pretty traumatic shit."

I folded my arms across my chest, narrowing my eyes at him.

"What does that have to do with anything?"

"I'm just saying that you're in a . . . vulnerable spot. Hey—" He held up his hands. "Don't give me that look. You are. And that's totally normal, but do you really think this is a good time to entertain the idea of anything with Jensen?"

My stomach soured as I felt heat spread across my cheeks. "Having him teach me self-defense and talking to him isn't entertaining anything," I said, and oh crap, that was a lie, because I'd so been entertaining the idea of kissing him.

Gavin raised his eyebrows. "Don't you remember what happened last time?"

I drew in a ragged breath as my fingers curled around the edge of the counter.

"Look, I'm just pointing that out. He has a history of making shit worse." He pushed off the counter and straightened. "I don't want to see you hurt, and he hurt you last time, at the worst possible moment in your life."

As much as I wanted to, there was no denying the truth to that statement. My gaze dropped and I shook my head. "It's not like that. I mean, it's not the same situation."

"You sure about that?" he asked quietly.

I nodded.

Gavin leaned forward, wrapping his arms around my shoulders. He dragged me forward, off the counter and to his chest as he hugged me. It felt good—maybe a little longer than I expected, but I soaked up the warmth. As wrong as it was, I took from him what I had wanted so badly from Jensen. I closed my eyes and breathed in the scent of fresh laundry.

"I know Jensen might be acting like he has some common decency right now, but just be careful around him," he said, squeezing me. "He's changed. We all have, but him especially. Just don't forget what he did to you."

GAVIN LEFT SHORTLY after Mom came home, and I hung out in the kitchen while she cooked up some fatty cheeseburger Hamburger Helper, and afterward, while I cleaned up the kitchen.

"I talked to Dr. Oliver today," she said as I loaded up the dishwasher.

It took me a few seconds to remember what she was talking about because my mind was so wrapped up in what Gavin had said. Closing the dishwasher, I turned around with a sigh and then dropped into the chair. "So, when's my appointment?"

"Next Friday, after school." She wiped a dishtowel across the table in front of where I sat. Admittedly, I was a messy eater. "I can go with you if you want."

That was the last thing I wanted. "No, thank you."

She wrinkled her nose at me as she tossed the towel into the sink. "You don't have to make it sound like it's the worst idea ever."

I laughed. "Well, it's not the greatest idea."

Mom narrowed her eyes, but then she tilted her head to the side, studying me. "Honey, you look terrible."

"Wow." I laughed again. "Thanks a lot."

Walking over to me, she placed cool hands on my cheeks. "Have you been sleeping?"

"Yes."

She tsked softly. "You're a terrible liar."

That I was. Sighing, I pulled free. "It's been a little hard sleeping."

"Maybe I should see if he could get you in sooner. Or I can get him to order a prescription for sleeping pills," she offered, turning to where she'd tossed the dishtowel. "They worked last time."

Last time.

I took a deep breath. "I don't need them, Mom."

But later that night, long after Mom had already gone to bed, I lay in mine, watching the shadows from the swaying branches outside dance across the ceiling. The TV flashed different colors every so often, the volume turned up just loud enough to drown out the creaks and groans the house made.

Perhaps the sleeping pills wouldn't be such a bad idea.

It was past midnight, and my eyelids were heavy, but sleep was elusive. I tossed and turned. I was too hot, the pillow felt too hard. My brain cycled through the conversation with Gavin and then Jensen, to the bird and beyond, to what happened on Saturday.

I wasn't sure what time it was when I tossed the covers off and climbed out of bed. The low blue light from the TV cast a glow across my bedroom. Weary to my very bones, I shuffled into my bathroom.

Flipping on the light, I crossed the room, my bare feet silent against the cool tile. I stopped in front of the sink, yawning as I turned the water on. Cupping my hands under the cool stream, I bent over, splashing the water over my face. It did very little, but I dipped my hands again and then scrubbed my eyes.

As I lifted my head, letting the water trickle between my fingers, cool air brushed along the back of my neck. I froze as my heart kicked against my ribs.

Water streamed into the sink, but *there*! I felt it again, across the base of my neck, a cool breath stirring the tendrils of hair. And then I heard it—a heavy footstep, like a boot connecting with the floor, followed by another.

Eyes shut and skin tingling, I slowly straightened. *Nothing is behind me.* It had to be the air kicking on and my ears playing tricks on me. *Nothing is behind me.*

Drawing a deep breath that didn't reach my lungs, I opened my eyes. Oh God, I was wrong—so very wrong. A scream rose in my throat.

It stood behind me, face covered in the stark white clown mask, and its black, empty holes where the eyes should be. Slowly, it cocked its head to the side and made a guttural tsking sound.

I spun around, stumbling back into the hard sink. He lurched at me, those glove covered hands reaching out—

Jerking up in bed, I gasped for air as my heart thudded against my ribs. Nightmare—it was just a *nightmare*.

"Oh my God." I pressed my hand against my chest.

No one was here. I was safe, but my poor heart hadn't registered that. Pressing my other hand against my chest, I sucked in several deep breaths.

Something about the room wasn't right, though. As my eyes adjusted to the darkness, I lowered my hands to the edge of the blanket, pulling it from where it rested around my knees. I tucked the comforter under my chin, glancing at the window. The curtains were still. That wasn't it . . .

The TV.

A knot formed under my ribs. The TV was turned off. I hadn't done that before I fell asleep, and I hadn't turned on a sleep timer. Hell, I wasn't even sure how to turn one on. Mom did it, I told myself. She had to have come in and turned it off.

I lay back down, curling onto my side as the sweat dotting my skin turned cool. My heart gradually slowed down, but I didn't close my eyes for any length of time.

I didn't fall back asleep.

EIGHT

RUNNING LATE THE next morning, I grabbed my Pop-Tart, kissed Mom, then raced for the door. I stopped before I barreled out, turning back to where she stood, pouring black coffee into her mug.

"Did you come in my bedroom last night and turn off the TV?" I asked.

Light blonde hair fell back over her shoulder as she looked over, her brows pinching together. "No. Why?"

The knot under my ribs grew twice its size. "I guess I must've set the sleep timer or something."

The only way I'd set the timer was by accident. I couldn't even fathom the chance that it could be something else. My brain was unable to cope with anything weird or stressful today. Saying good-bye, I headed out under the overcast sky.

By some sick twist of fate, I ended up parking next to Wendy's fancy, relatively new car, which looked to be a Lexus, but I refused to investigate the make of the car too closely, because it was likely that I'd fall on my face if she were seriously driving that kind of car. But I wasn't thinking about her pretty car as I climbed out a few seconds before her.

Wendy looked like a hot mess.

Her blonde hair was slicked back in a low ponytail and short strands had slipped free, hanging limply against ruddy cheeks. It was like she'd forgotten her powder and concealer this morning. Dark shadows bloomed under her eyes. She was wearing a loose t-shirt and sweats, something that I'd wear, but never expected to see her out in public in—especially the pink sweatpants.

She looked as bad as I felt.

Actually, I couldn't remember ever seeing her look so bad and I'd known the girl since elementary school.

She turned, and as she closed the door, her troubled gaze met mine. "Hey," she said.

I stared at her. "Hi." And I waited for some caustic, snotty re-mark, but when she simply walked toward the building, I was left standing there like an idiot.

Well, that was . . . unexpected. And just a little strange—kind of like a less-snarky alien or something invaded her.

School was uneventful other than Linds telling me that the "vol-unteer" meeting on Saturday was pushed back to the afternoon and would be at the old farmhouse that held the haunted tour every year.

There were no dead cardinals and Jensen didn't visit me during lunch, and I tried not to be disappointed by that. I had no reason to expect that he would, and it was probably better that he hadn't. Being friends with him was stupid enough. But I couldn't help but notice that Wendy sat her little butt down right next to him. I also noticed that Monica was absent from the table.

On second thought, I hadn't seen her all day.

"You should probably stop looking over at their table."

"Huh?" I turned my attention to Heidi.

Hair separated into pigtails, she looked adorable. With her baby face and freckles, she could pull it off. When I wore my hair like that, it looked like I had escaped an asylum. Picking at a granola bar, she grinned. "You keep looking over there. If you want me to believe that you're not interested in Jensen, you're going to have to try harder than that."

"I'm not looking at him."

"You checking out Brock or Mason?"

"What? No."

Her grin turned impish. "So, like I said . . ."

I stuck my tongue out at her, and she giggled. For the rest of lunch I resisted the urge to check out his table. It was only when I was ditching my tray and half-eaten food that I glanced over there again. Instead of my searching gaze meeting Jensen's, it was Brock who I ended up connecting with.

He wasn't smiling, and the expression on his face was unfathomable. The knot below my ribs expanded, and I quickly looked away.

"You okay?" Heidi bumped her shoulder against mine.

"Yeah," I said, forcing a smile that felt weird on my face. I needed to get some sleep tonight because my paranoia was at an all-time high. As we left the cafeteria, I glanced up the wide hall leading to the front entrance of the school. I squinted.

"Cops?" Heidi said, swinging her purple bookbag.

I nodded my head. Definitely cops, but not the school kind. They were deputies, and from this distance, I couldn't tell who they were, but one of them looked like Gavin's older cousin. "I wonder why they're here."

Heidi's delicate brows furrowed together. "I don't know, but I doubt it's about rainbows and puppy dog tails."

Wrinkling my nose, I pressed my lips together. "Yeah, I doubt it."

Curious about their presence, I dwelled on it throughout trig class. Heidi was right in her own little weird way. Deputies at the school didn't bode well, but there could be a million reasons as to why they were here. During art class, my last period of the day, I couldn't sit still as we studied a bunch of paintings of vases with flowers in them and then started our own versions. Nervous energy built in my system, like I'd chugged three Red Bulls.

It had nothing to do with my impending self-defense lesson.

At least that's what I kept telling myself.

Needing to drop off my books and grab my English text for homework, I headed to my locker with Linds, crossing paths with Gavin, who ended up tagging along. The black shirt he wore had more wrinkles in it than an elderly home.

"You should volunteer to help out with the haunted farmhouse this year." Linds eyed Gavin like he needed to have a reason to be where he was.

"Huh?" He frowned, appearing distracted.

"The haunted farmhouse," Linds repeated, sighing as I stopped in front of my locker. "You know. The thing we do every year that you never help with."

"Also the thing that Linds cons me into doing every year," I added, hiding my grin when she shot me a dirty look.

"Oh yeah. That." Gavin leaned against the locker beside mine. "You know, not interested."

Linds frowned, but like one of those tenacious small dogs, she wasn't ready to drop it yet. "You know, you should be interested. Volunteering builds good karma. And you want good karma, right?"

"I'm pretty sure volunteering for Habitat for Humanity brings good karma," he reasoned, glancing over at me with a slight smile on his face. "Not volunteering for a stupid haunted attraction on the other hand . . ."

"You're going to Hell for that," Linds replied.

"I'm not sure that's helping your case." Laughing, I opened my locker door and came face to face with a wide smile and black, empty eyes. A scream burst out of me as I leaped back, dropping my bookbag on the floor.

"What the hell?" Gavin pushed off the locker, swinging around so he faced mine. "Jesus."

Linds clapped both of her hands over her mouth.

Hanging from a rope off the small hook in the back of my locker was a nearly identical replica of the mask the attacker had worn—the same kind of mask I'd found on my bed but had disappeared as if it had never been there.

It had the same wide, red smile and large, empty eyes.

My heart kicked in my chest as I squeezed my eyes shut. Arms went around me, turning me away from the locker. It was just a stupid mask, but good God, seeing it again froze the blood in my veins. All I could see was the mask inches from my face and feel the hands around my neck, squeezing the life right out of me.

Someone smothered a laugh behind me. Or attempted to. Another person issued a harsh curse. I pressed my face against Gavin's chest, wanting to wash away the image of the mask. The trembling edge of panic crept over me.

"What's going on?" boomed the deep voice of Mr. Holden, our English teacher. "Hey, what is . . . ?"

Gavin stepped back, pulling me with him, and I knew the moment the teacher had arrived. I opened my eyes as Mr. Holden stopped in front of us.

"This is ridiculous!" shouted Mr. Holden, snatching the mask out of my locker. "Masks? Dead birds? These are not funny, people. Have some common sense."

As Mr. Holden raged on about the "seriously disappointing level of maturity" in the school, Gavin and Linds quickly ushered me away. We made it to the stairwell by the time I realized my face was still planted against Gavin's chest and his arm was around me. There was something too intimate about the embrace, so I pulled away, slipping out of his arms. I was a little embarrassed, because I felt . . . it felt weak, but maybe I was being too harsh on myself. I did almost die in the hands of someone wearing that mask.

"You okay?" Linds caught my hand, her dark eyes flashing.

"Yeah, it's just, I saw that and all I could think of was what happened. I wasn't prepared for that." As the initial shock of seeing the mask in my locker faded, anger grew like a fire-breathing dragon. "Who would do that?"

"I don't know." Gavin reached for the door, opening it. "Someone with an extremely sick sense of humor."

My hands were shaking as I went down the cement stairs. "It wasn't there before lunch. Someone had to have gotten in to my locker and put it there afterward."

"It wouldn't be hard to do." Linds tucked a tight curl behind her ear. "I mean, you hit those lockers in the right spot and they pop right open."

That much was true, but I didn't get why someone would do that. Like the dead cardinal, it was the kind of prank that was unnaturally cruel and not funny.

"They shouldn't have given the description of the mask in the news," Linds commented. "I get why they did it, but every idiot knows what it looks like now and they're doing shit like this. Kind of like that old movie in the nineties, where the killer wore the mask and then everybody at school started wearing one. Who knew people in real life would be just as stupid?"

Gavin snorted. "I would've wagered they would be that stupid."

"I don't get it, though," I said as we stepped into the warm air outside, my heart still beating too fast. "It wasn't funny. Knowing what happened to me, why would someone do that?"

Linds looked away, nibbling on her lower lip.

My breath caught as anger and a tangy fear warred inside me. "What if it wasn't a prank?"

She stopped, folding her arms around her waist. "What else could it be?"

"Maybe a warning?" I shivered in spite of the warm air.

"What kind of a warning?" Gavin found my hand, gently squeezing it when I didn't answer, because there was none. "It was a prank, obviously a really bad one, but that's all it was."

I squeezed his hand back, but the knot below my ribs had grown. I glanced over my shoulder, back at the school. Deep down, call it instinct or good old paranoia, but I knew that mask wasn't just a prank.

And maybe the cardinal wasn't either.

"WANT TO TRY something different?"

I nodded as Jensen's arms slipped from around mine. He stepped back as I faced him. We'd been practicing the whole bear hug thing again, and I was pretty sure I got it, but according to Jensen practice made perfect.

"What?" I asked.

Wearing nylon blue sweats and a white shirt that would've looked average on anyone else, he looked like a young celebrity caught leaving the gym. He brushed a lock of light brown hair off his forehead and grinned. Immediately, I was suspicious.

"Want to hit me?" he asked.

A surprised laugh escaped me.

"Hit me." He walked to where I stood and then laughed as I gaped at him. "Not every attacker is going to come from behind you. Some are going to come right at you, and you said you wanted to know how to fight so you've got to know where to hit."

"Oh." I placed my hands on my hips. "So kicking a guy in the balls and running isn't the best method?"

Jensen winced. "That would work, too, but I'm sure you'll want a little more in your bag of tricks."

I grinned, surprised by how relaxed I was. One would think this kind of class would be stressful, but since we'd begun, I hadn't thought about what happened with my locker or the nightmare I'd had last night. There really was something empowering in making a conscious decision to protect myself.

"I want to see what kind of punch you pack," he continued. "And don't worry about hurting me. I can take—"

Cocking back my arm, I punched him in the stomach. Dull pain lanced over my knuckles as I drew my hand back, shaking my fingers. Damn if his hard stomach didn't give one centimeter, but surprise did widen his eyes.

"How was that?" I asked, massaging away the twinge in my shoulder.

He tipped his head back and laughed. "You hit like a girl."

I scowled at him. "Well, I am a girl in case you've forgotten."

Lowering his chin, his gaze started at the tip of my bare feet and slowly made its way up to my lips. "Oh, I haven't forgotten. Trust me."

My frown slipped away. I had no idea what to say to that, because I felt like the kind of girl who would break out in a fit of giggles at any given moment around him, and right then, I wanted to be that girl.

"Nah, you actually did pretty good. I'm honestly just pretending that didn't hurt. You're throwing a punch wrong, though." He moved so that he stood behind me. "You have to throw from your stomach—not your arm. Doing it wrong is a sure-fire way of injuring yourself. See?" He placed his fingers on my right shoulder, over the tight muscles. "Aches, doesn't it?"

I started to tell him it wasn't that bad, because it really wasn't, but then the tips of his fingers pressed into my shoulder. Holy Cracker Jack, he hit the *right* spot. Like the kind of spot I didn't even know existed. My back arched as he moved his thumb in a tight circle. He moved closer, until the front of his leg brushed the back of mine. Warm breath danced along my neck, sending shivers skipping across my skin.

"I heard about the mask in your locker," he said after a few moments.

I tensed. "How . . . how did you hear about that?" He hadn't been around when it happened.

"Brock texted me." His other hand rose to my opposite shoulder, and I bit down on my lower lip to stop a sound that I would've been mortified over. "He said someone had hung it up in there."

I kept my eyes open, refusing to see that empty mask.

He continued to move his thumbs, loosening the muscles that had tensed. "I'm sorry that happened to you. Whoever did it is a dumbass."

A heartbeat passed. "You . . . you think it was a prank?"

His fingers stilled only for a moment. "What else could it be?"

I didn't answer, because voicing my suspicions out loud gave voice to how absurd they sounded.

"Ella?"

"Nothing," I said, turning my head slightly. "I was just . . . thinking out loud."

Jensen fell quiet after that. My muscles had long since loosened, but his magic fingers kept doing their thing. I wasn't sure how long he kept at it, but my skin felt toasty.

"Better?" he asked, his voice gruff as he slid his hand down my side.

Jelly had replaced my muscles, so I had no idea how I was supposed to continue. "Yeah."

He cleared his throat as he shifted behind me, putting some space between our bodies and resting one hand against the center of my stomach. I jerked at the contact. "Easy," he murmured, stirring the soft strands of hair at my temple. "Move your arm back—your right arm, like you're about to throw a punch."

I did what he asked while his fingers splayed across my stomach. His hand was so large that his pinky reached the band on my jeans. There was no way I could be unaware of that, of how close his hand was to the top button of my jeans.

"Now move your arm like you're hitting someone, but use your stomach to turn, to put the power behind the throw."

Biting down on my lip and forcing myself to concentrate, I did as he said, which turned out to be incorrect, because I had only *thought* that I had done what he said. Jensen took my left hand and placed it where his hand on my stomach had been and then he gripped my hips.

Oh dear.

That didn't help.

A tremble coursed down my legs. When I threw my next punch, he tilted my hips, and I finally got what he was saying. I also got a whole lot of other things that had nothing to do with his training. My imagination face-planted in the gutter.

We went through the motion a couple more times, taking longer than necessary, probably because I wasn't all that focused. When we finally broke apart and I turned toward him, my face felt like I'd been sunbathing during a solar storm.

His eyes were a brilliant shade of blue, shaded by thick, dark lashes, and I averted my gaze before I did something stupid, like tell him he had beautiful eyes.

"Want to get something to eat?" he asked.

The question caught me off guard, drawing my wide gaze back to his.

An uneven grin appeared on his face. "Based on the way you're staring at me, I'm going to go with you either didn't hear me or it's a resounding no."

"It's just that you haven't shown me where I should be hitting someone."

"I know."

When he didn't elaborate, I fiddled with the edge of my ponytail. "Okay. I thought we'd do that today. It's still pretty early."

"And that's why I asked if you wanted something to eat." He swaggered up to me, and I held my breath. He reached out, caught my fingers, and gently pulled them away from my hair. "You didn't eat much at lunch today." His gaze flicked away when my brows rose. "You were dropping off your tray. Half your food was still there."

"You noticed that?"

His gaze bounced back to mine. "I always notice you."

Again, I was struck absolutely speechless.

"And I'm actually attempting to delay my training sessions with you. You know, string them out so I have a reason for monopolizing your free time." Dropping my hair, he grinned at my dumbfounded expression. "You're surprised. Don't even try to say you're not. You've never been able to keep what you're thinking off your face."

"Well then," I murmured.

Jensen touched my injured cheek that was almost completely healed with the tips of his warm fingers. "I always liked that about you."

I raised my gaze and our eyes locked. So many things rose to the tip of my tongue. I was made of questions. He'd said he wanted to be friends, but he was awful touchy-feely to be considered a friend. And there was more to it, in the way he *did* touch me, how he looked at me, even the way he spoke.

And how he was looking at me and touching me right now.

But Gavin's warning from the day before was never too far from my thoughts. Jensen had broken my heart once before, and that's why he was so dangerous for me. That was the last thing I wanted to experience again.

My heart didn't have control over me, though. It wasn't like grabbing something to eat was a declaration of undying love. "Okay."

His lips curved into a sexy smile. "Good."

Feeling a little out of it due to the change of plans, I left to slip on my shoes and grab the bag that I had brought with me. The nervous hum of energy was back, whizzing through me like a hyper hummingbird.

Jensen locked up, and as we stepped out in the hall, he draped his arm over my shoulder. The light citrusy scent of his cologne enveloped me. I clenched the strap on my bag, telling myself this was completely normal behavior. Gavin did it all the time.

"Relax," he murmured directly into my ear. "I'm not going to bite you."

Apparently, I wasn't acting like this was normal behavior.

"Unless you're into that," he added in a low voice.

My head snapped toward his, and I sucked in a breath at how close our mouths were. His was tipped into a mischievous grin.

"That was pretty cheesy, wasn't it?" His thumb moved along my upper arm.

My lips twitched. "It was pretty cheesy. Also kind of creepy. Makes me think of a zombie."

"So, if I'm trying to get a beautiful girl to relax around me, offering to take a bite out of them isn't going to win me any points?"

"Probably not," I said. I started to smile, but his head tilted in a way that lined our mouths up. If he lowered his head a few more inches, well, we'd definitely be doing things friends did not do.

As he continued to stare down at me, something shifted in him, like it had when we sat on the couch. The playfulness was still there, but the muscles in his arm tensed, and with a little coaxing, he drew me closer. An inch or two separated our bodies, and I felt a little dizzy staring into his eyes.

"Well, I'm going to have to come up with something else," he murmured lazily.

"Like what?"

"Hmm . . ." His chin dropped another inch. So close. "Maybe a milkshake."

I laughed. "A milkshake?"

"Yeah. The diner across from here? They have awesome milkshakes. And cheese sandwiches."

My stomach grumbled. "I love me some grilled cheese sandwiches."

"I know."

That was sweet. "I think I like where this is—"

A throat cleared. I drew back, glancing toward the entrance. Deputy Shaw stood there, his form blotting out the light streaming in from the doors behind him.

Unease blossomed in the pit of my stomach. The look on his face was hard. Not like the friendly expression he had worn yesterday. He was working.

Jensen's arm slipped off my back, but he moved closer, slightly in front of me. "What's going on, Shaw?"

The casual way he spoke to the deputy told me he had some kind of relationship with the guy. Then it struck me. Shaw had remembered me from . . . from before, which probably meant he remembered Jensen too. Had they stayed in contact all these years? Or did Jensen remember that Shaw was Gavin's older cousin?

Shaw strode forward. "I need to talk to Ella."

"Why?" he asked, moving so he entirely blocked my body from the cop's.

Having no idea what was causing this response, and not wanting him to get into trouble, I stepped aside, meeting the deputy's dark gaze. "What's going on?"

Shaw stopped in front of us. "I have some questions I need to ask after the most recent event."

"Most recent?" I glanced at Jensen and then the deputy, confused. "What are you talking about?"

Surprise flitted across the deputy's face. "You haven't heard?"

"Heard what?" Jensen asked, stiffening.

Shaw scratched his jaw. "Well, hell, I thought you would've heard by now. Monica Graham is missing."

NINE

IN A DAZE, I followed Deputy Shaw into some kind of meeting room off the main hall of the warehouse. It smelled of burnt coffee. The room hadn't been in use for a while as there was a thin layer of dust on the brown table. Jensen sat beside me in an uncomfortable metal folding chair.

"She was last seen yesterday evening, visiting a friend's house after cheerleading practice," Deputy Shaw explained. "She left her friend's house in her car, but she didn't return home last night, and no one has heard from her since. Normally, missing person reports aren't filed within twenty-four hours, but in light of recent events we don't want to wait."

I thought of Vee Bartol, who would be missing three weeks come this Saturday, and then I thought of how ragged Wendy had looked this morning, which Monica's disappearance could've explained. Monica's parents had probably contacted Wendy last night, and she'd been more concerned about her friend than how she looked.

Now I felt bad for how I thought of her this morning.

"God," I said, because I didn't know what to say. "You really think she's missing? That she didn't just go somewhere?" After I said that, I realized how stupid it sounded. What seventeen or eighteen-year-old just up and left?

Shaw shook his head as he leaned back, the vest under his shirt making a crackling sound. Perched on the edge of the table, he folded his hands in his lap as he stared down at us. "It's not impossible."

"But unlikely. God, this is terrible."

Jensen's hand found mine under the table. After threading his fingers through mine, he squeezed gently. "It is terrible, and I don't mean to sound like a total jackass."

A wry grin formed on Shaw's lips. "But knowing you, you're going to anyway."

So they really, *really* did know each other.

"What does this have to do with Ella?" he asked, looking Shaw dead on.

My heart turned over as I met Shaw's steady gaze. "It's because of the attack Saturday night. The police think it's related to Monica's disappearance, right?"

"We have the state, county, and city departments involved in this," Shaw answered. "We're chasing down any possible lead we have, which leads me to you."

Drawing in a deep breath, I nodded. "Okay."

"It's unlikely that what happened to you has anything to do with Monica's disappearance, but I think it's smart to check out every possible avenue."

"That makes sense," I whispered.

"So we're taking everything into consideration, and I know you've already given your statement to the state police, but if you could walk me through what happened, it might shine some light on what's going on now. It might give us some answers. And maybe, if this does have anything to do with what happened to you, it could help Monica."

Jensen's grip on my hand tightened as he leaned forward. "Is it really necessary for her to go through that again?"

It was the last thing I wanted to do, but if talking about Saturday could help Monica, then I would deal with it. "It's okay," I said, taking a deep breath, preparing myself. "I can do this."

Jensen looked like he wanted to argue, but he didn't stop me as I began to tell my story. It wasn't easy, because it was all too real, too fresh, and I wasn't sure if a day would ever come when it didn't feel that way. I pulled my hand free from his hold and wrapped my arms around my stomach, stopping the chill that kept racing up and down my spine. When I got to the part where I'd fought to get free, Shaw listened with rapt attention, not missing a single detail.

Jensen reached under the table, placing a comforting hand on my knee. The contact grounded me in reality, in the right now.

"And then . . ." I glanced over at Jensen, who was watching me closely. "And then I remember Jensen picking me up and . . . and that's it."

Shaw nodded slowly. "And there was absolutely no way you saw his face or any distinguishing characteristics?"

I shook my head as my shoulders slumped. "The mask and wig stayed in place. To be honest, like Trooper Ritter pointed out, it could have been a girl for all I know." Tired, I reached up, rubbing the heels of my hands against my eyes. "I know that's no help whatsoever."

"No, it's helpful," he said, giving me a reassuring smile when I lowered my hands. "Now, a few nights ago, a call came into dispatch about a possible intruder at your home. The report filed said there was no sign of a break-in, but you said that the mask—the same kind the attacker was wearing—was on your bed and there was a note, saying something along the lines of it 'being your fault?'"

Jensen stared at me. "What? Why didn't you tell me that?"

Crap. "I . . . the cops didn't find anything, so I thought it was just my imagination. The window wasn't open and there was no mask on the bed when the police got there." My gaze swung back to Shaw. "I told myself it *was* my imagination, but I also think it's kind of hard to imagine all of that."

Shaw didn't answer immediately, and when he did, it was a totally vague response that wasn't him agreeing or disagreeing. Unease grew, slithering through me like noxious smoke. What if that thing had been in my house? I knew it was possible, but I'd been able to convince myself otherwise over the last couple of days. A shudder worked its way through my body, and Jensen's hand shifted, his fingers curling around my knee.

"How close were you to Monica?" Shaw asked.

"I wasn't at all."

His forehead creased. "But you went to school together since elementary, correct?"

"Yes." It was a little weird realizing that Shaw had done his homework. Then again, in a town this size, it wasn't hard to make the assumption that we'd grown up together. "But we were never close. We hung out in different crowds and she wasn't always . . ." I trailed off, thinking it would be work to finish that sentence.

"She wasn't what?" he coaxed gently.

I pressed my lips together. Monica, like Wendy and Shawna, had never been particularly nice to people. Up until this week, I'd never had a problem with any of them, but . . .

"Monica is popular, but she isn't the nicest person," Jensen answered truthfully, saving me from having to be the one to talk bad about her. "She had a tendency . . . ever since middle school, to pick on other kids."

"Like Penn Deaton?" Shaw asked.

I pressed back against the chair at the sound of his name. Hearing it roll over the deputy's tongue floored me.

"Yeah, like Penn," Jensen muttered, fixing his gaze on the wall.

The question might have sounded abnormal to anyone else, but it had been common knowledge after everything that Penn had been relentlessly bullied. Till this day, I could list those who, for whatever reason, had made Penn's life a living hell.

Monica Graham.

Brock Cochran.

Mason Brown.

Wendy Brewer.

My eyes widened as my stomach dropped to my toes. There was one more, and her name . . . was Vee Bartol. Until whatever stupid thing that had come between Vee and Monica during freshman year, those two had been thick as thieves.

Vee was missing. So was Monica.

But there were two more names I could add to that list. And although those two people hadn't bullied Penn, they had let him down. They had failed him in the worse kind of way.

"Do you think . . . do you think he has anything to do with Monica?" I asked, unable to say his name out loud.

"Not really," Shaw replied. "But knowing how everything turned out with Penn gives me a better understanding of what kind of person Monica Graham is."

His response should've relaxed me, but I was turning it over in my head, lost in my own thoughts until Shaw spoke again.

"What about you, Jensen?" he asked. "When we spoke to Wendy at school today, she listed you as one of Monica's friends. Do you have any idea why Monica might want to leave home, or if she was having problems with anyone?"

Jensen pulled his hand away as he rocked back in the chair, folding his arms. "Monica and I weren't that close, and honestly, when Wendy mentioned her not coming home last night while we were at lunch, I didn't think much of it."

He'd known that Monica was missing at lunch and hadn't said anything?

He shrugged one shoulder. "She and Brock have been dating on and off for a while. If anyone knows why Monica might want to skip town, it would be him."

Shaw nodded again. "We've spoken with him and there are still several other people we need to meet with." He looked over at me, smiling slightly. "I don't want you to be overly concerned.

Like I said, there is a small chance this has anything to do with what happened to you."

But there was no stopping my next thought. The guy hadn't managed to grab me, but he'd gotten Monica. My stomach roiled. I felt like hurling.

"Even if these things are related, the likelihood of him coming after you again is rare," he continued. "In any case I can think of, the attacker has never gone after a victim that got away."

Victim.

I hated that label, but what I hated more was the idea that Vee and Monica hadn't run away. That what happened to me Saturday night was connected to them, and that meant the attacker was hanging around. Visions of serial killers and the like danced in my head.

This couldn't be real.

I lived in a town were virtually nothing happened. Cows escaped farms and ended up on the Interstate. People got arrested because they were driving ATVs on the main roads. Sure, we had a drug problem, we had crime, and the random shooting here and there happened, but we were a safe community compared to other cities.

"There was a mask in my locker today," I recalled suddenly. "I have no idea how that slipped my mind, but when I opened my locker before I left the school there was a mask in there."

The deputy's gaze sharpened. "What?"

I told him about the mask in my locker. "One of the teachers took it. Mr. Holden. He said it was a prank, just like the cardinal in Wendy—"

"We were told about the cardinal by the administration, but as far as I know, no one knows about the mask," he said. "This is needed information. Thank you."

Shaw didn't have any more questions, and the three of us walked out together. Shaw called Jensen over to him for what was obviously a private conversation. "Wait for me?" Jensen requested.

"Sure." I headed over to where my car was parked. Jensen joined me a minute later. "What was that about?" I asked, watching the cruiser pull out of the parking lot.

It was late now, the sun turning the sky to a golden red as it set behind the mountains. Jensen frowned as he watched the cruiser disappear. "You're probably not going to like it."

I crossed my arms. "Try me."

"He wanted to make sure I kept an eye on you."

My mouth dropped open. "Come again?"

"Told you." He sighed. "He just wants to make sure you aren't running around a lot by yourself. Don't shoot the messenger."

Annoyed that the officer hadn't felt the need to tell *me* not to go traipsing through town, I shifted my weight. "So, he wasn't being entirely honest in there. He thinks what happened to me is related to Monica and Vee."

"Right now, I don't think any of them know what's really going on." Leaning against my car, Jensen rubbed his hands along his jaw as he stretched his neck from side to side. "Damn, this day has gone from weird to the absolute bizarre."

That was the understatement of the century. Opening my driver's side door, I tossed my bag into the passenger seat.

"Why didn't you tell me what really happened the night the police were at your house?" he asked, angling his body toward mine.

I gripped the door. "Why didn't you say anything about Monica?"

"I didn't think anything of it. Thought she just ran off or something. And I didn't want you worrying, especially after what happened with you Saturday night," he said, and that sounded pretty damn reasonable. "So why didn't you tell me?"

"Why would I?" I bit down on my lip. "The cops found no evidence of what I saw, and it makes me sound crazy. Maybe I am a little crazy."

He pushed off the car. "You're not crazy." Rounding the edge of the door, he placed his hand next to mine and lowered his head. "Ella, you've had a pretty extreme thing happen to you. If your imagination got away from you, no one is going to blame you for that."

My eyes met his. "What if it wasn't my imagination?"

His lips pressed together. "God, I don't even want to think about that."

"Me neither." I started to look away, but he cupped my cheek. The touch shocked me like touching a live wire would. My guard down, the next question slipped out. "Do you think what happened to me is related to Monica disappearing?"

His eyes held mine. "Truth?"

"Truth," I whispered.

"Shaw isn't going to tell you yes, because that could jeopardize the investigation. It could also needlessly scare you, but think about it. For the most part, Martinsburg is a pretty uneventful town, right? What's the probability of one girl going missing and another being attacked and she barely escapes?" When I winced at that, he smoothed his thumb along my cheek, skating under the pink, faintly scratched skin. "And then another girl goes missing? How can they not be related?"

And that was a damn good question, but that wasn't the only one that came to mind. My thoughts went back to that room, to the list of those who'd terrorized Penn all those years ago. Did it have anything to do with what . . . with what happened to him? But why and how? There were other connections between all of us. After all, we'd grown up together, but Shaw's innocent question had planted a very ugly seed in my brain.

Uncomfortable with where my thoughts were heading, I pulled away, pressing back against my car. "I'm going to head home."

Jensen let his hand fall to his side. "Rain check on grabbing something to eat then?"

I nodded. "See you at school tomorrow."

He stepped back, closing the door for me after I got behind the wheel. Sending him one last look, I pulled out of the parking spot, and when I glanced in the rearview mirror, Jensen was standing where I'd left him. His hands in his pockets.

Watching me.

"THIS IS SO scary." Linds paced in front of the couch. "It's like something in a movie. Or on one of those forensics shows."

Heidi sat beside me, her eyebrows arched. "Like Forensic Files?"

"What?" Linds stopped, head cocked to the side. "What is that?"

"A TV show," sighed Heidi.

She shook her head. "No. Like Criminal Minds or something— something people actually watch."

Both girls had showed up at my house a few minutes after I'd gotten home. I was shocked when I'd heard that Linds had picked up Heidi and drove here, and that she hadn't driven off the road, distracted by the arguing they usually do with each another. Linds had seen my surprised expression and had read it clearly.

"I'm not going anywhere by myself," she had said, stepping inside, and the door would've smacked Heidi in the face if she hadn't caught it. "I am not getting kiddie-napped."

"Like anyone would kidnap her," Heidi had muttered under her breath. "They'd return her after a minute."

Now Linds plopped down in the old, worn recliner. "This is really scary," she repeated. "Why would someone do this?"

"Question of the week." I twisted a section of my hair around my finger. "After talking to the deputy, I really don't think they have any idea."

"The thing is, there's no evidence." Heidi pulled a plastic bag out of her purse and opened it, picking out chunks of granola. Glancing at Linds, I saw her wrinkle her nose as Heidi popped one into her mouth. I grinned. She offered the bag to me. "Want some?"

I shook my head. "No thanks."

Heidi shrugged. "Anyway, there's no evidence, right? And if there is something, they might be keeping it quiet, because the person responsible for all of this is the only one who knows."

Linds hooked one knee over the other. "Did you learn that on Forensic Files?"

"Yep." Heidi grinned. "And from watching the ID Channel."

"Monica could've run off with her parents' landscaper," Linds suggested. "I mean, have you seen him? He's hot."

Despite the seriousness of everything, I laughed. "Well, I hope that's what's happening. I just don't want it to be what we fear."

"I don't want it to involve *you*," Heidi corrected, her hazel eyes more green than brown as she looked at me, a giant piece of granola between her fingers.

"I second that," Linds said.

"Thanks, guys."

"But you know the thing I don't get?" Heidi popped the granola in her mouth and chewed thoughtfully as we waited for her to continue. "Let's say these things are connected. I know, that's a terrible thought to consider, but what do you have in common with Vee and Heidi? I haven't lived here my whole life, but I don't think you guys were ever friends, right?"

"Ella has never been friends with Vee or Monica," Linds answered.

Heidi frowned as she rolled up her baggie. "So that's what I don't get. If it's connected, it has to be totally random then, right? It has to be completely random."

My gaze fell to the coffee table as I nodded absently. Yes, totally completely random. Except it would make much more sense if a clown mask hadn't ended up in my locker and then on my bed. And it would make sense if I didn't have anything in common with Monica and Vee.

But in a way, I did.

EVERYONE WAS BUZZING about Monica Graham at school on

Friday, especially when the police arrived in the afternoon to talk to a few more students. No one had heard from her, and I couldn't imagine what her family and those close to her had to be going through.

It was the same thing that Vee's parents must be experiencing.

What was sad about it is that no one had really mentioned Vee the whole first week of school. After her fallout with the cool crowd last year, no one really seemed to care what was up with her, but now?

She was the topic of conversation, right along with Monica.

I was exhausted by the end of the day, skipping out on Smoothie Fridays with Linds and Heidi, a ritual we'd started at the beginning of our junior year. When I got home, I climbed the stairs and found myself standing in front of my closet after dropping my bag on the bed.

I opened the door and dropped down to my knees, pushing the piles of jeans out of the way until I found the unopened shoebox, pieces of Christmas wrapping paper still clinging to the sides. Mom had taped the lid shut, as if it would pop open, I'd rip the wrapping paper off, and ruin the surprise.

But there was no real surprise to what was in the box. Mom got me the same gift every year and she would come into my bedroom after every Christmas and throw away the unopened box from the previous year.

I had no idea why I was doing what I was doing, but I rocked back on my heels. Drawing in a deep breath, I exhaled slowly then slipped my finger under the tape. Once the lid was off, I was staring at a pair of pristine black and pink sneakers.

Running shoes.

And the good kind with arch support, too. They had to cost a pretty penny, and these were like the fourth new pair I'd never worn, but Mom . . . she kept buying them.

The desire to slip those shoes on and lace them up kindled deep within my chest. Just the idea of heading outside and going for a run—running anywhere—and allowing myself to get lost in that burn was hard to resist.

But I didn't put them on. I closed the lid and placed them back in the closet, setting them down carefully, almost reverently.

Running was not going to happen anyway. At least not with a possible psychopath roaming around out there. Besides that, I hadn't slept more than three hours the night before and all I wanted to do was crash.

And that's what I ended up doing.

Curled up on the corner of the couch, I watched a marathon of Ghost Adventures with Mom, who had to have heard about Monica's disappearance, but didn't bring it up, and for that I was grateful. I didn't want to think about any of it. My brain needed a break.

I ended up falling asleep on the couch in the early morning hours and then waking up with cramped muscles. Glancing at the clock on the wall, I noticed I had about two hours before I was supposed to meet with Dad.

Throwing off the quilt, I swung my feet off the couch, stood, and then stretched out the tightness in my muscles. I could hear Mom moving around upstairs and smiled. On Saturdays, she'd recently taken to knitting as a hobby, holing up in her room with her needles and yarn.

I grabbed a glass of OJ and then climbed the stairs. Stopping at Mom's door, I knocked softly.

"Come in," she called.

Nudging the door open with my hip, I peered in. Mom sat on her bed, cross-legged. Holding two needles in one hand, she was trying to untangle threads of bright pink yarn.

"Morning," I said.

She smiled brightly. "You getting ready to meet with your father?"

"Yep."

"Good." She held up a swath of bright pink and green material.

"What do you think of this?"

I forced my expression to remain blank. I had no idea what it was that she was holding. One end was uneven and it was about a foot wide. "It's very . . . colorful."

"Isn't it?" She lowered her hands, eyes narrowing at her needles. "I'm making scarves for the girls at the bank. I think it will make a great Christmas present."

Yikes.

Taking a drink, I spun around and closed the door behind me before I had to admit that a five-year-old could probably knit something better than that.

I hesitated at my door for a second and then I forced myself to turn the knob. The room was how I'd left it yesterday, when I'd returned home from school, had stared at my running shoes, and then changed into my lazy, lounging clothes.

It was slightly cooler than the rest of the house. Placing my drink on the table next to my laptop, I walked over to the window and opened the curtains, letting the morning sunlight in.

I took a quick shower and walked back into my bedroom. It was strange, because I moved around like I was visiting a stranger's house. With time to kill, I found myself standing in front of my narrow bookshelf, the glass of OJ all but forgotten on my desk.

I don't know what made me grab what I did from the shelf, but my fingers skimmed over the thick spines, landing on a thin smooth one. I slid it out, not looking at what I held until I sat on the edge of the bed. Then I shifted my gaze to the blue and white yearbook—my middle school yearbook.

My fingers trembled as I cracked it open. Without skimming, I opened it right up to *that* section. Not the part where I looked like a little doofus. My eyes scanned down the list of names.

Penn Deaton.

An ache pierced my chest, forming a ball of remorse, sadness, shame, and guilt. It nearly closed off my throat, and I exhaled harshly as my gaze drifted down the row of colored photos, stopping on the fourth one from the left.

Tears pricked my eyes and I blinked them away as I stared at the young boy smiling back at me.

Penn . . . God, he had the best smiles. Big. Toothy. He hadn't cared that his front tooth was chipped. Well, he hadn't cared until middle school. He had the prettiest brown eyes, framed by heavy lashes, and hair the color of raven's wings. He'd always been small, and even in a picture that only showed his upper half, his shoulders were slim. Frail. I had no idea how much time had passed, but my cheeks were damp and I'd probably ruined the mascara I'd put on.

I smoothed my thumb over his picture, sniffling. I wished I could go back to the past and pay attention to the signs that had been there. I wished I could go back and we didn't do what—

Sucking in a sharp breath, I slammed the yearbook closed. It slipped from my hands, smacking off the floor. I stood up, stepping around it as I hurried into the bathroom. With shaking hands, I grabbed a makeup toilette and hastily wiped under my eyes.

Don't think about it. Don't think about it.

Fixing my face so I didn't look like I was coming out of withdrawals, I tossed the tissue in the bin then went back into the bedroom. I picked up the yearbook with two fingers, like it was venomous snake. I shoved it back into its place.

It was almost time to meet Dad.

Before I left, I picked up the small jewelry box off my dresser. I sat down on the edge of my bed, cracked it open, and rooted around for the bracelet Dad had bought me for my seventeenth birthday. It was a diamond tennis bracelet, really too pretty and fancy to wear, but I always slipped it on before I saw him. It seemed like the right thing to do.

A frown pulled at my lips as I nudged a pair of hoop earrings out of the way. Where was the damn bracelet? Unable to find it, I got up and checked the top of my dresser, thinking I might've

THE DEAD LIST 125

dropped it there after the last time I'd worn it, but other than some costume rings and faded receipts, there was nothing.

"What the hell?" I muttered, shaking the box.

I tried finding it again, but not only was it missing, so was the ring Gavin had bought me two Christmases ago—a white gold promise ring with a tiny speck of a sapphire. He had to work three months of odds and ends jobs to afford the ring. I had wanted to give it back to him when we broke up because it didn't seem right to keep it, but he'd insisted.

Both the tennis bracelet and ring were gone.

Had I misplaced them? I quickly scoured all the visible surfaces of my bedroom, but I came up empty. It was strange, because I was always careful with them. A niggle of unease gnawed at me as I closed the lid.

I placed the jewelry box back on the dresser, lingering just a moment longer, and then I left the room, stopping to close the door behind me.

TEN

SATURDAY LUNCHES WITH Dad were a biweekly tradition since the divorce. We always met at the same café downtown, sat in the same booth, and ate the same food.

Dad always ordered a grilled chicken salad—no croutons or salad dressing—and I always ordered a grilled cheese sandwich. We shared our potato chips, and we'd been coming here for so long that the waitress brought them out on a separate plate, placing it between us.

Neither of my parents had been that old when they got married and popped out baby Ella. Dad had been twenty-one and Mom had been twenty. They'd met in college, fell in love, and then fell out of it four years ago.

"How's the school year panning out?" he asked as our food arrived, brushing his fingers through the brown hair at his temple.

Turning out to be the seventh circle of Hell, all things considered. "It's looking really good."

"Your mother said you started taking self-defense classes?"

"I did. And that's going good too." I peeled the crust off the sandwich.

"And you're taking these lessons seriously, right?" He dipped his chin, pinning me with his best stern look, and my smile turned real. "I still don't look like I have an ounce of authority, do I?"

"Nope."

"I'm really going to have to work on that." He speared a piece of chicken. "So, I ran into Mr. Carver at the post office the other day."

I could feel the heat spreading across my cheeks.

"I didn't know that it was Jensen teaching you self-defense," Dad continued, and my brain started to backpedal from this conversation. "Mr. Carver seemed really happy about that. So was I. It's about time you two started talking again."

My eyes widened slightly as I stared at the chips.

Dad chewed thoughtfully. "You know," he said, pointing his fork at me. "It wouldn't hurt for you to start doing other things."

My eyes narrowed. If I were a cat, the hair along my spine would be standing straight up. I'd be hissing at this point, too. "What other things?"

He wisely changed the subject, but I knew it wouldn't last long. "The mark on your face is almost gone. How have you been with everything?"

"I've been okay." I popped a chip in my mouth.

"Your mother said you're going to be seeing Dr. Oliver next week."

Another chip flung its way into my mouth. "Yep."

"I think that's also a good idea." He paused, chasing down another slice of chicken. "I also think going away for college right now might not be—"

I sighed. "Dad, please don't start. I don't want to be living here for the rest of my life."

"Martinsburg isn't a bad place, honey."

"I know." Martinsburg was great, but I had to get away. Too many memories clung to this town.

Dad pushed his fork away. "Part of me can understand why you'd want to go elsewhere, with what happened all those years ago, but that's in the past."

I stiffened. "*Anyway.*"

He looked at me and then shook his head. "How's your mother?"

"Good. Still single."

His look turned bland. "Ella—"

"What?" I said innocently. "She hasn't gone out on a single date, and Mom's hot. You're losing your window of opportunity here."

"Honey, there's no window of anything. Rose and I are still together." He fished out a slice of radish. "And things are serious between us. You know that."

Rose.

She who shall not be named.

Around six months after my parents legally separated, Dad started seeing Rose. He swears to this day, along with Mom, that there was nothing happening between him and his *co-agent* at the realtor firm. Rose was a good ten years younger than Dad and seriously could pass as a college student.

The waitress swung by our table, refilling my Coke. I took a big ole hefty drink of it as Dad eyed me. "Is that diet?" he asked.

"Nope." I gave him a cheeky wide smile. "It's a hundred percent real soda pop with lots and lots of empty calories."

His brows furrowed. "Do you know how many throw-away calories are in that?"

I shrugged, but I did know. One hundred and forty to be exact. How did I know this needless information? Dad had told me already. Like about one hundred and forty times.

Dad wasn't a health nut. To people on the outside, they'd take one look at his trim physique and the OT he put into the gym, and think he was all about the health and fitness. But, oh no, Dad was a fat nut. In other words, he was petrified of getting the middle-aged paunch.

"I wish you hadn't given up the running. It's so good for you," he began. "You know, I can add you to my gym membership. You can even go with me after . . ."

Aaaand I just entered the eighth circle of Hell.

EVERY YEAR, THE Leadership of Blah Blah group partnered with the Future Farmers of Blah Blah group to put together the annual Halloween haunted hayride and farmhouse attraction where all the proceeds were donated to various charities. And every year since I had become a freshman and became friends with Linds, I got conned into volunteering.

The old farmhouse butted up to orchards, and during the fall, the whole place took on a creepy transformation as the leaves began to wither and the days grew shorter.

Parking my Jetta in a lot that was more weeds than gravel, I climbed out, wishing I'd worn something thicker than this thin paisley blouse and capris. The first weekend of September had rushed in cooler temps in spite of the cloudless, sunny sky.

I moved in and out of the dozen or so cars and headed for the farmhouse next to a wasted looking barn that had seen better days.

Laughter and conversation floated out of the open door and windows of the bottom floor. Wood groaned under my feet as I walked up the steps and crossed the porch. Peeking inside, I recognized several faces.

Brock and Mason were standing in front of a pile of fake pumpkins and other autumn decorations with identical confused expressions. Linds was with Ms. Reed, pulling various gross stuff out of huge boxes. Fake shiny pools of blood. Ropey intestines. Giant rats and bats.

Linds looked over at me, holding a brain in one hand and a heart in the other. "Hey! You made it. I was wondering if you were going to show up or not."

"Sorry. Lunch with Dad ran a little late." I smiled at Ms. Reed, who was in the process of scribbling in a thick notebook. "So, what do you want me to do?"

"Hmm . . ." Linds frowned into one of the boxes. "Right now we're just going through what we have, what we can use this year, and what we need to buy. Oh, how about this?" Tucking back a few stray curls, she bent over and reached into a box, pulling out something that resembled basketball netting.

She dropped it into my arms.

"What is this?" I asked, staring down at the knotted mess.

"Cobwebs. There's probably more than one set in there, but they're all tangled together." She bit down on her plump lower lip as she eyed me. "Can you take them apart and see how many are there?"

"That would be so helpful," Ms. Reed chimed in, and I pressed my lips together. Looking up at me, the pen she held stilled above the notebook. "Oh, and how are your self-defense lessons going with Jensen?"

Half the room went quiet, namely Brock and Mason. Oh dear. My cheeks heated. "It's . . . um, going good. Thanks for that."

She winked and my eyes widened. "I thought it would."

Linds arched a brow, and I turned, plopping down on an old stool near the window with my armful of fake webbing that smelled faintly of Halloween makeup. A smell I couldn't quite name, but it was distinctive, reminding me of what it was like to dress up and go door to door.

I missed those days.

I barely listened to the conversation around me, but every so often I'd hear Monica's name whispered, and it stirred up things I was doing my hardest not to think about. I'd rather focus on my dad's unending attempt at getting me to lose fifteen pounds. I kind of wanted to hold on to those pounds. Knowing my luck, if I lost weight, it would come off my boobs, but in all seriousness, I saw absolutely nothing wrong with what I weighed, so whatever.

A shadow fell over me. Brock stood there, his head tilted to the side. "Hey."

"What's up?" I tugged at the mess of fake cobwebs. The stringy stuff was balled into one giant knot. Ugh.

"Nothing much. Just helping out." Brock knelt next to me. "So . . . ?"

It was weird. Since his party, he hadn't talked to me, which I was totally okay with. Now I had no idea what to say to him. I finally found the edge of the webbing.

"You and Jensen hanging out?" he asked.

"He's teaching me self-defense," I corrected, yanking on the white string.

Brock chuckled. "That's a different way of saying it."

Frowning, I glanced up. "Huh?"

He met my eyes with a look that said I knew exactly what he was saying, but it was far over my head. "I can help you out with that, you know."

"The webbing?"

Brock laughed again. "No. With the self-defense stuff. I'm sure I can work in one or two . . . *practices* a week with you."

Suddenly what he was saying made sense and I wanted to wrap the netting around his neck. Not only was he suggesting that Jensen and I were doing more of a horizontal kind of training, but he thought I'd mess around with him, too? Anger moved in a slow burn through my veins.

I lowered the webbing to my lap. "It's really sad about Monica. I'm guessing you haven't heard anything new?"

His face paled and the blood rushed to his cheeks. "No. I haven't. But Monica and I weren't dating."

"That's right. You guys broke up a couple of weeks ago."

He stared at me a moment, the hue of his cheeks deepening, and then he muttered something under his breath. Straightening, he walked away and returned to Mason's side.

"What was that about?" whispered Linds, coming over to me

with a stuffed snake, its red eyes glimmering.

I shrugged, wrinkling my nose. "You don't even want to know."

"Let me guess. He was hitting on you?"

"Yep."

Her lip curled. "Doesn't surprise me. Real classy considering no one knows where his ex-girlfriend is."

"Exactly," I muttered, glancing over at the boys. A junior girl joined them, wrapping her arms around Mason. "What's with you and Mason?"

Linds' shoulders fell and she sighed, staring at the fake snake. "I don't know. He was all hot and heavy at Brock's party and he called me a couple days ago, but now . . . well, who knows?"

"We're supposed to be single and cool this year, remember?" I reminded her.

She grinned. "And how's that working out for you?"

"Still single." But my stomach did a little flop because I knew she was talking about Jensen.

"Uh-huh. But for how long?" Spinning on her heel at the sound of her name being called, she all but flounced away.

Pulling my hair up in a messy bun, I got to work, concentrating solely on untangling the mess. There was something relaxing about the mind-numbing task. Time passed, my brain empty, as I worked out all the knots, discovering that I had ten spider webs.

Covered in a thin layer of dust, I stood, brushing my hands across my rear. My gaze accidentally connected with Brock's, and he gave me a look that caused me to drop my hands off my butt.

Gee, he was most definitely worried about Monica.

Turning away from him in disgust, I came face to face with Ms. Reed and her perpetual smile. "We have ten spider webs," I told her.

"Great!" She immediately scribbled it down, then paused and looked at me. "Are you doing anything else right now?"

I knew I should've said yes. "No."

"Can you go upstairs and measure the workbench up there?" Ms.

Reed whipped a tape measure out of her back pocket. "We need to make sure it will fit our prop. I believe it's in the last bedroom."

Dammit.

Linds made a face behind her, and I resisted—barely—pitching the tape measure at Linds' girl parts.

"Sure," I grumbled.

"Sorry," Linds whispered as I stalked past her.

I shot her a death glare. "Your fault."

Passing Mason, who was now busy arranging the fake gourds and pumpkins into something truly repulsive, I approached the narrow staircase, having no idea where Brock had disappeared to.

God only knew what was upstairs in this old house. Probably a long-lost member of the Texas Chainsaw Massacre family.

Clutching the dusty handrail, I climbed the surprisingly sturdy steps. Dim light from the window at the top of the landing shined a faint glow down the long hallway. Dust was heavy in the air, dancing in the rays coming from the dirty glass window. Flowered wallpaper was peeling off the walls and missing in some places. All of the doors—six of them—were closed, and there were two at the end of the hall.

"Great," I muttered. Ms. Reed hadn't specified which bedroom and I really didn't want to randomly open doors.

It was kind of like turning over rocks that God had put there for a reason.

As I walked further down the hall, away from the only source of light, a chill of unease danced across my skin. There was just something creepy about virtually empty old houses.

I ignored it, trying the door on the right first. I pushed it open then jumped back, swallowing a scream.

"Holy shit." I clenched the tape measure in my fist.

A six-and-a-half-foot mummy was propped against the wall directly across from the door. Half of its papier-mâché face was crumbled away, caved in, and I wasn't sure if it was supposed to look like that. Dust clung to its white wrappings, giving it a frighteningly real look.

Cursing again, I scanned the room for said workbench but had no luck. I closed the door and spun around, wary of what I'd find behind door number two.

Hinges creaked as I inched the door open, the sound echoing in an unnatural way. Very little light entered the room, and in the thick shadows I could make out a shape that vaguely resembled a bench. There were other forms, things propped against the wall, others covered in cloth. Most likely more leftover props.

Feeling along the wall for a light switch, my hand sliced through a real cobweb. Squealing, I turned into a ninja as I flung the sticky material off my hand. Finally I found the switch and flipped it on.

The overhead light burst on brightly, and for a few moments everything in the room became visible—fake coffins with their lids closed propped against the wall, a very badly made vampire, more mummies, mannequins covered in soiled sheets, and the workbench, which had another prop tossed on it.

A flicker of white out of the corner of my eye caught my attention. Air froze up in my lungs as I spun toward the mannequins or whatever the hell was under those sheets. Had one of them moved?

My heart kicked against my ribs.

Just your imagination, I told myself. Forcing air into my chest, I started toward the bench, clenching the tape measure until my knuckles ached as I glanced around the room nervously.

The overhead light blinked suddenly, erratically, and then dimmed to a yellow glow, the bulb probably minutes from burning out.

Just my luck.

Wanting to get this over with, I shuffled around the draped sheets crammed next to the workbench, my lip curling in disgust. I had no idea what was on the bench. The pitiful light didn't reach this far across the room, and as thick as the shadows were around me, I'd be surprised if I could even read the measurements. I tugged out the tape measure—

Loose hairs at the nape of my neck stirred as icy fingers trailed across my skin.

Gasping, I spun around, causing the sheets to flutter around me. Dust flew into the air, clogging it. I stepped back, bumping into the workbench. Blood pounded through me as I stared at the sheets, watching them settle back into place.

I reached up and placed trembling fingers against the base of my neck. Cobwebs. Had to be cobwebs.

Throat dry, I turned back to the workbench and concentrated on my task. I had no idea what was on the bench. Wrapped in a dark blanket, its slender, stuffing filled legs were bound together with coarse rope, as were its arms. My gaze drifted over the length of the prop. It wasn't nearly as tall as the mummy, maybe a little over five and a half feet, close to my height.

A weird smell mixed with a musky scent radiated from the prop. I leaned over the bench, trying to measure its width, but the legs were in the way.

"Christ."

Putting the tape measure down, I grabbed the legs, totally planning on rolling the whole thing right off the bench, but . . . the legs were heavy. Solid. I lifted them with a grunt, and the smell, the sickly-sweet smell increased. Apprehension grew in the pit of my stomach, rising through me like smoke.

At once, I found it hard to breathe as my gaze slowly traveled the form again. My throat closed up. The blanket had loosened at the top, and was now barely folded together. I squinted as I stared into the gap. Something . . . something like dark hair curled around the edges of the blanket.

Oh God . . .

There was something else—something blood red and *feathered* in the center of the opening.

I leaned forward, my brows knitting together as I reached out with one shaky hand. *It's just a prop. It's fake. Totally fake.* My fingers caught the edge of the blanket, and with my heart pounding, I pulled the coarse material to the side.

A scream rushed up my throat, slamming to a stop as horror seized me in its icy grip. Jerking back, I opened my mouth wide, but no sound came out. I couldn't breathe and I couldn't look away from what lie unmoving on the bench.

Dull green eyes were fixed on the ceiling. Skin a ghastly shade of whitish-gray, all except the dark brown stain marring the corner of blue lips and the . . .

Oh God.

The head of a cardinal speared her lips, its small, feathered body disappearing into her grotesquely stretched mouth.

It wasn't a dummy.

The scream finally broke free, shattering the silence, and I didn't stop screaming. I couldn't.

I'd found her—I'd found Vee Bartol.

ELEVEN

POLICE SWARMED THE old farmhouse and barn. I wasn't sure how much time had passed, but the medical examiner's van had been parked there for a while and it seemed like forever ago that the officers had pulled me away from Linds and Ms. Reed, stashing me in the back of a cruiser.

People were questioned and then ordered off the property.

Yellow tape went up.

I'd given my statement to a trooper who appeared vaguely familiar and then to a deputy, who also appeared to be someone I felt like I should know. I'd heard enough to know this was being treated as a homicide, which became apparent from the moment I'd found Vee because people didn't simply die like that normally.

About every ten minutes or so, an officer checked on me. Someone had given me an unopened bottle of water. After taking one drink, it rested beside me, untouched.

I remained in the back of the cruiser, and no matter how many deep breaths I took, I couldn't get the scent of death out of my head. I pressed my hands to my face. Every so often, a tremor rocked me.

Vee was dead.

I hadn't been close to her, but that didn't lessen the shock or the horror seizing my insides in a tight, icy grip. She had been murdered. There was no doubt in my mind that was what had happened. She had been murdered and left there in the farmhouse to be found.

"How are you hanging in there?"

I looked up at the sound of the male voice. Dimly, my brain kicked on. "I know you."

"Yes." He knelt in the open door, watching me with steady, serious dark eyes. "You do know me."

"You're Deputy Shaw." I blinked. Like he didn't know who he was. "Sorry. My brain's not working."

"It's understandable." He reached into the car, squeezing my shoulder. "Just hang in there. We've called your mom to come get you. She'll be here soon."

"Thank you," I whispered as I leaned back against the seat, running my palms over my bent knees. Over his shoulder, my gaze found the coroner's van, still sitting there. "Is she still . . . ?"

"We can't move the . . . her until we've collected all the evidence." He squeezed my shoulder again. "That's probably not something you need to think about right now."

I nodded slowly. One image kept replaying over and over in my head, more often than the others. "There was a bird—a cardinal—shoved in her—"

"Now that's something you really don't want to think about, Ella." His hand slid away as he rose. Bracing himself against the door jamb, he dipped his head. "I know it's hard."

I almost laughed, but stopped myself. If I started, I wasn't sure I'd stop, and it would be the crazy kind of laughter. I glanced up at him, and it was like a memory unlocked itself from the depths of my mind. A bitter edged sensation of déjà vu slammed into me.

"I remember," I whispered, throat dry.

He tilted his head to the side. "Remember what?"

"You had me in the back of the cruiser last time." I knew the moment he got what I was saying because his eyes widened with understanding. "You waited with me until my parents showed up."

A moment passed. "I did. Hopefully we don't have to do that a third time."

He didn't say anything else but stood there like a silent sentry. How had I forgotten that was Deputy Shaw? Rattled by the realization, I sank back against the seat. I had seriously blocked out most of the details surrounding that night. That's what Dr. Oliver had said.

My stomach twisted around the water I had swallowed, and I closed my eyes, counting until the nausea passed.

It wasn't too long after that before Mom showed up. She parked her car near mine and then raced over to the cruiser. Shaw stepped aside as I climbed out. My legs shook as I took a step toward her.

Mom engulfed me in one of her huge hugs. "Oh, baby . . ."

I squeezed my eyes shut, inhaling her familiar rose perfume. Tears clogged my throat as I clung to her.

"You can go ahead and get her out of here," Shaw said, shutting the car door behind us. "If we need anything else, we know where to find her."

"Thank you," Mom said. She turned, keeping her arm tight around me. "Let's go home."

Numbly, I let Mom lead me to her Toyota. She stopped by my car, grabbed my bag out of it, then locked it before joining me. Squeezing my hands into fists, I focused on them as Mom turned the car around and drove out of the makeshift parking lot.

"Ella . . . ?"

I drew in a shaky breath. There was so much to be said, but there weren't enough words in the world to describe the shock and horror of finding a body like that. But worst of all, it hadn't been my first time coming face to face with one.

We didn't talk during the short trip home, and when she pulled up in front of the house, she ended up parking where I normally would because her spot was taken.

Slowly, I unbuckled my seat belt and opened the door. Mom

joined me, walking to the gate and opening it. I had a clear view of the front porch.

Jensen was sitting on the steps, his hands resting on his bent knees. He stood as we walked up the sidewalk. He didn't say a word as he strolled toward us, his long-legged pace eating up the distance, his pale blue, almost gray eyes fixed solely on me.

There was something painfully familiar about all of this.

But it didn't stop me. My lower lip trembled as he walked past Mom and wrapped his arms around me, holding me tight against his chest.

"I'm so sorry," he said. One hand traveled up my spine, fisting the hair at the back of my neck. "I'm so sorry you had to go through this."

The thing was, I found a body . . . for the second time in my life, and that was horrific, but nothing compared to what Vee had gone through, what her family would surely experience next. A shudder rocked through me as I dug my fingers into his sides. I don't know how long we stood there, but I heard the door shut quietly behind Mom. We were alone, as alone as we could be standing in the middle of our sidewalk, and we stood there in silence for several minutes.

Jensen guided me over to the steps, but when I went to sit beside him, he gently tugged me down into his lap, folding me into his embrace. There was a brief second where I thought I should protest this intimacy, but I wanted to be close to him. I wanted to feel the warmth and stability of just having someone hold me.

Inhaling his citrusy cologne and a scent that was uniquely his, I let it seep into every one of my senses. He trailed his hand up and down my spine in a continuous soothing slide, remaining quiet until I found my voice.

"I touched it," I whispered. "I touched *her* and I didn't even realize that it was real, that she was—"

"Shh," murmured Jensen, his hand stilling as he held me closer, tighter. "There was no way you could've known that."

I turned my head, resting my cheek on his shoulder. "Who would do that to someone?"

"A monster."

Taking several deep breaths, I loosened my grip on his shirt. "I don't think . . . she was dead long."

His chin grazed my forehead. "What do you mean?"

I swallowed hard. "She didn't look like she had been dead for long. I mean, she was missing for three weeks, but she didn't look that way or . . . or smell like that—" I cut myself off with a sharp inhale. "I'm not an expert, but I know she wasn't dead for three weeks."

He didn't answer immediately. "God, I don't even want to think it," he admitted, his voice rough. "That she could've been . . . held for that length of time and then murdered."

I didn't want to think it either, because that took all of this to a whole new level of terrifying. It wouldn't be a random thrill kill or anything like that. Not when someone was held for weeks and then killed. What could've been done to her during that time . . . ?

My stomach churned.

"And now Monica is missing," I said, a tremor coursing through me. "I don't care what anyone says. With Vee dead and Monica gone, it has to be related."

Jensen didn't respond right away, but he reached up with one hand, tilting my head back so that my eyes met his. "And you."

My heart skipped a beat.

"Whoever is behind this tried to grab you a week ago, but you got away." He pressed his forehead against mine, his chest rising sharply. "God, you got away."

I didn't want to think about it, but it was no use, because it was reality. The three of us were related to this—Vee. Monica, and me. He'd tried to grab me and had most likely gotten his hands on Monica while he still had Vee.

And she most likely had still been alive.

Shivering, I closed my eyes as Jensen's lips brushed over my forehead. "This is all so terrible."

"It is."

"She wasn't just dead," I told him, because I needed to say it out loud. "There was a cardinal in her mouth, Jensen."

He gave a little shake of his head. "Damn . . ."

"Just like the kind of cardinal that was in Wendy's bag." I bit down on my lip, thinking of the cardinals, the clown masks, and . . . *Penn*. "That's too much of a coincidence, isn't it?"

There was a beat of silence. "I want you to do me a favor."

I opened my eyes. "What?"

His thumb smoothed over my cheek as his gaze searched mine. "Let me take you to school and bring you home."

Drawing back, I shook my head. "But—"

"Or let Gavin or someone. I'm not trying to be pushy, I just don't want you to be alone right now," he explained. "And it's not because I don't think you can take care of yourself, but this is serious. This is real. Something terrible is going on and I want you . . ." He took a deep breath. "I want you to be as safe as possible."

How could I say no to that? I also wasn't stupid. This was serious, and the idea of going anywhere alone wasn't a good idea and not something I even wanted to do. "Okay."

A lopsided grin appeared. "Okay to me taking you, or some-one—anyone—other than me?"

"To you." I flushed, ducking my chin. "I mean, if that's what you want. You don't have to. I'm sure Gavin and Linds—"

"No, I want to. Not Gavin." Jensen's hand moved, his fingers curling around my hair. His hand lingered there a moment, and then he reached down, wrapping his hands around mine. He rubbed them between his. "Is your car still at the farmhouse?"

I nodded.

"If you want, we can go get it tomorrow. I don't think going out there tonight would be smart."

"I don't want to go back out there at all," I admitted. "I don't even want to see those buildings tomorrow."

"Then I'll take care of it. Nope—don't argue with me. I'll get your car here. I just need your keys."

When I nodded, he tucked my head under his chin. We sat there, listening to the chirps of the crickets and the wind moving among the branches. I was okay with him being here—more than okay—and right then our past together didn't matter.

Jensen was here when it mattered, but how had he known? I doubted it had hit the news that quickly that it was me who found the body. Discomfort tightened my muscles.

"How did you hear about what happened?" I asked.

"Brock texted me," he answered, his chest rumbling against mine. "He said that you found Vee's body."

I wondered if he'd also told Jensen how hysterical I'd been. How I screamed until my voice had given out. Strange thing was, Brock hadn't been around when I went upstairs and I didn't remember seeing him afterward either.

JENSEN PICKED ME up for school on Monday morning as offered. I had no idea how he got my car back to me on Sunday, but it was there before I even got up. We didn't talk about Vee or Monica on the way. Instead, it was a normal conversation. Well, as normal as making plans to go to the warehouse after school for more self-defense was.

When we pulled into the parking lot, he turned off the engine and looked over at me. With a baseball cap pulled low, the strong line of his jaw stood out. "You ready for today?"

I nodded.

"It's probably going to be a little rough." He reached over, poking my leg. "Not that you can't handle it."

A wry, tired smile twisted my lips. "I know. I'm as ready as I'll ever be."

"Okay." He pulled his keys out, leaned back, and grabbed our bags, handing mine over. "Let's do this."

Jensen and I walked into the building together. Any other day, this would've been the talk of the school.

But not today.

Everyone was talking about Vee. As the day progressed, there wasn't a pair of lips her name hadn't passed through. Grief counselors were called in, and throughout the day, long looks were sent in my direction. I knew people were talking, but very few approached me about it.

Mason was one of them. At lunch, he dropped into the seat next to me. "Hey," he said.

"Hi." I glanced over at Heidi, who looked as surprised as I felt. I picked up my plastic fork. "What's up?"

He wet his lips. "You got a second?"

"Sure."

Mason lowered his head and dropped his voice. "The cops made the rest of us leave Saturday before—well, before we could see anything."

"Jesus," muttered Heidi, dropping her hands on the table.

He ignored her while I tensed up. "What did she look like? I mean, I know that's a gross question, but I wanted—"

"Are you serious?"

Mason turned at the sound of Jensen's voice. One look at his face, and it was evident that he was angry. His pale eyes flashed a dark, thunderous color as he stared down at him. "What? I'm just—"

"Get the hell out of my seat." Jensen's knuckles were bleached white around the tray he held. "Before I get you out of the damn seat."

Standing up, Mason raised his hands as he glanced at Jensen and then me. His cheeks paled. "Look, man, I didn't mean anything by any of that."

"Whatever."

Mason hesitated for a moment and then spun off, hurrying back to his table.

"Your seat?" I asked, brows raised.

He took Mason's spot, placing his tray in front of him. "Yep."

I pressed my lips together, stealing a peek at Heidi. Her eyes were bouncing back and forth between us like we were her own personal tennis match.

"Thank you," I said. "But I could've shut him up."

Jensen raised a shoulder as he stared at what I was guessing was Salisbury steak. "I know, but seriously, what was I supposed to do when I was just walking along, minding my own business, about to have a seat and that dick is sitting here, asking a question like that?"

"Wait to see what I was going to do?"

Heidi snorted. "I, for one, am glad Jensen said something. I cannot believe he asked you that kind of question." She shook her head. "Didn't Linds get with him?"

"Yeah," I murmured. Sickened by Mason's crassness, I'd lost my appetite. And, as the day progressed, there were others like him, people who didn't give two craps about Vee, but were compelled by a sense of morbid fascination.

On Tuesday, the cops arrived at the school and, at the beginning of each class, a handful of kids were pulled out and sent to the office, which had my nerves stretched taut. The lack of sleep and everything else was getting to me.

Rain thundered off the windows and roof as I stopped by my locker after lunch. Jensen checked it out before I looked in it, inspecting the inside for something that would most likely ensure me a lifetime of therapy. When there were no masks or other creeptastic things, he leaned against the locker next to mine, his baseball cap pulled on backward, dark blond strands curling around the edge.

"If it's still raining after school, I'll pull the truck up to the back."

I smiled as I grabbed my art textbook. "Rain won't hurt me."

"Sugar melts," he replied, grinning slightly.

Rolling my eyes, I laughed softly. "Did you just compliment me?"

"Oh, that's right, I'm not supposed to do that. I'm supposed to be keeping it real." Those lips of his pursed thoughtfully. "I need to come up with a good insult. It's going to take me a while."

Smiling, I shook my head.

"Is your Mom still going out of town tomorrow night?" he asked, changing the subject.

I was so not looking forward to tomorrow night. "Yeah, she needs to since she stayed home last week. She wants me to go stay at Dad's, but that's not something I want to do."

"It would be smart." He reached up, adjusting the bill of his cap. "You shouldn't be staying alone."

"I know, but . . ." Staying with Dad meant staying with Rose and eating raw vegetables and being lectured on how I needed to do at least thirty minutes of cardio a day and—

"Hey!"

We turned at the sound of Linds' excited shout. She was speed walking down the hall, dodging students. The hem of her skirt fluttered around her slim legs.

"Hey." I shut my door as I shoved my book into my bag. "Aren't you supposed to be in class?"

"I'm using the bathroom." She slid to a stop between Jensen and me. "But I needed to come find you. It couldn't wait until—oh. Hey, Jensen. Whoa . . ." She stepped back, looking him up and down. "I like the baseball hat. It's a good—"

"Linds," I interrupted, tapping her shoulder. "What couldn't wait?"

Eyeing Jensen until he grinned at her, Linds' cheeks flushed before she got back on track. "Have you talked to Gavin?"

"On Sunday." He'd stopped by to see how I was, claiming he would've come by Saturday night, but he'd seen Jensen's truck out front. "We really didn't get a chance to talk yesterday."

"What about you?" she asked Jensen.

He shrugged a shoulder. "Nothing longer than a few seconds since Sunday. He actually went out with me to get Ella's car."

I blinked. Once, then twice. "Gavin went with you to get my car?"

"Yeah," he replied slowly. "Why wouldn't he?"

Why? Whenever Gavin and Jensen were in the same room together, it was like a contest to see who could out-stare the other the longest. "Well . . ."

"That's not important." Linds stamped her mule-heeled foot. "The police pulled me out of last period to question me again about Saturday. They'll probably get to you again," she said, and I winced, not looking forward to that. "Anyway, they asked me if I'd known that Vee had been seeing Gavin."

I gaped at her. At first I didn't think I'd heard her correctly. "Come again?"

"Did you know that Gavin and Vee were dating?"

It took me a moment. "What?"

"Exactly!" she whispered-yelled. "I had no idea and I'm assuming you had no idea either."

"No." I slipped my messenger bag up my arm. "They must've been mistaken. Gavin hadn't been seeing anyone since we broke up." I glanced over at Jensen, but he was staring at Linds, his jaw clenched. "Gavin wasn't dating Vee."

Looking me straight in the eye, Linds clasped my arm. "Yeah, he was. Supposedly all summer. And I heard them talking among themselves as I was being ushered out. He was with her the night she supposedly disappeared."

THEN

WE SAT IN a circle on the floor of the tree house, cross-legged with our knees pressed against each other. The sun was setting, splashing deep blues and violets across the sky. We didn't have much longer before we had to leave. Penn wouldn't climb down the wooden planks nailed into the tree at night, and even though it was summer, his parents wanted him back before dark.

The air was humid, and the thin wisps of hair that had escaped my ponytail stuck to my damp neck. I wanted to dunk my head in a vat of cold water as I nervously rubbed the palms of my hands along my legs.

I hated playing truth or dare, because inevitably, one of the boys—usually Jensen or Gavin—either asked an embarrassing question or suggested a dare that I'd end up getting called a girl for not doing.

Gavin waggled his brows at me, and I sighed. Another reason why I hated this game was the fact that I couldn't come up with a cool question or dare.

"Truth or dare?" I said.

"Truth!" he said boldly.

My brain whizzed as I searched for something to ask and I blurted out the first thing that came to mind. "Is it true . . . that you . . . ?"

Gavin leaned forward, waiting.

"Sleep with a fuzzy teddy bear?" I finished.

"What?" He sat up straight, glancing at Jensen, who grinned. "Are you serious?"

I shrugged. "Yeah."

"No." He sighed. "That's not true. And that was also lame, Ella."

I slept with a blue bear—a Care Bear, so whatever. I wrinkled my nose at him, and he grinned before looking at Jensen. "Your turn."

Tensing up, I held my breath.

Which meant it was also my turn. Moving my hand to the toe of my sneakers, I peeked at Penn and bit down on my lip to stop grinning. He wasn't even paying attention, staring off at the trees.

"Truth or dare, Ella?" Jensen said.

My heart did something strange in my chest, and I didn't understand the flipping motion as I turned back to him. I don't know why I said what I said. "Dare."

Oh my gosh, I wanted to take that back immediately. I knew better than to pick dare, but it was too late.

Jensen's lips split into a wide grin, and my heart did that weird flipping thing again. "I dare you to . . . kiss me."

My mouth dropped open.

"Ew," Penn said, and then he giggled, proving he was paying attention.

Jensen leaned toward me, his eyes a dark blue in the fading light. "That's the dare."

I stared at him. Kiss me? Kiss him? Like put our lips together?

"Duuude," Gavin murmured low. "She's not going to do it."

My gaze snapped to him. Why did he think I wouldn't do it? Because I was a girl? I wasn't chicken. My fingers dug into the toes of my sneaker as resolve straightened my spine. I looked at Jensen. "Okay. I accept your dare."

Jensen blinked thick lashes as if surprised, and I heard a strange, almost choking sound come from Gavin. Penn giggled again, and warmth spread across my face. Should I have gone with truth? Oh my gosh, I totally should've have—

"Okay." Jensen shifted, placing one hand on the old board behind me, and before I could say another word, he erased the distance between us and pressed his mouth to mine.

Jensen kissed me.

Our mouths were totally touching.

My eyes were wide and his were closed, and it was over in a heartbeat. Jensen pulled back, opening his eyes. He grinned at me, and I felt like I'd just run the length of Rosemont Avenue, twelve times.

"Okie dokie," Gavin said. "That was weird."

My lips tingling and cheeks burning with heat, I forced myself to turn to Penn slowly as Gavin spoke again. "Truth or dare, Penn?"

Penn's gaze darted around our group before settling on Gavin. We all knew he'd say truth, but I was barely paying attention. My concentration was centered on how Jensen's knee was pressing against mine. We'd kissed. Oh my gosh, Jensen and I had just put our mouths on—

"Dare!" Penn exclaimed.

Holy crap, my head swung toward him and my eyes widened until they felt like they'd pop out of my head. Neither of the other boys spoke, and I knew without looking at them that they shared identical expressions.

Oh, this was going to go bad, because Jensen and Gavin gave each other horrible dares. Like eating dirt and lying in the middle of the road and running naked through old Mrs. Towery's yard. And when I glanced at Gavin, I could see his brain working, coming up with something devious.

I couldn't let this happen.

Grabbing Penn's hand, I sprang to my feet and pulled him up with me, breaking our circle.

"Hey," Gavin said, craning his neck back. "What are you doing?"

"I'm done playing this game. Penn is walking me home."

Penn frowned thoughtfully. "I am?"

"Yep."

"Oh, you guys suck." Gavin shook his head. "It's still early."

I ignored him and waved with my free hand. "Bye!"

Stepping around Jensen, I started down the steps first so Penn could follow me, and thankfully, he did. He didn't hop down from the second step like I did. It wasn't even that far off the ground, but Penn was always super careful when it came to heights. Heck, he wouldn't step foot in the tree house without one of us with him. I still couldn't believe he even went in that tree house.

He hesitated, stretching his leg out until the toe of his black sneaker brushed the ground, and then he finally let go of the tree. I waited until he was beside me.

"Duuude," I heard Gavin say to Jensen again, but whatever else was said was lost in Penn and my shuffling along the leafy foliage as we began to walk back.

Shoving his hands into his pockets, he didn't say anything as he watched the thick limbs above us. "We didn't have to leave, you know."

"It's getting late."

"We still had plenty of time."

I jumped over a massive tangle of exposed roots. "I didn't want to play the stupid game again."

Penn glanced over at me. "You kissed Jensen."

My heart felt like it also jumped over those roots. "It was just a dare. It didn't mean nothing."

"Anything," he corrected softly, and I grinned at him. "I could've done the dare, you know. Whatever Gavin came up with, I would've done it."

"I know." I swung my arms wide as we continued to the road, trying my best to not think about that dare—the kiss. "That's not why I wanted to leave."

Penn knocked his shoulder into mine. "Liar."

"Nuh-uh."

"You know," he said, stepping around a large rock. "Summer's almost over. We head back to school in two weeks." The small smile on his face faded when I looked over at him. "I think this year is going to be different."

I didn't understand why, but a shiver of apprehension wiggled down my spine. "How?"

Penn pulled his hands out of his pockets, letting his thin arms dangle at his sides. "It just is. I don't . . . I don't think we'll be playing this game *again next summer."*

I halted, staring at him.

He walked a few paces ahead and then faced me. "Can I ask you something, Ella?"

I folded my arms along my waist and nodded.

"Do you really think we'll still be friends?"

"What?" Surprised, I stared at him.

"I mean, we'll still be friends in a year? In two? When we're in high school?" He reached up, running his hand through his messy, in need of a trim, hair. "Never mind. It's a stupid question."

"It was," I told him as I pushed forward, joining him. "We're always going to be best friends. No matter what."

TWELVE

LINDS HAD BEEN right. The police pulled me out of gym class on Wednesday afternoon, and I was led into a small conference room off the principal's office. First they went over everything that had happened when I found Vee's body, and then they talked to me about Gavin.

According to Trooper Ritter, Gavin had been dating Vee over the summer. *Did you know?* they asked. *Would there be any reason why Gavin wouldn't have told me?* I couldn't think of a reason. And why had Gavin and I broken up? Talking to them about the decline of our relationship was more awkward than having the sex talk with Mom, which had involved how to open a condom wrapper and all that jazz.

"We've been friends since we were little," I said, glancing back and forth between the two troopers. I wished Shaw was here. At least I was comfortable with him, but with Shaw being related to Gavin, I guessed he couldn't be the one to question me. "I mean, we were just better as friends than boyfriend and girlfriend."

"So you broke up with him?" Trooper Ritter asked.

I nodded, feeling uneasy with this whole line of questioning. "It was mutual."

"Now I'm a little confused," the other trooper stated. He rested his elbow on the table as he spoke. "If it was a mutual breakup, why didn't Gavin tell you that he was dating Vee?"

Knots formed in my stomach. That was a damn good question. One I didn't have an answer for. "I don't know. I really had no idea they were . . . they were seeing each other."

"And how does that make you feel?" he asked.

I glanced at Trooper Ritter, knocked off-kilter by the question. "How do I feel about them dating? I . . . I don't know." Really, I hadn't even begun to wrap my head around that. I'd never once heard Gavin even talk to her let alone be around her. "We weren't seeing each other anymore, so . . ." Or at least I assumed they started dating after we broke up, but who knew?

I didn't know anything anymore.

"Is . . . he a suspect?" I asked after they asked a few more questions about him.

Trooper Ritter smiled tightly, causing the skin around his eyes to crinkle. "Right now, everyone is a potential suspect."

That statement didn't sit well with me. When I was excused, I felt a little sick to my stomach, so I stood slowly. I hesitated at the door, turning back to where they sat, tilted together, both speaking in a low voice. "How . . . how did Vee die?"

Ritter glanced up, frowning. "That's not something we're at liberty to discuss right now."

I lowered my gaze. "Was it quick for her, though?"

He seemed to get what I was asking, and when I glanced up, his Adam's apple bobbed. Meeting my gaze, he didn't say a word, but it was all in his eyes, and what he didn't say that gave me my answer.

Vee didn't go quickly.

I WASN'T TOO surprised when Gavin showed up at my house after Jensen dropped me off. He looked worn out, as if he hadn't slept in as many days as I hadn't.

Without saying a word, I stepped aside and he shuffled into the foyer. His pale cheeks bloomed red as he glanced at me, our eyes meeting for a second before his darted away.

Gavin sighed, his shoulders tensing. "I'm guessing you've heard."

I studied him closely, trying to think back to a time when there weren't any secrets between us. It hadn't always been like this. Until the eighth grade, he was afraid of putting contacts in his eyes. He'd never been further out of state than Virginia or Maryland. This summer was the first time he'd gone to the beach. He wanted to be a graphic designer when he graduated college. I knew that the sides of his stomach were ticklish, and between the three of us—Jensen, him, and me—he was the only one who'd said that Penn wouldn't understand what Jensen and I had planned to do.

We hadn't listened to him.

My chest rose with a deep breath as I pushed those thoughts aside. "Why didn't you tell me?"

Turning so he faced me, he thrust his hand through his hair. "I didn't think it was important."

I gaped at him. "You didn't think it was important to let me know you were dating Vee? Especially after she went missing?"

"Her going missing had nothing to do with me," he said, his dark eyes flashing.

"I didn't say it did, but it's weird that you never said anything."

He dragged his hand down his face. "I know, but it wasn't something that I thought you'd like to hear about, you know? It wasn't like Vee and I were dating."

I stared at him as his words sunk in. "So you . . . were just hooking up?"

Closing his eyes, he nodded. "Just a few times, really, over the summer. It was nothing serious."

Wow. I didn't know what to think. I never thought Gavin would be into the 'just hooking up' thing. And I don't even know why I thought he wasn't. I didn't even know what I knew anymore. Walking around him, I went to the couch and sat down.

Gavin followed me. He didn't sit, though. He stood by the worn recliner that had belonged to Dad. He hadn't taken it with him when he moved. Why? Because he and Rose had purchased all new things for their home, you know, so they could have a fresh start.

"We ran into each other at the mall. It was after we broke up. I swear it was. I never messed around on you with her."

"Okay," I whispered. I believed him, but that didn't matter. It was neither here nor there at this point.

"I was . . . missing you and she was just there. One thing led to another and we hooked up. Like I said, it wasn't anything serious."

"But you kept hooking up with her?"

As he dropped into the recliner, he kept his gaze glued to the water rings on the coffee table. "Yeah, we did."

Again, I had no idea what to say. He'd been with her the night she disappeared and not once had he thought it might be something he wanted to share with people? The police? Her family? He could've talked to his cousin about it.

"The whole time you and I went out, we never had sex," he said quietly, and I stiffened at where this conversation was heading. He was correct. We didn't have sex, *sex*. But we'd done other things, and I'd enjoyed those things when they were happening. It was all the messy thoughts that had come afterward that I hadn't. "I thought that maybe something was wrong with me. That I was, like, universally unattractive."

"It wasn't that." I was quick to correct him. "It's just that you and I . . ."

"Are better as friends. Yeah, trust me, I haven't forgotten what you said." His shoulders rose and fell heavily. "But Vee was interested in me and . . ." He laughed hoarsely. "It wasn't a big deal. I never thought it would end like this."

I doubted many people did.

He looked at me then, features taut. "You're looking at me like you have no idea who I am."

"It's not that. It's just, you never seemed like the kind of guy who was into random hookups. That's more . . ." I didn't finish that train wreck of a sentence.

"More like Jensen." He took it there—right there. "I didn't say anything because of that. I didn't want you to know, because yeah, as stupid as it sounds, there's a part of me that still thinks there's hope for us."

Oh God.

I squeezed my eyes shut. Somehow this painfully awkward conversation just went from *icky* straight to *oh shit, get me out of here*. "Gavin . . ."

"Look, you don't need to respond to that or even think about it, especially right now." He slapped his hands down on his knees. "But I'm telling you that I have no idea why Vee went missing, and I sure as hell didn't have anything to do with it. You believe me, right?"

Forcing my eyes open, my gaze latched on to his. Those knots were back in my stomach, weighing me down. Deep down, I knew Gavin didn't have anything to do with Vee disappearing. I'd known him all my life, and the boy did not have something that . . . that evil inside of him. But I was disappointed. Not that he'd been hooking up with Vee, but because he hadn't told anyone and maybe that information wouldn't be helpful, but we'd never know now. "Yes," I said. "Of course."

Tension seeped out of his body and he all but slumped over. "Thank God. I don't care what anyone else thinks." He scrubbed at his jaw again. "My cousin—you know Jordan Shaw? One of the deputies?"

"Yeah."

"He told me—I mean, I don't know if he was supposed to do this or not, but they aren't looking at me too seriously, especially not after they interviewed me."

I picked up a throw pillow, tucking it against my chest. "Why?"

"They . . . man, they told me what happened to her. I guess to see how I reacted or something." Blood drained from his face, and my fingers tightened around the edges of the pillow. "God, I got sick." He broke off, laughing harshly. "I actually got sick."

"What . . . what did happen to her?" I asked.

He opened his mouth, closed it, then shook his head. "She was stabbed multiple times. Some of the wounds weren't deep. Like someone was torturing her. They showed me pictures. That's when I lost it."

"Oh God." I shouldn't have asked. I could've lived the rest of my life never knowing that.

"Worst thing? She was alive the whole time." He tipped his head back, throat working. When he spoke, his voice was hoarse. "She was killed within twenty-four hours of you finding her. They kept her alive."

I hugged the pillow to my chest, unable to fathom how someone could do that to another human being. I didn't know anyone like that and I didn't want to.

Gavin stayed a little while longer, and then he said something about getting home, talking everything over with his parents.

"Are you staying here by yourself?" he asked at the door. "Your mom is out of town, right?"

I was trying not to think about that. "I might go to Dad's."

"I think that would be a good idea." He drew in a deep breath. "Or if you want, I could stay with you."

"Thanks, but I'll probably head over to his house." I forced a smile. "But seriously, thanks for the offer."

"Yeah." His gaze searched mine and then he looked away. "I'll see you tomorrow."

"Bye."

I closed the door behind him, locking it and the deadbolt. Turning around, I leaned against it, my shoulders sagging. I believed Gavin, but was still shocked that he'd kept his relationship with Vee secret. Apparently, I didn't know him as well as I thought I had. And Vee? She'd been kept alive as I suspected—stabbed and most likely tortured.

I headed into the kitchen to grab a pizza out of the freezer. As it baked in the oven, I fielded a concerned call from Dad and then Linds, using the latter as the reason for why I wasn't staying at his house.

Mom would freak, and I was probably going to get next to no sleep. I was safe here, but just in case, I planned on sleeping with a baseball bat next to me. But as soon as the sun went down, I began to really rethink this whole staying by myself thing. Every noise in and outside of the house stretched my nerves to the point that when my phone chirped with a text from Jensen close to nine that night, I almost jumped out of my skin.

What r u doing?

A flutter started in my chest. This was a first. We'd exchanged numbers, but he hadn't texted me before. I sent back a quick: *Nothing.*

Did u go to your Dads?

I sighed, preparing myself for a text lecture. *No.*

There was a beat. *Want company?*

Holding my cell in my hand, I shook my head like an idiot. Being that it was close to nine, it was kind of too late to hang out. If Mom was home, she would've gotten all frowny faced about it, but like Gavin had offered earlier, it wasn't so much hanging out as it was peace of mind.

The flutter got crazy in my chest like a nest of bees were trying to find their way out. I'd turned down Gavin, and even with the Vee situation, he would've been the smarter bet.

Jensen was anything but the safer option.

My fingers trembled as I typed back the one word I shouldn't have.

Yes.

I SHOULD'VE CHANGED into something else before Jensen knocked on my front door. The sleep shorts barely covered my butt, and I wore nothing under the tank top and cardigan. Hell, the cardigan was longer than my shorts, but I'd spent those precious minutes freaking out and holding my phone to my chest, telling myself to text him back and say no.

But it was too late.

As I hurried to the front door, I admitted to myself that I hadn't wanted to tell him not to come over. And if I was being really honest, I wanted Jensen here.

God, I *really* wanted him here.

Feeling my cheeks heat, I opened the door and stepped aside. He strolled in, a grocery bag dangling from his fingers and a WVU baseball cap on backward.

He was dressed for bed, too, and I couldn't help but smile knowing he'd walked the three blocks to my house wearing plaid cotton pajama bottoms, an old Beastie Boys shirt, and Nike flip-flops.

Somehow he even managed to make that look sexy.

Jensen raised the bag as I looked up. "I brought something you're going to love."

My heart jumped stupidly, and I ignored it, fiddling with the sleeves of my cardigan. "Really?"

Smiling slightly, he nodded as he backed toward the stairs. "Yep."

"Can I see?"

"Nope." He winked when I frowned. "We're going upstairs, right?"

My gaze darted behind him. I hadn't really thought about that. It would be smart to just chill downstairs, but since I was doing a lot of stupid, why would I do something smart now?

"Sure." I headed around him, but somehow he ended up in front of me.

I was in awe as he walked down the hall, heading straight for my bedroom. I don't know why, but I expected him to have forgotten his way.

He hadn't.

Jensen swaggered right into my room like he had the hundred times before when we were younger, except then, he didn't make the room feel so small with his six-foot two-inch frame.

Looking around the room, he appeared to soak in the changes, and then smiled when he turned his startling blue gaze to my bed.

A sweet flush traveled down my throat.

"You still have it."

The hots for him? Because I did, really badly, and as I stared at him, I wondered if it was that obvious. I wondered if he knew I was thinking about the things I'd done and hadn't done with Gavin when we were together. Things I would jump into head first with Jensen.

"The Care Bear," he added. "God, you've had that thing for how long?"

I bit down on my lip. "I got it for my seventh birthday. So ten years."

"Ten years . . ." He shook his head as he wheeled around, spying the TV on its stand. "Perfect."

Curious as to what he was doing, I walked over to the bed and sat on the edge, tucking my legs against my chest in an attempt to not completely freak out on him.

He pulled a slender case from his bag, holding it between two long fingers. "Supernatural, season one," he announced.

My lips broke into a wide smile and I clapped. "Nice."

"Thought you'd approve." He quickly popped the DVD in and grabbed the remote. He joined me on the bed, his grin sending the bees in my chest into flight once more. "Now here comes the best part," he said as the title splashed over the screen.

Jensen pulled out two bottles of orange soda, a bag of dill potato chips, and a smaller bag of combos—the baked cheese kind.

My eyes widened as I stared at the items. I couldn't believe it. I raised my gaze, feeling a knot form in the back of my throat.

His half smile spread. "What?"

"You remembered," I whispered.

Handing over a soda, he shrugged. "Yeah."

"These are my favorite things—like my absolute favorite junk food." Not even Gavin remembered my love of orange soda and dill-flavored potato chips.

"I know." His lashes lifted.

The knot started to burn. "Thank you. I mean it. Thank you for . . . for all of this."

His eyes held mine for a moment, and then he picked up the combos. "Let's not let the epic late-night junk food fest go to waste."

I wanted to pounce on him, throw my arms around his neck, and hold on tight, like a barnacle.

But that would probably be awkward.

So I indulged in the fatty goodness as we watched the first two episodes of Supernatural. By the time it was past eleven, I expected him to bolt, but he didn't, and I didn't want to point the time out to him. I wasn't ready for him to leave. When I got up to use the bathroom, I nearly stumbled when I returned.

Oh sweet baby Jesus . . .

Jensen had changed positions, making himself all kinds of at home. The baseball cap was gone. Where? I had no idea. And I didn't care. Stretched out with his arms folded behind his head, he had his lower body tucked under the covers—*my* covers.

He cast me a sidelong glance. "Wanted to get comfortable."

And he had.

He also looked like he belonged there.

That half grin was back, and this time it held a wicked, mysterious edge to it. "Get comfortable with me?"

The invitation sounded so harmless and yet it did such strange things to my insides. As I inched forward, I told myself this wasn't a big deal. We'd shared a bed many times.

But that was back before I'd grown boobs.

Keeping my eyes glued to the hotness that was the Winchester brothers, I climbed onto my bed, shoving my legs under the covers. I didn't lie down. I was sort of frozen.

"Is Dean still your favorite?" he asked.

I nodded.

"You just like him because he's a smartass."

I nodded again.

A hand landed on my back, causing me to jump. "Whoa," Jensen murmured. "Relax."

"I am relaxed." I glanced over my shoulder at him, and he raised a brow. "I *am*."

He pulled his hand back, watching me closely. "Do you want me to leave? If so, I'm cool with that. Just tell me when and I'll—"

"No," I said quickly, and then I flushed, because I said it a little too quickly and loudly . . . and excitedly.

He chuckled. "Okay."

Turning back to the TV, I strung together an artwork of f-bombs. It wasn't like he was here for sex or anything like that, so I needed to chill out. Reaching up, I quickly unhooked the two buttons on my cardigan and slid it off my arms. I tossed it onto the floor and then lay back, tugging the blankets up, stopping short of folding them under my chin.

Neither of us spoke for a couple of minutes. We watched Sam and Dean narrowly escape a spirit who was drowning people in a lake, in bathtubs . . . and sinks.

Then Jensen flipped on his side, facing me. Ten seconds went by before I caved to the urge to look at him. I sucked in a soft breath. Lying like this, we were so close.

His hand rested in the miniscule space between us. "You haven't been getting a lot of sleep."

I focused on the neckline of his shirt. "Everyone keeps saying that to me. Do I look that bad?"

"No. You don't look bad. You just look tired."

A wry smile pulled at my lips as I placed my hands on my stomach. "That's a nice way of saying I look bad."

"Whatever."

I bit down on my lip. "I haven't been sleeping. With everything going on, it's hard to relax and I keep having nightmares. I know that sounds lame, but I haven't gotten more than a couple of hours of sleep a night, if that."

"It's not lame. It's understandable."

Lifting my chin, my gaze met with his. Okay. This was nothing like sharing beds when we were kids. There was something wholly intimate about him lying beside me, the citrus scent of his cologne, plus that—that *male* scent clung to the covers and every breath I took.

"Are you staying?" I asked.

"I'll stay as long as you want me here."

Something akin to pressure circled my chest, but it wasn't painful. It was pleasant and warm, and the sensation buzzed through my veins. "Won't you get in trouble?"

He laughed and a lopsided smile transformed his face. "Mom knows where I am. She's cool with me being here. She knows what's going on."

I arched a brow.

That grin turned downright naughty. "But she doesn't know I'm sleeping in your bed."

My cheeks heated as I choked on my laugh. "Yeah, I doubt she'd be happy with that."

Jensen laughed again as he reached over with his hand. His thick lashes lowered as he picked up my hand, wiggling his fingers through mine. That was the only part of us that touched, but I felt it in every fiber of my being.

"You're missing the start of the next episode," he murmured.

I'd been staring at him for Lord knows how long. Obediently, I cast my attention to the TV, and a smile formed on my lips. It wasn't long before my gaze wandered from the TV, falling to where Jensen's hand was wrapped tightly around mine.

THIRTEEN

I WASN'T SURE when I fell asleep or what woke me up, but I was wrapped in a toasty cocoon. I also couldn't move my legs, and something heavy and warm held me in place. Blinking my eyes open, my vision was slow to adjust to the darkness of my bedroom.

That was the first indication that something was up.

It had been over a week since I'd fallen asleep without the TV on. Then my snug cocoon shifted behind me, and a warm breath danced along the back of my neck.

My eyes peeled open.

Oh my God, my toasty snug cocoon wasn't a bunch of blankets.

Jensen was curled up behind me with one arm folded around my waist. One of his legs was tossed over mine, and I was tucked against his front. Not daring to move, I could feel his heart beating steadily against my back.

And that wasn't all. His hand rested against the curve of my belly, *under* my tank top. The flesh against flesh seared my skin and had my toes curling under the blanket. I closed my eyes, dragging in a shallow breath as sweet heat rolled over me. There wasn't a single part of me that wasn't aware of Jensen. How he held me in his sleep. How his leg was tangled in-between mine, pressing against the softest part of me.

My heart rate kicked up.

There was a fire in my blood, and I'd never felt like this with Gavin or any other boy. This was the spark I'd been missing, the feeling of not getting enough air, of my heart racing just because our bodies were tangled together. It reminded me of the rush that accompanied running.

Lying still was the most sublime torture.

But in those following moments, when my imagination ran wild and I pictured rolling over and kissing and touching and doing so, so much more, I realized something else.

Jensen was also very still.

His chest barely moved against my back, but his heart was beating faster, and his hand . . . his thumb moved in idle, slow circles just below my navel. Then he moved his leg just a fraction of an inch upward, and I sucked in a breath like it was my last.

Holy hot tamale . . .

"You're not asleep." Jensen's voice was deep and thick.

A tight shiver coursed up my spine. "No."

He didn't respond for a moment. I expected him to put some space between us, but he didn't. And I almost wished he would, because now that my senses were hyper-aware, I could feel *everything*. My heart started pounding even faster as a sharp burst of heat shot through the very center of me.

His chest rose against my back. A heartbeat passed between us and then he shifted.

Suddenly, I was on my back, staring up at Jensen, barely able to make out his features in the darkness of my room. His hand drifted away from my stomach and up my side in a slow slide that pushed all the air out of my lungs in one shaky rush. His hand landed on the pillow next to my head. His arms caged me in, and he lowered his body, stopping when our chests barely touched.

Our gazes locked. Something potent, tangible and infinite passed between us. The muscles in his arms flexed as his upper body came down a notch. He was all around me.

"It's too early to be up," he said, his head tilting to the side, lining up our mouths.

I had no idea what time it was and I didn't care. Nothing outside of this little space we'd created mattered at the moment.

"I was hoping that staying over with you would help you sleep better."

"I was sleeping perfectly." Slowly, I lifted my hands. My fingers trembled as I placed them against him. His stomach was hot and hard under the thin shirt he wore.

He jerked, and I started to pull my hands back. "Don't," he said as he came down on his elbow. With one hand, he reached down between us, placing his hand over one of my mine. The back of his knuckles grazed where my shirt had ridden up.

"Don't?" Don't could mean a lot of things.

There was a pause. "Don't stop."

Oh.

When he removed his hand from mine, I didn't pull my hands away. I don't know what made me do what I did next. Maybe it was the early morning hours and the darkness of the room that made everything seem surreal. Or maybe it was because underneath it all, I *was* comfortable with Jensen.

And maybe I simply wanted him.

I'd wanted him for so long.

I slid my hands down to where the shirt gaped away from his body, slipping my hands underneath it. His skin was scorching, almost like he was suffering from a fever, and he seemed to shudder when my fingers brushed over the taut lines of his lower stomach.

A deep sound rumbled from his chest, like a growl, and something deep inside me answered. I tipped my head back. Our noses touched and then our lips brushed together in an almost kiss. So many emotions rose and scrambled together—awe, hope, lust, and something deeper—something that had always been there.

"Ella." He breathed my name like it was a cross between a prayer and a curse. Resting his weight on one arm, he cupped my cheek with his other hand. He smoothed his thumb along my lower lip. "I never stopped thinking about you—about us. Not one day."

My heart rate sped up. "Not one day?"

"No." He pressed his lips to my forehead and then the tip of my nose. "And I know I *won't* stop thinking about us." A sweet, brief feel of his lips against the corner of my mouth as his lower body dropped wrung a gasp from me.

"Jensen," I whispered as my body seemed to take on a mind of its own, reacting without thought. My legs inched further apart, letting him in.

I sucked in a sharp breath. The thin material of our bottoms was not much of a barrier, and I felt like I was on fire. My skin was burning and my insides were melting.

His forehead dropped against mine, and for a long moment he held completely still above me. Then he moved, dragging his hand from my cheek down my skin to my waist as his hips rolled.

I dug my nails into his hips and tried to silence the soft sound rushing out of me, but I couldn't. He shuddered in response, and my body—my hips—responded. Curling one leg around his, I rocked against him, and then he was moving and I was moving. My head kicked back. His face dropped to my throat. I wasn't thinking about anything, only feeling the heightening tension curling deep inside me. I knew what was coming. I felt it before, but never this intensely. Not with my hands digging into his bare skin. Not with his hands sliding up my front, dragging my shirt higher and higher.

Jensen shifted slightly. His thigh was pressing hard against a very sensitive spot, and now we were moving more urgently. Our clothes were still on, but this was going to happen. I was chasing the tightening inside me until the tension built, reaching unbearable limits. Then it exploded. Wrapping my arms around him, I cried out as my body jerked and twisted against his.

I was still shaking, trembling when Jensen groaned, his cheek pressed against mine. "Ella, I'm going to have to get up, because I'm about—"

"Don't." I held him tighter and turned my head slightly, pressing a kiss to his cheek. "It's okay," I whispered in a voice I didn't recognize, and he seemed to know what I was saying, because he moved until he was stiffening and shuddering, my name a harsh gasp in my ear.

And then we were both finally still, our breaths panting and hearts fighting to slow down in the faint moonlight streaming through the window. I closed my eyes, still feeling like I was floating somewhere near the ceiling. None of this felt real.

Jensen lifted his head. I could feel his lips hovering over mine. We hadn't even kissed, not really, and . . ."I didn't plan on that happening, but—"

A loud thud against my bedroom window sent an unwelcomed jolt of surprise through me. My arms slipped off of him as I turned to the sound.

Jensen was off me and on his feet so fast that I wondered if he had wings or was some kind of superhuman. Sitting up, I realized my shirt was shoved up to my neck. I hastily pulled it down as my entire body turned beet red. "What was that?"

"I don't know." He prowled around the bed, making an unerring path straight to the window.

I rose to my knees, my heart beating for a different reason. "Jensen! What are you doing?"

"Checking out what caused that noise." He glanced over his shoulder at me, his features lost in the shadows of my room. "Stay there."

The heady warmth all but evaporated as he pushed the curtains wide. Icy fear built in my stomach, but I scooted to the edge of the bed as he peered out the window.

"What in the hell?" he muttered, immediately reaching down to slide the window up.

Unable to sit still, I climbed off the bed and crept toward him. Cool night air washed over my legs. I wrapped my arms around my waist. "What is it?"

Jensen didn't answer immediately, almost like he hadn't heard me. I reached out, touching his shoulder, and his eyes swung to mine. "I think you should go back to the bed, Ella."

I held his gaze for a moment, trepidation turning my insides into knots. "What is it?" I asked again.

Under the silvery light of the moon, Jensen's features were stark as he reached out, wrapping an arm around my shoulders. He pulled me against his side. "It could be a . . . a coincidence," he said, but there wasn't an ounce of conviction in his voice.

Craning my neck until I could see whatever it was, my breath started to come in short gasps. My gaze fell to the still form lying on the roof, mere inches from the now open window.

It was a bird.

I pressed my hand against my mouth as I stepped back. Even in the faint light I could tell what kind of bird it was.

It was a cardinal.

NEITHER OF US slept after that.

Jensen carefully disposed of the poor bird as the sun began to rise. He stayed in my house as I quickly showered and got ready for school, and I knew that couldn't have been comfortable for him because of, well, what happened before the whole dead bird thing. Just like I knew the walk to his house couldn't have been all that enjoyable.

"I'm not leaving you alone," he'd said.

I hadn't argued.

His parents had already left for work when we crossed the

driveway to his house. Like mine, it was an old two-story brick home renovated back when we were knee high to a grasshopper. Bright flowers in a cluster of reds, blues, and whites overflowed the flower boxes attached to the porch railing. Rose bushes climbed the ends of the porch, scenting the air.

I lingered on the wide front porch for a moment, struck by how many years had passed since I'd walked through these doors.

"You okay?" he asked, holding the door open.

"Yeah." I forced myself forward, caught between the past when we were two kids running in and out of this very front door, and the present us—the us that had been in bed together a mere hour or so ago, doing things we hadn't even discussed.

Drawing in a deep breath, I followed him inside. My first impression was that very little had changed since the last time I was here. His house still smelled of apples and cinnamon. Woven baskets were everywhere, some empty, others holding flower arrangements or odds and ends. His mom was into country—everything wooden and old looking.

"I'm going to take a quick shower." Jensen stopped at the stairs. "Make yourself at home."

"Okay." I placed my bag near the front door and glanced up. Our gazes connected, and I looked away, unsure of what was going on between us.

Jensen got halfway up the stairs and then stopped. Pivoting around, he walked to where I stood and clasped my cheeks with warm, steady hands. My breath caught as he tilted my head back, pressing a quick kiss to my forehead.

"I'll be right back," he said.

And he left me standing there like I'd forgotten how to breathe or walk. Raising my hand, I touched the center of my forehead as my heart kicked around in my chest.

What were we doing?

What had we done in that bed?

We hadn't had actual sex, but that was the closest two people could come to doing it with their clothes on. I had no idea what was happening, but this morning we'd crossed the line of friendship. I didn't regret it—quite the opposite, but . . . but outside of that dark room and bed there was a past.

Sighing, I moved further into the house, and it was like taking a walk through memories. Everything seemed the same as it had before they'd moved. A few things were in different places, but it was basically the same. I could easily remember racing through the rec room, plopping down on the beanbags that used to be in front of the TV, and grabbing a game controller.

I always kicked Jensen's ass at Mario Kart.

The dining room was only used for special occasions—birthdays and holidays. I walked down the short hallway that led to the kitchen, where I'd spent many evenings scarfing down pizza and sloppy joes.

Framed pictures lined the hall, most of them of Jensen's older brother Jonathan. I stopped, my gaze traveling over the photos of the good-looking older boy in high school pictures and random family photos.

God, Jensen looked so much like him, down to the strong jaw and full, expressive lips.

I glanced over the rest of the photos, one in particular catching my attention. An ache pierced my chest as my gaze traveled over the picture. It was Christmas, taken several years ago, when we'd just started middle school.

Gavin with his glasses, vaguely resembling Harry Potter, grinned at the camera. Jensen, taller than the rest of us, had his long arms wrapped around my shoulders. I wasn't looking at the camera. Nope. I'd been staring up at Jensen. And beside me was Penn. He had a wreath around his neck, his head poking out of the holly berries and twigs.

"Remember that Christmas? Gavin and Penn had a cranberry sauce eating contest. Both of them ended up eating so much that when they started hurling it back up, we thought they were dying."

Swallowing the knot in my throat, I turned at the sound of Jensen's voice. My lips parted. He stood there, tugging the sleeves out of a shirt, jeans hung low on his hips, revealing those fascinating indents and that amazing stomach of his. His hair was still wet, and curls clung to his forehead.

I looked away quickly, feeling my cheeks burn, which was ridiculous considering what we had shared. "That was fast."

"I'm quick like that." Grinning, he sauntered past me. "Want something to eat? I think we have Frosted Flakes. You still eat them?"

"Yeah." I followed him into the roomy kitchen that was different from when we were kids. It had been completely renovated, country style, with white cabinets and dark floors. I hopped up onto a barstool at the island.

He pulled the shirt on over his head and then set about making breakfast. Within minutes, a bowl of sugary flakes were set in front of me. "I think we need to let the police know about the bird."

"So you don't think it was a coincidence?" That was a stupid question, but I guess I was holding out hope that it was. Because if it wasn't a coincidence, there was a high likelihood that someone had been out on the tree, staring into my bedroom, watching us. There was enough moonlight to see what was happening.

I felt sick.

He propped his hip against the island, cradling his bowl of cereal. "I don't know, but why take any chances?"

"Agreed," I murmured, watching the flakes float in the milk. "I'll call Trooper Ritter on the way to school. He left me his number." Glancing up, I wasn't surprised to see he'd already finished off his cereal. "I just don't understand why someone would do this."

Or maybe I didn't *want* to understand why.

Jensen was quiet as he washed out his bowl and placed it in the dishwasher. "Do people ever have a reason for doing things like this?"

Words flew to the tip of my tongue, and I wanted to swallow

them back, but I couldn't. "I don't think this is something random. Like our town suddenly drew the interest of a serial killer," I said, watching the muscles tense under the back of his shirt. "And I know you don't think that either."

"I don't." He turned around, leaning back against the counter. "I just don't want to scare you."

"I'm already scared," I admitted in a whisper.

His striking face tightened. "I know. And I hate that."

"But that doesn't change anything. All of this is related. I know it is."

He shook his head as his jaw worked. "But what? You weren't friends with Vee and Monica. Other than living in the same town and going to the same school, you don't have anything in common."

I thought about the list of names I'd thrown together in my head, and as I stared at him, a sick feeling settled in the pit of my stomach. "But we do."

Jensen frowned. "How?"

It took a lot to say the name. "Penn."

He stared at me, his eyes widening slightly. "What?"

A chill took hold. "Penn loved cardinals. Even you pointed that out. Vee and Monica used to pick on Penn, remember? In middle school, they terrorized him. So did Wendy. And Brock and Mason—"

"Ella." Jensen pushed off the counter, thrusting a hand through his damp hair.

"And that day?" I continued, ignoring his warning. "We were just as bad as them. You know we were. You and I—"

"Stop." Jensen crossed the room, gripping my shoulders. A muscle ticked along his jaw. "I don't know what's happening, but it has nothing to do with the past, and Penn is *in* the past. This has nothing to do with him. It *can't*, Ella."

I met his pale stare. "Explain the cardinals then. Why them?"

"Who knows? But it can't be about him." His hands slipped over my shoulders as he took a step back. "Penn is dead, Ella."

I shot to my feet, suddenly wishing I hadn't said anything. I wheeled around, heading for the foyer. "We should leave."

"No." Jensen caught up to me, blocking the door to the hall. "I know you've let guilt eat up your life the last four years. I know that's why you started seeing the therapist."

My stomach dropped. How had he known about Dr. Oliver? He'd still lived here and we'd still talked at that point, but I hadn't told him. Gavin only found out once we started dating in high school.

"And now this guilt has warped into something else. How could it be about Penn? He's been dead for four years."

"I know how long he's been dead," I snapped, anger rushing to the surface.

His pale eyes flashed a deeper blue. "Then how in the world can this be about him?"

"I don't know!" I shouted, dragging in a deep breath. "Maybe someone is paying us back for what they did—for what *we* did!"

Jensen drew back as if I'd slapped him. He stared at me. "We didn't do anything."

A harsh, short laugh escaped me. "How can you say that? Because we did, Jensen. Gavin told us not to, that Penn wouldn't be okay with it, but we didn't listen."

"Oh my God . . ." He shook his head as he stared down at me. Varying degrees of horror and disbelief flickered across his face. "You think . . . ?"

He didn't have to finish that sentence, because I knew where it was heading, and so did he. I didn't look away as I struggled with my next breath.

Jensen snapped forward, clutching my cheeks once again. His wide gaze searched mine as he held me in place. "We didn't kill Penn, Ella."

I sucked in a breath. "We didn't?"

FOURTEEN

MENTIONING PENN WAS a conversation killer.

Jensen was stoic as he drove me to school, and we ended up having to park in the back of the lot. Rays of sun were just starting to break through the thick, gray clouds, lifting some of the chill in the air.

I walked ahead of Jensen, angry with him and with myself. I knew it sounded crazy, that anything happening today would have something to do with Penn, but Jensen hadn't needed to look at me with such pity either.

I shouldn't have said anything. And I shouldn't have let him stay last night, sleep in my bed, and everything that had happened in that bed.

Jensen caught up to me when I reached the door. Catching my arm, he tugged me out of the path of others. Several students stared in our direction with curious looks.

"What?" I asked, trying to pull my arm free.

His eyes narrowed. "I'm just letting you know that there are a lot of things we still need to talk about."

"I don't want to talk about Penn—"

"Not him. Not any of that." His hand slid up to my elbow as he dipped his head to mine. "I'm talking about us."

"Us?" I squeaked.

"Yeah, we need to talk about what happened between us this morning," he said. "Don't think there is a chance in hell I've forgotten about that."

Annoyed by the turn in conversation and, unfortunately, turned on by him, I dug deep, latching on to the irritation brimming in my veins. "Well, I have."

"Oh." Jensen laughed. "That's doubtful."

I gritted my teeth until my jaw ached. "There's nothing to talk about."

"There's a lot to talk about," he corrected, and then he smiled. "And we will talk."

"We won't be—"

Jensen hauled me against his chest and lowered his head until his lips weren't even an inch from mine. He was so close I could feel the warmth of his breath and almost taste his kiss. My eyes drifted shut as a riot of sensation rocketed through me.

When he spoke, his lips brushed mine. "Exactly."

My eyes popped open.

Jensen let go and winked. He caught the edge of the door, holding it open. "You better get inside or you're going to be late."

For a moment, all I could do was stare at him, and then I bounced out of it. "Jerk," I said, storming past him.

He laughed, and while that sound was all kinds of lovely, I wanted to drop kick him in the back of the head. Instead, I shot him a dark look before swinging around a cluster of people near the entrance to the gymnasium. As close as I was, I could hear bits and pieces of their conversation.

"It had to be him," a girl said. "He was dating her and no one knew?"

My spine stiffened.

A junior boy shrugged brawny shoulders. "Yeah, but come on.

Gavin? I don't think so."

"Whatever. If you're hiding a relationship, there's a reason," another girl argued. "Maybe she was pregnant and he killed her."

Oh my God.

"But what about Monica? Or . . . or *her*."

I pivoted around, pinning each of them with a look. "Gavin doesn't have anything to do with what's been happening."

Not giving them a chance to respond, I turned on my heel and picked up my pace. By the time I got to first period, I was ready to karate chop anyone who looked at me a second longer than I felt was necessary. The whole school had heard about Gavin's closet relationship with Vee.

God, that didn't look good.

None of this did.

I slumped in my seat as my thoughts unraveled, wandering back to the morning conversation with Jensen.

We didn't kill Penn.

He was right in the sense that we hadn't physically done something to Penn, but that didn't mean we were void of responsibility when it came to what had happened to him. We should've known better, but we had been selfish and so, so disloyal.

It happened in the fall before seventh grade, just when Jensen had started growing into his long arms and legs, and just when I started to really notice how he smiled, and how his eyes seemed to change color depending on his mood.

And I hadn't been the only one to notice.

Girls like Wendy and Monica started coming around our lunch table and hanging around our little group when we headed outside. Gavin, Penn, and I knew they were there for Jensen, even though he seemed to be oblivious to it.

I wasn't.

Maybe it was during those long afternoon breaks when I knew deep down that I would lose Jensen to the cooler and prettier girls.

Maybe that was why it had been so easy for me to forget about someone who'd been a friend to me since I could remember.

But it had happened the fall after we'd played truth or dare in the tree house, when Jensen had kissed me and Penn had asked if we'd be friends forever.

It was two weeks before Halloween, and for the last week or so, Penn had been *happy*. His birthday was coming up and his parents were planning on combining Halloween with the event, and in spite of how the kids were treating him at school, he was excited.

Then Brock decided to have a party at his house the same day as Penn's, and Jensen was invited. Looking back, I wondered if Brock had done it on purpose. It seemed childish, but from how others had treated Penn, to what Jensen and I had decided, I'd realized quickly that no matter how young people were, they were truly capable of anything.

Jensen had wanted to go to Brock's party. After all, his brother and Brock's were friends. But he hadn't wanted to go alone, so he invited me. And I hadn't wanted to let Jensen go to the party without me, not when Wendy and Monica would be there.

I don't know why it was so important that we go to Brock's party, other than us being stupid and young. But Jensen and I had planned on doing both—going to Brock's and then Penn's. When Gavin found out, he'd told us not to do it, that if Penn found out, he would be hurt, but we didn't listen.

So on the day of Penn's birthday party, Jensen and I went to Brock's, fully intending to leave early, but that wasn't what happened. Even though Jensen had stayed by my side the whole time, paying no attention to the other girls, we didn't leave early. I couldn't even remember why. We'd just lost track of time.

We'd missed Penn's party.

And the next day during lunch, Penn had found out where we'd been when Brock oh so casually mentioned it as he passed our table. To this day, I'll never forget how pale Penn got or how he kept saying it was okay when Jensen and I repeatedly apologized.

Penn had seemed fine, though. About two weeks passed and I'd all but forgotten about it, and then after school, I did what I always did. I slipped on my sneakers and went running. I was planning on meeting the boys at the tree house, so that's where I'd headed, but I was early. We were supposed to meet at 4:30 p.m., and it was 4:14 when I checked my watch as the tree house came into view.

I remembered slowing down and shaking the burn out of my legs, time seeming to crawl as I dragged in deep gulps of the crisp autumn air. I'd started to climb the steps when something on the ground on the other side of the tree caught my attention, and I remember letting go of the wooden planks, of walking around the trunk.

I'd found Penn lying on the ground.

He'd been lying face up, his body sprawled out, one leg under the other. His neck hadn't looked right. I'd never seen a dead person before that, but I knew he was dead. I knew that immediately.

There had been a belt around his neck.

A snapped rope on the ground.

The authorities said that he'd fashioned a noose out of a rope and belt, then hung himself from the tree. They said his weight had snapped the rope, but I couldn't believe it. I couldn't picture Penn going up in the tree house alone or climbing out onto the limb. I couldn't picture or understand why he would've done it that way, with a belt and a rope. That wasn't like Penn.

That wasn't him.

But then, like a nightmare unfolding, his parents found Penn's suicide note in his bedroom two days after he'd died. Supposedly only one sentence had been written.

I can't take it anymore.

An entire life summed up and ended in one sentence.

A lot of people had talked afterward. Why hadn't anyone known Penn had been bullied so badly? Why hadn't anyone seen the signs of depression? How could it have gotten to this point without anyone noticing?

None of those questions really mattered then, because I knew what had done it to him, what had pushed him over the edge.

We hadn't killed Penn with our own hands, but we had aided and abetted. We'd known that he'd been having problems—his parents fighting a lot, the kids at school picking on him. We'd been the proverbial straw that broke the camel's back, and there wasn't a day that had gone by that I hadn't wished we'd made a better decision.

That we'd chosen Penn.

JENSEN JOINED HEIDI and I at lunch, and by then my pissy attitude had faded into weariness. All morning everyone talked about Gavin. About Vee. And about Monica. In the eyes of our classmates, Gavin was a serial killer.

"I wish there was something we could do," I said, staring down at my lasagna.

"About?" Jensen asked, and I realized that I'd assumed everyone knew what I was thinking.

"About Gavin." I put my fork down, sighing. "Everyone is talking about him."

"They are." Heidi frowned. "And no one really talks to me, so if I've heard about it, that really does mean everyone is talking about it."

Well, that was reassuring.

I dared a quick look at Jensen. Chin tilted down, he was pulling his lasagna apart layer by layer, as if he were searching for something hidden in it. "We need to prove that Gavin didn't do anything."

Jensen looked up, his eyebrows raised. "And how would we do that?"

"That's a good question," Heidi added, twisting the long strands of red hair into a braid.

"I haven't gotten that far in my thought process," I grumbled.

"Well, considering that you're not Nancy Drew, and I'm not one of the Hardy Boys, I'm not sure exactly what we can do." One side of his mouth quirked up when I glared at him. "Look, I'm not being a smartass."

"You're not?"

"Okay, maybe a little, but let's look at this seriously. What can we really do? The cops are investigating it, and it's not like we can launch our own investigation. None of us know what to look for."

"Another good point," Heidi chimed in, and I was beginning to wonder if she was going to be of any help at all. "You can't go and check out the farmhouse. That's a crime scene, and the police would've pulled anything that could be considered evidence."

"And we can't get to that evidence." He poked at his lasagna. "Unless you know how to break into a police station, which if you did, that would be kind of hot."

I rolled my eyes.

"This is real life." Jensen's gaze found mine. "Not a book or a TV show where teenagers suddenly turn into seasoned investigators. We're not private detectives, and the last thing I want you to do is put yourself in danger."

There was very little I could say to that. Jensen and Heidi were right. None of us would even know where to start. Hell, I'd forgotten to call Trooper Ritter about the damn bird this morning, so I already made a lousy detective.

Heidi reached across the table, squeezing my hand. "The police will find something that proves Gavin had nothing to do with what happened to Vee. They probably already have, and when they find the person behind this, Gavin won't have anything to worry about."

"Okay." I forced a smile I didn't feel. "You're right."

Her green eyes lit up. "I know."

"Want my peaches?" Jensen slid his tray toward mine.

My gaze flicked from him to the fruit.

"You know you want it," he coaxed.

Heidi giggled. "That sounds remarkably dirty."

"Doesn't it?" He tossed her a careless grin, the kind that left a trail of girls in its midst. "Deliciously dirty."

Biting down on my lip, I tried to stop the smile from forming, because it felt wrong after our conversation. I picked up my fork, though, and scooped up the peaches. "Thank you."

"Uh-huh."

I took a bite of the sugary goodness and a bit of its juice trickled out, escaping the corner of my lips. I reached for my napkin, but I never made it.

"I'll get it." Before I could react, Jensen dipped his head, angling it so it looked like he was kissing me, and I thought that was what he was about to do.

I tensed up. Our first *real* kiss was about to go down in the school cafeteria.

Except he didn't kiss me, not really. Instead, the quick flick of his tongue caught the juice on my lower lip.

Holy peaches.

I gasped as heat zinged from my lips through my body.

Jensen pulled back, his eyes a crystal blue behind a thick fringe of lashes. "Mmm. Tasty."

"Oh dear," whispered Heidi, her hand pressed against her chest. "I think I just got pregnant watching that, and I don't even think I like boys."

My cheeks burst with heat. I was torn between climbing under the table, yelling at Jensen, and grabbing him and fusing our mouths together when a shadow appeared. In sort of a daze with my lip tingling, I glanced up.

Brock stood there, staring down at Jensen. "Yo, you got a second?"

He leaned back, cocking his head to the side. "No. Not really."

Surprise splashed across Brock's face and then he glanced at me. The hollows of his cheeks started to turn red. "You serious?"

"Do I look like I'm joking?"

Whoa. My eyes widened. What was up with the attitude?

Brock's expression darkened as his gaze settled on us, sending a chill right down my spine. "Whatever, man. Catch you later."

"Wow." Heidi's eyes were wide, watching Brock stiffly retreat back to his table. "He was not happy with you."

Jensen shrugged his shoulder. "I'm not worried about him."

The thing was, when I thought about the farmhouse and how Brock had disappeared, I kind of was.

IT WAS IN art class when I remembered I had an appointment with Dr. Oliver after school. Jensen offered to take me, and while I argued that I could take myself, he didn't relent until I begrudgingly allowed him to drive me there.

And wait for me.

He did promise me a smoothie afterward, which made agreeing not the hardest thing to do, because who couldn't use a smoothie?

Dr. Oliver's office was on Foxcroft Avenue, on the third floor of a brick building, and as I stepped off the elevator, I realized that a faint antiseptic scent clung to every breath I took.

My sandaled feet were quiet against the worn brown carpet as I made my way down the narrow hall that was all too familiar. The glass in the door up ahead was blurred out. Dr. Oliver took privacy very seriously.

I knew not to knock. There was no receptionist in the evening. I passed the potted palm trees and stopped at the second door that was cracked open. "Hello?"

"Ella?" Dr. Oliver called. "Go ahead and come in."

Taking a deep breath, I pushed open the door. The good doctor stood with his back to me, shaking a small can over his large aquarium. The guy was obsessed with his fish. I took a seat in front of his desk without being told.

"How are you doing today?" he asked politely.

Knowing he was going to do his shrink thing no matter which way I answered, I decided to go with honesty. "Tired."

"I imagine so. Your mother said you haven't been sleeping well?" He screwed the lid onto the bottle and set it aside. Turning toward me, he pulled off his wire frame glasses and smiled. He looked the same way as I remembered—dark trimmed beard, brown eyes, thinning hair.

I nodded. "I haven't been sleeping well."

"Because of the attack and subsequent situations, I imagine." He dropped into his chair, slipping his glasses back on. "You know the drill, Ella."

Swallowing a sigh, I slumped in the chair. Of course I knew the drill. Talk about my feelings. Talk about my fears. Blah, blah. I wanted to get this over and done with. There was a strawberry smoothie at the end of this dark cloud. So I told him how I felt—how I was scared. I admitted that I was having nightmares, that every little sound had me jumping out of my skin.

Dr. Oliver listened quietly, like he always did, fingers steepled under his chin. When I finished, he totally jumped right into the unexpected. "So you've been hanging out with Jensen Carver again."

My brows climbed up my forehead. Exactly how he went from my fear of being murdered to who I was hanging out with was beyond me. "How did you know?"

He smiled as he tapped a finger off his temple. "I'm psychic."

I stared at him.

Dr. Oliver sighed. "The window faces the front parking lot." He gestured behind him. "I saw you get out of his truck."

"Oh."

"Anyway." He drew the word out, and I cracked a grin. "When did you guys start talking? After the night of the attack?" When I nodded, his fingers went back to his chin. "And how is your relationship?"

I could feel the heat creeping across my cheeks. "It's okay."

"Uh-huh." There was a pause. "Becoming close with Jensen again, has that been stirring up anything?"

My lips pursed.

His eyebrow rose.

I sighed again. "A little bit, I guess. I mean, it's kind of hard not to think of . . . of him, but we don't talk about him."

"Maybe you two should."

I bit the inside of my cheek. Considering how talking about Penn this morning had gone, it wasn't something that I wanted to repeat immediately.

"I've always said that the way Jensen views what happened with Penn would be of value to you." Dr. Oliver lowered his hands. "He doesn't feel the same way you do."

It wasn't that Jensen didn't feel any remorse. I knew he did, but he was, as Dr. Oliver put it, pragmatic about things. Jensen believed that no matter what we had done or didn't do, Penn would've eventually taken his own life either way.

Penn was sick. I accepted that part of it. It had taken me a long time to realize that our one singular act hadn't driven Penn to take his life, but we had been the tipping point.

"Do you still feel responsible for Penn's death?"

The breath I exhaled was shaky as I met Dr. Oliver's stare. Part of me wanted to lie, because I knew if I said yes, this appointment was going to continue far longer than I wanted it to. But I guess honesty time was over. "Sometimes I . . . forget about it. I mean, not really completely forget, but I don't think about it."

"That's normal, Ella."

I winced. "It doesn't seem right though." I didn't want to continue, but Dr. Oliver was giving me a look that said he'd sit there and stare at me until I did. "I don't want to forget him—forget Penn. He was . . . he was my best friend. I grew up with him." My voice turned hoarse. "It's not right to just forget about him."

"No one is saying you need to forget him, Ella, but life does go on. It always has and will. Letting that happen is no disrespect to Penn's memory," he said patiently and then sat back, hooking one leg over the other. "You have to learn to let this guilt go."

Pressing my lips together, I folded my arms across my chest.

His gaze turned shrewd. "You did not kill that boy. Neither did Jensen. Choosing to go to one party over another does not make you responsible. It sucks," he said, raising his hands before pressing them together under his chin. "It was a series of unfortunate events, but nothing you two did equals ownership of blame."

I wanted to believe that so much. "What about Monica? Vee?"

"What about them?"

"They picked on him relentlessly. Are they to blame?"

Dr. Oliver didn't answer for a long moment. "When you bully someone, picking at them day after day, stripping away their self-worth and confidence, their very will to live, then you do have ownership of the blame. And what they did to him is very different than what you and Jensen did. You know that."

I nodded.

"I'm going to be up front with you," he said, and I schooled my expression blank. "What you're feeling—the anxiety and fear, even the nightmares, after a violent attack is normal. You're probably going to experience that for some time, maybe even until they apprehend the person responsible, but it's not affecting your daily life. So that's good. And I also think it's great that you're reconnecting with Jensen. In a way, getting to know him again is the right step for you to be taking."

"It is?"

He nodded, pulling a thick pad out of his desk. "It's all about finally letting your past go, and it's about time that you do that."

I hadn't really thought of it that way.

"But I am going to write you a prescription for something to help you sleep." He scribbled across the pad and then ripped the slip of paper off. "Sleep is important."

I took the paper. "So I'm okay?"

"As okay as any of us are." A quick smile flashed across his face.

My gaze dropped to his barely legible handwriting. "Can I ask you a question?"

He leaned back in his chair, hooking one leg over the other. "Have at it."

"You're a therapist, right?"

His eyebrow arched. "On some days."

I smiled at that. "What I mean is, you do this for a living, and with . . . what has been happening around here, why. . . . why do you think someone is doing this?"

"Ah . . . well, I don't think there's a simple answer to that question," he said. "There are people who kill for the thrill of it—thrill killers. There's no rhyme or reason. Their victims are usually random, and they tend to move about, not staying in one city or location."

"And you don't think that's the case here?"

"I don't think there's enough evidence to say either way, but I'd be surprised if that's what the police have on their hands. People kill for different motives—greed, love, hate." He paused, his gaze meeting mine. "Revenge. So on and so forth. And if the police can find a motive linking the murder to the disappearance and the attack, then they'll find their guy."

I turned that over in my head. "But what if there isn't a motive?"

Dr. Oliver leaned forward, the chair creaking under the shift in his weight. "Thrill killers are rare, Ella. There's almost always a motive. And most of the time it's what's staring us right in the face."

A chill tiptoed down my spine.

"I want to see you in three weeks," he said, reclining back. "Just in case you're not okay. Now get out of my office." He smiled. "Wife is making spaghetti for dinner. I don't want to be late."

I grinned at him in spite of the coldness his observation had left behind. "All right. Bye."

Leaving the office with my brand spanking new sleeping pill prescription in the pocket of my jeans, I slipped out the door, closing it quietly behind me. I headed down the hall, reading over the prescription. Sleeping pills. Would I take them? As haggard as I looked, I needed to.

Last night I'd slept pretty good. Even waking up as early as I did, I'd still gotten more sleep than I had in days. But it wasn't like Jensen could be my little bed buddy forever.

Of course, I immediately thought of this morning, of how he felt against me and what we'd done, and then at lunch, when he . . . Face burning, I slapped my hands over my cheeks as I turned the corner and walked right into someone.

Swallowing a shriek, I stumbled back, smacking into the wall behind me. Strong hands settled on my shoulders, steadying me.

"Whoa, are you okay?" Gavin asked.

I pressed my hands to my chest. "Oh my God, you scared me."

"Well, you were walking around the corner with your hands over your face. I doubt you would've seen anyone." A slight smile appeared. "You sure you're okay?"

"Yeah, I just wasn't paying attention." Looking up, I took in his pale complexion and the deep shadows under his eyes. "Are *you* okay?"

His brows knitted together. "Of course I am."

"You look . . ."

"Tired?" he supplied, and a dry laugh rattled out of him. "Well, as you know, school's been a bit of a bitch this week."

I winced. "Sorry. I really am sorry that you're going through all of this. It's not fair."

"Yeah, but I think Vee got the really unfair end of the deal."

"True." My stomach tumbled a bit.

Gavin's hands were still on my shoulders. "What are you doing here? Are you seeing Dr. Oliver again?"

I nodded. "Yeah, after everything, Mom thought it would be a good idea. I haven't been sleeping well, and I . . ." Then it hit me. I frowned. "What are you doing here?"

"Helping the parents. They're cleaning offices. I'm stuck with them for the evening." His fingers curled around my shoulders, tangling in my hair. "Actually, I'm glad I ran into you. Maybe we could grab something to eat. I'm sure my parents would understand."

"Oh, I . . ."

"I could really use a friend right now."

My heart hurting, I wrapped my arms around him, squeezing him tight as sympathy choked me. "I know, but I can't tonight. What about tomorrow after school?"

Gavin's arms circled me, and he dropped his chin to the top of my head. His chest rose with a deep breath. "What are you doing tonight?"

"Um, I'm going to get a smoothie with Jensen," I said, and Gavin immediately stiffened against me. "He brought me here. He's waiting outside."

"He's waiting for you," he repeated slowly. He drew back, dropping his arms. "So, are you and Jensen a thing?"

"What? No." I tucked my hair behind my ear. That was definitely not true. We were definitely a lot of something. "That doesn't matter, Gavin. We can do dinner tomorrow. Or maybe later tonight if—"

"Forget it." Gavin wheeled around. "I'll see you later."

"Wait." I pushed off the wall, following him down the silent hall. "Gavin, come on. Don't—"

"Don't what?" He spun around, face mottled. "Don't drop one for the other? Isn't that what you're doing? You dropped me at the end of last year, and now you're hooking up with Jensen."

I gaped at him. "Wait. It's not like that at all."

"It isn't? Could've fooled me. After all, you have a habit of doing this, right? You and Jensen both. Always moving on to something better. Isn't that what you did to Penn? And isn't that what Jensen did to you before?"

Getting slapped in the face would've felt better. Tears raced up my throat as I shook my head. He looked at me a second longer and said, "You two are really perfect for each another. Have at it."

FIFTEEN

LATER THAT NIGHT, after sharing a cup of warm tea and telling Mom about my appointment with Dr. Oliver, I tugged the blankets back from my bed. A slight citrusy scent clung to the pillows.

The prescription Dr. Oliver had written me sat on my desk. I wasn't sure yet if I'd get it filled. Yes, I wanted to sleep the entire night, but those things knocked me the hell out, and waking up from them always took an ungodly amount of time.

After changing into my pajamas, I went into the bathroom, washed my face, brushed my teeth, and did my nightly routine. I stepped back into my bedroom and stared at the bed. I took a deep breath and—

A soft knock on my bedroom window caused me to jump at least a foot into the air. I smacked my hand over my mouth. What the hell? Rooted to where I stood, I wondered if I was hearing things.

The quiet tapping came again.

Okay. The likelihood of a killer tapping on my window to come in had to be rare. That's what I told myself as I crept over to my window. Slowly, I pulled the curtains back.

My heart leaped in my chest.

On the other side of my window, Jensen was perched on my

roof. Grinning as if this wasn't abnormal or anything, he pointed at the windowsill.

For a moment, all I could do was stare at him. Then I glanced over my shoulder. My bedroom door was shut, but if Mom came in here . . .

It would not be pretty.

But I couldn't leave Jensen out on my roof. That would be . . . um, wrong I supposed. Shaking my head, I slowly eased the window open. "What are you doing?" I whispered.

"Watching the stars," he whispered back, his eyes glittering in the darkness.

I narrowed my eyes. "On my roof?"

"Why not?"

All I could do was stare at him.

"What?" His grin turned mischievous as he gripped the edges of the window. "Your roof is better than mine. And you know what else is?"

"What?"

"Your mother's hearing is better than my mother's. So you should let me in before she catches me on her roof."

I had no idea how him being inside my room meant that my mom wouldn't hear him, but I found myself stepping aside. Within the span of five seconds, he was in my room.

The first thing I noticed now that he was in my room, in the light, was that he was dressed for bed. "What are you doing here?" I asked.

Reaching around me, he grabbed the remote and turned on my TV. The volume muted our conversation. "I wanted to talk to you."

"That's why God made cellphones, Jensen."

His chin dipped as he stared up at me through thick lashes. "Silly Ella, God didn't make cellphones. Some extremely brilliant nerd probably did."

Rolling my eyes, I slapped his arm. "You shouldn't be here."

"Where should I be?" He took a step toward me.

I took a step back. "Not in my bedroom this late."

"Hmm . . ." He advanced on me, backing me up until I was pressed against the door. "Guess what else is better than mine?"

My heart pounded as he placed a hand beside my head. I stared at his arm, taking in the ropey muscles that disappeared under the sleeve of his shirt. "What?"

His head dropped low, his voice a shiver against my ear. "Your bed is so much better than mine."

I bit down on my lip as his mouth brushed my earlobe. "I'm sure that's not the case."

"It is." He reached around me again. A second later I heard the door lock, and blood thundered through my veins. "Did Gavin come over?"

I'd told him about running into Gavin when I was leaving Dr. Oliver's office. "No. I tried calling him, but he didn't answer."

"I'm not surprised." His hand settled on the curve of my hip.

"You're not?" The material of my sleep shorts was thin, like they had been this morning, and the heat of his touch was like a brand on my skin.

"Nope." His lips brushed the sensitive spot below my ear, and my knees went weak. "He doesn't like that you and I are together."

There was a hummingbird in my chest. The fluttering returned with a vengeance. "We are not together."

"Aren't we?"

My breath caught as his hand slid up, skating over my ribs, leaving a trail of fire in its wake.

Jensen's deep, low chuckle traveled across my throat. "After this morning, we are most definitely together. We just haven't worked out the specifics of our together-ness."

"Together-ness is not a word."

"Now it is." His hand slipped away from the door to cradle my cheek. He tipped my head back, and I thought my heart would burst from my chest. "So let's talk about the specifics."

My eyes locked with his, and I couldn't look away. "Can't this conversation wait?"

"Nope."

"You're going to get us into so much trouble."

"Where's the fun in anything if there's no risk?" His head dipped once more, and he placed a quick kiss against my wildly beating pulse. "And don't try to distract me. I'm on a mission. I want you."

My stomach did a backflip.

"I think that part is pretty obvious," he continued. "I couldn't even hold back this morning. When you told me it was okay, I just . . . lost it."

Oh Lord.

A throbbing pulse shot through me. I didn't need the reminder. What I did this morning—what he did this morning had not slipped far from my thoughts.

His eyes met mine once more as his hand dropped from my cheek to the other side of my ribs. He lifted me up as he pressed in, sliding one leg between mine. My hands clamped down on his shoulders at the shock of him.

"And you want me," he murmured. "I think that part is also obvious."

My fingers curled into his shirt. There was no denying that. Very few people in the universe would deny that. "I'm not into being friends with benefits," I whispered.

"Good. Because neither am I. Not with you," he added, his thumbs moving in slow circles. "Here's another specific. I don't share. It's just me. It's just you."

"Do you think I normally date more than one person at a time?"

"No." His lips pressed against my cheek. "But I just want to clarify that. And you know what else I want?"

By the way his body was pressed against mine, I had a pretty good idea of what he wanted. The same thing Gavin had wanted from me, but I hadn't been ready to give.

"Ask me," he said.

My breath shuddered. "What?"

"I want to be that guy—the one that when your phone rings, you hope it's me. The one who holds your hand in the hallway and at lunch. The guy who gets to hold *you*. I want to be the one who gets to touch you," he whispered against my cheek. "I want to be *yours*."

There was a swift swelling in my chest, and if he wasn't holding on to me, I knew I would float right up to the ceiling. His words were beautiful. Possibly the most poignant words a guy had ever spoken to me considering most were like hey, nice butt, let's make out. I doubted that Dr. Oliver had meant all of this when he talked about Jensen and I reconnecting, but I'd be a liar if I said that I didn't want this, that I didn't want to take those words and hold them close to my heart.

But I had wanted it before—before I really understood what I was feeling—and he had hurt me. "Jensen, I . . ."

"Don't tell me what you're thinking yet."

My eyes searched his. "When do you want me to tell you?"

"In a minute."

I raised an eyebrow. "In a—?"

Jensen's mouth was on mine before I could finish the thought. It was a whisper of lips, a brushing of his against mine, as if he were mapping out the feel, testing my response. When I didn't turn away, he swept his mouth across mine once more, and this time he kissed me.

He *really* kissed me, like we should've been kissing this morning, and I was swimming in raw emotions, swept away in a tide made of him and me and everything in our past and everything that could be our future. I kissed him back, following his lead, and his hands slid to my waist. There was no space between our bodies.

Holding me against him, he exhaled a soft moan, and his lips seared mine. He kissed me until we were both breathless, until my fingers were wrapped around the soft hair at the nape of his neck.

Jensen pulled back, resting his forehead against mine. His chest rose and fell in rapid, shallow breaths. "Now." His voice was deep, gruff. "Tell me what you're thinking now."

My brain cells had been blown. "I can't think."

I felt his cheek rise in a half smile as he reached up, turning off my bedroom light. Then he lowered me so my feet were flat on the floor and he grabbed my hand. He pulled me away from the door, to the bed. Down we went, our legs and arms tangled together, my heart pounding so fast. We lay facing each other, his breath warm against the top of my head, his heart drumming solidly under my hands.

"Can you think now?" he asked.

My brain was slow to come back online. The pleasant haze his kisses left behind clouded my thoughts. How close we were didn't help either. My lashes lifted and my eyes met his. He was watching me as if I was something valuable in his life, to be cherished—it was how he'd always looked at me in the past.

In that moment, the past intruded like an old friend you no longer had anything in common with. As I stared into his pale blue eyes, I suddenly wasn't sure about any of this, because there was so much between us.

Jensen seemed to sense the shift in me. "You *are* thinking."

"I am." It was hard to say the next words, because for so long I'd done nothing but run and hide from the past and from all the hurt. But I couldn't anymore. "There's a lot . . . between us, Jensen." My voice was low as I spoke. "And you say you want me, but you hurt me before. You . . . embarrassed me. I know it was a long time ago, but it's hard to let go of that."

He held my gaze for a moment and then rolled onto his back. Staring up at the ceiling, he cursed under his breath, the sound so self-deprecating. "You're thinking about that night."

The night.

The stupid dance.

I didn't like to think about it, because after everything with Penn, after all the years Jensen and I had known each other, he had made an absolute fool out of me before moving away.

"Yeah," I murmured, watching his profile. "I just don't understand. We were basically just kids, but why . . . why did you do it?"

Jensen didn't answer, and in the silence my mind whirled back several years, to when he invited me to the stupid Valentine's Day dance. I believed that it meant he liked me, too. Granted, we were like thirteen, but the dance had been a big deal. He had asked me at lunch, in front of Brock, Mason, the girls, and Gavin.

Even in front of the lunch lady with the frizzy hair.

I had my mom buy me this ridiculous pink dress, and I had gotten my hair done, and then the night of the dance, Dad had dropped me off, and Jensen . . . well, he never showed up. Everyone thought it was a joke. Gavin thought he'd done to me what we had done to Penn a year earlier, trading me in for something better. And Jensen had never told me why. Of course, I hadn't given him much of a chance. When he came to my house the next day, I wouldn't let him inside, and that was when I told him I never wanted to speak to him again.

"Why would you pull that kind of prank on me?" I whispered.

"A prank?" He turned his head toward mine sharply, eyes narrowed. "You really believe I'd do that to you? That asking you out was just some kind of game?"

"What was I supposed to think?"

"I never got the chance to tell you why I didn't show up that night." He shook his head, his gaze returning to the ceiling. "And I'm not saying that's your fault. I should've told you way before then, and you would've understood."

I frowned. "I don't understand."

His chest rose with a deep breath. "There's something about me—about my family you never knew. Hell, no one really knew.

It wasn't that I didn't want to tell you, but my parents . . . it was our dirty little secret."

"Okay. I'm really kind of confused. Dirty secret? What are you talking about?"

He opened his mouth and it was like he had to get his tongue around the words. "Jonathan—he was . . ."

Whoa. I wasn't expecting that this had anything to do with his brother.

Jensen shifted back onto his side, facing me. "Jon . . . he had issues, Ella. Not a lot of people knew. Only us and a few of his friends." He looked down. "Brock did, because his brother was close to Jon, but Mom and Dad were horrified."

"Horrified about what?" I asked.

He raised a hand, smoothing his palm down his face. "Jon had a huge drug problem."

I blinked once and then twice. "What?"

"Heroin," he spat the word out. "Started his sophomore year of high school. For a while he was able to function with it, and we had no idea. None at all. Not until he started getting strung out, stealing from them—from me. Once he took my birthday money our grandma gave me. Then it was obvious. They sent him to rehab, got him clean, and everyone thought he . . . you know, had escaped its clutches. He went to college, but he started using again."

Holy crap, I had no idea.

He frowned. "Our parents were so embarrassed by it. Like they did something wrong raising him and that's why he used. For the longest time, I didn't understand. Why? He didn't have a shitty life. He wasn't suffering from anything. He just tried it once and I guessed he was forever chasing that high. I don't know. It doesn't really matter. The night that he died in his sleep? He overdosed."

"Oh my God," I whispered. "I'm so—"

"Don't say you're sorry," he told me. "Heroin did that to him." There was a pause. "You know, I think people would be amazed by how many families are hiding secrets like that."

"Probably a lot." I had no idea what to say. This was something I never knew, and as many times as I had seen Jonathan, I never would have guessed.

"I was looking forward to going to that dance," he said quietly, as if he was talking to himself. "I liked you then, you know? As more than a friend. Had for a while, and well, I wish I had told you that. I wish I told you about Jon, but I didn't know what to say about him. Everyone looked up to him, even me. I thought eventually his . . . his problems would just go away."

A picture of a past I never knew existed started to form in my head. "Something happened that night."

"Yeah." His throat worked. "Jon had come home that afternoon all screwed up. He ended up getting into a fight with Dad because he'd taken money out of Mom's purse again. The fight was really bad, and Mom . . . man, she was nearly hysterical. Things got out of hand. The police were called, and before I knew it, the dance had already started."

Geez. I was floored. All this time I'd believed Jensen had pulled a nasty prank on me or had forgotten or a number of other lame things, but I'd never guessed this. Never had any reason to.

"I wanted to tell you." He looked at me again. "But . . ."

"But I didn't give you a chance." I squeezed my eyes shut. "When you showed up that weekend, I told you to leave me alone. And then you moved later that month. God, Jensen, I'm so sorry. About all of it."

"You don't have anything to apologize for." The tips of his fingers touched my cheek gingerly. "I could've told you what was going on before that night. I could've come back later on, but I didn't. None of that matters now."

But it did.

"So that's why I didn't show up at that dance, and that's why my parents moved. They wanted to get away. Anyway, like I said,

I wished I'd done so many things differently, but I can't go back in time. All I have is today and tomorrow, and I want a future," he said, closing his eyes. "I want a future with you."

Something tugged at my chest, and God, I wanted that future too. I wanted Jensen. I'd always wanted him and had missed him so badly during the years he was away, but to have him, I had to let go of the past.

Was I willing to do that?

Sitting up halfway, I stared down at him. Jensen had opened his eyes and was watching me warily with a bit of resignation churning in those beautiful eyes. I knew in that moment he expected me to tell him no or say I wasn't ready. And I knew he'd still stay with me, he'd still be there for me, and an even deeper part of me realized that he wouldn't give up.

He'd wait.

But I didn't want to wait.

I didn't want to live in a past full of hurt and pain, guilt and misunderstandings anymore. I wanted today and tomorrow, especially when there was such a powerful reminder that not everyone had tomorrow. I wanted a fresh start and I wanted that with him.

"I want that too," I said, and my heart thumped in my chest. "I want to be with you."

For a long moment, Jensen didn't move, and I wasn't sure he even breathed. Then he slipped two fingers under my chin, tilting my head down. "For real?"

"For real," I whispered, knowing that I was making the right choice. "But can you . . . can you forgive me?"

His brows furrowed. "What would I need to forgive you for?"

It seemed obvious to me. "I didn't give you a chance to explain. I didn't even want to listen. It was selfish and cold—"

"You didn't know. I had ample opportunity to tell you about Jon and I didn't." His gaze searched mine. "There's nothing to apologize for. Okay?"

I wanted to apologize again, because I felt like a bitch, but I nodded. "Okay."

"Thank you." Jensen's arms swept around me and he pulled me down, snuggling me close to him, and that's how we stayed.

That's how we fell asleep.

LIKE THE MORNING before, I woke a little too early to get ready, but surprisingly well-rested and toasty.

Really toasty.

I'd fallen asleep in Jensen's arms, my head tucked under his chin, my leg cradled between his. My heart did a little jump in my chest. Our conversation from last night was replaying itself. As was the kiss we shared.

Jensen had thanked me for being with him, for giving him a chance, and I was kind of blown away by that.

It took me a few moments to realize that Jensen wasn't asleep. At some point, his fingers started moving up and down the curve of my spine. My hands were still folded against his chest and I could feel his heart kick up, matching mine.

"Morning," I murmured.

"Mmm . . ." That seemed to be all he was capable of saying, but he was definitely awake enough to move. One hand trailed up my side, skipping to my bare arm, and then the tips of his fingers found their way to my jaw. He tilted my head back, and my gaze met his sleepy, heavily lidded one. "Morning."

Before I could say anything else, Jensen lowered his head and kissed me. There was a flutter of panic. I hadn't washed my face or brushed my teeth, and I knew I looked like a hot mess, but the infinite tenderness of his kiss swept away those concerns. The kiss was slow and sweet, an exploration, and I was lost in him.

When he finally lifted his mouth from mine, I had pressed the length of my body against his, and he was half on his back. He slid his hands down my back and then lower, eliciting a gasp from me.

"I need to get out of this bed or . . ."

My heart tripped up as I stared down at him. "Or what?"

He kicked his head back, his hair wonderfully messy. "Or we're going to switch positions, repeat the morning before, end up really late for school, and most likely busted by your mother in a very awkward way." He stretched up, kissing my parted lips. "Oh, and this time, we'd probably be naked, so . . ."

A heady flush traveled down my body. Being busted by my mom in that kind of situation was mortifying, but I didn't move. I touched his cheek, running my fingers over the slight stubble.

"Not probably." His lips curled up in a lazy smile. "We'd most definitely be naked."

I bit down on my lip. My stomach hollowed at the thought of there being nothing between us.

My voice was low, barely a whisper when I spoke. "I've never done it before."

"What?" One hand traveled up my back. He gently tugged on my hair. "Get naked?"

Gavin and I had been together for a while, and we'd experimented in lots of ways that involved getting naked, but . . ."No. Not *that*."

An eyebrow rose, and then his lazy smile vanished as his eyes widened slightly. The look was almost comical. "Wait. You and Gavin never . . . ?"

I shook my head.

"Not even one time?"

"Nope. We did stuff, but not that," I said, and he looked so floored one would think I'd admitted to being the Easter Bunny. "Is it really that hard to believe?"

"Hell yeah," he murmured, splaying his hand across my cheek. "How the hell did he manage to keep his hands off of you?"

I shot him a bland look.

"Sorry. I just thought . . ."

"Going that far, well, it never seemed right." I shrugged. "Not once. Not like . . ."

"Not like what?" Jensen swallowed hard. "You and me?"

"Yeah."

He stared at me for a moment and then squeezed his eyes shut. "Damn. That does not help."

"Help with what?"

"Not getting you naked."

Unable to suppress my grin, I rolled off him and he groaned. "Sorry?"

"Uh-huh." He threw an arm over his eyes. "Did I tell you you're beautiful in the morning?"

I smiled. "No."

"You are." He shifted his arm, opening one eye. "The best thing ever to see first thing in the morning." Then he sat up. Leaning over, he kissed my forehead. "I better get going."

"Yeah," I whispered, caught up in the swelling-chest thing. I knew that feeling had a name. A four-letter word. Something I'd felt for Jensen for a long time, even when I wanted to hate him.

Jensen rose fluidly and I followed him to the window. He stopped there, turning to me. His voice was low, his grin wicked. "You know, I'm sure I can hang out for a few more minutes. If you're going to shower, I can help."

"Oh no." I smacked his chest. "I do not need that kind of help."

He straightened, putting his hands on my hips. "I think you lie. I think you want that kind of help."

My cheeks burned, because yeah, I sort of did. "You better go."

Jensen chuckled before he dipped his head, kissing me like it was the first time and the last time. My heart was going crazy in my chest by the time he broke away and climbed back out my window.

And it didn't slow down.

Not when he showed up to take me to school or when he folded his hand around mine as we walked inside. He seemed oblivious to the questioning stares. Some were confused, as if they couldn't figure out what he was doing with me. Others just openly gawked.

Linds was waiting for me at my locker, her head tilting to the side as we drew closer. Her gaze dropped from my face, to our hands, and then back to my face again.

"Did I miss something?" she asked.

Jensen grinned. "Miss what? Me? Yes."

"There has to be a newsletter that I haven't subscribed to." She pinned me with a look. "Because you two are holding hands."

Who knew holding hands was such a big deal?

Across from Linds, Wendy and Brock were standing together. Whatever conversation they were having with one another had grinded to a halt. I shifted, uncomfortable with the extra attention. I started to pull my hand free, but Jensen wasn't having it.

"That we are," Jensen said.

Linds' eyes widened to the size of mini spaceships. Beyond her, Wendy jabbed her elbow into Brock's side, who was now joined by Mason. We were gathering an audience.

My cheeks heated, and my tongue twisted around the simple words that explained what Jensen and I were, but apparently he was more of a show than tell kind of guy.

His knuckles brushed under my chin, tipping my head back to meet his lips. The kiss was not quick or chaste, and really not school appropriate. Not when my lips parted, and he took that kiss to a whole new level.

Wendy's inhale was like a crack of thunder, and I knew I should've pulled away from Jensen. Kissing like this was not something we should be doing at the given moment, but the taste and feel of him had this wonderful ability of making the world disappear around us.

"Holy crap," Linds said, her voice an excited whisper.

My face was flaming as Jensen pulled back. "Does that answer your question?" he said.

"That and then some," she replied, grinning at me.

I had the wild notion to laugh, and I didn't know why, but I smiled and turned, my gaze colliding with a pair of dark eyes.

Gavin.

He was staring like one or the both of us had walked up to him and punched him in the gonads. His face was pale, the shadows under his eyes darker. His expression tightened, and then he wheeled around, stalking off in the opposite direction.

LINDS HOUNDED ME for details on Jensen and me the moment I walked into art class. She was convinced that we'd been having this torrid, secret love affair, and that did sound more interesting than the truth.

Miss Reed, art teacher extraordinaire and guidance counselor of the year, was making a beeline straight for our side of the class-room, her hands smoothing over her paint covered smock. I tried to make myself as small as possible. At the beginning of every class, she sent two students to the storage room to grab the paintings we were working on, and I was feeling incredibly lazy.

Her gaze landed on Wendy. "You and Mason can go grab the paintings, please."

Wendy's breath huffed out. "I'm not feeling well. Can someone else do it? Please," she whined.

I rolled my eyes.

"Ella? Mason?" she said, planting her hands on her full hips. "Your turn. You know the drill."

Dammit.

Linds wrinkled her nose. "Lucky you."

There was nothing 'lucky' about the way she said that, and Mason cut her a look. "I heard that."

She smiled sweetly. "And I don't care."

Eyes wide and lips pursed, I stood and headed for the door before I got caught up in their royal rumble. Mason ended up in front of me, smacking the door open and letting it swing back. I caught it before it knocked me on my butt.

"Thanks," I muttered.

He glanced over his shoulder, his blond hair swinging. "Sorry," he grumbled, and I thought he might've sounded a little sorry.

We headed back toward the drama classroom, where the entrance to the storage room and the backstage of the theatre was. Knowing my luck, half the paintings would still be wet.

"So you and Jensen hooking up or something?" he asked, punching open the door.

I frowned at his back. Hooking up in guy lingo could mean a lot of things. "We're dating."

"Dating?" He actually held the door for me this time. "That's interesting."

My brows furrowed as I walked behind him, heading down the narrow hallway. It smelled like mold and turpentine back here. "Why's that interesting?"

He shrugged as he thrust a hand through his hair. "I don't know. He just doesn't date girls, you know? He hooks up with them. That's about it."

I resisted the urge to tell Mason that was not the case with us, but the lengthy explanation would be wasted on the brain cells he'd smoke away later.

He headed into the storage room, walking past the easels and stacks of paintings marked with earlier class periods. "I think it just took everyone by surprise 'cuz didn't he like invite you to the eighth grade dance and then stand you up?"

"Wow," I said, staring at him as I came to a complete stop. He remembered that? "Way to just throw that out there."

"Sorry." This time he didn't sound sorry. He sounded smug. "I mean, it's just weird."

It was weird. I got that. It was also probably why Gavin was so shocked that I was even friends with Jensen after that, but I knew the truth now.

Sighing as those ugly memories managed to resurface, I tucked my hair back behind my ear. That was in the past—a past that I had all wrong.

Except no matter how much I told myself that, my chest felt heavy. It didn't take a lot to remember how I felt, how heartbroken I'd been. I always thought it was a nice, hefty dose of karma after what I'd done to Penn.

The sound of footfalls intruded, which was weird, because Mason had stopped and I wasn't walking. I looked over my shoulder, frowning as I scanned the room. Tubes and cans of paint were stacked waist high among the paintings, props from plays, and costumes.

A wicked sense of déjà vu hit me upside the head. My skin crawled like a hundred ants had descended on me, their little legs digging into my flesh. It was the same feeling I had in the farmhouse, right before I'd found Vee's body.

Chills skated down my arms as I stared at the costumes hanging from wire racks, half expecting them to jump out at me. Nothing was out of place. Nothing happened, but the sensation of being watched gave me the creepy crawlies.

"Here we go," Mason announced, finding the stacks of paintings from our class. I turned, finding him staring at me like I needed to be patted on my head. Of course, someone was watching me. Mason. *Dumbass.* "I can probably get most of these. I just . . . *holy shit!*"

I gaped as he jumped back from the paintings, his hands rising up like he had a fleet of cops pointing guns at him. "What?"

He shook his head, pointing.

I followed his gaze and felt the floor under my feet shift. The paintings, they were all destroyed, the canvases slashed open with something jagged and sharp. Red paint had been splattered across them, like a gruesome crime scene. But that wasn't the most messed up thing.

Oh no. Not at all.

I stepped back, my eyes following the row of paintings. Placed side by side, they spelled out two words.

You're next.

SIXTEEN

NO ONE KNEW who or how the paintings got destroyed, only that it shook up an already nervous student body.

The staff claimed it was a prank yet again—a stupid, misguided prank from someone who had absolutely no class. That was possible. After all, how could it be something else—someone with truly nefarious intentions? Because if the same person responsible for the attacks did it, how would they have known who would go pick up the paintings?

Anyone could've picked them up, reading the 'You're Next' message sprawled across them in red paint, so it couldn't have been left there for just one person.

The thing was, anyone could get into the storage room. Hell, they really didn't even need to be a student. The door was rarely locked, and the doors to the outside were only locked when after school activities ended. Prank or not, it was doubtful the staff would ever find who was responsible for the disturbing display.

Like the clown mask in my locker and the dead bird in Wendy's bag, it was something that went cold and unexplained. But the police were at the school almost every day. We saw them heading into the administrative offices when we were in the halls, and sometimes we caught glimpses of their cruisers in the parking lot.

But it wasn't just the local or state boys that sporadically showed up. There were a few in suits that I imagined were on the federal level, and my suspicions were confirmed when I was pulled out of class one afternoon and interviewed all over again.

F.B.I.

Wow.

But they weren't the only ones to descend on our small town. So did the media. News stations from the surrounding cities and states popped up. I watched the evening news whenever I could, but nothing they said was new.

Over the course of the next week or so, the night Jensen climbed in through my bedroom window was rinsed and repeated. He would scale the tree and come through the window, and he would always kiss me as he locked the door and turned off the lights before pulling me into bed.

Except on Wednesdays.

He used the front door then.

With him, I didn't need to use the prescription sleeping pills. The prescription was still on my desk unfilled. And some evenings, he'd leave when Mom popped her head into the living room, and then he'd return through the window thirty or so minutes later.

Jensen and I were boyfriend and girlfriend, something I had stopped fantasizing about ages ago. But we were.

Not everyone was happy about our together-ness. Gavin hadn't spoken to me since the night I had Dr. Oliver's appointment. He sat clear across from me in English and didn't return any of my calls or texts. And that hurt something fierce.

I didn't get it. He'd been dating Vee and I hadn't freaked out on him when I found out. When I explained this to Linds when she was at my house one evening, she looked at me like I was half stupid.

"It's pretty obvious," she said, kicking her legs out to the side, stretching. "You didn't freak out because you see him as a friend, but honey, he doesn't see you that way. That's why he's freaking."

I wanted to deny it, but as time passed and Gavin made no attempt at talking to me, it was really obvious and it sucked.

And then there was the stuff I did my best not to dwell on. It was heading into the second week since Monica had disappeared, and there had been no leads in her disappearance or who had killed Vee. Obviously Gavin wasn't a suspect. Not that anyone at school had determined that on their own, but common sense said that the police would've arrested him by now if they had any evidence pointing in his direction.

Things hadn't returned to normal, though, not that I had expected them to. Candlelight vigils were held for Monica and in Vee's memory. The hallways at school were subdued as the month of September slowly crept by.

Would the killer ever be found? Had he or she left town? Would Monica ever resurface, alive or dead? No one had the answers, and it seemed as if no news was just as frightening.

But on Friday morning something happened that proved that news was worse than no news. It started as whispers in second period, like a virus that was slow to spread. At the end of third period, Jensen was waiting for me out in the hall. I knew immediately that something was up.

His class was downstairs.

"What's going on?" I asked.

Jensen took my hand, glancing around as he led me to the alcove with a view of the football field. "You haven't heard?"

Knots formed in my stomach. "Heard what?"

A muscle thrummed along his jaw. "People are saying that Wendy didn't come home from school yesterday."

"Oh no," I whispered, squeezing my eyes shut. "It's not just a rumor?"

"No. Mr. Vicks confirmed it last class. He asked if anyone might have information about her whereabouts, to please come forward."

He squeezed my hand. "She's gone and . . ."

"And so is Monica, just like Vee." I shuddered.

Jensen tugged me into his chest, and I wrapped my arms around him. This wasn't over, not that I truly believed it for one second, but this was a brutal slap in the face to everyone.

The warning bell drove us apart, and I went to my next class in a daze. By the end of the day, the news had broken wide open. Another girl was missing.

Another girl who had picked on Penn.

I squeezed my eyes shut as I stood in front of my locker. This didn't have anything to do with Penn. It couldn't.

Jensen touched my arm. "You okay?"

"Yeah." I opened my locker. "Can we hit the warehouse? I'd like to—"

"Ella!" Linds shouted from down the hall, causing several heads to turn. She hurried up to my side, placing her hands together under her chin. "Can I ask you a huge favor?"

"Sure." I shoved most of my books inside my locker, keeping only my English text for homework. "But it better have absolutely nothing to do with haunted anything."

Her face fell. "Actually, that's on hold until we find a new location. Obviously, no one wants to go to a fake haunted house that actually might be . . ." She trailed off, shaking her head. "Anyway, no. I'm not asking about that. Mom and Dad are out of town, visiting my aunt. Can you stay with me? My parents won't be back until tomorrow night. Please? Pretty please?"

Jensen stiffened beside me, and I glanced over at him. One look told me he was not happy at all with the idea of me spending a night alone with Linds. It only made me a little uneasy, but common sense told me there was safety in numbers. Everyone who had been attacked had been by themselves.

"Come on," she pleaded. "We haven't hung out in ages. And we can rent stupid comedies with Ryan Reynolds in them. Sorry."

She glanced at Jensen, smiling. "He's hot. So are you, but he's Theo James hot."

"I'm trying not to be too offended," he deadpanned, and I grinned.

"Anyway, we can get a ton of junk food. I'll go to the store and get whatever you want. We can even invite Heidi," she added, and that was a big deal. *"Please."*

She was right. We hadn't hung out in a long time. Closing my locker door, I slung my bag over my shoulder. "Yeah, you know, I think that would be a good idea."

"Oh!" she squealed, throwing her arms around me. "Thank you!"

"I've got a few things to do first," I said, once she stopped strangling me. "But I can come over around seven or so."

"That's perfect. Gives me enough time to go shopping after practice." She sprinted forward, hugging me again. "Thank you!"

After Linds headed off in the opposite direction, I turned to Jensen. He didn't look thrilled. "We'll be okay," I told him.

He nodded. "Maybe I can—"

"Girls' night," I said, even though the thought of him coming over to Linds' house didn't sound like such a bad idea.

"Yeah, yeah." He took my hand, squeezing it gently. "I'm really going to work your ass during training now."

That sounded kind of dirty.

He glanced down at me, eyebrows raised. "And not in a way you'd enjoy."

"Boo," I murmured.

Chuckling under his breath, he took his sweet time walking beside me as we made our way outside. Since I didn't have to be at Linds' until seven, we had time to spare.

The weather was cool and the scent of fall was in the air as we trekked up the slight hill leading to the parking lot. It seemed like the leaves had begun to change to gold and red while I was in class, or I was just that unobservant.

"Jesus," Jensen growled, dropping my hand as he came to a standstill.

Up ahead, a few kids were hanging around, snapping pictures of a car. My jaw dropped when I saw what they were snapping with their camera phones, and anger coursed through me like bitter acid.

We were a few feet from Gavin's car. It wasn't fancy, just an old Honda, but Gavin loved that baby, practically bathing it more times than he did his dog. Spray painted across the hood, the windshield, and the trunk was one word in blood red paint.

Murderer.

MY STOMACH MUSCLES were killing me.

Jensen hadn't been kidding when he said he was going to work my ass today. I'd lost count of how many kicks and punches he made me do, working with the punching bag. Right now, I wasn't doing much of anything other than watching him slam his wrapped fists into the bag.

His shirt was off.

I was officially distracted.

The ropey muscles of his back tensed and rippled as he swung. His skin glistened with a fine sheen of sweat, and under the rim of his backwards baseball cap his hair was damp.

My mouth dried.

The dips. The knee jabs. The punches. He was absolutely stunning as he moved around the bag, working it like I imagined a pro boxer would.

Jensen backed off, lowering his arms as he glanced over his shoulder at where I stood. His pale blue eyes glimmered, and that was the only warning I got. He spun and rushed right at where I stood in the center of the mats. I knew in the back of my head this was a test of sorts—practicing self-defense moves when an attacker was coming at me from the front, but there was something about having a six foot and then some dude rushing your ass that made you take a moment to react.

I kicked back a leg, bracing myself, and I raised my hands, picturing the "punch and run" points—what Jensen had dubbed them. Throat. Eye. Solar plexus. Groin. Other ouchie parts. I was going to go for the solar plexus with my knee since I had more strength in my legs.

I brought my knee up, but Jensen easily avoided the direct hit. His arms went around mine, clamping them to my sides, and I slammed the heel of my foot down on his, a little harder than I attended, but he shifted at the last second, and my foot hit the mat.

Cursing under my breath, I went for the groin. Obviously foreseeing my next move, he rolled his weight, and I went down, thrown off balance and cussing like a cracked-out sailor.

Jensen shifted, taking the brunt of the fall, but the air still wheezed out of my lungs when I landed on top of him. Laughing, he rolled me onto my back and leaned over me, his hands planted into the mat on either side of my head. He was sweaty and gross, but I didn't care.

"Do you kiss your mother with that mouth?" he asked.

"I kiss you with it."

"True." He dipped his head, brushing his lips over mine as he spoke. "And I kind of like it when you talk like that."

"Why doesn't that surprise me?"

"Nothing about me should surprise you." He shifted his weight to one arm, scooping up a loose strand of hair that had escaped my ponytail. He brushed it back. "You almost got me."

I scrunched up my nose. "Almost doesn't quite count."

"It doesn't." Jensen settled his hips between my legs. His hand got distracted, sliding down my face, to my neck, and then to the curve of my shoulder. "But it's close. I've had years of practicing. You've had a month tops."

"How did you get so many years of experience doing this?" I

asked, biting down on my lip as his fingers traced the curve of my collarbone.

"I didn't tell you?"

"No." My breath caught as he abandoned my collarbone and went for the V-neck of my shirt. We'd touched and kissed a lot since we made this relationship official, but we hadn't yet had a repeat of the first morning. I think we were kind of starting over, taking things . . . slower.

Slow was torturous in a really fun way.

"I started at the end of eighth grade, during the summer." His gaze veered away from mine, to what he was doing with his finger. "I had a lot of . . . anger in me."

"You did?"

His finger dipped under the hem of my shirt, causing muscles deep inside me to clench. Even though we were at the warehouse, I knew no one would come into the rooms. At least no one had yet. So I wasn't too worried about getting caught.

"Yeah. You know, with everything that happened with Penn. I never thought it was our fault." He lifted his chin and the clarity of his eyes held me. "But that doesn't mean I didn't feel anything. I was pissed at him, at myself, at a lot of things that had nothing to do with him."

I figured the 'a lot of things' had to do with his brother. I never knew any of this, so I watched him quietly as his gaze went back to his hand. He was silent for a long moment.

"One night I ran into Shaw. I was mouthing off, and instead of knocking me into next week, he got me involved in Krav Maga, and long story short, here I am."

"God, that has to suck for Shaw—the whole Gavin seeing Vee thing and people thinking the worst." I smoothed my hand over his jaw. "So you've known Shaw that long?"

He turned his head, kissing the center of my palm. "Yeah, he came around a few times after . . . Penn. I think it's because he isn't close to Gavin, so he was helping me when he probably wanted to help Gavin. And he did help me, you know, center some of that anger."

I smiled. "I'm happy to hear that. I didn't know that you were having problems."

"I know you think I didn't feel anything just because I don't think of it the way you do, but that shit with Penn tore me up for a while." His gaze moved back to mine. "I know you don't like to talk about Penn, but you've got to understand, we didn't do that to him." He caught my chin as I started to look away, forcing my eyes to his. "I'm not saying we were completely devoid of responsibility. We weren't. But we were just kids. We made a stupid decision, and Penn . . . God, as much as I miss him, he was sick. You know he was, Ella. It went beyond what was happening at school."

I drew in a deep breath, causing my chest to press against his. Penn did have problems, bouts of extreme hyper happiness and then long stretches of sullen moods. The crap at school and his parents fighting hadn't been the catalyst for his behavior switches. Sometimes it would happen when he was with us and nothing had gone wrong. Dr. Oliver once told me that he believed Penn might've suffered from a disorder—a sickness aggravated from outside influences—and that if he'd gotten help, things most likely would've been different. I'd never really took those words to heart, thinking someone that young couldn't suffer that way, but that was dumb of me. Depression could strike at any age really, but Penn always seemed to bounce back from whatever was plaguing him. Not a day went by without him smiling.

"I know," I whispered.

"We were the icing on the cake, you know? That's all we were. I'm not saying if he had gotten help or if we had seen the signs, it wouldn't have turned out differently, but we didn't put the rope around his neck," he said in a quiet, serious tone. "We didn't bully him. We made a stupid call. And I do hate that we were the icing, but we were not at fault for what he did."

I thought about what Jensen said, *really* thought about it. That he and I were the icing on a fucked up cake, nothing more and nothing less. The decision we made had been wrong, but Jensen was right—so was Dr. Oliver and my mom and dad. We didn't put that rope around his neck.

Then I thought of the psycho—the monster, the whatever—that was stalking our town. Whoever was behind that horrific mask was also solely responsible for his own actions. Not me when he tried to grab me. Not Vee. And not Monica or Wendy. Tears crept up my throat.

"Ella?"

I blinked away the wetness. "I don't know if I'll ever not feel guilty, but you're right. We didn't do it. We made a shitty choice, but we didn't do it."

"We didn't," he repeated softly.

It wasn't like an angel suddenly appeared, harking and glowing and whatever it was that angels did. There was no big realization. Just a little bit of the pressure I carried with me since Penn's death eased off. Not a lot, but some. I guess it was a start.

It was something.

"You were distracted earlier," he said, trailing a finger over the bridge of my nose.

Before Jensen had handed me off to the punching bag, we practiced evasive techniques, but admittedly my head had not been in it. "I was thinking about Wendy."

Jensen didn't respond immediately. "I've been thinking about her, too. We weren't close, like we didn't, um . . ."

"Talk?" I supplied.

"Yeah. That." Holy crap on a chip, the centers of his cheeks actually pinked. "We didn't talk a lot, and I know she could be a terror when she wanted to be, but she doesn't deserve what is happening. I hope they find her and I hope she's okay."

"Me too." I obviously wasn't close to her, but that didn't change the fact I prayed she would show up tomorrow alive. "I was also thinking about Gavin—about his car and what they did."

"It's messed up."

"It really is," I said, once again wishing there was something that I could do.

"Maybe after I drop you off at Linds', I'll swing by Gavin's," he suggested. "Talk to him."

Surprised, I stared up at him. That was so going to be an awkward time, but the fact that Jensen was willing to go where he was not wanted to make sure Gavin was okay warmed me in a way very few things could.

That swelling was back, along with the haunting four-letter word I wanted to scream at the top of my lungs. "Thank you." I stretched my neck, kissing the corner of his mouth.

Jensen's eyes held mine for a moment and then moved up my body. He turned his head so our lips lined up. He kissed me gently, and a shudder rolled through me. There was something infinitely tender in the way he coaxed my lips open. My arms looped around his neck as my breath caught in my throat.

The kisses changed and deepened into a slow-burning caress, sending shivers all through my body. When he left my mouth and dropped hot little kisses down my throat, my insides started sweltering. His hand traveled to my hip and my fingers moved through his hair, letting the silky locks sift through my fingers.

A deep sound rumbled up from his chest as his tricky fingers made their way under my shirt. I sucked in a sharp breath as his hand coasted up my side, his thumb smoothing over the cup of my bra.

"God, I feel . . . crazy in the best way when I'm with you," he said in a low voice that sent shivers curling down my spine. "You have no idea how much I missed you—how I hated seeing you with someone else, knowing you should've been with me."

"I felt the same," I whispered, my lips feeling swollen and warm.

Sometimes I couldn't believe that we had made our way back to each other. There were many moments when it didn't feel real. Like it was some kind of fantasy that I would wake up from.

His eyes reminded me of the bluest oceans. "You did?"

I wet my lips, drawing his attention. "I tried not to think about you with Wendy or someone else. It made me jealous and it hurt, because I—" I cut myself off before I said too much.

"You what?" he prodded, moving his thumb in a way that made me really wish we were somewhere more private and we had the whole evening to ourselves.

Forcing a smile, I shook my head. "I'm just happy we are together now."

Jensen studied me for a moment and then kissed the tip of my nose. He lifted himself off of me. Climbing to his feet, he took my hands and hauled me up with him. "We should probably get going."

We straightened up, turned off the lights, and I waited just outside the doors as he locked up. Jensen grabbed my hand, pulling me toward his chest. Over his shoulder, I could see that a couple of the doors to the other rooms were open. My gaze drifted back to his. The expression on his face was serious.

"What?" I asked.

His arms wrapped loosely around me. "I don't like what's going down tonight."

"Me staying with Linds?"

"Yeah." He dropped his forehead to mine. "No one's there but you and her. With everything going on, it worries me."

"I'll be fine." I tapped his cheek with my fingers. "She has an alarm system. It'll be turned on. Besides, everyone—including me—was by themselves when . . . well, when it happened."

"I know, but maybe I should come over, too." He caught my hand, pressing his lips to the tips of my fingers. The tiny, innocent kisses caused my heart to skip a beat. "It could be a really interesting slumber party."

I laughed, pulling my hand free. "Oh my God, you're such a perv. No."

"I wasn't talking about that." He waggled his brows, and on anyone else it would look ridiculous, but he managed to make it look strangely hot. "Although—"

"Don't even finish that sentence."

Laughing softly, he dropped his arm around my shoulder, tucking me against his side as we headed toward the entrance. "But seriously, I would feel better if I was there."

"I know, but Linds and I haven't spent any time together lately. And I even think Heidi is coming over. We need this." I pushed open the door, glancing up at the cloudless sky. "A girls' night."

Jensen still wasn't happy, but he relented when I promised to keep in contact, lock doors and windows, set the alarm, hide the keys and all sharp objects. We swung by my house to grab some clothes and check in with Mom. When he dropped me off in Linds' development, he leaned in, giving me a not so quick kiss that left me rethinking inviting him.

He drew back, his fingers lingering on my cheek. "Text me later, okay?"

"I will." I started to pull away, but then kissed his cheek. "Let me know how things go with Gavin."

"Will do."

I climbed out, grabbing my tote full of clothes and stuff. Giving Jensen a little wave, I headed up Linds' driveway. Her neighborhood was newer and nicer than mine, each house built within the last decade. It had the whole *Stepford Wives* thing going on.

Without looking behind me, I knew Jensen was still at the bottom of the driveway, waiting for me to head inside. As I crossed the neatly trimmed yard, the front door opened.

"Perfect timing," Linds said, stepping aside and holding the door open. "I just ordered pizza. Extra mushrooms."

"You rock."

Linds' gaze flicked over my shoulder. "You know, he's allowed to come in."

"I know, but you and I haven't spent a lot of time together. So no boys allowed."

She shrugged as she closed the door. "Yeah, what happened to that whole being single our senior year? Apparently, I'm the only one following that rule."

My grin turned sheepish. "Sorry, but I . . ."

"I wouldn't turn down Jensen either." Pulling a hair tie off her wrist, she pulled her tight curls up into a ponytail. "He could eat crackers and Chinese food in my bed and I'd be all right with that."

I giggled. "At the same time?"

"Yep." She sat on the arm of the sectional couch. Linds' parents had very minimalistic tastes. Unlike Jensen's house or mine, there was nothing cluttered about it. Everything had a place, and it was either black, white, or beige.

I was always afraid of ruining the furniture.

"So you guys talked it all out?" she asked.

Dropping my bag on the shiny hardwood floor, I filled Linds in on everything, stopping when the pizza arrived, then continuing again as we demolished the large pepperoni and extra mushroom goodness.

"I didn't know about his brother," she said, frowning. "How did none of us know about his brother?"

"I don't know." I rubbed my full belly. "God, I wish I did. I feel so bad for Jensen and his family, having to go through that mostly alone."

"Yeah, but he could've told you what was up. You guys were best friends for so long. So don't feel too guilty." She stood, dropping a black and white checkered pillow on the couch. "I mean, I get why it's not something one would want to broadcast to the world, but he could've told you. It would've saved you a lot of pain."

True, but I hadn't really given him the chance to tell me when it mattered most. There was nothing I could do about that now, and my decision to stop living in the past meant that I had to stop dwelling on it. I had to cut Jensen and myself a break.

"Hey, where's Heidi?" I asked, changing the subject.

She shrugged. "I have no idea. She didn't respond to my text. You know I'm too high strung for her."

I rolled my eyes as I stood. "She's never said that."

Linds crossed her arms.

"Okay, she might have said something like that." Glancing at the time, I sighed. It was already past eight, and I doubted Heidi would come out. "I'll text her, but do you mind if I take a shower real quick? Jensen and I—"

"Worked up a sweat?" Her eyes widened. "Did you guys have sex before you came over?"

"Oh my God, no." I laughed. "We were at the warehouse. The whole self-defense thing."

"Uh-huh. I'm beginning to think the whole self-defense lesson thing is code for sex."

"Whatever." I tossed a pillow at her.

She caught it, grinning. "Yeah. Use my parents' though. My bathroom is a hot mess."

"No surprise there." Smiling at the dirty look she sent my way, I grabbed my bag off the floor. "I like your parents' bathroom anyway. The shower could fit like five people."

"It's sweet, right?" She dropped the pillow on the couch. "I'll go make us some popcorn. And dip. Cheese dip. And you will eat. A lot."

There was always room for cheese dip.

Hurrying up the wide staircase, I headed down the hall toward her parents' master bedroom. The double white doors were open and the room smelled like fresh linen. I stepped into the adjoining bathroom, sighing.

The shower had three separate showerheads.

Heaven.

I sat my bag on the tiled ledge around the Jacuzzi tub and dragged out my shower stuff, fresh clothes, and an old terry cloth robe that reached my thighs. Since I was normally too lazy to towel myself off, I sort of enjoyed dripping dry.

Stripping off my clothes, I rolled them up in a messy ball and shoved them into my tote. I reached through the gap between the wall and the blurred glass doors, turning on the water. I stepped under the multiple jets, barely able to contain a groan of envious pleasure. I could live in this shower; it was that awesome.

I took my time, like I always did when I used her parents' shower, lazily washing the shampoo and body wash off, letting the conditioner soak in longer than necessary.

But there was cheese dip waiting for me.

Tipping my head back under the streaming water, I closed my eyes as the shower did its thing.

I stilled, my fingers in my hair, my eyes wide open.

Under the steady stream of water, I wasn't sure what I'd heard at first, but something had snagged my attention. Lowering my chin and arms, I peered out the glass doors as the water beat down on me. The room was blurred, distorted through the glass.

The bathroom doors were cracked open, leaving a small gap between them. Tiny bumps spread along my flesh. I swear I'd shut them behind me, but it was possible the doors hadn't latched into place. Turning away, I quickly set about rinsing the rest of the conditioner out of my hair, hating how easily I could be rattled.

Not that I doubted anyone would blame me.

The sound came again and my eyes popped wide open as my heart lurched in my chest. The bathroom light flicked off, and I turned to the doors just as a dark blur passed through them. The doors eased shut. The click of the latch was like a crack of thunder.

My heart stopped in my chest.

"Linds?" I called out and waited.

There was no response.

My hand shook as I reached over, turning off the water. My hair was plastered to my back as I opened the shower door. Holding my breath, I quickly scanned the bathroom. "Linds?" I called again, but would she have done this, turning the light off on me? I didn't think so.

Dripping onto the mat, I picked up my robe and quickly slipped it on, belting it at the waist. I crept forward, the tile cool and slippery under my feet. I stood at the door, straining to hear something, anything—there was nothing but silence. Every muscle in my back tensed up as I grabbed the knob and yanked it open.

My heart lurched in my chest as I came face to face with the ghastly white mask, empty black eyeholes, and the open, grotesque red smile.

SEVENTEEN

I JERKED BACK out of shock. He was *here*! Horror poured into my bloodstream like an ice storm.

The mask tilted to the side as it raised a hand, waving its finger back and forth. A gruff tsking sound came from behind the mask.

Then he sprang forward.

I backpedaled, my feet slipping over the wet tile as a scream tore from my throat. A glove covered hand clamped down on my arm. I pulled back, nearly wrenching my arm from its socket.

He roared into the bathroom, a booted foot hitting one of the puddles as I twisted, ripping my arm free. The loss of contact threw him off balance, and his foot slipped on the wet tile. He went down on one knee.

I tore out of the bathroom, gripping the door and slamming it shut. As I whipped around, the doors exploded open behind me. I took another step and arms clamped down on my waist. Before I could even react, I was airborne.

I slammed into the bed, my hip hitting the bedpost. A sheet of soaked hair obscured my vision as pain knocked the air out of my lungs, but instinct was screaming through me, digging out all the time I spent in the warehouse with Jensen.

He was on me, his hands circling my throat and pressing down with his weight. I sunk a good inch or so into the mattress. All I could see was the terrifying smile, the empty eyes, and behind the hood, the frizzy, fake hair. My mouth was wide open, but I couldn't get any air into my lungs.

Panic tried to dig its claws into me, but I refused to cave to the terror. Before he could trap my legs with his, I rolled my hips, lifting my knee. With everything I had in me, I shoved it into his groin.

He grunted as his fingers loosened. Air streamed into my throat, and this time I pulled both my legs up, slamming the heels of my feet into his calves. His weight shifted, and I was able to roll out from underneath him.

I fell off the bed, wheezing as my knees slammed into the floor. I didn't stop. Pushing up, I ran across the bedroom, throwing open the door. My feet smacked off the hardwood floor in the hallway.

"Linds!" I screamed her name over and over, fear amplifying when there was no answer.

Had he done something to her? Was she hurt?

I reached the stairs just as I heard his booted feet connect with the floor behind me. The hairs on my arms rose as I raced down the steps, taking them two at a time. Two steps from the last, my foot slipped and I went down. Catching myself on the banister before I broke my neck, I ignored the screaming pain tearing through my muscles. Straightening, I gained my balance as I reached the foyer.

Weight crashed into me from behind and I went down, my knees and hands smacking the floor. A hand burrowed into my hair, roughly trying to turn me around. I twisted at the waist, brought my knee back, and kicked him in the chest.

He let go, and I launched to my feet. Already on his, he moved around me, blocking the front door. His chest was moving up and down, the hood fallen on broad shoulders, the wig slightly askew.

I *almost* charged him—*almost* went with a punch to the throat, but he reached behind him, brandishing something that glinted in the foyer light.

A knife.

A long, thick, and wickedly sharp knife—the kind serial killers coveted.

Screw that.

Whipping around, I darted for the nearest exit, which was the garage. I screamed for Linds, and I also just screamed. With every step I took I could practically feel the knife slicing through my back, ripping through cloth and flesh.

I slid across the kitchen floor, slamming into the door leading to the garage. Yanking on it, I realized it was locked. My pulse nearing stroke territory, I reached down, turning the little lock. As I opened the door, I glanced over my shoulder.

Clown Face wasn't there.

Not wasting any time, I stepped into the dark garage, letting the door shut behind me. I dragged in a breath, and immediately I started coughing. At first I couldn't make sense of the gas smell, the sound, or why I couldn't breathe. I didn't understand what was happening, and then I did.

The car in the closed garage—a Lincoln sedan that belonged to Linds' mom was running.

I pulled up the loose collar of my robe, coughing into the material as I started to turn away, looking for the button to open the garage door, when I realized the car wasn't empty.

There was a form in the driver's seat.

Eyes starting to burn, I ran to the side, across chilly cement, then cried out in horror.

Slumped behind the wheel was Linds.

Oh my God.

Somehow there was a part of my brain that was still functioning. I knew these fumes had built up in the garage, that it was deadly, that it had been on purpose, and that I needed to get Linds out of the car and into fresh air. I reached for the door. It was locked—so were the passenger and the back doors. A new kind of fear took hold, settling in my gut, adding to the weight already pressing down on my chest. Instinct spun me around, and I rushed back to the wall, slamming my palm down on the button.

Nothing happened.

I hit it again, and again, and again, and still the door wouldn't open.

Hacking now, deep body shaking coughs, I whirled around, searching for anything. Spying a shovel in the shadowy corner, I grabbed it and went back to the car.

Arms shaking, lungs seizing up, I swung it hard, shoving the heavy, sharp edge into the back window. Glass shattered. Tossing the shovel inside the car for nothing more than having a weapon nearby, I crawled through the window.

Tiny pieces of glass snagged my robe, scratching my skin as I wiggled through. Once inside, I grabbed Linds by the shoulders, and it seemed like forever before I was able to move her, shoving her into the passenger seat.

Climbing over the center console, I gripped the steering wheel. The inside of the car was starting to spin, my arms almost too weak to hold up so that I could reach the gearshift. Squeezing my stinging eyes shut, I slid the gear into reverse and slammed my foot on the gas.

The car roared to life, jerking backward, and then the tires squealed in the darkness. It lurched and sped out, hitting the metal garage door. It rattled, but did not give.

God, this could not be happening—this could not be happening.

Hand tingling, I slipped the gears into drive, went forward, and then slammed it back into reverse again. The car roared back, and this time metal and plastic gave way. The car flew into the driveway as the airbag deployed, popping into my face and pushing Linds' body back. White dust clouded everything and, for a moment, I couldn't see. One side of the car went up over a brick flower box and then down before the car coasted to a stop, half on the driveway and half in the grass.

Shoving the air bag down, I dragged in deep gulps of clean, cool night air. Stunned and dizzy from the lack of oxygen, I leaned back against the seat and turned to look at Linds.

She was half in her seat, half against the floor, her head turned away from me. She wasn't moving, and I didn't know if she was alive or . . .

I reached for her, my fingers brushing her clammy skin. "Linds," I croaked. "Linds, wake up."

Nothing happened, and in my foggy thoughts, I knew I should get her out of the car, get her into the clean air. I had to—

There was a knock on the driver's window.

Screaming hoarsely, I twisted around, my stomach tumbling as a familiar face peered in at me.

Brock.

"What the hell is going on?" he asked.

Hands shaking, I hit the unlock button and pushed open the door. I all but fell out, and would've eaten grass and cement if he hadn't caught me. What was he doing here? I tried to think past the pain in my chest and head as he steadied me.

"Ella? Jesus Christ, is that Linds in there?" His voice pitched. "What's going on?"

"What are you doing here?" I asked, stumbling free.

"I live two houses down." He glanced at the wrecked garage door. "I was just getting home. I heard the screams."

He heard the screams, but as no one else had come rushing to help us, did no one else hear? It didn't matter right now. Stumbling around the front of the car, I barely held myself up. "You need to the call the police. *He* was here. I think Linds is hurt—hurt bad."

"What?" He started to lean into the car.

"Call the police!" I shouted until my voice gave out.

"Okay. Okay!" He backed up, pulling a slim phone out of his

back pocket.

I stopped paying attention to him as I reached the passenger door. By some luck, I'd hit the unlock button, and the passenger door sprung open.

I reached for Linds. "Please be okay," I whispered, getting my hands under her arms. "Please, *please* be okay."

Breathing in the fumes had weakened me, and I couldn't lift her. Raising my head, I swiped at the tears. "Please help me."

Brock was beside me in an instant, slipping the phone back into his pocket. "Move out of the way."

I didn't want to, but I did.

"The police are on the way," he said, reaching in and easily scooping Linds up. Her head lolled against his chest like there were no bones or muscles in her neck at all. "I didn't know what to tell them."

When he placed her in the grass, I dropped to my knees beside her, glancing up at the house. Then I placed my hands against her neck, not really sure if I was hitting the right spot, but when I found a pulse, I almost collapsed. "He was here," I said, my voice scratching out of my throat. "He was inside the house. He did this."

"The . . . the guy that attacked you before?" Brock glanced behind me, and I could make out the distinctive hum of voices. "He was here?"

I nodded, folding my hands around Linds'. Turning my attention to her, I held on for dear life. "Please be okay. Please. Please."

It wasn't long at all before the sounds of sirens grew louder, and then there were police covering the lawn, hands pulling me away from Linds as EMTs rushed forward.

"She was in the car—in the garage with the car running," I told them, my mouth dry. Those hands turned me around, and I was suddenly staring up at Shaw.

"Ella, what happened?" he asked.

"He was here—he was inside the house while I was taking a

shower." The story spilled out of me as tears welled, blinding me. "I couldn't get the garage door to open, so I drove the car through the door."

"That was good. That was smart." He started leading me away from where the medics were working on Linds. Another ambulance was pulling up to the house. A crowd was gathering on the sidewalk, their dark forms blurring together.

I dug my feet in, coughing. "Is she okay? Please, tell me she's okay."

"They're doing everything they can." He wrapped an arm around my waist, turning me around. "We need to get you looked at."

"I'm okay," I wheezed.

"Doubtful. You were in that garage, too. And you're bleeding."

I am?

Shaw handed me off to an EMT, and after curt instructions, an oxygen mask was shoved on my face. The EMT, who had spent an ungodly amount of time shining a bright light in my eyes, helped me tighten the belt around my waist. God only knows how many people had gotten a way too personal look at me, but I couldn't bring myself to care.

As the medic inspected the scratches on my knees and hands, Shaw cornered Brock near a Japanese maple tree. Other officers were there, huddled around him. They were demanding to know what he was doing here.

Brock gave them the same answer, but my stomach churned relentlessly. Could be a convenient answer.

But then they were wheeling Linds out, and under the street lamp, her normally deep brown skin was a deep, hideous gray.

"Is she okay?" I asked, moving the mask.

"She's alive." The medic placed the mask back on my face.

I started to lift it again. "I want to go with—"

"You're staying right here." Shaw's head snapped around like the Exorcist. "Sit there, shut up, and suck up the oxygen."

Damn.

I sat there, I shut right up, and I sucked up oxygen until the medic checked my pulse and then pulled the mask off.

"You're lucky," the EMT said, standing up. "Only a few scratches and some bruises. You could be dead."

Not like I needed that wake-up call. "I want to see . . ." I trailed off as one of the deputies came out the front door, carrying the clown mask. I climbed out the back of the ambulance, my legs shaking.

"Whoa." The medic grabbed my arm. "I want you to sit still for a little while longer."

The officer carrying the mask halted in the driveway. "Oh, look, the state boys are finally here."

Within seconds, green uniforms swarmed the front yard. I recognized Trooper Ritter. He took one long look at me before heading toward were Shaw was standing with Brock.

My stomach cramped as the new officers gathered around Brock, and then Shaw broke away, striding toward me.

"How are you feeling?" he asked.

Wrapping my arms around myself, I willed my teeth to stop chattering. "I'm okay, but Linds—"

"They took her to the hospital, and you'll be able to go check on her soon, but I need you to focus on me right now. Okay?" When I nodded, he shifted his stance. "When did Brock show up?"

My gaze darted over to him. "After I drove through the garage door. He knocked . . . he knocked on the car window."

"Did he say why he was out here?"

I licked my lips. They felt impossibly dry. "He said he lives a few houses down. That he heard screaming . . . wait." I took in his shrewd gaze. "Do you think Brock . . . ?"

"I want you to stay here." He clamped a hand down on my shoulder and continued without answering my question. "I'll call your—"

"Don't call my mom," I pleaded. "Please. I don't want her to see me like this—see the garage and all the police. Please. I'm okay, and I don't want her to freak out. *Please.*"

He shifted again, jaw hard. "Okay."

"Can you . . . can you call Jensen?"

Shaw stared at me a moment and then nodded. "Yeah, I can call him." He started to turn and then stopped. "You got some clothes in there?"

"In the bathroom."

"I'll send someone up. Meanwhile, follow me."

I followed him over to where his cruiser was parked. Popping the trunk, he pulled out a dark blanket.

"It's clean," he said, shaking it out. "I promise."

At this point I didn't care if it had been in a stinkbug infested crack house. I stood still as he dropped the blanket over my shoulders. It covered more than the robe. Relieved, I tucked the edges of the blanket close.

I didn't want to stand out here by the flashing lights of the cop cars, too close to the prying eyes of the neighbors. I saw Shaw on his phone, and I hoped he was calling Jensen. He spoke briefly to another deputy who turned and headed up to the open front door.

I shivered.

Had they called Linds' parents yet? I squeezed my eyes shut, rocking back slightly on my numb feet. I should be there with her so that when she woke up she wasn't afraid. And she would wake up. She had to. I couldn't allow myself to think anything else.

A few minutes later, an officer came to stand with me. I didn't recognize him. He was a deputy by the looks of his uniform. I was learning they all wore different colors and oddly shaped hats. He didn't speak, and I realized dumbly that I was probably under guard.

"Holy shit!" yelled a voice from within the garage.

I turned just as a deputy stumbled out, bent at the waist, clasping his knees. He gagged. Someone yelled something. The officer standing with me frowned. "Stay here," he ordered.

He rushed over, joining the cops who were standing at the back of Linds' mom's car. Officers raced back and forth in the driveway, and whatever they were saying was lost in the roaring of the blood in my ears. I stumbled forward, my arms and legs shaking. No one noticed me as I approached the group huddled around the back of the car, the same car Linds had been trapped in, might've died in.

No. Linds was alive. Shaw said as much.

"What's going on?" Brock demanded from where he stood by the tree, but his voice sounded so very far away. "Come on, someone tell me what the hell is going on."

Legs trembling, I crept forward, drawn to whatever it was that had the cops freaking out. An officer stepped aside, turning his head to speak into a microphone attached to his shoulder. "We got a signal eighteen out here. I need the M.E. stat."

I could see around him, see inside the trunk, see what was folded up in there waiting to be found.

"Oh my God," I whispered, my hands rising to my mouth.

"Shit." Shaw spun around and was suddenly in front of me, blocking the view of the trunk, but it was too late. He turned me away, but I'd already seen it.

Monica.

I saw Monica folded into the trunk, her hands tucked under her chin like she was sleeping, and that's how she looked. Peaceful. Asleep. All except for the cardinal shoved into her mouth.

EIGHTEEN

LIGHTNING FLASHED ACROSS the sky, splintering the darkness. A crack of thunder chased after it, so loud and so close that the windows in my bedroom rattled.

"Ella."

I wrapped my arms around my waist as I turned. Jensen stood in the doorway, and I knew he'd been there longer than I realized, standing silent and still like a sentry. He'd been a constant presence since he'd arrived at Linds' house.

I took a step toward him, my legs shaky. I didn't speak and neither did he as he crossed the distance between us. Taking me in his arms, he held me close to his chest, easing some of the chill that had invaded my bones and senses.

Tonight had been one of the worst nights of my life.

Jensen's lips brushed my forehead. "Everyone is downstairs."

It was late, more like early morning, and under normal circumstances, Mom would be flipping out, but tonight was far from normal. The wind picked up and the tree outside rattled like dry bones.

"Gavin showed up," he continued, smoothing a hand down my back. "Heidi's here, too. Your mom made hot chocolate."

I drew back as another flash of lightning tore up the sky. "She'll wake up, right?"

"Yes." Conviction strengthened his voice. He kissed my forehead. "She will."

A coma.

That was what the doctors said. Linds had inhaled too many fumes and her body had shut down. Her parents were with her at the hospital and since she was in intensive care, anyone outside of her family wasn't allowed in her room.

"I still can't believe it. He was in that house. He was in the bathroom when I . . ." I couldn't finish that sentence without wanting to hurl.

Jensen's muscles rolled as he carefully placed his hands on my cheeks and then kissed my forehead. Moments passed before he said a word. "I hate this. I hate that you're in danger, and you are. There's no telling each other anything different." His voice turned deeper, rougher. "This is twice now that he . . . he almost got you."

That was the reality of the situation. There was no more pretending or looking at this statistically. Twice now the . . . thing had come after me.

I took a deep breath. "We should go downstairs."

He nodded, and I started around him, but he caught my hand, stopping me. "Are you okay?"

A weak smile tugged at my lips. "I'm just a little sore. I'll be fine."

"That's not what I mean."

Of course. The poor excuse of a smile faded. "I really don't know what to think or feel. I mean, how am I supposed to feel?"

"Scared? Confused?" His hand slid up to my elbow. "Angry?"

"I feel all of those things." And I had felt them before, after finding Penn, but there had also been a lot of guilt attached to that.

His gaze searched my face intently for a moment and then he nodded once more. Taking my hand in his, we headed downstairs. Mom was in the dining room we rarely used, on the phone with my father. Her voice was tight and she turned away as I walked past, lowering her voice even more.

In the living room, Gavin and Heidi sat on the couch. They both looked up as we entered, Gavin's gaze lingering on our joined hands. I started to pull free, but Jensen wasn't having that.

Jensen sat in the recliner and tugged me down into his lap. He grabbed a cup of untouched cocoa and handed it over to me.

"You look okay," Gavin said, and then winced. "I mean, you don't look like you just went toe to toe with Mike Myers."

My brows rose.

"Okay. None of that came out right." He scrubbed his hand through his hair. "Can I start over?"

"That might be a good idea," Heidi murmured.

"It's okay." I smiled at him. "I'm fine. Just a little bruised up, but Linds . . . she's not okay."

Heidi placed her cup on the coffee table. "And the cops seriously have no suspects?"

"There really hasn't been any evidence left behind." Jensen's hand moved up and down my back as he spoke. "Except . . . well, the bodies."

"How do you know it was a guy?" Heidi asked.

I looked at her sharply and, for some reason, a chill radiated over my skin. I shook my head. "It was a guy. I mean, I don't know of any girls that can pick me up and toss me like a baseball."

Jensen stiffened behind me.

"It's definitely a guy," Gavin said, almost distractedly as he stared at the closed blinds.

"Yeah, most murderous psychos are men." Heidi twisted the end of her braid between her fingers. "At least they are in TV and movies."

I cracked a grin at that, and then sipped my cocoa.

"Something is going on, though," she said, dropping the edges of her hair. "He's totally jumped out of his pattern."

"What?" Gavin frowned.

"'There was a pattern." Heidi straightened when we all looked at her. "What? I can't be the only person who saw this."

"Apparently you are," Jensen said.

"It's really obvious. Or, at least I think it is," she said. "Don't most serial killers follow a pattern? They do in the movies and in books."

Well, *that* was some hardcore proof right there.

"Look. Vee was missing for two weeks, right? The night it marked two weeks, you were attacked. The night of Brock's party. Then Vee's body was found a week later, a few days after Monica went missing. And then, two weeks later, Wendy goes missing and . . . well, Monica is found."

"Holy shit." Jensen straightened a bit. "You're right. The timeline."

She nodded. "But tonight threw the pattern off completely. He went after Ella and tried to kill Linds."

I winced.

"Sorry," she said softly. "But locking someone in a car in a garage with said car running is pretty clear-cut."

"I know." I took another drink, but it soured in my stomach. I placed it aside. "Okay. Let's say there is a pattern. Why would he go off it?"

She shrugged. "I'm not a serial killer, so I really don't know."

"Maybe he's just done with it," Gavin said, shifting his gaze to where I sat.

"Or he's just getting sloppy," Jensen commented.

"I don't think it's that. Maybe he had this grand plan but decided to speed it up. Get it over with. Or maybe . . . maybe he thinks the police are close to finding out who he is."

Jensen leaned around me, frowning. Gavin looked at him for a moment, and something seemed to pass between them. I had no idea what it was, but Gavin looked away with a shrug. "Does the pattern really matter?" he asked. "To me, it's the why behind it all."

The why. That was a big deal. Something Heidi said nagged at me. Two weeks. It kept replaying over and over in my head. Two weeks.

"Maybe he doesn't like girls," Heidi said, delicate brows knitted together. "I mean, he's gone after only girls."

That was pretty scary, but I didn't think it was just that. I glanced up, my eyes meeting Gavin's, and it clicked. I stood suddenly, unable to sit.

"What?" he said, watching me.

I paced to the middle of the room. "Two weeks, right? You know what else took two weeks?" My heart pounded in my chest as I turned to Jensen, and he shook his head. I knew he had an idea of where I was going with this. "Penn."

"What?" Gavin exclaimed.

Heidi looked confused. She'd known about Penn, but she hadn't lived here when all of that went down.

"No, Ella. This has nothing to do with him," Jensen said, leaning forward with his hands on his knees.

"Why would it have to do with him?" asked Heidi.

Taking a quick breath, I filled her in on what had happened—about Brock and his friends and then what . . . what Jensen and I had done. "Two weeks after the party, Penn killed himself. It was exactly two weeks."

"But that could be a coincidence." Heidi wrapped her arms around herself, looking more disturbed than she sounded.

"Could it? I mean, Penn loved cardinals."

"Ella—"

"What?" I cut Jensen off. "It's not impossible."

"Penn is dead," Gavin said, and I swore to God, I wanted to smack someone. "I know you know that, so why do you think it has anything to do with him?"

Shaking my head, I crossed the room and peeked through the blinds. I couldn't see anything but the front porch railing and the hedges, but I knew a cruiser sat on the street. The police said they'd have a presence here. Just in case.

Just in case he tried for a third time.

"Maybe someone wants revenge," I said, turning around to face them. "Look at everyone who has been attacked or gone missing. Vee and Monica teased him in school. I know what I did." My heart thumped heavily as I glanced at Jensen. He looked away, a muscle thrumming along his jaw. "Linds didn't, but she was with me."

"But who would want revenge? His family doesn't live around here anymore," Gavin said. "And to be honest, I think it's awfully convenient that Brock just happened to be outside tonight."

I folded my arms across my chest, shivering. "The police questioned him. They were suspicious, but they let him go."

"That doesn't mean he's not a suspect," Gavin insisted.

Jensen rolled his shoulders as if he was trying to work out a kink. "But if this has to do with Penn—"

"You think that now?" There was no hiding the derision in my voice.

He held up his hands. "I'm not saying I do or I don't, but why would it be Brock? He was a total dick to Penn."

"And yet, you're still friends with him," Gavin commented.

Jensen looked at him blandly but didn't respond.

"Whatever," Gavin muttered.

I ignored them. "Maybe he's doing it because he feels guilty for what he's done."

"Well, if it does have to do with Penn, that just leaves you, Jensen, Brock . . . and who else?" Gavin frowned. "There's someone else."

"Mason," Jensen muttered.

He nodded slowly. "He'd be in danger, too."

"Does it matter why?" Heidi asked suddenly. She stared down at her hands as she spoke. "To me, it doesn't. Because no matter what the reason is, it doesn't justify what's happening. It won't ever change what this person is doing, and I think, in a way, knowing why cheapens the memories of those affected. As if stamping a reason on why someone is murdered somehow changes the fact that they're dead. It doesn't."

Heidi had a point.

Mom showed up after that. It was time for everyone to hit the road. I really didn't like the idea of any of them leaving. I hugged Heidi goodbye.

Gavin stopped at the door and turned to me. I could feel Jensen's eyes on us. "I know it didn't sound like it earlier, but I think you're on to something."

I lowered my voice. "About Penn?"

He nodded, looking over my shoulder. "I don't know how or why, but I . . . I believe you."

I closed my eyes out of relief. At least someone didn't think I was completely crazy. "Thank you."

Gavin started to walk away, but stopped and faced me. "I'm sorry about the way I reacted—about you and Jensen."

The change in subject caught me off guard. "It's okay."

"No, it isn't. It was a douche move on my part. So I'm sorry," he said again. "I'm not going to lie. It sucks thinking of you two together, but I *am* happy for you."

He reached out to squeeze my hand, but I sprung forward and wrapped my arms around his shoulders. I hugged him tight, a move he returned. When I pulled back, I swallowed the knot in my throat. "Be careful."

"You too."

I watched him walk off the porch and down the sidewalk, joining Heidi by the gate. He was going to take her home so she wouldn't be alone. I don't know how long I stood there, but when I finally turned around, Jensen was waiting.

"Your mom said I could stay."

"Downstairs," Mom's voice traveled from the hallway above. "He can stay here, but downstairs."

"Got it." Closing the door, I turned to Jensen. He was leaning against the archway that led into the living room, his hands in his pockets. I lowered my voice as I approached him. "You think I'm crazy, don't you?"

"I've always thought you were a little cray-cray."

My eyes narrowed.

He flashed a half grin. "I don't think you're crazy, Ella. I just don't know what to think about all of this. I mean, Penn?" He laughed under his breath, but there wasn't any humor to it. "It's like we're dealing with something that's not flesh and blood."

"Sometimes I wonder if we are," I admitted quietly. "There's something almost inhuman about it. Like there is no humanity there, behind that mask. I mean, I know it's a living, breathing person and all, but how can someone do what he's doing?"

"I don't know."

And I wondered if we'd ever know, or if we'd have a chance to find out before he picked us off, one by one.

I shuddered, knowing that was a terrible way to look at this. "I'll get you some blankets and stuff."

"I'll be waiting."

Turning, I hurried up the stairs, not surprised to find my mom waiting outside of her bedroom. In her arms were blankets and a pillow. She'd been amazing through all of this, but I knew her. I knew none of this could be easy.

Hell, how could it be easy for anyone?

I slowed down as I approached her.

"I'm okay with him being here," she said, pinning me with the 'parent' look Dad could never perfect. "Frankly, I'm only allowing it because I trust both of you, and I know it makes you feel better knowing he's here, but I'm serious. He stays downstairs and you stay upstairs."

If Mom only knew . . .

"Okay. We'll behave." I took the stack from her. "Thank you."

She patted my shoulder. "Take this down to him and then get

your butt back up here. And tomorrow we need to talk about other arrangements."

"Other arrangements?"

"Tomorrow."

I hid my groan. I knew what the other arrangements would be. Sending me to stay with my dad. There was nothing I could do about that right now.

I carried the pillow and blankets to where Jensen waited on the couch. Dropping them on the arm, I smiled slightly. "Here you go."

He tilted his head back. "I can sneak up once your mom goes to bed."

"I don't think that's a great idea since she knows you're here," I pointed out.

"Boo." He took my hand, threading his fingers through mine. "A kiss before I say goodnight?"

I let him pull me down, and when his lips pressed against mine, the swelling pressure in my chest returned. The kiss was sweet and slow, but as his hands settled on my hips and slid up, stopping below my chest, it became stronger, deeper. When he kissed me, it was easy to forget the bad stuff, to pretend that everything was okay.

Those kisses had the power of building their own little world and blocking out everything else, but we weren't in our own bubble. I knew Mom was probably waiting upstairs.

"That's a perfect kind of goodnight," I murmured against his lips when I pulled back.

"But it doesn't make you want to say goodnight, does it?" He kissed the corner of my lip, and his breath was warm, tantalizing. "You better head up there before your mom kicks me out."

Mom would have a coronary if she came downstairs in the morning and saw us snuggled together. Then again, considering all that had happened, I wasn't sure if she'd be that concerned about it.

But I wasn't willing to take that risk.

I wanted Jensen here, and not just because I felt safer knowing he was nearby, but because I hoped he was safer too. If we were right about whoever was behind this having gone off his own pattern, and if I was right and it did have to do with Penn, then Jensen was in as much danger as I was.

"Goodnight," I said, kissing his cheek, but as I tried to stand, he held on. "What?"

"Can I ask you for a favor and you won't get mad at me?"

"It depends."

He leaned back against the couch. "I want you to steer clear of Gavin."

My brows arched. "What?"

"It's not because of jealousy or any crap like that."

I stared at him. "If it's not jealousy, then what is it? Wait. You don't think he's responsible for any of this." I drew back, eyeing him. "We've known Gavin since we were kids, Jensen."

"I know, but . . . you trust me, right?"

"Of course."

"And I trust you," he said, holding my hand and placing it against his chest. "But I don't trust anyone else right now, because it seriously could be anyone at this point. And that scares the shit out of me. Because it could be someone we trust."

THEN

PENN SQUARED HIS *shoulders and smiled wide. The glassiness of his eyes faded and I let out the breath I was holding.* "It really isn't a big deal, Ella."

He was lying. If it wasn't a big deal, his eyes wouldn't be so shiny. Guilt was like a pool of churning acid in my stomach. I'd never really experienced that feeling before, not to this extreme. I didn't like it.

"Can you and Jensen just forget about it?" He stood up from where he had been perched on his bed and picked up a large, colorful book about birds. "Because he's apologized like ten times since Monday."

I bit my lip, resisting the urge to squirm. "It's because we do feel bad. And we really did plan on coming, but—"

Penn held the book to his chest and closed his eyes. "I know. You guys feel sorry. That's all that matters. And it's not a big deal. It's not like someone died because you didn't come to my party." He laughed and opened his eyes. The shininess was completely gone. He smiled as he gave me a lopsided shrug. "Everything is okay."

NINETEEN

IT COULD BE anyone.

Those words haunted me over the weekend, even though I spent most of it trying to do normal things after checking in with Linds' parents. She still hadn't woken up and there had been no change in her status.

I didn't know what I'd do if Linds didn't wake up. It hurt, and it was too scary to even consider that. All I could do was tell myself that wouldn't be the case. She would wake up, and she would be Linds again.

Luckily, Mom hadn't discussed other 'arrangements' yet. Not that I was totally against staying with my dad, but I didn't want Mom to be alone.

After checking in with his parents on Saturday morning, and then again on Sunday, Jensen had returned, and we'd spent the better part of the day curled up on the couch watching the DVDs of Supernatural he'd brought with him. But even the Winchester brothers couldn't distract me from the direction my thoughts were taking.

It could be anyone.

Jensen was right. Over the course of the day, I mentally went over the list of suspects. I ruled out any females, even though Ms.

Reed had been the one to send me to the storage room and upstairs at the farmhouse. I'd *felt* the attacker. It was a man or an extremely masculine woman with absolutely no chest to speak of.

Seriously unlikely.

I knew it couldn't be Gavin. That would be like thinking it was Jensen. There was no way you could grow up with someone and not know they were hiding the fact they were a serial killer.

At least I hoped so.

So who did that leave? Brock? It just didn't make sense for it to be him unless it had nothing to do with Penn or guilt was driving him.

When we were halfway through season three of Supernatural, Mom ran out to the grocery store to pick up something for dinner and Jensen shifted. Somehow I ended up under him.

"What are you doing?" I folded my hands together under my chest, attempting to behave.

Shifting his weight onto the arm beside my head, he arched a brow at me. "You haven't been paying attention to the TV at all."

He was too damn observant sometimes. "Yes, I have."

"Uh-uh. Your body has been as tight as a bowstring this entire time. I'm afraid you're going to snap in half. Talk to me."

My eyes met his and I sighed. "Why do you have to be so observant?"

"I'm just that skilled."

A grin pulled at my lips and then disappeared. "I think we need to warn Mason."

Jensen didn't respond.

"I know you don't think it has anything to do with Penn. Maybe it doesn't," I said. "But I'd feel better if we warned Mason. Maybe even Brock."

He sat up, pulling me into a sitting position along with him. "And it would make you feel better to . . . warn them?"

Brushing the hair out of my face, I nodded. "It would."

"Okay." He smacked his hands down on his knees. "We can do

it tomorrow at school. I can get Mason at—"

I jumped at the sudden shrill ringing of the house phone traveling from the kitchen. Jensen groaned. "It's probably someone from one of the news stations."

They'd been calling all weekend, and I knew it was only a matter of time before they were camped out in front of my house. Teenagers getting attacked and murdered was big news. I got that, even understood the attention, but I didn't understand what the reporters thought I could say to them. The police had informed me quite bluntly to keep my mouth shut and not speak to the media. Not that I had any desire to mug it up for the camera.

Frowning, I stood and hurried into the kitchen, expecting it to be yet another reporter that had gotten ahold of our home phone number. The damn thing never rang before all of this happened.

Picking up the receiver, I cleared my throat. "Hello?"

Silence greeted me.

"Hello?" I turned, spying Jensen standing in the doorway. I shrugged and raised my brows. "Anybody there? Look, if this is a reporter, I don't have anything to say. Nothing at all."

Jensen frowned. "Just hang up."

Sounded like a good plan. I started to move the phone away from my ear when I heard it—a guttural whisper that raised the tiny hairs on my arms, barely audible over the sudden rush of static.

"*Murderer* . . ."

Ice drenched my veins and I froze. "What?"

The click of the call disconnecting was like a gunshot in my ear. I stood there, eyes wide as Jensen crossed the distance between us. He took the phone out of my suddenly limp fingers.

"Hello?" He scowled as he lowered the phone. "No one is there. Did someone say something?"

"I don't know." I wrapped my arms around myself. "I thought I heard someone say 'murderer.'"

A cold mask of anger slipped over Jensen's face as he glanced down at the phone. He hit a button. "It says unknown caller. The number is probably blocked."

"I don't know if I even heard correctly." I left the kitchen, brushing past Jensen. Stopping at the window, I parted the blinds. Like before, I couldn't see the street, but I wondered if the police were out there.

Murderer.

I shivered as Jensen came up behind me, wrapping his arms around my waist. "You're not—" he started.

"I know." And I really did. All those years of carrying so much heavy guilt now seemed so pointless, and I wasn't going to let someone else dump that on me again.

SCHOOL ON MONDAY morning sucked more than it normally did. It had rained all the way to school, and the halls of the building felt unnaturally cold and unwelcoming.

Unwelcoming except for the crisis unit that seemed to be permanently parked in the school, which meant I spent most of third period meeting with grief counselors.

A whole lot of awkward ensued.

Cops were crawling all over the school, both local and federal, and there were no more quick glimpses of them. There was no mistaking their presence. Media was camped outside, interviewing any student that got within grabbing distance of them. The attention, the whole atmosphere was surreal.

After eating a quick lunch with Jensen and Heidi, I waited out in the hallway while Jensen finagled Mason away from the ever-dwindling table he sat at. Brock was noticeably absent, something that had my stomach twisting.

Was he skipping school?

Or had he gone missing?

I leaned against the wall beside the trophy case, wondering at what point did I go from worrying if a kid didn't show up for class if that meant something bad had happened to them?

Jensen rounded the corner, walking beside a surprisingly mellow looking Mason. His blond hair was pulled back in a short ponytail, his hands shoved deep into his ripped-up jeans.

He saw me and frowned. "What's up?"

I straightened, glancing at Jensen, who thrust a hand through his hair. I started to just put it out there, but it was Jensen who spoke first.

"Where's Brock?" he asked.

Mason shrugged. "I don't know. Haven't heard from him since Saturday. He was worried about the shit that happened with Linds and what the police thought. He's probably hiding out at home."

I seriously hoped so. "After everything that has happened, I think you have to be careful."

He looked at me, and then his gaze flipped to Jensen. "I have to be careful?"

"Yes." I nodded just in case he didn't understand me. Taking a deep breath, I decided to just get it over with. "Remember Penn?"

Mason's brows flew up. "That nerdy little kid that offed himself a few years back?"

My hands curled into fists. "His name was Penn—"

"Yeah, I remember." Mason glanced behind him quickly, into the cafeteria. "What about him?"

"I don't know if you've noticed this or not, but everyone, with the exception of Linds, who has been attacked, had something to do with Penn."

He pulled his hands out of his pockets, brushing a strand of hair back from his face. "Yeah, like who?"

"Vee, Wendy, and Monica all picked on Penn." Jensen folded his arms. "So did Brock, and so did you."

A confused smile appeared on Mason's face as he glanced back and forth at us. "So?"

My brows rose. How many brain cells did this boy burn on a regular basis? "So? What we're trying to say is we think the killer is going after people who picked on Penn. That means you and Brock . . . wherever he is . . . could be in danger."

Mason opened his mouth, looked at Jensen, who arched a brow at him, and then looked back at me. He laughed. "Are you fucking crazy?"

Jensen spun so quickly that he was a blur. Slamming his hands into Mason's shoulders, he pushed him into the wall. "You might want to rethink that statement."

My eyes widened. "Jensen!"

"What?" Mason raised his hands. "That's completely—"

His hands curled into the front of Mason's shirt. "I'm serious. Think very carefully about what you say next."

"All I'm saying is who thinks about that Penn kid?" Blood drained from Mason's face. "No one does anymore."

No one thinks about Penn anymore? God, the well of sadness that opened up in my chest was almost too much. I grabbed Jensen's arm because it really looked like he was about to punch Mason.

"Come on," I said, shaking my head, done with this.

Jensen slowly let go of Mason, and as he turned, dropping his arm around my shoulders, his eyes glittered.

Mason pushed off the wall and backed away. "Look, I'm not trying to be ignorant. Just Penn? That's crazy."

"Shut up, Mason." Then to me, Jensen asked, "You okay?"

I nodded. I did what I felt I needed to do, and I didn't care if he thought I was a lunatic. I warned Mason, and now it was up to him to take it seriously. I really hoped he didn't have to.

AFTER THE SOMEWHAT disastrous and embarrassing attempt at warning Mason, the school day ended with no more drama llama visitations, and Jensen and I headed to my house.

"I don't regret saying something," I said as he turned onto my street.

He glanced at me. "Well, I regret not punching him in the face."

My lips twitched. "Sorry. I couldn't let that happen."

"I'm sure I'll get another opportunity," he muttered, squinting at the windshield.

I let out a low breath as we pulled to a stop in front of my house, behind my lonesome Jetta. Mom wasn't home yet, wouldn't be for several hours. When he turned off the engine, I didn't move. At least there were no reporters hiding in the bushes.

"Do you think he's got Brock or . . . ?" I trailed off, unable to finish the sentence.

Jensen sat back, clenching the keys in his hand. "Or Brock made a run for it because the police are on to him?"

I nodded.

"I don't know, but if it is him?" Jensen shook his head. "Besides the fact that it's messed up in so many different ways that I can't even think about it right now, it might be a good thing. Because if it is him and he's hit the road, then you're safe."

"So are you."

He tilted his head to the side. "I'm not worried about me."

I frowned. "You should be. We all should be worried."

"I'm too worried about you to really give it a thought."

"While that's sweet and all, I kind of want to punch you in the face."

Jensen laughed. "Wow."

"I don't want you to do something careless and put yourself in danger." I leaned over and kissed his cheek. "And I really don't want to punch you in the face, but if you do something dumb and get hurt, I'm going to, and you taught me how to punch. So it'll hurt. Okay?"

He chuckled again. "Okay. You ready to head in?"

"Yep." I reached back and grabbed my bookbag. "You hungry?"

"Always."

I climbed out and waited for him to join me, and then we hurried down the walkway. The dark, fat clouds looked ready to burst at any second. "I think we have some leftover pizza from last night."

"Perfect."

I took another step, and a fat drop of cold rain landed on my nose. "Crap."

Halfway to the porch, we broke into a run, but we weren't quick enough. The clouds ripped open and chilly rain poured down on us, soaking my shirt by the time we reached shelter.

"Oh my God," I gasped, slopping my wet hair out of my face. "That is cold."

"Cold?" His gaze hit below my neck. "I really don't feel cold at all."

My gaze followed his and my cheeks heated. I slapped his chest. "You're such a dog."

Shoving his hair back from his forehead, he grinned. "You love me."

The air caught in my throat as my gaze locked with his. *You love me.* The rightness of those three words were shattering, the truth undeniable. I loved Jensen. I had loved Jensen for years. That was no big surprise, but I was *in* love with him too.

His grin started to fade. "What are you staring at? Can you see my nipples through my shirt? I doubt mine are as—"

"No." I flushed, turning away as I dug my keys out of my bag. "I'm not staring at anything."

"You were."

I rolled my eyes as I shoved the key in the lock.

Jensen stepped right up behind me, pressing his fingertips lightly into my hips. "Then what were you thinking?"

"I wasn't thinking anything."

His breath was warm against my neck. "You're such a terrible liar."

Opening the door, I escaped inside, putting space between us. "You're terribly annoying."

Jensen laughed as I dropped my bag inside. "Where are you going?"

I stopped at the base of the stairs. "I'm going to go get changed." And recollect my scattered, overly emotional thoughts. I knew Jensen cared about me. Deeply. But love? He hadn't said that and we'd just gotten together.

But we'd known each other forever.

His lashes lowered, giving his eyes a heavy look. "Need help?"

I started to tell him no, but my heart leaped and parts of my body coiled tightly. I wet my suddenly dry lips. I really needed to say no. Mom wouldn't be home for a couple of hours, but . . ."Sure."

Oh goodness.

Jensen blinked once and then twice, staring at me like he honestly hadn't expected me to say yes. He cleared his throat, extending his arm. "I have no words. After you."

Laughing loudly, I whirled around and headed up the stairs. The laugh . . . God, it felt good. That moment of feeling free, I clung to it, but when I reached the landing and turned to see Jensen a step below me, I swallowed hard.

"You know." His voice was deeper than normal. "That shirt is going to have to go first. It's soaked."

My hands opened and closed at my sides. "It *is* wet."

"Glad we're on the same page with that." His eyes were fastened on mine as he came up the last step, stopping in front of me. "Need help?"

It was like someone else was in control of my body. I nodded.

He hesitated for a moment. "Thank you," he said in a low voice, and I didn't understand what he was thanking me for. He brushed my wet hair back from my shoulders. "Do you have any idea what you do to me?"

My throat dried and I shook my head.

Jensen didn't follow up on that statement as he slipped his hands under the hem of my wet shirt. As he lifted it up over my head, my heart felt like it stopped beating in my chest. He made a deep sound in the back of his throat as he draped my shirt over the railing.

I closed my eyes and forced myself to breathe normally so I didn't end up passing out because that would surely be a mood killer. But it was hard. I was standing before him in my jeans and bra, and I knew the latter, being as damp as it was, showed more than it probably covered.

"You're beautiful."

My eyes flew open. His stare was latched on to my face which was not where I thought it would be. My throat closed up, and I stood still as the tips of his fingers skimmed the sides of my stomach, running all the way up to my throat and then my cheeks. Who knew such a light touch could cause my knees to shake?

He tilted my head back and brushed his lips against mine. It was quick and soft, but it zinged all the way to my toes. He brushed the back of his fingers across my cheeks, sweeping up any lingering drops of rain, and then his lips found mine again, taking it deeper and longer.

His lips didn't leave mine as his hands skated back down, sending a series of shivers through my body. My fingers found the damp ends of his hair as his hands settled on my hips. Without breaking contact, he lifted me up. His lips caught a surprised gasp as I wrapped my legs around his waist.

I leaned into him, sliding my fingers through his hair. The feel of his damp shirt against my flushed skin sent a riot of sensations through me.

Jensen walked us to my bedroom. I didn't know what was going to happen once we were inside, but I was curious—beyond curious. I wanted to know. I wanted to experience this with him.

I wanted to feel alive.

And I wanted to feel that with him and only him.

My bedroom door was cracked open, and when my back bumped into it, it drifted the rest of the way. Kissing me deeply, he eased my legs off his waist and my feet to the floor.

He lifted his mouth from mine. "Ella, I want you."

Air caught in my throat. "I can tell."

He rested his forehead against mine. "I'm sure you can." He dropped his trembling hands to my waist. "But I don't want to rush you. I mean, I'm ready. I've *been* ready, but I want you to be—"

"I'm ready," I said, and the moment I said it, I knew it was true.

Jensen drew back and his eyes were wide. "Are you . . . are you sure? We don't have to."

"I know we don't." Taking a deep breath, I unhooked the first button on my jeans and pulled down the zipper. "But I'm sure."

Jensen briefly closed his eyes as he made this deep sound and then he clasped my cheeks. Tilting my head back, he kissed me. There was nothing slow or soft about it. I felt branded, scorched all the way through.

He pulled away to ask, "Do you have a condom? I don't."

"I do," I admitted. He drew back, surprise filling his features. Biting down on my lip, I shrugged. "When Gavin and I were together, I got some just in case. Well, Linds got me some." I shook my head. "It doesn't matter. I have some."

"It's okay. You don't need to explain." He smiled. "I'm just glad you have them."

Turning, I went to the nightstand and opened the bottom drawer. I rooted around under the socks until I found the small box. I pulled out a wrapper without looking at it. Linds had gotten me one of the boxes that had a ton of different kinds—kinds I almost died looking at. I laid it on the nightstand and then looked at Jensen.

He stepped forward again, closing the small distance between us. I backed up until I felt the bed behind me. My heart was racing as I reached down and wrapped my fingers around the hem of his wet shirt. Wordlessly, he lifted his arms. I pulled his shirt off as he toed off his sneakers and socks. My shoes came off next, and then I undid his belt, my fingers trembling as I pulled it through the loops. Our jeans hit the floor.

Jensen unhooked my bra, carefully dragging the straps down my arms. The moment that hit the floor, we were chest to chest. I sucked in an unsteady breath at the feeling.

"If you want to stop at any moment, you tell me." One arm circled my waist. "Okay?"

"Okay," I whispered.

Cupping the back of my neck, Jensen guided me onto my back. My damp hair spread out along the pillows, and he climbed over me, slowly lowering his body onto mine, his hips settling between my thighs.

Everything slowed down.

The kissing. The touching. The way we started to explore each other. It started with just the tips of my fingers grazing over his taut skin, and then I grew braver and it was my entire hands. He did the same, easing slightly to the side so we had room. Every place he touched, it felt like he was starting a fire. My breasts. My stomach. And then lower, and he touched me in a way that had my back pressing down into the mattress and my hips lifting up. When the last of our clothing ended up on the floor, it was almost too much and still not enough. Not even when we were chest to chest again, hip to hip with nothing between us. Not when we started moving and rocking against one another. Not when the way we started clenching at each other sped up, becoming less careful.

Then, with our breaths coming in short pants, mingling together, and our bodies trembling against one another, we broke apart. Jensen grabbed the silver foil from the nightstand, and I watched him slide it on, my pulse pounding erratically.

"Remember," he said in a thick voice that stretched my nerve endings raw. "We can stop at any moment."

"I know." I spread my hand across his smooth jaw. "I trust you."

Those eyes were like azure jewels, and then . . . then we started all over again. The kisses though, they were infinitely more, and when his hand left me, and I was really, really ready, we came together.

There was pain.

A sharp twinge radiated down my legs. There was no stopping the gasp, and the concern that filled Jensen's eyes nearly brought tears to mine. He waited. We waited. Jensen kissed my forehead, the tip of my nose, and the lids of my eyes. He kissed the corners of my lips and the space just below my ear.

And then, slowly, there was no pain.

There was something else. Something fulfilling and empty all at the same time. Something that drove both of us. Something that guided our hips, our hands, and our mouths. Something that was dangerously wild and beautifully out of control.

That spinning feeling, the sensation of a coil tightening and tightening deep within me returned, and I chased it again, lifting my hips and legs. I held him tight, seeking his mouth as the tension broke, lashing out and throwing me over the edge, taking Jensen with me.

When it was over, our bodies were slick and the pounding of our hearts were slow to calm.

Jensen eased away as he palmed my cheek. "Are you okay?" he asked, his voice rough. Every so often, a tremor would course through his hand, then his entire body. It was the same with me—brief, sweet aftershocks.

Swallowing, I nodded then whispered, "Yes."

He smoothed his thumb along my lower lip. "It didn't hurt . . . too much?"

"No." I forced my eyes open and smiled. "It was . . . it was perfect."

His smile stretched across his face. "Yeah. Yeah, it was."

Tipping my chin down, I watched him through lowered lashes as he shifted onto his side next to me. His skin was flushed, his features soft in a way I'd never seen them before. He still held my cheek, and we didn't speak for a long time.

I rolled onto my side, leaning over and kissing the space above his chest. "I think I need to shower," I said, feeling my cheeks heat.

"Yeah?" He reached up, tucking my hair back behind my ear. "Want company?"

I nodded.

A lopsided grin formed. "Let me grab our clothes."

Jensen was the first to get up, and while he picked our clothes up off the floor, I tried to calmly walk into the bathroom and not run since I was completely naked. I had been naked, but being naked on the bed was different than prancing around the room naked.

I'd just turned on the shower when Jensen entered the bathroom behind me, closing the door. He dropped our clothes into a pile and then walked up, wrapping his arms around me from behind. He kissed my cheek, and my eyes drifted closed at the feel of him against me.

I smiled.

I'd never showered with a boy before. Obviously. Before today I would've thought it would be weird and awkward, and when we first stepped into the shower and bumped into each other, it *was* awkward.

But I was comfortable with Jensen.

We wouldn't have done what we just did if I hadn't been.

The shower took a little longer than it should've. We got distracted with each other, kissing and indulging in a more slippery exploration that was stirring up that swollen feeling again.

But I knew we were running out of time. "Mom will be home soon," I said, my voice thick. "We should . . ."

"Yeah." He kissed me one more time. "We should start behaving."

A small grin appeared on my lips, because I doubted Jensen knew how to behave. We rinsed off the last of the body wash and then I stepped out, grabbing a towel since I had no idea where my robe was.

Changing into my clothes took a while too, because I couldn't stop watching Jensen. He was just . . . yeah. Wow.

It was only once he was completely dressed that I realized I'd forgotten to grab a shirt, so I was left in my bra and jeans once again.

And that seemed to really please him. "I am not complaining," he said.

"Of course not."

Grinning, he wrapping his arms around me and started backing me up. "What we just shared? I . . . I really don't have words for it," he said. "I just want you to know that it meant a lot to me."

I stared up at him.

He reached around and opened the bathroom door. Steam crawled out into the bedroom as cold air rushed to greet my damp back. "I've never really felt like that before," he said, and that faint flush was back, creeping over his cheeks in a way I found extremely adorable. "You have to know that I—*Christ*."

The shock of the word spun me out of my haze. Jensen wasn't staring at me, his attention was focused behind me. I started to turn, but his arms folded around my back, pressing me against his chest so tightly I could barely move.

"No," he said. "*No*."

"What?" My pulse picked up as unease took root in the pit of my stomach. I tried to turn again, but it was impossible to break his hold.

Jensen started backing up, and I managed to slide my hands between us. I pushed hard against his chest. "Ella!"

I was able to twist around enough to see my bedroom. My gaze darted to the rumpled blankets and then to the foot of my bed. My horrified gaze rose to the ceiling fan.

A body hung from the fan, arms and legs limp at its sides. The ghastly white mask was secured in place, a red frizzy wig covering its head.

My mouth worked soundlessly as I pressed back against Jensen. I got hung up on its neck, how the head hung at an unnatural angle, and what was wrapped around it.

TWENTY

JENSEN PULLED ME out of my bedroom and down the hall. Blood buzzed in my ears and my heart was beating too fast. I didn't get a good look at the body, but I knew it was a guy.

There was a guy hanging in my bedroom.

"He's been in here," I said, and it was stupid, because it was obvious, but I couldn't stop saying it. "He's been in here again, while we were . . . oh God."

"I know." Jensen snatched my shirt off the banister, shoving it into my hands. "Get this on."

My hands shook as I dragged it over my head, wincing as the cool, damp cloth clung to my skin. There was a good chance it was inside out, but I didn't care. We started downstairs, but I stopped, turning to where the house phone sat on a small table in the hall outside the main bathroom.

"Wait." I picked up the cordless phone, hitting the button. A busy signal greeted me. "What the . . . ?"

My stomach dropped.

The other receiver, the one downstairs, had to be off the hook.

"It doesn't matter. My cell is in my truck. Or we can grab yours from your bag."

I dropped the cordless phone and hurried down the steps, feeling like at any given moment, a giant half spider, half human would try to snatch me from behind.

Before we hit the foyer, Jensen stopped and peered around the railing, toward the living room, and then did the same on the other side, looking into the dining room. He snatched up my bag and then grabbed my hand again.

As we ran out of the house, he dug out my phone and called the police. He spoke to them as he stowed me away in the truck, and then climbed into the other side. "We'll stay out front. Okay." He disconnected the call and handed the phone over. "They're on their way."

I dropped my phone in my lap, staring out the window. The rain had stopped.

"Oh my God . . ." I pressed my hands to my face, bending over. "Who do you think it was?"

He squeezed my shoulder. "I don't know, but Brock . . ."

Brock was missing, meaning he could've just gone from suspect to victim in a nanosecond. My fingers curled into my hair as my stomach cramped with nausea. The afternoon had gone from something wonderful to a horror show in a matter of seconds.

And who knew how long he'd been in the house. He could've been hiding while Jensen and I were in the bedroom. He could've been . . . could've been watching.

My stomach twisted.

"It'll be okay," Jensen said, and he said it again and again.

I looked up, lowering my hands, and my gaze met his. "Someone is hanging in my bedroom. This stuff is not coincidental."

"I know." He removed his hand as he tipped his head against the headrest, staring out the window.

"And someone was in there while we were—"

"I know," he repeated, jaw tight.

The police showed up then, parking their cruiser in front of

Jensen's truck, blocking him in. A county one appeared behind us. I twisted around, recognizing Shaw. Jensen and I glanced at each other and climbed out.

The city officer reached us first. "There's a . . . a body hanging in my bedroom," I said. "I don't know who it is."

"Stay here." The officer's face was stoic as he turned to Shaw. "You ready?"

Shaw looked at us like he wanted to lock us up in one of those oxygen bubbles before he nodded. Then they disappeared into the house.

Wrapping his arms around me, Jensen pulled me against his chest. I went, closing my eyes. "I'm going to have to call Mom."

"I can do it for you."

I closed my eyes. "I need to. I don't want her to hear your voice and think something's happened."

Jensen dropped his chin to the top of my head and fell quiet as he held me. I opened my eyes, trying to see the body in the room, but the details were too fuzzy.

"Shaw's coming out," he said.

I turned in his arms, my chest locking up. The look on his face made me not want to ask, but I had to. "Who is it?"

He stepped in front of us and took off his hat. Running his hand over his head, he frowned. "It's not . . . it's not anyone."

Confusion swamped me. "What do you mean?"

Shaw lowered his arm. "It was fake—a dummy. Probably a prop left over from the Halloween thing you guys were working on."

"Fake?" I whispered. My brain did not comprehend the word.

Jensen tipped his head back, blowing out a deep breath. "Thank God."

"Obviously someone was trying to scare you," he went on, lowering the volume of his radio. "And it worked. They must have gotten in through your window. Officer Brandis is up there. We're going to get a crime unit out here to dust for prints, and then we'll take the damn thing down."

I stepped away from Jensen, letting the words sink in as I tugged my still damp hair back from my face. Fake. Someone had broken into my house to hang a fake person.

I didn't even know what to do with that.

"It could be a prank, but with the recent events I think you should find someone else to stay with," he suggested.

"I think that's a good idea." Jensen placed his arm over my shoulders. "You could stay with your dad."

Shaw nodded. "I think that would be a great idea. He lives in town?"

"On the other side, near Shepherdstown. In the development . . ." As Jensen explained, my attention drifted toward the house.

The body had been fake.

But the warning was clear.

"BUT MOM—"

She placed her hands on her hips. "I don't want you staying another night in this house. I want you at your father's."

I shifted my weight. "But what about you?"

"I'm going to head back to the office. I'm going to get someone out here tomorrow with an alarm, and then I'm going to stay with my sister." She paused, frowning. "And I think I'm going to apply for a gun permit."

My lips pursed. "But—"

"Honey, I can't stay at your father's and I don't want you in a hotel room. No more arguing. Get your stuff."

I was seconds away from stomping my feet. I wanted to stay with my mom. I wanted her, but that wasn't happening. So I resorted to pouting.

She ignored that. "Her father won't get home until eight." Mom glanced at Jensen, who was sitting quietly on the recliner, minding his own business. It was like she had decided he'd be my babysitter. If she knew what had gone down this afternoon, he would probably be the last person she trusted around me. "Neither will Rose."

"I'll stay with her."

"Good." She shot me a look that said get moving.

I sighed. Jensen headed upstairs with me. An officer was still in my bedroom, messing with the window. Thank God the dummy had been pulled down and removed. I still hesitated at the door.

I had no idea how I'd ever sleep in this room again.

Or this house.

"Let's get this over with," Jensen said, eyeing the officer.

Feeling out of it, I grabbed a tote from my closet and started shoving clothes into the bag. Every so often, a tremor shook me. I felt kind of numb, and I felt too much. Anger. Fear. Confusion. More anger.

I wanted this to be over.

Grabbing a couple of sweaters, I turned away from the closet as the hangers rocked back and forth.

I wanted to know who was doing this.

Bending down, I grabbed some socks, and then I moved on to stashing undies into my bag.

I wanted to know why this was happening.

Except there were no answers, and the police had no idea who or why someone was doing this or when it would be over. No one even knew if Brock was on the run or dead. No one knew anything.

I rose, my gaze falling to the bed, to the messy sheets. What Jensen and I had done felt like hours ago, another lifetime ago.

"I'm done," I said, shoving my clothes into the bag.

Jensen arched a brow. "Are you sure? Any other clothes you want to punch?"

"Maybe."

One side of his mouth quirked. "Well, don't let me stop you."

I picked up my tote from the bed, slinging it over my shoulder.

As we left the room, I glanced up at the fan and then to the window. No matter how any of this turned out, things would never, ever be the same again.

And my blood boiled because of that.

I left my room and tried not to kick a wall as I did so. The cordless phone was still off the charger in the hall. I placed it back in its holder. Who knew why the phone in the kitchen had been taken off the receiver. Just some other way to mess with our heads.

"We can go to my house for a little while. Mom and Dad won't be home till late. Both are at the office," he said as we headed down the stairs.

"Okay." I breathed out. "That'll be fine."

He stared at me when we hit the foyer and then nodded. Turning, I walked into the kitchen and said goodbye to Mom. She promised not to hang around the house too long. I hugged her twice before I left.

It felt kind of lame driving the three blocks to Jensen's house. Overcast clouds looked ready to dump rain again. I left my tote in his truck and slid out of the seat, closing the door behind me. I looked over the yard, biting my lip. Thick hedges blocked the street, but I couldn't shake the feeling of being watched.

Could be something.

Could be paranoia.

We passed under the old black walnut tree, watching so we didn't step on any of the shells. Jensen fished out his keys. "Stick close to me. I want to check out the house."

My stomach did a flip. "You think he could be here?"

"I don't think so, but I want to be careful."

That was smart. Come to think of it, we should've had one of the officers scope out the place. A little too late for that, though. I stuck close to Jensen as he checked everywhere in the house, the doors, and the windows. By the time we made it upstairs to the last room, his bedroom, there was about an hour left until my dad would get home.

It had been so long since I'd been in his bedroom that I took the time to check out his room to settle my thoughts.

The walls were bare of any sports' posters, but a WVU flag was tacked to the wall above his headboard. As Jensen brushed past me, picking up socks and God knows what else, I turned to his desk. Papers covered the top, and I recognized an English assignment. Sticking out from the bottom of the notebooks was a University of Maryland handbook.

My breath caught.

Jensen was kicking a pair of sneakers into the closet when I turned around. The center of his cheeks were pink as he straightened and walked to his bed. Plopping down, he patted the spot next to him.

I pressed my lips together, thinking of the handbook. "Do you think we'll make it there?"

His brows knitted. "Make it to where? Your dad's house?"

"No." I wished it were that simple. "To University of Maryland."

"What? Oh babe . . ." He sat up. "I promise you we'll make it there."

"That's . . ." That was sweet, but he couldn't promise that. No one could. And graduating and going away to college seemed so far away. Hell, Thanksgiving break didn't seem possible.

I couldn't shake the feeling that we were running out of time. That the fake dummy was more than just a warning, more like a prelude.

God, I didn't want to think about anything, and the only thing I wanted to feel was that crazy warmth I'd felt earlier in the afternoon, because who knew if we'd get a chance to feel it again?

I don't know what made me do what I did next, but when I met Jensen's questioning stare, I just stopped thinking altogether.

Standing in front of him, I took a breath I didn't need and reached down, pulling my shirt off over my head before I could think twice.

"Ella." Jensen gripped the edges of the bed as his gaze dipped from my face. "What are you doing?"

"Nothing," I whispered.

His gaze dropped again. "That sure does not look like nothing."

My legs felt like jelly as I walked forward and placed my hands on his shoulders. He tipped his head back, his throat working as I climbed onto his lap, putting a knee on either side of his hips. His hands settled on my waist as I lowered myself down.

He opened his mouth, but before he could say something that would surely introduce logic into what I was doing, I kissed him. Making a deep sound, his hands flattened against my lower back. Our lips parted, the kiss deepening. And I wasn't thinking. All I was doing was feeling.

Breaking contact long enough to pull back, I grabbed his shirt, and he lifted his arms, helping me pull it off. My gaze traveled over the golden skin of his shoulders, across his chest, and the ridges of his stomach.

Wow. Me likey.

When I dragged my eyes back up, he grinned at me.

I pressed against him, practically climbing inside him. His skin was so much warmer than mine, tighter. I reached a hand up, threading my fingers through his hair. Heat swept through my veins, and if I could stay here with him like this, I could almost believe that we were two normal teenagers facing everyday stuff.

The kiss deepened, his lips parting. A deep, sexy sound rumbled up from his chest, and his other hand wrapped around the back of my head.

"Ella." His voice was soft against my lips.

"Don't," I whispered as I shifted my hips closer to his.

His hand tightened on the back of my head and then he rolled. I was on my back in a second, and the feel of his body pressing against mine was a shock to my system.

My stomach dipped in a pleasant way, but then he started to

pull back. An almost desperate edge rode me. I gripped his arms, holding him close, wanting to get lost in the feelings from earlier, wanting not to think.

Our eyes locked. His were like the ocean in the morning, glittering under the sunlight. My breath caught in my throat. The intensity in his stare . . . it almost undid me. Jensen's mouth crashed into mine, his kiss sweeping me up into that place I wanted to be, where there was only him and me. Our legs tangled together. His hands skimmed over my body and we kissed like we'd never done it before, kissing like it might be our last. I trailed my hand down his chest, the tips of my fingers traveling over the dips and planes of his stomach. I reached the button on his jeans and went for it.

He caught my wrist. "Ella . . ."

"What?" I tried again, but he pulled my hand away. Rolling his weight onto one arm that trembled, he pressed my hand against the center of his chest. His heart pounded under my palm. "Jensen?"

"What we did this afternoon was . . . was perfect, Ella. And God knows I want you again," he said, lifting himself. "But not like this."

He was speaking a different language. "What?"

Jensen closed his eyes. "We can't do this now."

Damn if we couldn't. "Why? We already did, and I'm okay. I can do it again. I really would like to do it again."

He groaned. "I'm sure I'm going to be asking myself that question over and over again."

I couldn't help but smile. "So?"

"So . . ." He made another deep sound as he let go of my hand. I kept it there because I liked feeling the steady pound. He smoothed his thumb along my jaw. "It's really simple."

"It doesn't seem simple. I want this, but you—"

"Oh, I wanted it this afternoon. I totally want it again, and I want it more than anything else. God, I can't believe I'm saying this." He shook his head. "But this isn't right. Not like this. Never like this, when you're scared and angry and confused. Because you're the first girl I've ever fallen in love with, Ella, and you'll be the last girl I ever love."

I tried to take a breath, but it got stuck in the ball of emotion that suddenly formed in my throat. My hand curled against his chest as I stared into his eyes. "You . . . you love me?"

He rested his forehead against mine, dragging in a deep breath. "I would think that would be pretty obvious by now, but yeah, I love you and then some."

Tears rushed to my eyes, and I lifted my head, kissing him with everything that was in me. "I love you, too. I don't think I ever stopped. I'm *in* love with you."

Jensen shuddered. "Hearing that . . ." His voice was gruff, raw. "There are no words—hey, why are you crying?"

"I'm sorry." I laughed, feeling stupid. "They're not unhappy tears. I promise."

He caught the tears with his lips, and then he rolled onto his side, gathering me close. I snuggled up, closing my eyes. My cheeks felt warm—so did the rest of me. I smiled as he dropped little kisses across my cheeks and the bridge of my nose. We stayed like that for a while, talking about college, about what classes we wanted, and how we planned to make sure we shared enough.

We planned.

We kissed.

We explored one another like it was the first time. He traced the curve of my stomach, the strap of my bra, and the indent of my navel. I did the same, fascinated by how his skin could be so soft and hard at the same time.

We didn't go any farther than that and it was exactly what I—what we—needed. The promise of tomorrow, the belief that it would be there, and we would have time to experience what we had once more.

"We need to get heading over to your dad's," he said finally.

I sat up, handing over his shirt, and he helped me into mine, which took longer than if I had just put it on myself. But I wasn't complaining.

We walked downstairs, hand in hand, stopping at the front door for a quick kiss that caught me by surprise. When he pulled away, I wanted to hold on to him. The idea of him coming back here, where I wouldn't know if he was okay or not, was going to drive me insane.

Between worrying about him, about Heidi and my mom, and Gavin and Linds, I was going to develop a stomach ulcer on steroids.

Jensen flipped on the porch light, and we stepped outside. The night had grown chilly and the breeze cut through my thin shirt. I went down the porch steps, and the feeling came out of nowhere once more. The hairs on the back of my neck rose. I looked around, sucking in a gasp as my gaze fell on the black walnut tree.

A swift curse from behind alerted me to the fact that Jensen had spotted what I was staring at. Hanging from the tree was another damn dummy with a clown mask and wig. It was too dark to tell the color of the wig.

"This is . . ." I shook my head. All the happiness of the moments spent entwined vanished like a smack in the face.

Jensen edged around me, going down a step. "It wasn't there when we came in."

Anger rose in me, hot and bright. It swelled alongside the fear and confusion. And I was tired of being afraid. I didn't care if he was hiding somewhere, watching, and getting off on this. I pushed past Jensen and stalked up to the dummy.

"Ella!"

Wind whipped my hair around my face as I reached up, grasping the edge of the clown mask. The plastic was cool under my finger-tips. Slipping my fingers into the gap of the wide smile, I pulled as hard as I could. The mask didn't give for a moment, and then the strap holding it in place snapped.

"Holy shit!" shouted Jensen as I stumbled back. Suddenly he

was behind me, his hands on my shoulders, yanking me backward.

The mask slipped from my fingers. "Oh God," I whispered.

What hung from the tree wasn't a prop or a dummy.

It wasn't fake.

The glassy dark eyes were real.

The slack jaw was familiar.

It was Brock.

TWENTY-ONE

BROCK'S BODY SWAYED back and forth. I didn't want to believe what I was seeing, that it was truly him hanging up there, the clown mask on the ground in the damp grass and dirt.

I pressed the back of my hand against my mouth, swallowing hard. I told myself to look away, but I couldn't.

"We need to call the police," Jensen said, and his voice sounded so far away.

I murmured something along the lines of agreeing, but both of our phones were in his truck. My feet were rooted to the ground.

"Come with me," Jensen urged, and when I didn't move, he took my hand. He didn't ask if I was okay because who would be after seeing that?

My body felt numb as we hurried to his truck. Jensen grabbed his cell out of the glove box. I turned to his yard. With the thick hedges and trees, you couldn't see Brock's body from the sidewalk or the road, but how had someone gotten it there without being seen?

Unless Brock had walked himself into the yard and done it himself.

That was possible, especially if he was the one behind it. I didn't know what to think as I stared at the hedges, my fingers twitching.

"Let's go inside," he said, glancing around the street, his gaze extra sharp. As we headed back into the yard, Jensen maneuvered me so I wasn't walking closest to the tree.

I forced myself not to look.

Jensen called 911 as he unlocked the door. I barely heard what he said to them as I drifted into the living room. A few moments passed, then he came in behind me. "They'll be here soon. Told us to stay inside and lock the doors."

Running my hands over my face, I nodded. "Oh God, I . . ."

Jensen placed his hands on my shoulders. "It's going to be okay. This is—"

Somewhere in the house, a floorboard creaked. It was not the normal sound of a house settling, but a slow deliberate measure of footsteps. The air halted in my throat.

"Jensen," I whispered.

He placed a finger over his lips and stood so still that I wondered if he was breathing. I strained to not move, to listen.

The sound came again. Wood groaning.

"I don't know where it's coming from," he whispered. My eyes rose to the ceiling. "I want you to go outside, okay? I want you to go right to my truck and—"

"No," I hissed, grabbing his arm. "I am not leaving you in here. If I'm going outside, you're coming with me. It's as simple as that. You are not—"

The footsteps came again, sending ice through my stomach.

Jensen wrapped his hand around mine. He pulled me along behind him, stepping around the couch. We crept down the narrow hallway, turned to enter the kitchen—

Jensen drew up short and I plowed right into his back. He cursed, and I saw it—saw the thing standing in front of the kitchen table, clown mask in place, head tilted to the side.

It made that God-awful tsking sound.

The next couple of moments were a terrifying blur. Jensen

twisted at the waist and pushed me hard enough so that I stumbled back several steps and lost my balance. I went down on my knees and immediately raised my head, peering up through a sheet of hair.

Jensen was in the kitchen with the killer. He went right after him, balls to the wall with no fear. But terror swelled inside me as he swung at him, and the killer easily avoided a punch that would've knocked him into next week.

Too easily.

I pushed to my feet, screaming as Jensen landed a punch in his stomach. The attacker doubled over as he staggered a step to the side and then straightened. They circled one another in some kind of macabre dance.

Spinning around, I searched for a weapon. Remembering the heavy iron candlestick holders in the living room, I spared Jensen one last look. His back was to the kitchen doorway.

"You're not getting out of this house," Jensen warned.

The thing made a sound, something inhuman, but much like a laugh. It was deep and low and animalistic. It sent a chill right to my marrow.

I raced into the living room, heading for the hutch near the foyer entryway. Tossing the white candle out, I grabbed the heavy holder. Dimly, I could hear the sound of grunts, of flesh connecting with flesh, and off in the distance, the sound of sirens grew steadily closer. I darted back down the hall.

Jensen twisted to the side, breaking free from the grip around his neck. The quick movement threw him off balance, and the thing in the mask slammed his hands into Jensen's chest, shoving him back.

A scream built in my throat.

Jensen grabbed the back of the chair to catch himself, but the thing swung his arm out. Something was in his hand—a wrought iron pan, heavy, and capable of a lot of damage. He swung hard, and the crack as it connected with the side of Jensen's head caused a scream to erupt from me. Horror seized me as Jensen crumpled like a paper sack.

He went down.

And didn't move.

No. No, no, no.

I wasn't thinking as I raced toward where Jensen lay, sprawled out on the kitchen floor. I dropped to my knees, clutching the candlestick as I cried out. My gaze darted up to where the attacker had been standing. He was gone. The backdoor was open.

The candlestick slipped from my fingers as I grasped Jensen's shoulder. "Jensen? Oh God, please open your eyes. Please!"

His eyes were sealed shut. A trickle of blood ran from his temple, over his ear. I carefully touched his head, and my hand came back wet and red.

"Oh my God, no." Tears blurred my eyes. I shuddered. "No, no, no."

Footsteps echoed down the hall behind me. I grabbed the candlestick and spun at the waist, ready to knock out anyone who was coming near Jensen.

Gavin stood in the hall, his eyes wide. His chest was rising and falling hard. "What's going on?"

My thoughts raced. How did he get in here? Why was he here? Where was the killer? I stood, breathing heavily.

He stepped into the kitchen. "What—?"

"Don't come any closer." I held up the candlestick.

His gaze darted back to me, and he turned at the sound of high pitched sirens arriving out front. My gaze quickly moved over his face. Along the left corner of his mouth, the skin was an angry shade of pink like he'd been in a recent fight. Too recent.

Horror exploded in my stomach as I stared at Gavin. Too many coincidences. My brain clicked off, and instinct roared to life—to protect Jensen, to protect myself. He started to take another step toward us and I swung. The base of the candlestick caught him in the side of the head. A look of surprise flashed across his face as he stumbled into the side of the fridge. Down for the count.

Something in my chest broke. The candlestick slipped from my fingers, clanging off the floor. I dropped next to Jensen. Through the tears, I could see that the river of blood along the side of his head had increased.

I didn't know what to do, how to help him.

I smoothed my hand along his cheek, whispering his name, telling him that I loved him over and over again.

The front door burst open, and officers piled into the kitchen within seconds. I looked up, my hands shaking. "Help him. Please."

"Christ." A younger officer knelt down on the other side of Jensen as he glanced to where Gavin lay. He hit a button on his shoulder radio as he checked for a pulse. I couldn't bring myself to do that. "What's the status on the ambulance?" he asked.

The static reply made no sense to me. "Is he alive?"

"I've got a pulse." He looked over my shoulder. "What about the other one?"

"I got a pulse over here," answered another officer.

I clutched at Jensen's shirt. He was alive, but a hit to the head could be serious—could end up being fatal.

"What happened?" the officer demanded.

A tremor rocked my body. "We went outside. He was taking me to my dad's, but we saw . . . we saw Brock's body, so we called the police. They told us to wait inside and we did. But he . . ." I didn't look at Gavin. I couldn't let myself think about that right now. "But he was in here. Jensen tried to fight him off."

"Okay. Do you know what he was hit with?"

I nodded at where the pan rested a few feet from the door. "I didn't even see him grab it. It all happened so fast."

It all had happened too fast.

The EMTs showed up after that. One of them grabbed my shoulders, physically moving me out of the way and putting me down in a chair. I couldn't stay seated, so I stood, but I kept out of the way as they checked Jensen over. Another set worked on Gavin.

A stretcher was brought in. Words were spoken at a rapid pace. Jensen was loaded up and strapped in. An oxygen mask was placed over his pale face.

"Is he going to be okay?" I asked.

No one answered.

They started to wheel him out of the room, and I followed after them. When I reached the front door, Shaw blocked it. "Is he going to be okay?" I demanded.

"They're going to take good care of him."

That wasn't good enough for me. "I need to be with him."

"We need you here, just for a little while."

"No." I started to brush the hair back from my face, but saw that my fingers were covered in blood—Jensen's blood. "Oh God." I wiped my hands across my jeans, dragging in deep breaths. "I need to go with him."

Shaw took my arm, pulling me outside as the EMTs came through with Gavin. The deputy's gaze followed their progress, his face paling.

"It was him," I whispered, feeling sick even saying it. This whole time I never, ever thought it was him, couldn't even wrap my head around it being Gavin. It didn't make sense to me, but God, it hurt—it cut so deep. "He showed up right after I thought the attacker had disappeared. He pretended like he didn't know anything, but I saw . . . it looked like he'd just been in a fight and Jensen had been fighting . . ." I trailed off, seeing Brock's body in the tree. They hadn't cut him down yet. I turned, squeezing my eyes shut.

He looked down at me, and I could tell he was struggling with keeping his face blank. Gavin had been my best friend for what seemed like forever, but he was also Shaw's family. They weren't close, but this had to be hard for him. "Is it possible Gavin ran into the attacker?" Shaw asked. "And fought him?"

"What?" I opened my eyes.

"That's a possibility," he clipped out. "Gavin could've been try-ing to protect you. God." He scrubbed his hand through his hair. "This is going to kill his father—the whole family if it was Gavin."

"If?" I shuddered, shaking my head. "But . . ."

But it could be possible that it wasn't him. Gavin did live right down the street, just like Brock lived next door to Linds. He could've randomly shown up. It wasn't impossible and I . . . I had hit him pretty hard.

And that also would mean the killer could still be out there.

I didn't know how much time passed as I went through another round of questions. Jensen's parents were notified, so they never showed up at the house. They'd gone where I wanted to be.

Finally, after Shaw spoke with a couple other officers, he ush-ered me toward his cruiser. I drew in a deep breath. "I want to go to the hospital."

Shaw shook his head. "We need to get you someplace safe."

"The hospital will be safe!" I dug in my heels. "I want to be with Jensen."

He opened the door, pinning me with a look. A moment passed. "Fine. Just get in the car."

"Thank you." I could've hugged him. Kissed him.

I climbed into the backseat, wiping my hands against my jeans. It felt like I couldn't get the blood off.

Shaw didn't say anything as he eased away from the curb and started toward King Street. When he made a left, I frowned.

"I thought we were going to the hospital."

He didn't answer.

I sat forward. Breathing heavily, I grasped the cage as I stared out the window. My thoughts whirled as I focused on Shaw in the front seat. Stopped at a red light, he sat there, grasping the steering wheel until his knuckles bleached white, and then he slowly, finger by finger, let go.

My fingers curled around the steel. "I want to go to the hospital.

That's where we're going, right?"

"I'm not taking you to the hospital."

"What?" I whispered.

"I'm surprised you lived on that street after everything. Wasn't it hard?" he asked, his voice sounding off.

I frowned at the strangeness of his tone, the absolute flatness.

The cruiser started forward again, traveling under the underpass. We could get to the hospital from here, but . . ."Considering how you want to move away from here and get away from all reminders of what happened four years ago, I'm surprised you just didn't move in with your father when he left."

My frown started to slip. "How . . . how do you know I want to move away?"

"Everyone knows that, Ella. You haven't made it a secret." There was a pause. "It's funny how people deal with things—stuff that they brought on themselves. Some think they have no fault, you know? None at all. They just keep doing what they do, blissfully ignorant. Others get angry."

The next breath I took froze in my lungs. My fingers eased off the steel.

"And there're people like you." At another stoplight, he twisted around so he faced me. The coldness in his gaze stopped my heart. "So riddled with guilt that you can't even say his name without wincing."

"His name?" My pulse sped up.

His gaze met mine. "Penn."

I drew back from the steel cage as I stared at him. Part of my brain was processing what was going down, knew what he was saying and what a precarious position I was in, but the other part flat-out refused it. Couldn't even wrap itself around the idea.

A smile appeared on his face, and then he made the low guttural sound that had haunted me since the very first time I'd heard it. He tsked under his breath. "It's time to pay your dues, Ella."

TWENTY-TWO

OH MY GOD . . .

It was Deputy Jordan Shaw.

Part of me rebelled at the idea, but it was him. He was the monster. The killer among us. As I stared at him, pieces started to click together in a horrifying chain of connections.

Shaw had been one of the officers to respond to the call at Penn's house. He lived in this town, knew it inside and out. He'd been at the school when the bird had been placed in Wendy's bag. He'd been at the warehouse when Jensen and I had talked about me staying with Linds'. And he'd been at school when the mask was placed in my locker, but how did he know to get into my window? Unless he'd been watching when Jensen did it? And him being a cop? He knew how to get away with what he was doing, could hide evidence if there was any, but I didn't understand. Why? Why would he do this? He was Gavin's cousin, but why would he do this to us? I couldn't think of a reason.

Shit. Shit. Shit.

Over and over again, that one word replayed in my head as I reached for the door and realized there was no handle, no way out.

Shaw laughed, and there was something menacing and mocking

about it. "You're not escaping this time."

This time.

The hairs rose all over my body as my head swung back to him sharply. Coldness rooted deep in my stomach. I was trapped.

"You walked right into it. I'm thinking I probably should've gone this route from the beginning." He grinned then. "If I'd known how easy it would be, it would've saved me a lot of trouble, but then again, where's the fun in that?"

I swallowed against the rapidly building nausea. "The fun?"

One shoulder shrugged, and his attention flipped back to the house, back to where Gavin was. Oh God. *Gavin*. He was hurt—hurt badly, could be dead, and I . . . I had helped Shaw take him out.

He chuckled. "Thinking of Gavin, huh? You know, he was the only one out of you little shits that really cared about that kid. Who never screwed him over."

My heart was beating fast now, trying to climb out of my chest. "We cared about Penn."

"Sure didn't seem like it."

"Why?" I asked. "Why are you doing this?"

"Why?" he mimicked, and then turned back to the steering wheel.

Shaw didn't answer. The cruiser lurched into motion, pulling away from the curb. I had to get out of here. That was the only thing I could focus on, but as I glanced around the dark interior, I noticed nothing I could use to break a window.

Nothing other than my feet.

Leaning back against the seat, I pulled my knees back and slammed my feet into the window. The thud sent a jolt up my legs, but the window didn't give. I did it again, totally prepared to jump out of a moving car.

Shaw laughed. "That's reinforced glass, honey. You aren't going anywhere."

I switched positions, pushing against the back of the seat. Pulling my knees back, I kicked the cage. The steel rattled, but like with the glass, nothing gave. I kicked it again, and then again.

"Knock it off," he warned, glancing back at me as the houses sped by outside the cruiser. "Or I will pull this car over, and our time will be cut short."

Pulling the cruiser over would give me a chance to escape. That was my only opportunity, so I kicked the cage again and again, until my feet and knees ached.

At the red light, he reached down to his side, unhooked something, and a second later, a red dot appeared on my chest. I sucked in air, stilling.

"This is a taser," he gritted out. "It won't kill you, but it will hurt like hell. And if it makes it through the cage, you're going to wish you had listened to me. So stop."

Shaking all over, I decided pushing it wouldn't be wise. I'd never been tased before, but I'd seen videos, and it didn't look like fun. Not to mention, I had no idea how long the effects of a taser would last. I couldn't risk being out of it when he opened the car door.

And he had to open the car door at some point.

I settled down, conserving my energy. I couldn't let myself think about Gavin or Jensen.

"That's a good girl," he murmured.

The desire to kick his head in was almost too strong. Taking several deep breaths, I turned my attention to the window. The streets were virtually empty, lit by the streetlamps. I recognized where we were. Downtown. Ironically, we passed the police station.

It wasn't long before we reached Rosemont Avenue. Confused, I twisted toward Shaw. Was he taking me back to my street?

Yes.

We drove down my street, passing my house by a block, and then he turned into a narrow alley I hadn't gone down in years. I absolutely refused to go there, because it led to the back entrance of Penn's house. Ice drenched my veins.

Shaw pulled the cruiser off to the side, tires crunching over gravel. The car crept under the carport that was still standing and virtually hidden by overgrown bushes and trees. No one would see the car, and as late as it was, I doubted anyone would even be awake let alone looking out the back window, seeing through the jungle of overgrown branches and weeds.

"Why here?" I asked.

Shaw killed the engine. "It's where it all began. Seems fitting that it's where it all should end. When I'm done with you . . . well, that just leaves two more."

Mason. Jensen.

I had no idea where Mason was, but oh God, Jensen would be in the hospital, virtually unprotected. No one would stop Shaw from walking in there, but there'd be witnesses. "You're not going to get away with this."

"That's probably the most cliché thing people can say."

"Others saw you take me!"

"I'll say I dropped you off at your father's. Then I'll pay them a little visit." He laughed again, the sound cold and flat. "Of course I'm going to get away with it. Do you think I don't know how to cover my tracks? How to make a death look accidental?"

My heart stopped again. He was talking about my dad and Rose and Jensen.

"And up until ten minutes or so ago, you had no idea it was me." He smirked. "I will get away with it, and it's not because I'm smart or a cop. It's because I'm doing the right thing."

"Doing the right thing? You're killing people!"

"I'm cleaning up this damn mess."

Cleaning up this mess? I wasn't following.

"It's the right thing to do." His brows rose and then he turned, opening the car door. "You do anything stupid, you're going to regret it."

My heart was back to pounding so fast that I was worried about having a heart attack. I was planning a whole lot of stupid. I'd only have one chance to get free. My hands were shaking as he rounded the car, his form bulky and heavy in the shadows. He reached for the door.

I rolled onto my back as he opened it, kicking out with both of my feet. My sneakers caught him in the midsection. I don't know if it was the impact, or simply surprise that I would attempt something, but he stumbled several steps back, and I didn't waste any time.

Survival was the only thing I could focus on. I wriggled out of the back seat, and the moment my feet hit the gravel, Shaw was right in front of me. I didn't think. I swung from the waist, slamming my fist into the same area where I'd kicked him—the solar plexus.

Shaw doubled over and I spun, opening my mouth to let loose an ear piercing scream. The sound tore through the night, but a hand clamped down on my lips, muffling the cry before it could gain any traction.

A knee slammed into my back, taking me down. I hit the gravel hard, my palms skidding across the small, sharp stones, ripping open my skin. Sudden pressure smashed my face down. Pain lanced across my cheek.

"I should kill you now," he seethed into my ear. Reaching up, he gripped my arm. "I told you to behave. I doubt it was that hard to understand."

He wrenched my arm back, tucking his knee against my lower back. His fingers dug into my other wrist and then both arms were pinned behind me. The slap of cold steel around my wrists caused my stomach to churn with panic.

He hauled me onto my feet, roughly turning me around. Pain exploded along my jaw, knocking me backward. My knees gave out under the shock. Blood pooled in my mouth. Dimly, I was aware that he had hit me.

Shaw lifted me up, dragging me toward the back steps with his hand over my mouth. He fished out a key. The hinges groaned as he opened the door and then shoved me inside. With my hands secured behind me, I lost my balance and went down on the kitchen tile.

He closed and locked the door behind him, his boots pounding off the floor as he approached me. He grabbed a handful of hair, hauling me to my feet. "Does it look like you remember?"

My eyes darted around the kitchen. With the exception of a table and two chairs, the room was bare. "No." My jaw ached around the word.

"Yeah, because a family used to live here." He led me forward, his hand wrapping tightly around my forearm. "A mother and a father and a son. They were happy for the most part."

"No, they weren't," I whispered.

His grip tightened until I gasped. "I said 'for the most part,' didn't I?" He led me into the dark hallway. My eyes had barely adjusted to the minimal light coming in through the front windows. "Did you ever wonder why this house never sold?"

I felt sick, close to throwing up. "Yes."

"I always thought it was the bad vibes. For years it's sat on the market. Rumor has it they're demolishing it at the end of the year. How do you feel about that?"

"I . . . I don't know."

"Seems like the whole town would just rather forget about the kid. God knows I'd love to." He spun toward the stairs, and I balked. He pushed hard, and I fell forward, cracking my knees off the second step. He caught my arm before I ate the step above. "What? You don't want to go upstairs? Too bad."

I had little choice. He all but carried me up there, down the hall and past the wooden railing that seemed to bow out over the foyer. The door to Penn's old bedroom was closed.

"Remember when we first met?"

Squeezing my eyes shut did nothing to change the past, so I forced them open. I'd been too upset to really pay attention to the stream of officers that had poured into the woods, who had disappeared among the trees, and seemed to never come back out.

"I was the first officer on the scene." He turned me around so I was facing him. Half of his expression was lost in the darkness. Down below, something squeaked and scurried across the floor, its nails making quick tapping sounds.

My lower lip trembled. "And I . . . I found him."

"You helped put him there."

I jerked back into the wall, stirring up dust.

"You and the rest of them," he said, leaning in until his breath stirred the hair around my temple. "Brock. Monica. Wendy. Mason. Jensen. You."

My breath rattled out of me. For the longest time, I carried that guilt. I always would, but it had lessened because I finally began to let it go. "Jensen and I—we didn't do what Brock and them did. We went to a party. That's all—"

"That's all? Really?" Shaw tsked, and the sound turned my blood cold. "You don't blame yourself anymore?" When I didn't answer immediately, he gripped my chin until I cried out. "Do you still blame yourself?"

My legs shook as I held his gaze. "I will always . . . feel responsible."

"But?" he sneered.

"But I loved Penn, and I never meant to hurt him."

His head tilted to the side, his fingers digging into my flesh. "But you did."

"It was just a party. That was all. We didn't go to his party!" I shouted, and for the first time—for real—I believed what was coming out of my mouth. "I will *always* feel bad, and I will *always* wish I could go back and make a different decision, but Jensen and I *didn't* kill him."

"The thing is, you can't go back." He sounded almost sad about that.

Chest rising and falling heavily, my chin notched up. "I know."

Shaw wrenched open the door and pushed me hard, and then

again, once we were inside the room. Something hit me in the thighs, and I toppled over onto a hard, springy mattress that smelled of sweat and other things I didn't want to think about.

I rolled up, using my feet to push myself across the bed. Walking in front of the bed, Shaw bent at the waist, and a second later, a soft halo of light illuminated the room. A battery-operated lantern had been turned on.

Penn's bedroom . . . it wasn't like it used to be.

The single window was covered with a board. Everything except this rotten bed had been removed from the room. Spray painted across the wall in red were names. Names repeated a thousand or more times.

Vee.

Brock.

Mason.

Wendy.

Monica.

Jensen.

Ella.

Over and over again, our names took up every square inch of the room—even the ceiling. It was obvious that Shaw had done this and hadn't been worried about anyone finding it.

He really was crazy. Not like that should come as a surprise.

My gaze settled back on him. He watched me from the foot of the bed. One word came out of me. "Why?"

"Does it matter?" He held a black duffel bag in his hand. "Maybe seeing a young boy dead messed me up?"

I looked around the room for an escape, but he stood where he could get to the door quickly.

"Some scenes stick with you." He paused, pulling something out of the duffel bag. "As part of an investigation for any unattended death, we have to talk. I talked to you. I talked to Jensen. I talked to my cousin. I talked to Penn's parents and yours and the school.

I heard what was done to Penn."

"It had to be hard. I know it was hard, but what you're doing—"

He stared at me, his fingers clenching the edges of the duffle bag. "In middle school, when you and Gavin were just tiny kids, there was this boy named Eddie Stevenson. A lot of the other kids picked on him. So did I. We were relentless."

"You . . . you harassed him?" I didn't get how this was connecting to why he was *murdering* people.

"Yeah." He ran his other hand over his head, rubbing the back of his neck. "He went home one day. Hung himself. It was my fault. It was all of ours and there wasn't a damn thing I could do to fix that. To go back and change things. Because I was an asshole, some innocent kid died. This . . . this shit here is different, but in the end it's really the same."

My gaze darted toward the door and then back to him. There was not enough room.

"I'd managed to do my best to forget about it. Like you." His hand lowered and he pulled something out of the bag. The mask. My stomach tumbled. Its white plastic face shined eerily in the dim light. "Actually, you and I are a lot alike."

"I'm nothing like you." I stared at the mask.

"That's what everyone says. You hid from what you did. So did I. Up until that call that afternoon. I couldn't hide anymore."

I shuddered as he reached up, pulling the mask on over his head, shielding his face. Every living breathing nightmare roared to life before me. White face. Dark empty eyes. Wide, red grotesque smile.

"All of you went about your lives," he said, his voice different behind the mask. Deeper. Scarier. "*Almost* all of you."

"I don't understand." My hands were starting to go numb. "You waited four years to do what? Take revenge for Penn? You didn't even know him."

"It's not for Penn." He came around the side of the door, inching closer. My muscles tensed as I drew back. "It's never been for him."

"What?" I couldn't take my eyes away from the mask.

His head tilted to the side, so eerily familiar. "I've got to clean this mess up."

"Oh my God," I whispered. He was more than just crazy. He'd taken a trip into insanity land and there was no coming back. "How did you pass the psych exams to become an officer?"

He reacted so fast that I barely saw him move. His fist snapped out, catching me along the temple, knocking me over. I landed cheek first against the soiled sheets, pain radiating across my face and down my throat.

"Does that answer your question?" he asked, straightening.

Blood leaked out of my mouth as I squeezed my eyes shut. My head swam like I'd been dunked underwater.

"Too bad I don't have as much time to spend with you as I did the others." His hand smoothed down my arm, forcing my eyes wide. He pulled back, slipping gloves on. "'I wanted them to experience what he did."

"You want all of us . . . to die."

"Something like that." He gripped my arm, dragging me across the bed. "It's necessary at this point."

I kicked out, but he caught my leg with his other hand. He yanked hard, dragging me right off the bed. My back hit the floor, knocking the air out of me. Stunned, I stared up at him as he towered over me, the horrible clown mask in my face. I knew I was covered in bruises, but it's not like that was going to matter by the end of the night.

I knew he was going to kill me. There would be no weeks of me being missing and experiencing God knows what at his hands. But through the pain and the fear, I knew I had to keep him talking if I had any hope of figuring a way out of this, because I didn't want to die, not like this, in a house that once held good memories but had been perverted into madness.

He placed me on my feet, keeping a hand on me as he turned

to the closet door. Sore muscles in my back tensed as he opened it. My gaze tracked up to the bar that had been readjusted higher—too high for someone to reach on their own—and stopped on the belt hanging from it.

Oh God, my legs shook. My memory flashed back to the tree outside of Jensen's house, to the two legs swaying back and forth. Was he going to make me hang myself?

Shaw guided me forward, but I couldn't go in there. There was no way in hell. "Why Linds?" I asked, trying to stall.

"She got in the way." The pressure on my back increased, tipping me forward. "So, in a way, that's your fault."

That didn't hurt like he intended it to. What happened to Linds wasn't my fault. It was Shaw's fault. But panic was clawing at me. Every part of my body shook. He reached for the belt.

"Wait!" I shouted.

He halted.

"Why . . . why the mask?"

For a moment, I imagined he was smiling behind the mask. "I was scared of clowns as a kid."

Whoa. That just took this to a whole new level of crazy. "You're a killer."

"I didn't kill them. I'm not a murderer."

I gaped at him.

"They put the rope around their necks. Not me," he explained, and a new kind of horror surfaced. "They made that choice. Just like you will."

My gaze bounced to the thick belt. "They . . . you made them hang themselves?"

"After a while, they begged for it."

The smugness in his voice made my skin crawl. From what I'd known, the bodies had borne marks of torture, and while I'd known how Brock had died, now I knew how the rest had. The things he had to have done to them to make them cave would haunt me.

Another well placed shove had me stumbling forward. I was almost in the closet when I turned toward Shaw. Suddenly, I thought of all those afternoons spent with Jensen. I'd taken those classes to defend myself and, dammit, I was not going to go down without a fight.

And I sure as hell wasn't letting him put that belt around my neck.

Like Jensen had instructed the first time we practiced together, I pretended to be weak. I swayed on my feet, and the hand on my back moved to grab for my arm, but in those tiny seconds, I brought my leg up and slammed my heel into his foot. I knew it wasn't pain that caused him to jerk back. It was surprise, but that was enough.

Using everything in me, I brought my knee up, connecting with his groin. It wasn't the first time I got him there, but hopefully, it would be the last.

Shaw doubled over, gasping for air.

I spun around, practically leaping forward. Throwing the door open with my elbow, I pushed through and hit the hallway running.

"Shit."

The sound of his voice was too close, and a second later, his body connected with mine. My waist hit the banister and I doubled over. The railing shuddered under my weight. Wood creaked and groaned, and my heart dropped into my stomach. It was going to give, and I would fall to the foyer below.

Shaw grabbed ahold of my arm and I twisted violently, slamming my shoulder into his chest. He rocked into the banister, and this time wood splintered. The cracking reverberated through the house. Half of the railing snapped, falling down to the foyer below. It landed with a heavy, broken thud.

His hand grasped my arm, but I kept pulling until his hold slipped. He teetered on the edge, his arms out wide and that damn mask . . . the smiling clown face. He reached for me as he started to tip backward. His fingers grazed my arm.

A heartbeat passed and my eyes locked with the dark holes.

"You think this is over?" he asked.

I stepped back out of his reach. "Yes."

And he . . . he went right over, disappearing into the darkness that seemed to reach up, wrap its arms around him, and pull him down.

A thick, wet thud echoed in the otherwise silent house.

Breathing heavy, I crept toward the edge, twisting my wrists in the handcuffs, and peered down below. In the sliver of moonlight slicing across the floor, I saw Shaw. He lay with one leg twisted under him, his neck resting at an unnatural angle. The clown mask was still secured on his face, smiling up at me.

He didn't move again.

TWENTY-THREE

EVERYTHING WAS A blur as I climbed down the dusty stairs, careful not to misstep and lose my balance. Without my hands to break my fall, I'd be on that floor like Shaw.

I didn't want to look at him, but I had to as I reached the landing. Moving slowly to his side, I stood and waited, watching his chest. Minutes had to have passed, and when I didn't see it move, I let out a ragged breath of relief.

As I backed away, I kept an eye on him anyway. All I could think about was all those horror films where the bad guy seemed to come back to life. But Shaw didn't get up. With the exception of my footsteps and the distant scurry of mice, the house was silent.

Running out of the house and to a neighbor's zapped me of all my strength. The adrenaline faded once I convinced them I wasn't an escaped criminal. While I waited for the police, sitting on the couch inside an older couple's house, all the aches and pains started to blossom across my body. The only part of me that didn't hurt was my hands, but I couldn't feel them anyway.

"Would you . . . like something to drink?" the older woman asked.

I huddled down under the blanket she'd draped over my shoulders. "No . . . no, thank you."

Things were a heady mess after that.

The police showed up. I gave my statement as they found keys to unlock the cuffs. My wrists were bleeding and rubbed raw, but I hadn't even noticed. I told them about Shaw and some officers disappeared back out the front door. Trooper Ritter showed up, and there were EMTs. When one of them helped me stand up, my legs gave out and the world went fuzzy.

When I opened my eyes again, I was staring up at a plain white ceiling. Not the kind in the elderly couple's house. My gaze was slow to drift down, over the pea green curtains and the little table to my right where a ceramic pitcher sat with empty plastic cups.

I was in a hospital room.

When did that happen?

Sensing another presence in the room, it hurt to turn my head to the left, but I did, and was rewarded with a beautiful sight.

Jensen sat on the edge of my bed, his hands folded in his lap.

My heart turned over heavily. He was alive, and he was up and moving around. Emotion clogged my throat as I stared at him.

His chin was dipped down, and several dark blond locks fell over his forehead. His hair was darker along one side of his head, matted with dried blood.

I didn't speak, but he seemed to become aware of me. He lifted his chin, and eyes the color of dawn met mine. Relief splashed across his face.

"Hey," he whispered, one side of his mouth curling up. "There's my beautiful girl."

"Hey you," I croaked and started to smile, but my lips felt too tight and hurt. I raised my other hand, reaching for my lips.

Jensen caught my fingers. "Nah, babe, don't do that."

"What's wrong with my mouth?"

"Your lip was split. There are a couple of stitches." A dark look crept across his striking face as his gaze dipped to my wrist. It was heavily bandaged, but a bit of red had stained the cloth. "God,

Ella . . ." He choked off, closing his eyes as he bent his head, pressing a kiss to the center of my palm. "When they told me you'd been brought in, I feared the worst."

"I'm okay." I pressed my hand against his cheek. "Are you? I was so scared. I thought—" My voice broke. "I thought I'd never see you again."

"My head is harder than it looks." His eyes opened, the blue a startling color of the ocean. "Are you? Because they told me what happened—they told me who it was and what he admitted to you."

"He's . . . he's still dead, right?"

Jensen frowned at that question, and I got that it sounded weird, but whatever. "He's dead, dead," he told me.

I drew in a deep breath and winced. "That hurt."

He shifted closer, his movements slow. "You're pretty banged up, Ella. Busted lip and eye. Half your face is swollen. The nurse said your ribs are bruised."

"How about you?"

A soft, tired smile appeared. "Bruises. A contusion. They're keeping you in here for observation—both of us."

"I bet I look terrible."

"You look freaking beautiful."

I snorted. "So you have a concussion then."

"No." He bent down, kissing my forehead. When he straightened a little, he swallowed hard. "I know he hurt you, but did he—"

"No." I knew where the question was heading. "It wasn't about that. He was . . . he was out of his mind, Jensen. The things he said, I . . ."

"It's okay. They told me. You don't have to go through it again." Smiling again, he glanced over his shoulder. The bruise along his temple was ugly and mean. "Your parents have been here, but they went to grab some food with Linds' parents. You've been asleep for a while."

"I have? It felt like minutes."

He watched me intently. "If he wasn't dead, I would've killed him for what he did to you."

"No," I whispered, an ache piercing my chest. "You don't want that on your hands."

The look on his face said he disagreed with that. "Can you roll on your side?"

"Yeah, I guess so. Why?"

"I need to hold you right now and I'm going to make this work." He glanced at the narrow bed and frowned. "Somehow."

My heart turned over happily. "I'm not sure the nurses and staff will appreciate that. Wait. Are you even supposed to be out of your room?"

His eyes sparkled. "No. But I'm still in the hospital and that counts for something, right?"

I laughed, ignoring the pain pounding in my ribs. "I'm not sure they'll think that."

"I don't care." Standing like a man four or five times his age, he made his way to the other side of the bed. "Let's do this."

It took a while for me to get onto my side without killing my ribs, and then even longer for Jensen to lie down.

"Ow," we moaned at the same time, and Jensen chuckled as he readjusted himself so I wasn't resting against his ribs. "We're both kind of pathetic, aren't we?"

"Yeah." I smiled in spite of the stitches. It was good being almost in his arms. He really couldn't hold me, but we made it work, lying as close as possible. His warmth, his very presence, chased away some of the darkness from the night. "But I love you."

His lips brushed along the nape of my neck, eliciting a shiver from me. "But I love *us*."

THE NURSES DID chase Jensen off, back to his room with adoring expressions on their faces. I think I rolled my eyes so far back they almost rolled out of my head. They also chased off my parents after an hour or so of my mom, my dad, *and* Rose clucking over me like worried hens.

After they left, it was a few hours shy of morning. I was hovering back and forth between asleep and awake when I heard the door creak. Figuring it was one of the nurses checking on me, I opened my eyes into thin slits. The pea green curtains fluttered.

It wasn't a nurse who walked in.

I started to sit up, but my body screamed in protest. "Gavin?"

"Don't sit up." He came to the side of the bed, sitting down just like Jensen had. His gaze drifted over me. "You look terrible, Ella."

He didn't look much better. His forehead looked a bit swollen, and it was purple from where I'd hit him in the head. Oh dear.

"Gavin, I'm so sorry. I thought—"

"You thought I was the killer." He smiled as he reached across the bed, wrapping his hand around mine. "It happens."

My brows rose. "I don't think someone mistakes their friend as a killer that often."

"Well, with everything going on, it's easy to imagine." His shirt stretched over his shoulders as he shifted, the material over his arm torn. "Let's not talk about that now."

He was taking this very well, or maybe he just got one good look at me and felt too bad to really make me feel guilty. "Okay," I said, squeezing his hand. "Did you have to sneak past the nurses?"

"Yeah, but I needed to see you." He paused, pulling his hand free. "I tried to come by earlier, but you were with Jensen."

Before, I would've felt a tidal wave of embarrassment and awkwardness, but after everything, I couldn't muster the feeling. "The nurses ran him off. He should be let out tomorrow. Me too."

Gavin reached up, scrubbing his hand carefully through his unkempt hair. "God, Ella, I can't believe . . . things have ended up here."

I closed my eyes briefly. "Me neither, but I'm glad you're okay."

His lashes drifted shut. "I think you're mistaking what I'm

saying."

Confused, I tilted my head toward him. "How?"

He leaned down, placing one hand next to the shoulder furthest from him. The closeness wigged me out a little, but he was my friend, and I *had* knocked him over the head not too long ago. "I have a secret to admit," he whispered.

Something in the way he said that caused tiny knots to form in my stomach. "What?"

"Shaw wasn't the only one," he said, and my eyes widened. "And he sure as hell wasn't the brains behind any of this."

My body jerked and I started to sit up, but Gavin moved incredibly fast, smacking a hand over my mouth as he climbed onto the bed, forcing his weight down on my legs.

A slow smile curled his lips, turning a familiar face into something I'd never seen before. My heart kicked against my chest frantically as I breathed heavily out of my nose.

"Oh, you look so, so surprised. Come on, you can't be that dumb. Why would Shaw do this if it wasn't for me?" He lowered his head until our faces were an inch apart. "Shaw has always been a bit of a loose cannon, but he cared about his family—about me, more than I ever knew. Didn't know until I was thirteen actually."

I dug my fingers into his hand, trying to dislodge it, but there was no moving him. All I could think about was what Shaw had said right before he fell to his death.

You think this is over?

It had been a warning—a warning that I hadn't even noticed. And it made sense now—the mask in my locker, my bedroom window—things that Shaw couldn't have known or done. The footsteps we'd heard upstairs at Jensen's house. That was Gavin.

He chuckled low in his throat. "Ah, I see you're putting it together. You've always been a smart one. It was cute how you defended me right up until you swung at my head. But it worked out in a way. Shaw got you, but it didn't end the way I wanted. He was supposed to be the one to take you out," he said, dark eyes locked on to mine. "Because I thought it would be too hard for me to do it, but you know what? It's really not that hard."

Oh God . . .

"I started planning at the beginning of summer. We tried it with Vee, and when that worked out perfectly, we tried to grab you. But damn, Ella, you've got nine lives or something." He drew back as I swung my arms at him. He caught one and pinned it down beside my hip. "And it was so much fun messing with you. The night with the mask in your bedroom? That was me. The dummy hanging in your house? All me, baby."

The smugness in his voice chilled me to my very core. I fought back, trying to catch him, but he kept out of my reach. The blows I landed bounced off his arm and chest to no avail.

"I watched you." He paused. "I watched you and Jensen. You wouldn't give it to me after all the time we spent together, but all Jensen had to do was smile in your direction and you opened your legs right up. Yeah, so this is actually a lot easier than I thought it would be."

His lip curled in disgust. "And this whole time, you never saw what was right in front of your face. I think Jensen was beginning to see it, but not you. For all those years after Penn, I hated all of them—even you at times. But I still loved you."

My eyes widened further.

"But I have to do this. I had to do all of this. Shaw understood. It's the only way for me to make amends." His hand moved off my mouth and then circled my neck, cutting off my air and ability to scream. Panic roared through me, surging like an out of control storm. I couldn't breathe.

"Don't worry. When I'm finished with you, I'll take care of him. Or maybe I won't. Seems fitting he'll have to live the rest of his life without you." One shoulder shrugged like he was discussing the difference between salt and pepper.

My eyes darted around the room frenziedly, landing on the heavy ceramic water pitcher. Could I reach it?

"Do you want to know why?" he asked, his lips brushing my bruised cheek, startling me. "Why now? Why four years later?" Then he leaned down again, his fingers loosening around my neck, allowing some air in. His mouth then brushed my ear as he whispered, "Penn didn't kill himself."

Everything stopped.

He waited until my wide eyes found his. "Penn wanted to go look at birds and he didn't want to wait until you and Jensen got there. So I went with him. I was still pissed about you and Jensen skipping his party for Brock's. Hell, I was more pissed that Penn let it slide. He never stood up for himself. *Never*. And I was so sick of him being a doormat for everyone. I told him that. I told him that you two couldn't really be his friends after bailing on him, and he started to cry. *To cry*, Ella." His eyes took on an unfocused, manic look. "I don't even know how it happened. I told him to stop crying. But then he said—he said that he trusted you two. That he knew you were really sorry and that *I* was the bad friend for even bringing it up. *Me*. And that was such bullshit, because I didn't bail on him. But he never trusted me. It was always you. It was always Jensen."

Oh my God.

"I pushed him," Gavin said, closing his eyes. "I pushed him, not that hard, but he lost his balance. He fell, Ella. He fell, and I panicked. I didn't mean to hurt him. I just wanted him to stand up for himself. I wanted him to see that I was the better friend. It was an accident. I didn't know what to do. I ran home and I . . . I called Shaw. He came right over. He knew that I was in trouble. That no one would believe it was an accident. He helped me cover it up, got the belt and rope, planted the note in Penn's bedroom. And he helped me now, too. He knew it wasn't my fault."

Cleaning up the mess. Shaw had said that.

"It wasn't my fault." Gavin's fingers tightened on my throat again. "None of this would have happened if they didn't bully Penn. If you and Jensen hadn't chosen them over Penn. You all forced me to do this, because I had to somehow make it right. You all made me do this. So I created a list—a dead list."

My thoughts whirled with the reveal. Penn never killed himself. It had been Gavin—Penn had been his first victim. All that guilt . . . none of it mattered now.

Self-preservation consumed me.

I stretched out my arm as I fought to get him to let go of my other, hoping that would distract him. The tips of my fingers brushed the handle of the pitcher as the edges of my vision started to turn black. Blood rushed into my ears, drowning out whatever crazy crap Gavin was spewing. My fingers wrapped around the handle.

"And I think you know this already," Gavin said. "You're on it."

I swung the pitcher at his head, the impact shattering the ceramic. Bits of sharp pieces flew in my face and across the room. His hands loosened immediately, and I sucked in air as he rolled off the bed, hitting the floor.

Scrambling from the bed, I hit the call button as I backed up. The IV in my hand caught and then ripped free, but I barely felt the pain.

Gavin climbed to his feet as I edged away, through the curtains. He charged forward, blood running in rivulets down his face.

"That's the second time you've hit me in the head, Ella. That's not very nice."

"You're trying to kill me," I gasped out.

His eyes narrowed. "Good point."

And then he leaped forward.

I didn't think as I raised the part of the pitcher that had remained intact, the handle and its ragged, wickedly sharp edges. Gavin smacked into me—into the broken handle. Red gushed everywhere.

He stumbled a step, his arms rising to his slashed throat. He looked at me with eyes wide, as if he couldn't believe what I'd done. Then his mouth opened like he was trying to speak, but nothing but blood came out.

He smiled.

Gavin *smiled* as his legs buckled and his knees hit the floor.

I backed up until I hit the wall behind me. My legs gave out and I slid down the wall, clutching the jagged piece of ceramic in my trembling hand, shaking all over as I watched the puddle of dark blood under Gavin spread further.

THEN

THE FOUR OF us lay side by side on the floor of the tree house, staring up at the bright and dewy green leaves. I was sandwiched between Penn and Jensen, and Gavin was on Penn's other side. I really had no idea what any of us were doing, but I was happy and I was smiling.

"What do you guys want to do when you grow up?" Penn asked, tapping his fingers off his belly.

Gavin made a choking laughing sound. "Not clean offices, that's for sure."

I didn't think cleaning offices and houses was that bad. His parents seemed to enjoy doing it.

"Then what?" Penn persisted.

"I don't know," he grumbled. "It's a stupid question."

Jensen elbowed me in the side as he said, "It's not a stupid question. I want to be a coach or maybe a teacher. I could be both."

"Oh man, that really is lame. A teacher?" Gavin laughed again. "You'd be stuck in school forever."

"So what?" Jensen tilted his head, and I could tell that he was grinning. "You get summers off."

I giggled, thinking I liked the way he thought.

"What about you?" Jensen nudged me with his elbow again.

Wiggling my toes, I thought real hard about that. High school was so far away, college even further. It was like forever from now, but I plucked the first thing out of my head that came to mind. "I'd like to be a veterinarian."

"And save all the turtles in the world?" Jensen teased.

Gavin laughed. "We could help you. Okay. I guess . . . I guess I'd like to be a doctor. They make a lot of money."

My lips split into a wider grin and then I turned my head toward Penn. "What about you?"

Penn stared up at the blur of tree leaves and the dazzling light peeking through them. He shook his head slightly and then said, "I want to be a teacher and a veterinarian and a doctor. I want to be everything."

TWENTY-FOUR

THE COPPERY RED and golden leaves dazzled under the bright sunlight as a cool breeze circled through the front yard, stirring the hair around my shoulders. Behind me, the front door opened, and I willed myself not to jump.

Over the last four days, every little noise had me almost coming out of my skin. A deep childlike part of me expected another killer to resurface, even though I knew there wasn't anyone else.

They found Wendy in Penn's old house. She was in another bedroom, and she was surprisingly still alive. I didn't understand how or why. No one knew and we would probably never know, but she was alive and in the hospital, and I guessed that was one silver lining in the dark clouds.

And the media attention was beginning to fade away, turning toward some other tragic situation in some other small town. Things were starting to return to normal.

Jensen sat down beside me on the porch step, and when I looked over at him, I couldn't help but see the deep purple bruise along his temple. It seemed to never want to fade. Then again, my face still looked a bit like hamburger meat.

"Your mom is planning on making chili for dinner." He smiled.

"She asked me what my favorite soup was. I went with chili."

I laughed softly. "Mom's in love with you."

"Just like her daughter, huh?"

"Something like that."

Jensen leaned in, brushing his lips across mine. He kissed me softly and carefully, aware of the tender corner of my mouth. When he broke contact, he pressed his forehead against mine.

"So what do you want to do today? We have all Sunday for ourselves."

Jensen and I hadn't been back to school since everything had gone down. Monday would be our first day back. Part of me was looking forward to the return to normalcy, but I knew there'd be a lot of looks, a lot of questions.

A lot of memories.

"What are you thinking?" he asked as he shifted toward me.

My gaze roamed over his face and then over the yard. Leaves fluttered to the grass. "Why do you think he did it?" It was the first time since that night that I had asked the question. I couldn't bring myself to really talk about it before then.

There was a beat of silence. "Gavin?"

Swallowing against the burn of tears, I nodded. "Why do you think he just didn't tell the truth when it came to what happened to Penn? He might not have been in that much trouble."

"God, I hate to say this, but he was messed up. None of us saw that and we all . . ."

We all carried guilt, thinking we had driven Penn to kill himself. Worse yet, that was what his family had believed for four years. Now we all knew the truth, but there were still so many questions.

"We may never know." Gently tugging on my arm until I stood and sat between his legs, he wrapped his arms around me from behind. Both of our bodies were well on the way to healing, but every so often, one wrong move would have us creeping around like we were destined for the retirement home. My lips were still sore, as was my cheek. Jensen was still getting a mean headache once a day.

I rested my head against his chin. "He said you were beginning to see it—to see him."

"It was just some of the things he said, but I don't think I really believed it was him, that it could be him." He sighed. "Even though Gavin and I hadn't been close in years, I never would have thought he'd do this—that he'd plan it out . . . that he'd kill people. The thing is, we're never going to know why. Not really. And we've got to move past that."

Tears pricked the back of my eyes. Gavin had taken all those answers to the grave. That was something else I tried not to think about—how Gavin and Shaw had died. It sucked knowing it was by my hand, but there was no guilt. I protected myself—I saved myself.

As crazy as it sounded, I . . . God, I found myself missing Gavin and then I'd remember everything he'd done. He'd killed Penn, accident or not, and then he helped kill Vee, Monica, and Brock. It was a confusing mix of feelings that I guessed I would sort out one day.

"I know," I said finally.

"It's going to be hard," he said, when I tilted my head back and our eyes met. "His parents . . ."

That hurt, too. They had no idea the darkness their son was hiding. From what I could tell, they hadn't been aware of any of it. They'd been completely in the dark like the rest of us, and they had to be hurting far worse.

"You don't think—"

"No," I said, already knowing what he was going to ask. "I don't blame myself for . . . for any of this. Shaw and Gavin did what they did." I closed my eyes as his fingers threaded through my hair.

Jensen's arms tightened and he didn't respond, but I knew he was relieved to hear that. I wasn't telling a load of crap, either. Over the last couple of days I'd done a lot of thinking. I had to. My gaze returned to the sky, and I thought about the night it had all started for me, staring up at the stars thinking they looked like tiny tiki torches.

I'd been so excited about my upcoming year and the knowledge I'd be leaving, going away to college soon. I wanted that night back.

I knew I could have it back.

It would just take a little time.

And probably a bit of therapy.

Okay, a lot of therapy.

The door behind us opened, and we turned. Mom stood, clutching her cellphone in her hand. "Linds' parents just called."

MY HEART RACED the whole way to the hospital and up the elevator, Jensen holding my hand tightly as we hurried down the wide hall. The door to her room was ajar. I stopped, almost too afraid to go through it. Looking up at Jensen, he smiled and nodded.

Letting go of his hand, I pushed open the door and the waterworks began almost immediately. Tears spilled down my face and I didn't even care.

Linds was sitting up in bed. She was awake. She was *alive*.

Our eyes met, and I rushed forward, almost knocking her dad out of the way to get to her. I almost joined her on the bed, that was how tight I held her, and nothing—nothing felt better than her hugging me back.

I talked to her, muffling words that didn't make any sense whatsoever, and she did the same. I wasn't sure how much time passed before Jensen placed a hand on my back.

"Come on." Amusement colored his tone. "She probably needs to breathe."

Reluctantly, I sat back on the edge of the bed, wiping my hands under my eyes. "I'm sorry. I'm just so happy."

"Me too," Linds sniffed.

Jensen made a sound as he sat behind me. "If you two are so happy, why are you both sobbing?"

"You're a boy," I grumbled, looking around. Linds' parents had left. "You wouldn't understand."

"I guess not." He looped his arms around my waist and peered over my shoulder. "I'm happy to see you awake, Linds. You're looking good."

A wobbly smile appeared on her paler than normal face. "If I only knew being in a coma would get you to tell me I looked good, I would've done it a lot sooner."

I laughed, so damn relieved, because this was Linds—she was okay and she was normal. I wiped under my eyes again. "God, I am so happy."

"Me too." She leaned back against her mountain of pillows. "And I'll be even happier when they tell me I can eat something."

"It will probably be a cup of jello," Jensen said.

Linds frowned. "Oh God, I want a Whopper."

He rested his chin on my shoulder. "I doubt that's going to happen."

"You're a dream crusher." She sighed as she looked at me. "I owe you a huge thanks."

I frowned. "Why?"

"Why?" Her eyes widened. "Mom and Dad told me what you did—you drove the car through the garage door to get me out. Man, I wish I was awake to see that part."

My cheeks flushed. "I didn't do it by myself. Brock helped get you out of the car, but he's . . ." I trailed off, unsure of how much Linds knew."

She shifted in the bed. "Dad told me about him and about that cop." Her lower lip trembled. "He told me about Gavin."

"Yeah," I whispered, because I had no idea what to say about that.

Jensen's hand flattened against my stomach, and he moved his thumb around in a slow, steady circle. "How are you feeling?" he asked, changing the subject.

As Linds answered his question, we had another visitor. Heidi.

I wasn't surprised to see her since I'd texted her on the way to hospital, but I was a wee bit shocked when she walked to the bed and actually hugged Linds instead of throwing granola in her face.

"I'm glad you're, like, not dead or anything," Heidi said.

Linds glanced at us and then back to her. "Um, thanks?"

I laughed, and some of the darkness of the last couple of months eased off. Jensen's embrace tightened, and I smiled. Even though it hurt for reasons that cut deeper than the physical, the smile spread until my entire face ached.

My eyes met Linds' and she winked as Jensen brushed his lips across my cheek. Carefully leaning back into his embrace, I glanced at Heidi. Her hair twisted into pigtails, she looked like the Wendy's chick as she stared down at Linds, and for once, she looked like she wanted to be near her and not running in the opposite direction.

That was a major change.

Hell, we all changed, especially me. I wouldn't give credit to Shaw or Gavin for that. The weight I carried with me was lighter, and, in a way, I had the memory of Penn to thank for that.

I had my friends to thank.

And we all were alive, our futures waiting for us.

AFTER STAYING WITH Linds in the hospital, I came home. Like the last time I'd done this, I wasn't sure what led me to my closet door or what had me opening it, but I dropped to my knees and pushed the piles of jeans out of the way. I found the shoebox. Standing, I took it over to the bed with me and sat down. As I opened the lid and pulled the shoes out, I thought about Penn. The twinge of pain deep in my chest was still there, and even though I knew now that he never took his life, it didn't lessen the pain of losing him. If anything, it increased it.

But I couldn't go back.

Out of the four of us, only two of us remained. Jensen and

me. I wondered sometimes if any of us spent any time in that tree house thinking it would just be the two of us. That at any point in our young lives we thought this was how things would turn out.

But I knew we never thought that. Or maybe Gavin did, long before that fateful afternoon in the tree house with Penn, but that's not something I'll ever know.

I want to be everything.

Taking a deep, biting breath, I slipped my sneakers on and laced them up. I could do that for Penn. Maybe not become a teacher, a veterinarian, and a doctor, but I could do *this* for him.

I pushed to my feet, wiggling my toes in the sneakers, and then I walked out of my bedroom, down the stairs, and out the front door. I stood on the porch for a moment and looked up at the cloudless, blue sky. I smiled until I *felt* it, until it was real.

Then I stepped off the porch and went running.

ACKNOWLEDGEMENTS

I WANTED THANK my amazing agent Kevan Lyon, especially on this book. You know why. Another big thanks to my foreign rights agent Taryn Fagerness. I want to also say thank you to Wattpad who hosted TDL on their website for several years. You guys are amazing. Thank you Kara Malinczak for her editorial awesomeness and to Christine Borgford at Type A Formatting for finally turning TDL into a book, book. Another round of thank yous goes out to cover models Mikey Lee and Tara McMichen, photographer Reggie Deanching (R & M Photography), and cover designer Sara Eirew. All of you did an amazing job bringing TDL to life.

None of this would've been possible with the support or friendship of Stacey Morgan, Stephanie Brown, Hannah McBride, Sarah J Maas, Andrea Joan, Laura Kaye, Jillian Stein, Liz Berry, Jay Crownover, Kathleen Tucker, Cora Carmack, Jen Frederick, and many, many more. Of course, thank you to my family and to Loki . . . and Diesel. Not sure why I'm thanking the dogs, but don't question me.

And finally, thank you, the reader. Without you, there would be no point to this. Every reader, every reviewer—thank you!

ABOUT
JENNIFER L. ARMENTROUT

Jennifer L. Armentrout is the # 1 New York Times and International best selling author who lives in Martinsburg, West Virginia. Not all the rumors you've heard about her state are true. When she's not busy writing, she likes to garden, work out, watch really bad zombie movies, pretend to write, and hang out with her husband and her hyper Jack Russell named Loki.

She writes young adult contemporary, science fiction, and paranormal romance for Spencer Hill Press, Entangled Teen, Disney Hyperion, and Harlequin Teen. Don't Look Back was nominated as Best in Young Adult Fiction by the Young Adult Library Association. Her book Obsidian has been optioned for a major motion picture and her Covenant Series has been optioned for TV.

Under the name J. Lynn, Jennifer has written New Adult and Adult contemporary and paranormal romance, including the # 1 New York Times best seller Wait for You. She writes for Harper-Collins and Entangled Brazen.

For details about current and upcoming titles from
Jennifer L. Armentrout,
please visit www.jenniferlarmentrout.com